BEHEMOTH

By David Meyer

ACKNOWLEDGEMENTS

Creating a new story is, for me at least, an incredibly solitary journey. But that doesn't mean I'm alone along the way. With that said, I'd like to thank all of you fans, booksellers, and librarians for reading my books and recommending them to your friends, family members, and customers. Without your support, this journey would've ended a long time ago.

Also, many thanks to Julie, my muse, for your love, inspiration, and editing work on *BEHEMOTH*. And finally, thanks to Ryden for being a part of my life.

The curtains are about to open. So, take your seat. Get nice and comfortable.

Welcome to the world of *Apex Predator*.

Welcome to *BEHEMOTH*.

CHAPTER 1

Date: Unknown; Location: Unknown

This can't be heaven, Bailey Mills thought as bright rays of waning moonlight filtered through her half-opened eyelids, *so it must be hell.*

For a moment, she lay still in the swamp, inhaling the odors of clay, rotten oranges, and bird droppings. Tall blades of green grass, partially trampled, surrounded her. Farther back, she saw a layer of orange-barked trees, forty to sixty feet high and dripping with yellow-green fruit. More trees, towering and ancient, lay beyond the fruit trees. The view reminded her a little of that Thomas Cole landscape adorning the bedroom wall of her ex-boyfriend's Hamptons getaway.

And she hated that painting.

With a soft groan, she lifted her face off of the soggy soil. Clenched her teeth as a searing ache struck the back of her skull. Closing her eyes, she took a few deep breaths and tried to think. Where was she? How had she gotten there?

Gradually, the pain dulled. With some effort, she pried her eyes back open and stared out at the small marshy clearing, the four-foot tall reeds, and the multi-layered forest. Twisting her neck, she looked for a sign, any sign, of civilization. But all she saw was more foliage, more nature.

Her brain clicked into high gear as she tried to remember the sequence of events that had led her to this place. She recalled waking up late on the morning of June 18, 2016. Then a late lunch and three or four cocktails with her besties at Bullish Bistro, Manhattan's newest hotspot. Afterward, her driver, Gregory What's-His-Name, had driven her back to her five-story brownstone. She would've preferred a night on the town, drinking and dancing herself into oblivion at the invitation-only Carlyle Lounge. But instead, she'd sacrificed her evening to attend the Galeton Charity Ball, a boring annual extravaganza to raise money for conservation projects throughout Africa.

She glanced down at her clothes, confirming they were the same ones she'd worn to the ball. A slinky black dress, stained with grime, covered her carefully sculpted body. Matching high heels, a stylish silver necklace, and a couple of chunky bracelets on her right wrist completed the look. It was an eye-popping outfit, well suited for a charity affair.

But completely useless in her present situation.

Her brain continued to churn, searching for additional memories. But it came up blank. She didn't remember the party or if she'd even gone to it.

A wave of dizziness swept over her. Queasiness erupted in her stomach, the sort of queasiness one feels after imbibing way too many mojitos and mai tais. The first few pangs of regret rocked her grumbling belly. She must've done it again. That was the only explanation. She could already imagine the headlines crisscrossing the *New Yorker Chronicles* as well as the countless other celebrity sites that loved to hate her. Stuff like *Billionaire Bailey Humiliates Herself at Charity Ball!* and *The Boozing Bad Girl Strikes Again!*

She understood the public's fascination with her. At least to an extent. She possessed fabulous wealth despite never working a day in her life. Plus, she was blessed with supermodel looks. Her eyes were blue like the ocean. Her tanned skin was flawless. Her long blonde hair, perfectly styled at all times, lacked split ends or frizz. And of course, her rail-thin body, ample chest, and long legs were the stuff of fantasies.

Indeed, she was America's favorite—and sometimes its least-favorite—spoiled little princess. The gorgeous party girl with oodles of inherited money. Desired by men. Despised by their girlfriends.

She enjoyed the attention. But it embarrassed her a bit. It wasn't like she was curing old age, inventing the next great gadget, or creating art that touched the soul. She was, if all the layers were stripped away, little more than a professional partier.

Gingerly, she touched the top of her head. A slow grimace crossed her face as she felt the grime packed into the layers of carefully pinned locks of hair. It would take her personal hairstylist hours to clean it. Hours!

Her feet screamed in protest. Reaching down, she slipped the heels off her manicured peds. Slowly, she massaged the soles of her feet. Then she rose to a standing position.

Her stomach grumbled, but the only thing resembling food—the yellow-green fruit, much of which lay rotting in the marsh—creeped her out. They might've smelled like oranges, but they looked like bumpy tennis balls. Plus, they appeared to emit some kind of milky white sap.

Gross. Just ... gross.

A cool breeze chilled her mud-drenched torso. Tiny flies buzzed around her, nipping at her perfect skin, ignoring her repeated attempts to drive them away.

The more she thought about her situation, the more confused and frightened she felt. The Galeton Charity Ball was always held at the historic Quimros Hotel on the Upper West Side, not far from Central Park. But this wasn't Central Park. Not even close. It was an honest-to-goodness forest with nary a skyscraper to be seen.

Panic engulfed her, stretching through her veins and streaking deep into her heart. Clutching her shivering shoulders, she turned in a circle. There was no way she'd wandered into a forest by herself. Someone had taken her here. But who? And why?

"Ohhhh, my head … hot damn …"

Heart pounding, Mills whirled toward the unfamiliar voice. A grizzled older man stood about ten feet away, wobbling on unsteady legs. He sported thick glasses, a fat face, and a gray beard.

He wasn't cute or stylish and he didn't project much in the way of wealth or power. No, he was the sort of hapless loser Mills would've ignored as she and her besties swished their way down Madison Avenue. But here, in this strange, ancient forest, she was grateful for his company. "Hey," she called out. "Over here."

The man gave her a suspicious glance. "Who the hell are you?"

She blinked. "You don't recognize me?"

"Should I?"

"I'm Bailey Mills."

He stared at her.

"You know, *the* Bailey Mills."

"Well, I'm *the* Brian Toland." He cleaned his glasses on his shirt. Looked around. "Where the hell are we?"

"I was hoping you could tell me."

"Last I recall I was in my office. Hunched over my keyboard, pecking away in the dark."

Mills frowned, trying to make sense of it all. "You're a writer?"

"Damn straight."

"I hate writers."

A smirk crossed his wrinkled face. "A hatred for the humble scribe, my dear, is clear evidence of a pathetically primitive mind."

"I ... what?"

"Uhhh ..." A new voice, feminine and hard-edged, drifted out of the clearing.

Toland's head swiveled to his right. "Who's there?"

After several seconds with no response, he trekked toward the voice, his shoes squelching repeatedly in the marshy soil.

A bit of reflected light caught Mills' eye. Casting a glance at the ground, she saw her purse, a one-of-a-kind black clutch. Falling to her knees, she popped it open. Her pulse slowed a bit as she caught sight of her satphone.

She pressed a button and the screen came to life. The battery was low, less than ten percent of full power. Wasting no time, she initiated a call to her bestest bestie, Rachel Crossing, and lifted the device to her ear. A slow frown creased her face. She tried another bestie. And then another one.

"Where'd you go?" Toland called out.

Ignoring him, Mills tried to make another call. But the battery died and the screen faded to black. Frustrated, she threw the satphone into the muck and climbed to her feet.

Right away, she spied two women standing with Toland in the deep grass. The first woman, at least from the chest-up, was a hot mess. She wore a baggy green sweatshirt, no accessories, and not even a touch of lipstick. Her hair, clipped close to her scalp, was dyed canary yellow.

The second woman was older, in her mid-forties, and gave off the vibe of an overworked businesswoman. She wore a cheap blue jacket, likely part of a pantsuit, and a bobbed hair cut. Her makeup—pale red lipstick and severe eyeliner—was boresville.

"My phone didn't work." Mills felt her jaw begin to quiver. "All I got was static."

"That's not surprising." The businesswoman glanced over both shoulders. "From the looks of it, we're a long way from the nearest cell tower."

"This isn't some cheap smartphone," Mills retorted. "It's a satphone. It gets coverage anywhere on Earth."

The businesswoman arched an eyebrow. "*You*'ve got a satphone?"

"Of course."

"That's interesting." Toland stroked his jaw. "My phone's acting funny too."

Mills cocked her head. "How so?"

"I can't call anyone. Can't email or text either. Plus, the date and time are all messed up." He chuckled half-heartedly. "It thinks we're in a different century."

"Which one?"

"One that won't happen for about 4,000 years."

Mills didn't know what to say.

"I know you." The hot mess' eyes widened. "You're Bailey Mills."

"That's right." Mills offered her a sweet smile. "I'm glad at least one of you knows who I am."

"Yeah, I know you alright. I despise you."

Mills' smile faded.

"Enough." Toland waved at the hot mess and the businesswoman in turn. "This is Tricia Elliott and Randi Skolnick. Ladies, this is Bailey Mills. Apparently, she's famous if you care about that sort of thing."

A low growl rang out.

Mills' spine turned to jelly and she rotated in a quarter-circle. Some dense berry bushes occupied one edge of the clearing. The bushes rustled as if a breeze had caught hold of them.

But there was no breeze.

Another growl filled the still air.

Mills took a step backward.

The bushes rustled again and she saw an animal, shrouded in green leaves, little red berries, and shadows. Its shoulders were roughly four feet off the ground. Its body was five to six feet long. It possessed a stubby tail, high shoulder blades, and short, powerful limbs.

Mills backed up farther, joining the others in a tight group.

"What is that thing?" Elliott whispered.

"I think it's a cougar," Toland replied tightly.

"Are cougars dangerous?" Mills asked.

"Of course, they're dangerous, you dolt. Cougar is another name for a mountain lion."

The bushes parted before Mills could reply. The creature emerged. Paws stomped on wet leaves, crushing them underfoot. Its body curled and curved, pulsating with life. Its head turned. Its jaw lifted upward. A roar filled the pale night sky.

Mills wanted to rub her eyes, to erase the terrifying vision before her. But she couldn't even blink.

"That's no cougar," Toland whispered as the group ducked their heads beneath the tall grass. "It's a ... hell, I don't know what it is."

"I know what it is."

Mills' eyes flitted in the direction of this new voice, a low-pitched smooth sort. She saw a man in his late twenties. He was clean-shaven and wore stylish eyeglasses. His outfit, skinny jeans and a t-shirt featuring a cartoon T-Rex complaining about short arms, screamed hipster.

"Well, what is it?" she mouthed.

"I've only seen something like it once before." The hipster stared at the creature's long, curving teeth. "But not in the wild."

"Where then?"

"In a museum. Those teeth are a dead giveaway. They could only belong to a *Smilodon fatalis*."

Mills shivered at the name.

"In other words, it's a saber-toothed tiger." The hipster's voice rang cold. "And it's been extinct for more than 10,000 years."

CHAPTER 2

Date: June 19, 2016, 4:06 a.m.; Location: Upper East Side, New York, NY

The sudden cry, brimming with terror and anguish, reverberated through the steel and concrete canyon. It was the cry of the helpless, the cry of the pathetic. The cry of a creature who'd nearly run out of options, nearly run out of time.

It was the cry of fleeing prey.

Zach Caplan halted at the corner of 73rd Street and York Avenue. His eyes closed over. His head tilted skyward and he perked his ears. The cry had rung out from half a block away, filling his brain with its strangely pleasing resonance. There was something horribly wonderful about the cry of prey, about the roar of a pursuing predator. Horrible because of death's finality. Wonderful because death, in so many ways, fostered new life. For the first time in forever, Caplan felt at home.

Another cry—the cry of now-hopelessly cornered prey—rang out. Caplan's fingers, thick and heavily calloused, curled tightly around the rungs of several cotton tote bags, stuffed with canned goods, peanut butter, apples, and other items from his weekly late-night shopping trip to Jerry's Emporium. The cry belonged to a man, heavily wounded by time's arrow. A man who once might've bested the predator—most likely a mugger—that now accosted him.

But a man who now stood no chance.

Caplan's eyelids snapped open. A tall brick building, grayish from years of neglect, filled his line of sight. Five stories up, he saw a familiar window, caked with dirt and dust. A tiny light behind the window called out to him, begging him to ignore the cries. Begging him to do what he always did on nights like this one, namely drag his groceries up several flights of cracked stairs to his sorry excuse for an apartment. To eat a late-night snack in front of his old television. To grab a few restless hours of sleep on his lumpy, threadbare couch. To dream of a do-over, of a chance to get things right this time.

A third cry, far more desperate than the first two, filled the air. Caplan had heard that same cry thousands of times in his life. It was a final grasping of straws, a last-ditch call for help. In less than a minute, it would be over. The mugger, suddenly richer, would flee the scene. At best, the old man would lose his valuables.

At worst, he'd lose his life.

Caplan's face grew piping hot. Yes, this was how nature worked. The strong and the smart survived, the weak and the stupid died. But it wasn't right. It hadn't been right five months ago. It certainly wasn't right now.

His fingers uncurled. The cotton bags dropped to the sidewalk, crashing against the concrete. Spinning toward 73rd Street, he broke into a mad dash.

His powerful arms pumped like pistons. His breaths came in short, brief bursts as his long legs carried him down the sidewalk. He didn't look like a runner. But similar to the antelope, he possessed quiet, deceptive speed.

Caplan didn't match any of the popular stereotypes for handsome men. He wasn't, for instance, blonde with blue eyes. Instead, his hair was jet black and curly to the point of untamable. As for his eyes, they were as green as freshly watered grass.

On the other hand, he wasn't tall, dark, and handsome. He stood an inch shy of six feet. His skin, although darkened from years of sun exposure, wasn't too many shades removed from that of an albino. And his face, rugged and weathered from the elements, was a far cry from the youthful pretty-boy look so prevalent in modern media.

Halfway down the block, he heard light scuffling and heavy grunts. Turning right, Caplan raced into a dark alley. He ran in near-silence. His breathing was barely audible. His waterproof trail-runners slapped the concrete with the lightest of touches.

Fifty feet away, he saw two shadowy figures struggling behind a couple of metal garbage cans. Light glinted wildly as they fought for control of a large handgun. The predator, outfitted in a black hoodie and dark jeans, was gigantic. Easily six foot four and possessing the powerful neck and shoulders of a linebacker. The other man—the prey—was frail and old. Outfitted in bright-checkered pants and a sleek green polo shirt, he looked like a wealthy golfer far removed from his natural habitat.

Caplan's senses kicked into overdrive, focusing on the alley as a whole. Spilt trash—pizza boxes, opened envelopes, wadded-up diapers—littered the ground, indicating the trashcans had been recently moved. The air smelled of body odor, but it didn't seem to come from the struggling combatants. Rather, a curious mixture of expensive colognes surrounded predator and prey. Metal groaned as the western fire escape, one of two abutting either side of the alley, shifted back and forth.

Caplan knew what it meant. And his primal instincts told him to break off, to rethink his strategy. But he was no longer listening to them. He was listening to new instincts, ones that had formed five months earlier. Ones that told him to dish out as much pain and anguish as humanly possible.

Lowering his shoulder, Caplan crashed into the predator. Jets of fire shot down his arm, across his chest. Ignoring the searing pain, he kept at it, pushing forward with all of his strength.

The predator didn't yelp or moan. Rather, a surprised grunt escaped his lips. Releasing the gun, he toppled to the ground with all the force of a full-grown tree trunk.

The prey stumbled backward, trying to maintain control of the gun. But he jolted as his rear struck the concrete and the weapon, a 9mm pistol with fully supported ramped hammer-forged barrel, hit the ground and skidded into the darkness.

Caplan rolled to his feet. The predator jumped up to face him. Lips twisting into a sick grin, the predator stepped forward. Forming a fist out of his right hand, he reared back like a baseball pitcher.

The heavy fist slammed into Caplan's jaw with bone-breaking force. Caplan whirled in a circle and dropped to the ground. Stars exploded in his head and a dizzy spell nearly sent him into the land of darkness.

The predator appeared, hovering over him like a wraith. Caplan picked himself off the ground. Rose unsteadily to his feet. He had no strategy, no plan of attack or retreat. All he had was an overwhelming desire to release months of pent-up aggression.

Before the predator could launch another attack, Caplan ran forward, throwing fists with reckless abandon. A right one slammed into the predator's stomach. A left one struck the man's right cheek.

Absorbing the blows, the predator backed up a few feet. His eyes tightened into tiny orbs.

Rage took over Caplan as he threw more punches. A right cross to the belly. A left uppercut to the chest. The predator hunkered down, trying to ward off the barrage. But a fist to the mouth stunned him and another one to the solar plexus sent him reeling toward the old trashcans. Metal clattered as he smashed into them and fell to the ground.

Shifting his gaze, Caplan saw the prey crawling into the darkness. Hurrying forward, he grabbed the old man. Pulled him to his feet and stared into his eyes.

"What are you doing?" the prey said. "The gun—"

"Who are you?"

The prey opened his mouth to respond. But rattling metal bars stopped him short.

Caplan didn't need to look to know what was above him. He'd noticed the signs. The shifted trashcans, the misplaced odors, the groaning metal. But he had no desire to flee. Just to fight to the bitter end.

Twisting around, he ran toward the west wall at full speed. At the last second, he kicked his feet against the brick and shot upward. His fingers closed around a rusty metal bar.

Fire escapes were an increasingly rare feature in New York City. Aesthetically unpleasing and considered highly unsafe, many architects had replaced them over the years with fireproof interior stairwells. The ones that remained, the dinosaurs, had been reworked to allow easier ladder deployment.

Caplan pulled himself onto the fire escape. Two men, wide-eyed as all hell, stood before him. One was short with curly black hair poking out from under his hoodie. The other was basketball-tall with long legs.

Caplan jumped. His hands closed around an overhead bar. With a sudden lurch, he launched himself forward. Feet extended, his body soared like a missile into the curly-haired man.

Screaming like a banshee, the man stumbled backward. He lost his balance and seconds later, his head slammed into the metal bars. His eyes rolled into the back of his head and he fell still.

Caplan landed in a crouching position. He started to get up but a sharp kick struck his side. His pain sensors erupted and he stumbled to a knee. A second kick, a brutal one, caught the top of his skull and he crumpled to a heap on top of the metal bars.

A hint of copper snaked into his nostrils. He touched the side of his head. It felt tacky, sticky.

The fire escape rattled and trembled. Caplan felt a breeze and rolled to the side. The baller's sneaker slammed into the bars, narrowly missing his head.

Caplan lashed out with a kick. It missed its mark, but managed to drive his attacker back a few feet.

Fighting off dizziness, Caplan lifted his back off the bars.

The baller backed up another foot. His eyes glittered like gold.

Caplan shot a quick glance at the ground. The predator remained still among the fallen trashcans and mounds of garbage. The prey remained glued to the concrete, seemingly frozen with fear.

A surge of anger appeared in the pit of Caplan's stomach. It swirled upward, outward, spreading to all corners of his body.

Rushing forward, the baller unleashed yet another vicious kick. Caplan could've blocked it. But he was too angry, too enraged to think straight. Wading forward, he ignored the sneaker, letting it crunch against his left thigh. And then he was on top of the man, overwhelming him with his weight. The baller lost his balance and toppled over the safety rail.

Caplan fell with him.

Air rushed in Caplan's ears as they hurtled to the ground. Less than a second later, the baller's side smacked sickeningly into one of the trashcans. The impact sent Caplan flopping onto the concrete and he slid forward, knocking aside rotten vegetables, beer bottles, and slimy tissues before coming to a halt.

For three full seconds, he lay on the concrete, dazed and bloodied. His pulse raced non-stop. His pores, opened wide during the fight, caused sweat to streak down his grime-covered face.

The baller stirred. Kicked his legs slightly. Jerked his arms as if he were a newborn.

Caplan crawled to the man. Saw blood oozing from the guy's forehead. Felt it splatter against his palms and slip between his fingers. His breathing sped up. He felt an uncontrollable lust in his heart.

A lust for blood.

Caplan grabbed the baller's hair. Swung a heavy fist at the guy's nose, busting it open and causing blood to spurt out of the nostrils like water out of twin faucets.

The impact stung Caplan's hand. But he reared back and delivered another thundering punch to the man's face. And another one. And then another one.

After a few more punches, he released the hair and watched the man's bloodied face sag to the concrete. Standing up, he swung around to face the prey.

The old man stood slack-jawed in the alley, shifting his gaze between the baller and Caplan. Then he started backing toward the fallen pistol. "Thank you," he said. "I don't know what I would've done if you hadn't showed up."

A single look into the man's eyes told Caplan everything he needed to know. His body ached from the blows he'd sustained as he strode forward. His hands were in desperate need of ice baths.

The old man stooped to pick up the pistol. But Caplan's boot pressed down, pinning it to the concrete.

The old man looked up. Gave Caplan a confused look.

Caplan smiled. Shifted sideways.

And slammed his left fist straight into the old man's kisser.

The old man's head snapped back. His legs folded under him and he was unconscious before he hit the ground.

"Thought you could pull a con job on an innocent, huh?" Caplan whispered between breaths. "Thought you and your boys could draw in prey of your own with that little performance of yours? Well, guess again."

For a moment, Caplan stood over the vanquished old man, breathing rapidly and allowing his adrenaline to ease. His ribs hurt and he could feel blood trickling down the side of his face. It wasn't his first fistfight, but it was definitely one of the more painful ones. He'd taken a tremendous beating. And for what? To punish some gang of thieves for trying to prey on good Samaritans?

He crouched next to the old man. Patted the guy's pockets until he'd located a wallet. Pulling it out, he peered at the man's license.

"James Corbotch?" With a frown, he tossed the license—clearly fake—onto the old man's unconscious form. Then he marched out of the alley, still frowning. He wondered what kind of confidence trick the old man had intended to pull with the license. And what kind of gullible person would actually believe it? After all, James Corbotch wasn't just another Joe Schmo.

He was the richest man on the planet.

CHAPTER 3

Hunger pangs hit Caplan's stomach as he half-walked, half-limped into his tiny, dilapidated apartment. His groceries, along with the cotton tote bags, had disappeared by the time he'd gone back to retrieve them. It pissed him off to no end. This was why he hated the city, hated everything about it. There was always some lowlife waiting in the shadows, looking to take advantage of a good Samaritan.

He slammed his door so hard paintings would've rattled in their frames if he'd actually owned any paintings. After locking the dual-bolt mechanism, he dragged himself to his couch and eased himself into its lumpy cushions. The sofa, a three-seater purple mess he'd bought from the local Kettler Thrift Store, was an eyesore. But what did he care? All of Manhattan, from the shocking amount of waste to the soulless skyscrapers, was an eyesore.

A dull ache sprung up in his jaw. Gently, he touched the tender skin. While he hurt all over, the predator's punch hurt most of all. He wondered about that. After that first strike, the predator had hunkered down and taken Caplan's punishment. Why? Why hadn't he fought back? Wasn't the whole point of the scheme to draw in a good Samaritan? To trap that person and rob him?

A few doubts entered Caplan's brain. On one hand, he knew a scam when he saw it. And a single look into the old man's steady, calculating eyes had confirmed it. But maybe he'd gotten the scheme wrong. Maybe they weren't trying to rob him. Maybe they were trying to capture him, use him for something. Like steal his organs or one of the countless insane crimes he'd read about in the free subway newspapers.

Caplan's side started to hurt. Then his belly stung. Lifting his shirt, he checked his wounds. He wasn't anywhere near hospital shape, but he still required medical attention.

Wincing, he stood up and trudged to the bathroom, cursing his bloodlust the entire way. It had felt therapeutic in the moment, but he was paying for it now.

As he neared the bathroom, he cast a glance at a tall dresser. The wood was heavily splintered and covered with stains. It wasn't fit for a homeless shelter, let alone an apartment. But so what? It held his clothes just fine.

An unframed photo atop the dresser caught his eye. Two small rocks propped it up. It showed a young woman, backed by a forest of willows, pines, and oaks. She wasn't smiling. Instead, she looked like she'd always looked, as if she were about to bitch someone out. Her pupils, sharp and blue, were surrounded by eye shadow. Her nose was a bit big for her face, but certainly not unbecoming. Her cheeks were rounded at the top and angular all the way down to her pointy jaw.

His gaze flitted to her long blonde hair, shiny and swept back into an updo. The updo glittered under intense sunlight.

He stopped and stared at this gorgeous creature. This woman he'd once loved with all his heart and soul. This woman that he'd ripped out of his life five months ago. Not because he loved her any less, but because he no longer deserved her.

Some sins, after all, could never be forgiven.

"I don't know what you're doing right now, Amanda," he whispered under his breath. "But I hope you're happy."

CHAPTER 4

Date: June 19, 2016, 4:28 a.m.; Location: Hatcher Station, Vallerio Forest, NH

The air whipped as Amanda Morgan swung the rifle butt in an arc, cracking it against Secretary of State Barbara Slayton's skull. Secretary Slayton, all eighty-three years of her, slumped to the ground. Blood seeped from the back of her head, staining her bluish-white hair and oozing across the hardwood floor.

The screams and shouts halted. The other prisoners, clad in silk suits and formal cocktail dresses, backed into the center of the room. One by one, they found their seats at the circular tables.

Morgan inhaled a deep breath as she faced the prisoners. A ripped white lab coat hung limply from her well-toned body. Her blonde hair was scraggily and damp with sweat. "Consider that a warning," she shouted. "Next person who disobeys an order gets a bullet in the face."

The prisoners swapped uneasy looks.

Morgan's eyes drifted to the room itself, known internally as the Eye. Giant monitor banks, one per wall, shifted video feeds every fifteen seconds. She saw wild horses, bison, and zebras grazing in steppe grasslands. Asian and African elephants, along with deer, grizzly bears, and jaguars, weaving their way through dense forests. Mountain goats and camels feeding gracefully on the foliage of arid mountains, keeping watchful eyes out for mountain lions and other predators.

Normally, workstations, desks, and computers covered the floor space between the monitors. Well-trained rangers used them to maintain a distant eye on the various ecosystems that made up the Vallerio Forest. But hours earlier, the room had undergone a transformation. The normal occupants had been shuttled off to their quarters for the evening. Their workstations and desks had been pushed to the sides of the room. Circular tables, covered with white cloth and surrounded by chairs, had taken their place. Extravagant food and the finest wines had been wheeled in on fancy carts. A party celebrating ... something ... had commenced.

Axel Eichel, Managing Director of the International Monetary Fund, sat up straight. A longtime member of the Socialist Party and hailing from the 5th arrondissement of Paris, he was both beloved and despised for his gentle handling of the continuing European debt crisis. "We'll behave." He eyed the room's other prisoners. "You have my word."

"Good, good." Morgan licked her lips. There were twenty-one prisoners in total. Four top-level Vallerio Foundation executives. And seventeen guests who wielded an incredible amount of power between them. Besides Eichel, their ranks included four prominent politicians from four separate continents, five high-ranking members of the United Nations, four bankers, and three directors of major global businesses. The prisoners, a curious combination of nationalities, came from all ends of the political spectrum. Social progressives sat alongside social conservatives. Neoconservatives rubbed elbows with anti-war liberals.

Deborah Keifer, a stern bird-like woman and president of the Vallerio Foundation, glared at Morgan. "What do you want?" she asked, her voice dripping with disdain.

Ignoring her, Morgan glided across the room. She stopped next to Charlie Lodge, one of the world's foremost geneticists and a five-year resident at Hatcher Station. "Watch them closely."

"But that guy said—"

"That guy is a bureaucrat," she said, finishing his thought with her own. "In other words, a born liar."

Lodge's breaths sped up to the point of hyperventilation.

Morgan looked into his eyes. Saw his fear, his anxiety. "Are you sure you can handle this?"

He tugged at his lab coat. "It's just that, well, I've never shot anyone before."

"Me neither." She patted his shoulder. "I'll send some backup."

Morgan walked to the door. Pushed it open and entered Hatcher Station's central core, better known as the Heptagon. The Heptagon, consistent with its moniker, contained seven equidistant walls. Separate doors were mounted in the middle of each wall. One door led outside to several rings of security fences and, farther back, the vast Vallerio Forest. The other six doors led to Hatcher Station's various sections, including the Galley, the Barracks, Operations, Research, the Warehouse, and of course, the Eye.

"Fei." Her gaze turned to Fei Nai-Yuan, a brilliant Chinese-American geophysicist. "Charlie needs help."

Nai-Yuan, equipped with one of the many rifles seized during the coup, gave her a brisk nod. With quick steps, he made his way into the Eye, shutting the door behind him.

Morgan strode across the Heptagon, passing a collection of bound guards along the way. They sat in a circle, backs to the middle. Six people, a mixture of scientists, technicians, and rangers, kept them in check with rifles. The station's primary physician, Dr. Ankur Adnan, moved silently about the guards, checking their stitches and rebandaging their wounds.

She grasped Research's doorknob. As she opened the door, a distinct humming noise, the product of computers and machinery, filled her ears. Strong heat reached out, causing a thin layer of sweat to bubble up all over her body.

She paused, giving herself a moment to adjust to the sudden temperature change. Then she strode through the doorframe, paying no attention to the mounted *Stop: Restricted Access, Research Only* sign.

She walked through the maze of tables and machinery. A metal hatch, roughly three feet on each side, occupied the room's far right corner. Other than some giant hinges on one side and a handle on the other side, the hatch was perfectly flat with the floor. A small computer screen was embedded into the metal. It showed ever-changing strings of digits and letters, bright green against a black background.

Two women sat at a long table near the hatch. Their gazes were fixed upon laptops. Their fingers swept over the keyboards, pecking keys at a high rate of speed.

Morgan cleared her throat. "Well?"

"Nothing yet," Bonnie Codd said without looking up.

"You've been at this for hours."

"We're making progress."

Morgan rubbed her forehead. Normally, the hatch—which was controlled by computers far beneath them—took mere minutes to open. Unfortunately, this was no normal situation. "How much progress?"

Codd clucked her tongue in disapproval. "If you're in such a hurry, why don't you try that back entrance you mentioned?"

"Because it's just as hard to open from the outside. Now, how much progress have you made?"

"Do you see that thing?" Codd nodded at the hatch. "It's two-feet thick, made of the latest torch and drill resistant metals. Thermal lances couldn't touch it. I don't think even an atomic bomb could crack it."

"I know. But—"

"The only way into the Lab is to penetrate a whole bunch of mechanical and electronic locking mechanisms. And that's a lot easier than it sounds."

"I need you to go faster. It's only a matter of time before the Foundation figures out something's wrong here."

Zlata Issova, who served as Codd's right-hand woman at Hatcher Station, arched an eyebrow. "Do you think they'll attack us?"

"Not right away," Morgan said, trying to hide the doubt in her voice. "Not while we've got hostages."

The two computer experts stared at her with hooded eyes.

"Let me worry about the Foundation." Morgan nodded at the hatch. "Just get us down there so we can access the communications network."

Codd and Issova exchanged looks. Then they returned to their keyboards.

As they worked, Morgan gently touched her waist. Pain shot up and down her right side, but she didn't feel sorry for herself. She deserved the pain. After all, she and the other researchers weren't entirely blameless in all this. They'd challenged God, challenged His grip on time itself.

And some sins, unfortunately, could never be forgiven.

CHAPTER 5

Date: June 19, 2016, 8:01 a.m.; Location: Central Park, New York, NY

"Good morning, folks." Suppressing a yawn, Caplan stared across the wide expanse of Central Park's Great Lawn. Nineteen shining faces, clearly pumped up on copious amounts of coffee, stared back at him. "And welcome to the Zach Caplan Survival School. This particular class, Urban Survival Basics, will run for the next eight Saturdays."

A couple of smiles greeted his words. Most were broad and curious. But some, as always, were smirky and self-satisfied. Inwardly, he groaned. Introductory sessions were always the worst. In order to reel in the fish, he offered them for free. As a business strategy, it worked wonders, doubling his paid attendees. But it also had a dark side. Namely, the fact that it brought in the cynics.

"I've got a question." A dude, outfitted in jeans and a tight t-shirt, folded his arms across his chest. "Why do you do this?"

Here we go, Caplan thought. "Do what?" he asked.

"Rip people off."

An uncomfortable silence filled the air.

"Let me guess," Caplan replied. "You hate survivalists, right?"

"I think they're stupid, dangerous hillbillies." The dude flashed a grin at a heavyset guy. "But I don't hate them."

The guy, clearly friends with the dude, roared with laughter.

"What you call stupid, I call smart." The words, repeated many times over the last five months, rolled easily off Caplan's tongue. "Back in the 1950s, people built bomb shelters in order to survive nuclear fallout. When inflation ran wild in the 1970s, they ditched paper money for gold. A few decades later, they bought canned goods and generators when Y2K looked like it might cause food shortages and blackouts."

"Interesting," the dude replied in a voice that indicated the exact opposite. "What's your point?"

"Those people weren't stupid hillbillies. They were ordinary, intelligent people, preparing for difficult times."

"Which never happened."

"But that doesn't mean something couldn't have happened." For an instant, Caplan's mind snapped back to the Vallerio Forest. To five months ago. To that part of him that no longer existed. "If something goes wrong, a little preparation just might save your life."

Exhaling softly, Caplan shifted his gaze to the other students. "Now, let's talk about what you can expect from this class. Urban Survival Basics isn't meant to prepare you for a minor terrorist attack or a measles outbreak. It's in case something truly bad happens. Something that destroys civilization."

The heavyset guy smirked. "How often does that happen?"

"More often than you think," Caplan replied smoothly. "Think of the Anasazi, the Mayas, the Khmer Empire, the Roman Empire, the Soviet Union."

"And yet, here we are, more civilized than ever," the dude said, finding his tongue. "Those people didn't need bug out bags or canned goods to survive disasters. They just picked up the pieces and moved on with their lives."

God, he hated the cynics. Why didn't they just let him teach his classes in peace? "Not all of them. Many people— the ones who didn't see it coming—perished. Modern civilization is built on the backs of those who were prepared." Caplan smiled. "The survivalists."

The dude exchanged frustrated looks with the guy. Together, they ambled away from the group.

Caplan turned his attention back to the students. "So—"

"I've got one more question for you." The dude whirled around. "You're a survival expert, right?"

Caplan nodded.

"Then how come you only teach urban stuff? How come you don't teach wilderness skills?"

Caplan's mouth moved, but no words came out.

A grin creased the dude's lips. Whirling around, he and the guy hiked across the Great Lawn, chortling loudly with glee.

Caplan's blood rushed to his head. It wasn't the questions that bothered him so much as the thoughts they provoked in his head. About his career at Hatcher Station, deep within the Vallerio Forest. About the life he'd left behind.

His hands formed into fists. He was sorely tempted to chase after the dude, to beat the man senseless. But he forced himself to breathe slowly. To allow his anger to ebb. *You've got a class to teach*, he reminded himself. *Money to earn, rent to pay.*

Caplan took another breath. "Urban Survival Basics isn't about growing urban gardens or installing solar panels. On the other hand, it's not about fighting off hordes of enemies with your fists and feet. It's about two things, evasion and escape. Evasion from authorities, terrorists, criminals, zombies, you name it. Escape from captivity, escape from the city."

He paused, allowing his words to register with the students. "Let's face it ... New York sucks." A few half-hearted chuckles rang out. "If the shit ever hits the fan, this is probably the worst place you could find yourself. It's overcrowded and under-resourced. Urban Survival Basics will teach you how to handle that. Over the next eight weeks, we'll cover a variety of topics. The building and planting of supply caches. The creation of fake papers and IDs. Stealth movements, including buildering and parkour. Checkpoint crossing via disguises and the aforementioned false documents. You'll learn how to pick locks, break zip ties, and bust out of temporary urban prisons. And you'll learn how to steal an abandoned car and start it without keys."

He noted the excitement, the enthusiasm amongst the students. He wasn't surprised. His students were, by and large, rich urbanites. They bored easily and were always on the lookout for a new experience. His classes promised that and a whole lot more.

"After seven weeks of training, you'll be given the opportunity to show what you know," Caplan continued. "The last class will consist of a real-world scenario. All of you will be restrained and locked down somewhere in New York City during a mock disaster. You'll have to break out, gather resources, evade agents trying to recapture you, and escape the city. And you'll do it all without the use of cell phones or computers."

The students' excitement level jumped a few notches. If there was one thing urbanites loved more than unique experiences, it was an excuse to temporarily escape the drudgery of social media and constant connectivity.

Caplan wiped his hand across his brow, relieving it of sweat. The temperature, a balmy seventy-four degrees

Fahrenheit, didn't bother him. What bothered him was the lack of shade, the lack of trees.

He sniffed the air, but was unable to get a good whiff of anything. The grass barely registered in his nostrils. The few surviving trees, the ones that had so far avoided the recent die out, were seemingly odorless. He missed the smells of the outdoors. The real outdoors, not the well-groomed artifice of Central Park.

"Today's session will focus on knowledge-gathering and prep work," Caplan said. "We're going to discuss recent riots and large-scale terrorist attacks. We'll look at how authorities work, how they lockdown cities and establish checkpoints. Then we'll move on to caches. I'll show—"

"Is this session full?" The voice was familiar, but somehow tougher, stronger. Like it was packed full of nails. "Or have you got room for another student?"

Whirling around, Caplan fixed his gaze at the old man from the fake mugging. His fingers curled into fists. He forgot the students, forgot the session. "You little—"

"The student's name is Amanda Morgan."

Caplan's brow cinched tight. Amanda? His Amanda?

"She's always getting herself into trouble. So, I'd like to sign her up for your class." The old man inhaled deeply. "I think you're the only one who can help her."

CHAPTER 6

"Spill it." Caplan pushed the old man away from his students. "Now."

The old man turned around and rubbed his bruised jaw. Then he smoothed down his gray sport coat and tailored white shirt. "Take it easy, son."

Caplan wasn't in the mood to take it easy. Grabbing the man by the collar, he pulled him close. "How do you know Amanda?"

"She works for me."

"Liar." Caplan shook the man hard. "You staged that mugging. Then one of your cronies followed me back to my apartment. That's the only way you could've found out about Amanda."

"You're right about one thing. The mugging was staged. But it was also necessary. I needed to vet you, to see you in action."

"What the hell are you talking about?"

With surprising strength, the old man broke free of Caplan's grip. "Let's start over. My name is James Corbotch."

"And I'm Leonardo da Vinci."

"I'm serious."

"No, you're a con artist."

James Corbotch, the elderly patriarch of the Corbotch family, was one of the most enigmatic people in the entire world. His vast holdings, known to most people as the Corbotch Empire, had its origins in the family's seventeenth century banking business. Over the years, it had spread its wings across the globe, gobbling up countless enterprises along the way.

Little was known about James. Some said he lived in the French Alps, wiling away his years with a bevy of buxom beauties. Others thought he owned a chain of private South Pacific islands from which he hosted island-hopping fetish parties for the rich and famous. Still others believed he lived like a hermit, moving from hovel to hovel, doing everything in his power to keep a low profile.

Personally, Caplan wasn't sure what to believe. Maybe all those things were right. Or maybe they were all wrong. All he knew was that the man in front of him was *not* James Corbotch.

The man pulled a wallet out of his back pocket. He passed a business card to Caplan.

Caplan glanced at the card. Constructed from elegant cardboard, it held just two lines of text. The name *James Corbotch* on the first line. And a phone number on the second one.

Caplan crumpled the card in his fist. "This is your proof?"

"Not all of it." Corbotch flashed his license and several other cards in front of Caplan's face. "See?"

Caplan ignored them. "You're boring me."

"Perhaps this will convince you." Corbotch took a deep breath. "Your name is Zach Caplan. You used to work as Chief Ranger at Hatcher Station, the Vallerio Forest's lone outpost."

Caplan's eyes tightened. That information was strictly confidential. Nobody outside of Hatcher—not even his closest friends—knew it.

"For three years, everything was fine. You were liked and respected. You grew close to Amanda Morgan, a biologist of the highest caliber. But all that changed five months ago when Tony Morgan, Amanda's brother, vanished while conducting an unsanctioned visit to Sector 84. An exhaustive three-day search turned up his abandoned vehicle and some bloody scraps of clothing, but nothing else. Since he'd stolen the keys from your workspace, you took it hard, choosing to tender your resignation. Then you moved here, to New York City, where you proceeded to open an urban survival school."

"How … how do you know all this?"

The old man didn't blink. "Because I own the Vallerio Forest. It's been in my family for as long as we've been on this continent."

"Nice try. The Vallerio Foundation owns it."

"Yes. But I own the Vallerio Foundation through various trusts and dummy corporations. For reasons that aren't relevant to this conversation, I disguise my affiliation through a lot of legal mumbo-jumbo."

Caplan heard the man's words, heard the veracity behind them. He could scarcely believe it. Yet, he knew it was true. The man standing before him was indeed James Corbotch, the perennial top placeholder on Acton's annual ranking of the globe's wealthiest people.

"When you left, you sat for an exit interview with Ms. Keifer. At that time, you informed her that you'd never return to Hatcher Station. I believe the expression you used was, 'I'll rot in hell first.'" Corbotch paused. "I'm here to change your mind."

Caplan thought about what Corbotch had said, about how Amanda Morgan needed help. The very thought sent bolts of electricity shooting through him. "Why the mugging?" he asked. "Why didn't you just talk to me?"

"Like I said, I needed to vet you."

"For what?"

"For a multi-layered crisis situation. I wanted to see how you'd react, how'd you handle it."

Caplan rubbed his sore jaw. "So, those guys ...?"

"Part of my personal security team." Corbotch offered a bare hint of a smile. "Of course, I instructed them to take it easy on you."

That was easy? Caplan thought, rubbing his sore jaw. "So, how'd I do?"

"You passed with flying colors. You showed courage and persistence. You spotted hidden threats, used the environment to deliver creative attacks, and even uncovered my duplicity." Corbotch paused. "In short, you're exactly what I need."

Caplan felt a spot of darkness enter his heart. He didn't care for Corbotch. And he certainly didn't like being lied to and manipulated either. "The feeling isn't mutual," he said, turning to leave.

"She needs you, Zach."

Caplan paused. Slowly, he twisted back to Corbotch.

"Last night, a team of armed terrorists seized control of Hatcher Station along with a group of visiting dignitaries. Amanda Morgan, along with dozens of employees, was on the premises at the time."

"Impossible. Hatcher is protected—"

"—protected by multiple layers of top-notch security," Corbotch said. "Yes, I know. But that doesn't change the facts."

Caplan fought to control his emotions. "How'd it happen?"

"The details are unclear. All we know for certain is that the assault started around eight o'clock. The terrorists seized the Warehouse and disarmed most of the guards.

Fortunately, a couple of guards eluded capture and locked themselves into the Lab. They've been using the communications equipment to keep my people apprised of the situation."

Caplan's forehead started to ache. Gently, he kneaded it, massaging away months of mental pain.

He'd never actually seen the underground Lab. And the scientists who worked there were forbidden to talk about it. He'd once asked Morgan about it and her cryptic response still haunted him. *Let's just say we're doing something important, Zach,* she'd said. *Revolutionary, even. It's going to change the way we perceive this world's past, present, and future.*

"Why Hatcher?" Caplan asked. "Were they after the dignitaries?"

"If it's a kidnapping-for-ransom, it's an awful quiet one. So far, we haven't heard a peep from the terrorists." Corbotch shrugged. "Regardless of their goals, they're currently holding dozens of people—including Amanda—at gunpoint. That's where you come in. You worked at Hatcher. You know its layout and its security systems."

Caplan frowned. "What exactly do you want from me? Want me to sketch everything out for the police? That's easy. Just let me—"

"Actually, the authorities won't be involved in this matter. For reasons I can't discuss, this needs to be handled carefully and with great discretion." A crafty look formed on Corbotch's visage. "In other words, I don't want sketches. I want you."

Caplan's frown deepened.

"As we speak, my personal security forces are prepping to infiltrate the Vallerio. They've got firepower and experience. What they lack is ground knowledge of Hatcher Station and its security systems. That's why I need you to go with them. You'll be handsomely compensated, of course."

A whirlwind of emotions swept through Caplan. He thought about Morgan, thought about how much he missed her. He thought about the offer, thought about what he could contribute to the mission. "No," he said at last.

"But—"

"If you want maps, sketches, I'm your guy. But that's it."

"Amanda needs you."

"Yeah, like an axe to the head. Don't you remember what happened to her brother? How he died because of me?" Caplan shoved Corbotch's crumpled-up business card into his back pocket. Then he spun on his heels and walked away. "Get lost. I've got a class to teach."

CHAPTER 7

Date: June 19, 2016, 8:15 a.m.; Location: Central Park, New York, NY

As Caplan hiked back to his students, he shot a glance over his shoulder. Given the time of day, the Great Lawn was unusually busy and he saw all sorts of people. Men and women, decked out in faded uniforms, played softball on one of the diamonds. Kids flew kites and kicked soccer balls. Their parents, sprawled out on the grass with little picnic baskets, ate bagel sandwiches and sipped mimosas.

But Corbotch was nowhere to be seen.

Upon reaching his students, Caplan stared at them through hollow eyes. Memories of Amanda Morgan filled his brain. The way she tipped her head when she laughed. The feel of his hand on the small of her back. Her breaths heating up his ear. Her body moving in time with his.

"Thanks for your patience." Forcing the memories to a tiny corner of his mind, Caplan offered his students a fake smile. "Now, let's talk about today's agenda. Namely, knowledge gathering and prep work. Nine times out of ten, brains trump brawn in crisis situations. Knowing how authorities or criminals tend to secure and control areas is paramount to escaping them. And having access to resources—tools, bottled water, food, and weapons—is often the difference between life and death. While everyone else is raiding grocery stores for scraps, you'll be securing and utilizing pre-planted caches."

Thoughts of Morgan roared out of the corner of his mind. He remembered watching her sleep at night. Her little snores, her shallow breaths. He recalled his arms around her and hers around him. Bodies intertwined under cotton sheets, pressed so close together he could almost feel her heart beating inside his chest.

"Today's, uh …" Once again, Caplan pushed the memories into the deepest recesses of his mind. This time, he tied them down with heavy mental restraints. "Today's class, by necessity, may seem somewhat dry at times. That's why we're going to spice it up on occasion. Over the next few hours, I'll offer impromptu demonstrations of survival skills. You'll see me use parkour to cross an entire block without ever touching the sidewalk. You'll watch as I break into a car—don't worry, it's owned by a friend—and start the ignition without keys. And you'll see plenty of other stuff, too. Stuff that all of you will be doing over the next eight weeks."

The students stared at him with bright eyes. The things he'd just mentioned were red meat to bored rich folks. For the most part, they didn't care about how authorities worked or optimal survival strategies for a real-life disaster.

They just wanted to see and do cool stuff.

"I need a volunteer." Caplan scanned the eager faces, settling on a fresh-scrubbed masculine one. It belonged to a rapidly aging, twenty-something year-old man. The man's wrinkled visage indicated he worked in one of those hundred-hour week professions, probably investment banking or law. His jittery limbs and nervous manner hinted at a burgeoning Adderall habit. "Think you can handle it?"

"Sure." A crooked smile creased the man's wrinkled face and he stepped forward. "But can you handle me?"

The students tittered.

Caplan grinned. "What's your name?"

"Dalton. Dalton Nevins."

Dalton Nevins, Caplan repeated inside his head, storing the name in his memory banks. He found it useful to recall as many student names as possible. It made people feel like they were friends and friends were far more likely to become paying customers.

"Okay, Dalton." Caplan reached into his pocket and pulled out a strip of rigid nylon with a built-in ratchet on the far end. Small teeth ran down one side of the strip. "Do you recognize this?"

Nevins' head bobbed. "It's a zip-tie."

"Very good." Caplan held out his wrists, side by side, and touched them together. "Put it on me."

Nevins took the zip-tie. Awkwardly, he wrapped it around Caplan's wrists and pulled one end through the ratchet.

"Really?" Caplan shot a wink at the other students. "Is that the best you've got?"

Laughter rang out and Caplan grinned devilishly. Of course, this was all part of the act. He needed the zip-ties to be tight. The tighter, the better.

Nevins' jaw tightened. Grabbing the zip-tie with both hands, he cinched it tight.

As the nylon strip dug into Caplan's flesh, he felt other ties, mental ones, enclose his heart. They squeezed so hard he thought the vessel might burst inside his chest. What the hell was he doing? Was he really going to keep teaching like nothing had happened?

Caplan held up his wrists for everyone to see. "You've probably seen zip-ties in plenty of movies and with good reason. They're fiendish devices. This particular set is extra tough and comes with a rating of 200 pounds." He paused. "Here's the problem. Any forward movement of the zip tie will cause it to cinch even tighter. And any attempt to pull my wrists apart causes the ratchet to lock. So, how does one escape them?"

Truth be told, escape was a simple matter. He'd deliberately held his wrists side by side while Nevins had applied the zip-tie. The resulting position, one of four basic ones, was the easiest to break.

Using his fingers, Caplan shifted the ratchet until it was directly between his wrists. Without warning, he swung his arms downward. His wrists hit his belly and he propelled his elbows backward, as if to touch them behind his back. The impact overwhelmed the ratchet, busting the zip-tie and sending it flying to the ground.

Like always, the students exploded into applause. And like always, Caplan took a mock bow. But something was different this time. Normally, he felt invigorated by the demonstration. This time, however, he felt empty. Hollowed out.

Picking up the broken zip-tie, he stuffed it into his pocket. "And that's how …" He trailed off. The mental ties binding his heart cinched tighter and tighter.

"Zip-ties are …" He trailed off again.

He couldn't do this. Not today.

"Thanks for coming," he said awkwardly. "Unfortunately, something's come up. I'm going to have to postpone the rest of this session."

The bright eyes faded away. Darker ones, curious but annoyed, took their places.

"Did you hurt yourself?" Nevins smirked. "Did I make it too tight?"

"No," Caplan mumbled. "I just … I need to take care of something. I'll be in touch with all of you soon."

Without another word, Caplan strode forward. The students parted, making way for him.

As he hiked across the Great Lawn, he heard the students chattering amongst themselves. Some sounded irritated, others were downright angry. He didn't blame them. He'd wasted their time and he doubted he'd see any of them ever again.

He walked farther, passing the softball players, the kite flyers and their parents. He passed dogs on leashes. Men, women. Old folks, youngsters. As always, people surrounded him.

But at that moment, he felt utterly, painfully alone.

CHAPTER 8

Date: June 19, 2016, 8:33 a.m.; Location: Upper East Side, New York, NY

Caplan sprinted down the sidewalk, dodging a pair of walkers and startling an elderly woman as she walked out of a flower shop, bouquet of white roses clutched in her gnarled fingers.

Halfway down the block, a truck pulled out of a garage, effectively blocking his path.

Caplan quickened his pace. His trail runners pounded the sidewalk as he sailed past a group of men in casual suits.

With a sudden leap, he sprung off the ground. Colliding against the moving metal, his shoes kicked furiously, transforming his forward momentum upward. His fingers latched onto the roof. With his feet still kicking the truck's side, he pulled himself onto the roof, rolled across the flat metal, and dropped off the other side. It was a perfect pop vault, one of the basic moves he taught in his parkour-centered classes. Unlike most practitioners, Caplan hadn't learned the move while living in the city.

He'd learned it in the wild.

Caplan had spent most of his life in the outdoors. He loved to run and had often taken advantage of the solitude and natural beauty provided by nature. It felt so free, so uplifting. But over time, that feeling began to change. He grew tired of running the well-beaten path. Of running around obstacles, of avoiding them. He'd longed to take his own path. And so he did.

Many years ago, he'd started experimenting with jumps and vaults, leaps and swings. He'd taught himself to cross over dense bushes, to leap rocks with nary a touch, and to scale trees. And he'd taught himself to leap from tree to tree, to move great distances without ever touching the ground. He was exceedingly good at it. Even better, he found the whole thing therapeutic. Running and jumping with reckless abandon freed his mind, giving it a chance to wander.

As Caplan darted down another stretch of sidewalk, he felt his mind break free of the chains he'd wrapped around it. Memories—ones he'd kept at bay for months—flooded his brain. They swarmed within him, around him. They consumed him.

Consumed his very soul.

CHAPTER 9

Date: January 6, 2016, 1:12 p.m.; Location: Hatcher Station, Vallerio Forest, NH

"I need a favor, buddy. But you're not going to like it."

"Hang on." Zach Caplan typed a few more keys, bringing up one of fourteen cameras operating within Sector 76. An image of grassland, covered with four inches of snow, appeared on his monitor. He studied the grassland, a popular corridor for many of the Vallerio's animals, for fresh tracks. Seeing none, he whirled around in his chair and eyed the newcomer with suspicion. "Forget it."

Tony Morgan popped a frown. At six feet, two inches and a hefty 220 pounds, Tony was a giant of a man. Between his set jaw and a few days of stubble, he reminded Caplan of a former football player. But Tony had never played traditional sports, preferring instead to focus on outdoor activities like cycling, kayaking, and caving. "But I haven't even told you what the favor is," he replied.

"You're the one asking for it. That's all I need to know."

Tony shook his head in mock sadness. "Is this how you treat all your friends?"

"Only the ones who keep asking me to break the rules."

"I swear this is the last time. It's just that—"

"Wait, let me guess." Caplan tapped his jaw in mock thought. "You're making a wreath, but ran out of leaves. Or maybe you need to collect droppings to fertilize your pretend garden. Or maybe—"

"Laugh all you want," Tony said, "but every single one of those trips had a purpose."

"A bullshit purpose."

"Maybe so." He smiled. "But they still had purpose."

Chief Ranger brought with it certain responsibilities, including control over the keys to *Roadster*, Hatcher's primary ground vehicle. Equipped with four-wheel drive and numerous other off-road features, it was well suited for the Vallerio's varied terrain.

But while Caplan maintained physical control of *Roadster*, actual control rested in the hands of Deborah Keifer, the president of the Vallerio Foundation. Anyone who wanted to use the vehicle had to file a specific research request with her. If she approved it—which was rare—Caplan would receive a notification from her office. It was then his job to select the appropriate date and time for the outing, based on weather conditions and animal movements.

Caplan took a deep breath as he spun back to his keyboard. "Did you file a request with Deborah?"

Tony hesitated. "Umm … yes?"

"And she approved it?"

"Do we really need to do this?"

Caplan looked at him for a few seconds. "What's in it for me if I help you?" he asked.

"A bottle of Hamron's Horror."

Caplan's ears perked at the name of his favorite scotch. "I was kidding."

"I know. But it's still yours if you give me the keys."

Caplan liked Tony, liked him a lot. The guy hadn't even batted an eye when Caplan had started dating his sister. But he'd made a mistake by letting Tony take *Roadster* out for an unauthorized spin a few weeks back. Ever since then, the guy wouldn't leave him alone.

"Where to?" Caplan asked.

Again, Tony hesitated. "Sector 84."

Caplan's fingers flew across his keyboard. Within seconds, six video feeds appeared on his screen. They showed a heavily wooded area, drenched in snow. Like the grassland in Sector 76, this particular stretch of snow was pristine. "Not much activity," he said. "What's your interest in 84?"

Tony pursed his lips and arched both eyebrows in comical fashion.

"I see," Caplan said slowly. "You're not interested in 84. So, why do you need *Roadster*?"

"I just … need a break from this place."

Caplan sympathized with that. Hatcher Station was a neat place to live, but he often felt cooped up within its walls. He longed to run through the Vallerio, to explore it. To see it for real rather than over video feeds.

On the other hand, rules were rules. They existed for a reason. Keeping the Vallerio free of human influence allowed Hatcher's staff to observe and record nature at its wildest. The scientific benefits were immeasurable.

"So, what do you say?" Tony asked. "Can I take *Roadster*?"

"Yes," Caplan replied after a moment. "But I'm coming with you."

CHAPTER 10

Date: June 19, 2016, 8:40 a.m.; Location: Upper East Side, New York, NY

The loud honk reverberated in Caplan's ears. Memories of that crisp, cool January day vacated his mind. He became aware of his surroundings. The hot pavement under his trail runners. Pulsing, swirling heat upon his chest. The smell of engine exhaust mixed with New York's standard grab bag of gag-inducing odors.

He swiveled to the right. Fixed his gaze upon a well-waxed sport utility vehicle. A couple of dings, nothing big though, lined its shiny red surface. Its chrome wheels glinted in the early morning sun. Waves of heat emanated from its hood.

Like so many of its brethren, the SUV had most likely been purchased for fashion reasons rather than functional ones. The concept, like so many other aspects of civilization, was utterly foreign to him.

Desk jobs, retirement plans, farmer's markets, organic groceries, art exhibitions, Broadway shows, celebrity tours … he'd dealt with them all in one form or another over the last five months. And while he rarely saw value in any of those things, he didn't dismiss them either. After all, he was the weird one. The fish out of water, so to speak.

More honks rang out, joining forces to form one mighty blaring noise. Caplan felt eyes, dozens of them, staring in his direction. Shifting his gaze, he looked past the SUV. Cars and taxis were lined up as far as he could see, filling the air with electrical heat and noxious fumes.

"Get out of the road, asshole!"

Caplan glanced at the red SUV. The driver, a petite brunette in a tight black shirt stared back at him from behind the windshield. Her tiny hands held the steering wheel in a death grip. Her jaw quivered in fury.

What was it with these city folks anyway? Always in a hurry to go nowhere, always angry at the slightest delay.

As Caplan trudged across the street to the waiting sidewalk, a second wave of loneliness crashed over him. He missed Amanda Morgan. Tony Morgan, too. And he missed all the other people who lived and worked at Hatcher Station. More generally, he missed being around people like himself. People who sought out the wild rather than artificial parks. People who preferred nature's clock to that of mankind. Five months ago, leaving it all behind had seemed like his only choice. A bit of penance for sins that could never be forgiven.

But had that really been the right move?

Rubber squealed as the red SUV shot into the intersection, turned left, and disappeared from his life. The stream of cars and taxis followed after it, their drivers burning his ears with shouts of "jerk" and "dumbass." And then they too were gone. Bystanders, attracted by all the commotion, turned away. Life in the city went on, same as before.

Caplan hiked past a small Thai restaurant and stopped next to a brick wall. He placed his back against it and tipped his head upward. He took deep breaths. Shallow breaths. And deep breaths again.

Now that he thought about it—really thought about it— he found himself doubting his decisions. His decision to leave Hatcher Station. His decision to relocate to Manhattan. And most recently, his decision to turn down Corbotch.

He frowned. He felt a physical imbalance, not unlike the one experienced in Hans Christian Andersen's famous tale, *The Princess and the Pea*. Reaching into his back pocket, he pulled out a crumpled mass. He smoothed it and stared at the name *James Corbotch*.

Stared at the phone number beneath it.

He pushed away from the wall. Took another deep breath of New York's foul oxygen. Then he started walking again, slower and with purpose. Maybe he'd been wrong five months ago. Maybe forgiveness was in his reach.

Maybe it was something he could earn.

CHAPTER 11

"What are we going to do?" Bailey Mills' heart pounded against her chest with continuous ferocity. "We can't stay here forever."

The hipster with the T-Rex shirt studied the clearing from their perch high up in the strange fruit tree. Below, the saber paced around the trunk at a wide distance, growling softly. "If you've got a suggestion, I'm all ears."

Mills didn't have a suggestion. In fact, she could barely think straight. Hours ago, she had raced across the clearing with Toland, Skolnick, Elliott, and the hipster. While the saber watched, they'd scaled one of the orange-barked trees and taken refuge among its yellow-green fruit. Then they'd waited. And waited.

And waited.

"Maybe we can—"

Wood splintered and cracked loudly, like gunshots. Shrieks rang out and Mills felt herself swaying and swinging back and forth. Then the tree's branches, stretched to the breaking point by the extra weight, collapsed in a sudden flurry of noise and commotion.

Mills and the others plummeted to the earth, smashing tall reeds to the ground. Mud splattered everywhere. Chirping in unison, birds took flight from nearby treetops, scattering to the winds.

For a moment, Mills lay in the mud, dazed and disoriented. Then she remembered the saber, remembered how it had stalked them for the last few hours. *Get up, you idiot*, her brain shouted. *Get up and run!*

Skolnick shrieked, causing even more birds to shoot into the sky. The saber, which had watched them fall from ten yards out, turned to look at her.

Skolnick, out of her mind with fear, stood up. She raised her voice a few decibels until she was screaming at the top of her lungs.

Mills' throat ran dry. Despite hours of quiet whispering with the others, she still had no clue how a long-extinct creature had suddenly come back to life. Eventually, she'd just accepted it as reality. But now, back on level turf with the saber, she found herself wondering about it all over again.

Rising to her haunches, Mills stole along the edge of the clearing to a patch of undisturbed grass. Then she chanced a quick look at the saber.

The beast hadn't left its position. But now its head was cocked to the side. Its eyes, orange and deadly, shifted a few degrees as they followed the now-fleeing Skolnick into the forest.

The saber's teeth gnashed together. Then a giant roar rang out. Paws slapped the earth as the beast tried to race forward. But it slipped on the wet mud, losing precious seconds in the process.

"Run," the hipster shouted. "Run, damn it!"

His words cut through the thick air like a hatchet. And within seconds, Mills was running, running for her life.

Brian Toland raced into the surrounding forest, hot on Skolnick's heels. Tricia Elliott was next to clear the boundary.

Mills' bare feet skidded in the slippery mud. Somehow she kept her balance long enough to reach the forest, followed closely by the hipster. But as she passed under the canopy of thick branches and fruit, a new problem arose. Rocks, some sharp and some just hard as hell, littered the ground. More than once, her bare feet crunched on these unforgiving objects. And yet, she continued to run, propelled by that most primal of fears.

Prickly bushes, dripping with berry-like fruit, lay beyond the initial layer of trees. Fortunately, she was able to avoid them by following the lead of those in front of her. Confident in her path, Mills shifted her eyes to the ground. Carefully, she directed her feet, soaked with blood and wet dirt, over the rocky terrain.

She ran into a different section of forest, one laced with pine trees. Behind her, she heard damp leaves smooshing against mud. Heavy, constant breathing. Wet twigs snapping dully underfoot.

She yelped as something sharp grazed her left thigh. Looking down, she saw the saber running next to her, its horrible jaws snapping at her leg.

It paced alongside her for a few moments. Then it dropped back and fell in behind her. Spitting and snarling, it sprinted forward.

The hipster grabbed her right arm and yanked her, forcing her to the right. The saber, already airborne, tried to compensate by shifting its massive head toward her.

Twisting her neck away from its curving teeth, Mills lashed out with her left arm. Her fist crashed harmlessly into the beast's tough hide, glancing off it with little force. But it was just enough to direct the jaws away from her exposed face and toward empty air.

Landing on all fours, the saber roared again as it tried to whirl around on a three-inch carpet of pine needles. But its momentum carried it forward, causing it to smack solidly against an ancient tree trunk.

Mills shot the hipster a grateful look.

He gave her a grim one in return.

She tried to run faster. But her feet, which had seen far more nail salons than jogging paths, felt sore and tired. Her lungs were on fire. Meanwhile, her toned upper body, sculpted for looks rather than function, screamed for a break from the physical exertion. Only sheer terror kept her from falling to her knees and succumbing to a horrible fate.

Pine needles stung her feet and thin branches whipped at her face as she followed Elliott and the others through a patch of dense cedars. Her brain yelled at her, demanding more speed. Or, at the very least, a plan of escape.

It occurred to her that Skolnick, firmly in the lead, was in a pretty good place at the moment. It brought to mind an old truism. To survive, Skolnick didn't need to outrun the saber.

She just needed to outrun everyone else.

Mills fought back the rising panic in her chest. Why was she sticking with these people anyway? It wasn't like she knew them. Then again, what else could she do? Go off by herself? She wouldn't survive a day in this place without help.

Swiveling her head to the rear, she saw trampled needles, some torn up turf, and a few mossy rocks. Plus, about a billion flies that continued to nip at her sweat-drenched skin.

But no saber.

Air rushed and a blur of movement caught her eye. Shifting her gaze to the right, Mills saw the saber streak past her, dodging between pines and prickly bushes.

"Look out," Mills gasped. "It's—"

The air swirled loudly, drowning her out. Thundering noises rose above the current—*thump, thump, thump*—as the ancient beast galloped past Elliott and Toland. Racing ahead, it coiled up into a tight spring of tendons and muscles.

Then it lunged at Skolnick.

The businesswoman screamed as the saber knocked her to the ground. Her head snapped back, striking a weather-beaten rock. Her tongue lolled out of her mouth and she went limp.

Mills ground to a halt. The others did as well. For an excruciatingly long moment, she stared at the saber, at the unconscious Skolnick. Wondered what—if anything—she could do.

Ribs cracked as the beast's paws, large and heavy, crunched down upon Skolnick's chest. Lifting its head to the canopy, the saber roared.

Chills ran down Mills' spine. Then something touched her shoulder. She started to jerk away, before realizing it was the hipster. "It's me." He raised his voice to a soft whisper so the others could hear him. "Everyone, back up. Slowly, quietly. Keep your eyes on that ... thing. And whatever you do, don't turn your back."

Swallowing, Mills stared at Skolnick. "What about her?"

The saber roared again. Neck muscles wrinkling, it stabbed its head at Skolnick. Its long teeth sank into the woman's belly. Blood exploded outward, coloring the damp leaves a dark crimson. Multiple organs slid to the ground, slipping and skittering across the mud-drenched needles.

Mills gasped, her hand flying to her mouth to cut it off. Not that it mattered. The saber knew about her. Knew about all of them.

Wordlessly, she and the others followed the hipster on a slow, cautious retreat. The saber watched them for a minute or two. Then it dipped its jaws to Skolnick's corpse.

Blutchk. Spluuch. Pluuchk.

Mills fought back the urge to vomit. Her brain whirred and clanked like well-oiled machinery as she forced herself to concentrate on the future, on survival. She lacked food and water, shelter and weapons. Even worse, she lacked the skills to produce any of those things.

If she hoped to survive, she needed to contact the outside world, to get help. But how? Her satphone had failed and died. And the presence of a saber-toothed tiger, long extinct, indicated they were in some remote region, far removed from civilization. An area yet to be explored by modern man.

In short, she had no resources, no skills. No means of communication and not even a prayer of anyone stumbling upon her. She might last another hour, another day, another week. But that didn't change the horrible truth that had begun to permeate her brain.

Death was coming for her.

It was just a question of when.

CHAPTER 12

Date: June 19, 2016, 8:54 a.m.; Location: Hatcher Station, Vallerio Forest, NH

Father Time, Morgan thought, *is one vengeful bastard*. Of course, that didn't change her culpability. After all, she and her fellow scientists had challenged the mythical timekeeper on his own turf, not the other way around. So, they bore at least some responsibility for all the evil that had been subsequently released into the world. And like it or not, a reckoning was coming.

It was just a matter of time.

Over twelve hours had passed since the initial uprising. Twelve hours since she and her allies had raided the Warehouse, seized the arsenal, and forced most of the opposition into submission. And yet, she had surprisingly little to show for it. Just rooms full of people—agitated dignitaries, grim-faced guards, and her increasingly nervous allies—as well as a hatch that refused to open. Unfortunately, full control of the station—and more importantly its communication systems—had eluded her.

Head down, she paced back and forth across the brightly lit room. Hoping against hope, she waited for shouts from Codd and Issova. Excited shouts, shouts of success. But all she heard was the continuous, quiet pecking of fingers on keys.

A burning sensation reappeared in her right waist. Breaking off her pattern, she walked to the room's southeastern corner and slipped into the hidden dead space between a pair of filing cabinets.

The burning sensation morphed into searing pain. Gripping her waist, Morgan inhaled a sharp breath. *Keep it together, Amanda,* she thought. *You've got to keep it together.*

Shrugging off her tattered lab coat, she let it drop to the floor. Then she pulled up her crimson stretchy tee and peered at her waist. Her bandages, a rush job by Dr. Adnan, were soaked through with blood.

Tentatively, she gripped a bandage and peeled it back, exposing a deep, jagged gash. She'd received it during the uprising, a not-so-generous gift from one of Hatcher's now-subdued guards.

Gently, she probed the wound, right where the knife had first slit her skin. Her head spun in circles and she nearly passed out from the pain.

She pulled the bandage back over the wound and picked up the lab coat. Folded it into a wad and held it tight against her waist.

Morgan leaned against one of the cabinets. It felt refrigerator-cool and its smooth surface soothed her nerves. Staring off into space, she thought about the long, torturous path that had brought her to this place, this time.

It had all started with Tony's disappearance in Sector 84, an isolated woodland area within the Vallerio Forest. His apparent demise destroyed her, sending her into a tailspin of misery and despair. After several days of moping and grieving, anger erupted within her. She'd entered the Barracks and made her way to Tony's area. Then she'd turned destructive, throwing things, breaking things. That was when she discovered it.

The package.

While flinging books to the floor, she'd heard a mysterious clunk. Pausing for a moment, she saw an old leather-bound copy of the Jules Verne classic, *Journey to the Center of the Earth*. She'd picked it up and cracked it open. Inside, she'd discovered a hollowed-out interior, filled with a thick brown envelope.

With great trepidation, she'd opened the envelope. Inside, she discovered a treasure trove of papers. All night, she'd sat on her brother's bed, reading his scrawls about 48A. First with skepticism. Then with curiosity.

And finally, with fear.

The next day, she'd returned to work, ignoring the pleas of others to take more time, to properly mourn her brother. She began viewing Hatcher's video feeds—the ones for the far corners of Sector 48—in secret. That day, she adopted his quest to unearth the truth.

Day-by-day, week-by-week, month-by-month, Morgan studied those feeds, confirming the existence of 48A. Eventually, she recruited Codd and Issova to her cause and they discovered the sector's hidden feeds. After that, the truth became impossible to ignore. She, along with the other researchers, had been recruited to Hatcher Station on an epic quest to push back the boundaries of time. But someone had corrupted their work. Twisted it, changed it. Turned it into something unholy.

One by one, she'd brought scientists, technicians, and rangers into the fold. They scoffed at first but that quickly changed as she showed them indisputable evidence of wrongdoing.

A few people had wanted to go public with the information. But Morgan convinced them otherwise. Hatcher's guards controlled the Lab and with it, the building's external communications equipment. Since their loyalties lay with the Foundation, she knew they'd never let the truth out into the open.

Leaving Hatcher was a difficult, but not impossible task. However, taking evidence from the premises was a different story. Guards subjected exiting employees to multiple searches, relieving them of any and all items prior to departure. So, the odds of escaping with even a shred of evidence were nonexistent. And thanks to the gravity of the situation, Morgan suspected anyone caught trying to do so would wind up dead.

So, she offered an alternative plan. On June 18, Hatcher was scheduled to host a group of high-powered dignitaries. During the dinner, she and the others would stage a bloodless uprising. They'd seize the arsenal, conquer Hatcher, and use the Lab's communications equipment to release their evidence to the proper authorities as well as to the media.

Unfortunately, her plan had gone off the rails. The bloodless uprising quickly turned into a protracted gunfight. During the battle, one of the guards had managed to alert the Lab. The Lab's guards had proceeded to shut the hatch, effectively sealing off the communications equipment. They'd probably contacted the Vallerio Foundation as well and Morgan knew fresh forces couldn't be far off.

A bolt of pain shot through her waist and she clutched it a little tighter. For some reason, the pain made her think of Tony, of how much she missed him. What she wouldn't give to have him by her side again.

"Amanda?" Codd's voice sounded crisp and cold like an ice storm.

What now? Morgan thought, barely containing her irritation. She'd spent the last few hours in Research, fulfilling resource requests on behalf of Codd and Issova. Some water here. Another laptop there. It was necessary, but mundane work.

"Yes?" she called out.

"We're in," Codd replied.

Morgan snapped to attention. "You mean …?"

"Yes. The hatch is ready to open."

Morgan donned the lab coat. Still clutching her waist, she squeezed between the file cabinets and hiked to the door. She shouted out instructions and a group of armed scientists gathered around her.

As she led the group into Research, thoughts of Zach Caplan, strangely enough, filtered into her brain. To make his unauthorized trip, Tony had stolen car keys from Caplan's unlocked desk drawer. Apparently plagued with guilt, Caplan had left Hatcher a few days later without speaking so much as a word to her. She understood his reaction. Still, his absence had only added to her pain. Losing her brother was hard enough. But her boyfriend, her soul mate? Well, that was enough to rip her heart asunder.

Morgan caught sight of the hatch. It looked the same as always. A three-foot square section of metal plating with hinges on one side and a built-in computer screen. Codd and Issova, still sitting at the same table, continued to work on their laptops.

"Well?" Morgan said impatiently. "What are you waiting for?"

Codd typed a command into her keyboard. Metal shifted, grinding quietly against metal. Air rushed like a wind tunnel.

With a loud click, the hatch yawned open. As always, air blasted out of the shaft, the result of multiple blowers that helped keep airborne particles from entering the Lab.

Morgan peeked into the shaft, seeing the familiar metal ladder descending into relative darkness. "Do yourselves a favor." She flashed a wary look at the small group of armed scientists as she lowered herself into the shaft. "Be ready for anything."

CHAPTER 13

Date: June 19, 2016, 9:06 a.m.; Location: Upper East Side, New York, NY

Caplan pressed the phone to his ear as it continued to ring. *This ain't rocket science, James*, he thought in frustration. *The phone rings, you pick it up.*

The phone rang again. And again. Before it could ring yet again, he pushed an on-screen button, ending the call. Gritting his teeth, he stared at his yellow, heavily flaked ceiling.

The phone vibrated in his right hand. Glancing down, he saw the words, *Unknown Caller*, blinking on the screen. His left forefinger itched to accept the call. But he hesitated. *This ain't rocket science, Zach*, he scolded himself. *The phone rings, you pick it up.*

But he didn't pick it up. And eventually, the call went to voicemail.

Slowly, he sank into his lumpy sofa. Folded his tough, weathered hands in his lap and stared at them so hard his eyes started to hurt. He hated this place, hated this city. So, why was he suddenly reluctant to leave it behind?

Steeling his brain, he put all thoughts of Tony Morgan out of his head and focused on just one thing.

Hatcher Station.

He knew Hatcher like the tiny bumps, folds, and veins in his hands. He recalled the electric fences, the makeshift garage, and the building's massive sprawl. The Heptagon-shaped interior along with its seven wings—the Galley, the Barracks, Operations, Research, the Warehouse, the Eye, and the entranceway—also came to mind.

But what didn't come to mind were weaknesses. Besides a couple of rooftop vents, Hatcher contained no hidden entrances or secret doorways. And the building was rock solid, having been built to withstand earthquakes, blizzards, forest fires, and cyclonic nor'easters. Just how much help could he realistically offer to the situation?

Sighing, Caplan leaned against the cushions. They weren't exactly comfortable, but they still felt nice against his tired body.

On the opposite end of the couch, he saw his laptop. Low on processing power and over a decade old, it was a far cry from the expensive gadgets he saw everyday on the city streets. But it was more than enough to maintain his simplistic Zach Caplan Survival School website.

He thought about the morning's session and how he'd cancelled it. How he'd left all those potential students in the lurch. He needed to send them an apology as well as a veiled plea to give him another chance. Half-heartedly, he reached for the device.

Brrrinnnng!

Caplan's hand froze a few inches from the laptop. His eyes flitted to his phone. But it didn't tremble, didn't light up.

Brrrinnnng!

It wasn't a phone call, so what was …?

Brrrinnnng!

Ahh, it was the buzzer. Which meant someone was at his door. Caplan couldn't remember the last time he had a visitor at this time of day. It had to be Corbotch.

He started to stand up, but the laptop caught his gaze. For a moment, his eyes flicked back and forth between the device and the front door. A series of stark choices, all intertwined, bombarded his brain. Teach survival skills or use them? This apartment or Hatcher Station? Manhattan or the Vallerio? Civilization or nature?

Brrrinnnng!

Caplan pushed himself off the lumpy cushions. He rose to his feet and with one last fleeting look at his laptop, strode across the room. He checked the peephole, unlocked the bolt, and opened the door.

James Corbotch—looking cross and tired—stood alone in the shabby hallway, surrounded by peeling paint and moldy picture frames. "Well?" he said. "Are you going to invite me in?"

Caplan stepped out of the way and Corbotch strode into the apartment. His gray sport coat shimmered gently under the harsh halogen lights. Sweat stains covered the front of his tailored white shirt. "I got your call."

Caplan frowned. "How'd you get here so fast?"

"I was in the neighborhood."

"Well, uh, … look, I'm still trying to—"

"The situation has changed."

Caplan recognized an edge to the man's voice. His fingertips began to tremble from nervous energy. He drummed them against his sides, but the energy refused to dissipate. "Yeah?"

"My people just received another garbled transmission from Hatcher Station. Most of it is gibberish, but we were able to decipher enough of it to determine that the terrorists breached the Lab."

"So, that's it." Caplan felt strangely numb. "They've got control over the entire building."

"Not necessarily. The Lab's guards are well trained and have plenty of provisions. At the very least, they should be able to put up a spirited defense. But that won't matter if we don't get to Hatcher in time."

"In time for what?"

"How much do you know about the Lab?"

"Almost nothing," Caplan admitted. "Research was strictly off-limits during my tenure."

"There's a computer-controlled hatch at the far end of Research. It opens to a vertical shaft. Gas valves line all sides of the shaft. They're designed to blow air upward. It's one of several mechanisms used to keep airborne particles out of the Lab." Corbotch's mouth crinkled at the edges. "The communications aren't working right, but my people are still able to remotely monitor the Lab and its systems. So, we know that when the terrorists hacked into the security program, they accidentally triggered a switch in gases. Instead of oxygen, a particularly nasty biological agent known as HA-78 filtered out into the shaft."

Caplan's eyes narrowed to slits. "How nasty are we talking about?"

"Anyone exposed to it will die within eight hours of contact. Since dispersal happened mere minutes ago, that works out to roughly five o'clock."

Caplan gawked at him. "Why would you allow something that dangerous at Hatcher?"

"The details aren't important. Suffice it to say, HA-78 plays an important role in Research's work."

"Can your people shut down the gas?"

"They already did, but it's too late. The valves released enough HA-78 to cover every inch of Hatcher Station and then some. Without the proper treatment, every person within that building will die in eight hours."

Caplan closed his eyes. Took a deep breath.

"I didn't mean for this to happen," Corbotch said. "But now that it has, I'm going to do everything in my power to save Amanda and every other person at Hatcher. Will you help me?"

Caplan thought about Tony's death. He thought about his guilt and his self-imposed banishment to Manhattan. But most of all, he thought about Amanda Morgan. He thought about how he'd felt about her and how he owed her for what had happened to Tony.

"Okay." He opened his eyes. "I'm in."

CHAPTER 14

Date: June 19, 2016, 1:14 p.m.; Location: Prohibited Airspace, Vallerio Forest, NH

"Hold still." The voice overflowed with disdain. "This won't hurt a bit."

A thick hypodermic needle slid into Caplan's arm. It pierced his skin with excruciating slowness. Liquid eased out of the needle and trickled into his bloodstream.

Seconds later, the predator from the alley—real name, Julius Pearson—yanked the needle out of Caplan's arm. He tossed some cotton balls, a bottle of rubbing alcohol, and a few bandages onto Caplan's lap before returning to his seat.

Caplan wet one of the cotton balls and swiped his arm. Then he used a bandage to plaster it to the pinprick. "Took you long enough." Caplan ignored the urge to rub his aching arm. "What's the matter? My skin too tough for you?"

"Possibly," Pearson replied. "Let's try one of your eyeballs next."

Corbotch frowned. "Can the two of you please try to get along?"

Pearson hesitated before offering a hand across the aisle. Caplan took it and immediately found his fingers crushed by the man's meaty grip.

"That's better," Corbotch said. "You know, I really think you'll be friends before this is over."

Caplan hid his pain behind a deadpan expression. "I can't wait."

"Yes, well ..." Corbotch shot Pearson a cooperate-or-die look before glancing in Caplan's direction. "That shot is fast acting. By the time we land, you'll be fully immunized against HA-78."

Pearson released the grip and Caplan retracted the wounded appendage to his body. At that exact moment, his seat jolted. Hard. A throbbing ache rippled through his forehead. He clenched his teeth, fighting it with all his strength. The pain subsided, only to be replaced by whirling dizziness.

God, he hated this. People didn't belong in the sky. It was unnatural, an affront to evolution's whims.

"I've got a question," Caplan said. "Why didn't you immunize Hatcher personnel before now?"

Corbotch sighed. "The HA-78 vaccine, along with the antibiotic treatment you'll be carrying, just completed its last round of testing. We were scheduled to roll it out next week."

"And the CDC was okay with that?"

Corbotch merely smiled.

Before Caplan could continue that line of questioning, his vision turned blurry. Concentrating hard, he twisted his head, studying the interior of the corporate helicopter. A Rexto 419R3, according to Corbotch. And from the looks of it, designed exclusively for the ultra-wealthy.

The cabin featured four extra-wide seats, two to a row. The rows faced each other, allowing for easy conversation. Corbotch, shrouded in shadows, sat across from him and with his back to the cockpit. Pearson sat to Corbotch's right.

Looking down, Caplan saw an exquisite sand-colored leather seat beneath his jeans. The carpet was plush wool and carefully coordinated to match the seats. A minibar, stocked with top-shelf liquor, had been custom-made for the rotorcraft and built into one side of the cabin.

Caplan's throat ran dry. Working his tongue, he tried like hell to get some moisture into his cottonmouth. "Where are we landing?" he asked.

"A small clearing, roughly half a mile from the station," Corbotch replied.

"Which sector?"

"Sector 23. Not many animals live there and the clearing is free of cameras. As you can see, we've thought this through from every angle."

"Good." Although unbuttoned, the collar of Caplan's black Henley shirt started to tighten around his neck. His jeans felt stiff and inflexible. His feet sweated buckets, soaking his long wool socks and sturdy trail-runners. "Very good."

Reaching to the bar, Corbotch picked up a bottle of Hamron's Horror. He dropped some ice cubes into a clean tumbler. Tipped the bottle toward the glass, filling it with copper-colored scotch. "Would you like some?" he asked.

Why the hell not? Caplan thought. "Sure."

The helicopter vibrated again. Caplan clutched his plush armrests. He waited for the vibrations to settle down, but instead they increased in intensity.

"Hey Derek," Corbotch shouted. "What's the deal?"

"We've got high winds and a little turbulence, sir." Derek Perkins—the curly-haired man from the alley—kept his gaze fixed on the front window and his hands on the controls. "A storm is on the horizon. Unfortunately, I don't think it's going to pass anytime soon."

Corbotch exhaled an annoyed sigh. Then he picked up an empty tumbler. Filled it with ice cubes and scotch. Silently, he passed it across the aisle.

Caplan took the tumbler. Tipped it to his mouth. A swig of Hamron's Horror swept over his tongue. It tasted smoky and burnt his throat as he swallowed it down.

"So, how do you like my little slice of nature?" Corbotch asked.

Caplan glanced out the side window. His eyes widened. How could they not? The Vallerio Forest, far beneath him, was widely regarded as one of the world's most mysterious places. As a boy, he'd gobbled up numerous books about it, about the strange myths and legends surrounding it.

He gazed intensely upon the trees, the leaves. But his keen eyes failed to breach the outer foliage. Even after three years of living in its midst, he was still amazed by the forest's darkness, its impenetrability. It seemed almost impervious to all forms of light.

"It's just as I remembered it," Caplan replied.

"And I assume you recall what we're doing down there, right?"

Abruptly, a glint of brightness knifed its way through the foliage. Caplan did a double take as he traced the light to its origin. *Oh, my God*, he thought. *The fence.*

The glinting light vanished and Caplan's brow furrowed into hard ridges. A giant electric fence famously cut off the Vallerio from the outside world. Similar fences, much smaller ones, surrounded Hatcher Station. But the fence below him, which marked the southern edge of Sector 48A, was another entity altogether. For Sector 48A—Tony's name for it—didn't exist, at least not on paper.

Caplan inhaled slow, sharp breaths. Images of that cold January day flitted quietly through his mind like an old black and white movie. "Sure," he replied after a moment. "You're running a private—and secretive—animal sanctuary. Lions, tigers, bears, and God knows what else."

"That's not a terrible description. But to be more precise, it's a massive Pleistocene rewilding project."

Caplan shrugged. He'd heard those words before, but had never paid them much attention. Unlike the eggheads who populated Hatcher, he hadn't asked a lot of questions. He'd just focused on his responsibilities as Chief Ranger, namely managing the Eye, watching over the forest, and overseeing the occasional field expedition.

Corbotch frowned. "Didn't you go through orientation?"

"Yeah, ranger orientation. For the most part, we talked about day-to-day operations. As for the Vallerio, we were just told to consider it an open zoo."

"I see. Well, think of rewilding as the opposite of civilizing. The idea is to return large-scale areas to natural states."

Caplan nodded. "Like a nature preserve."

"Not exactly. Forest rangers and conservationists manage preserves intensely. They chop down new trees. Encourage overgrazing to control animal populations. And so on." Corbotch's eyes shone brightly in the dimly lit cabin. "They do those things because they're afraid of change, of evolution. You see, nature doesn't exist in a steady-state equilibrium. It's always changing, always evolving. Rewilding takes advantage of that fact. In contrast to a preserve, a rewilded area is distinguished by a lack of management. It involves establishing a natural area and then stepping back from it. Letting nature take over, free from human influence."

"What's the point? I mean, it sounds great and all. But is there any real benefit to it?"

"Actually, yes." Corbotch adopted a thoughtful look. "Have you ever heard of the *Maclura pomifera*, or horse apple tree?"

Caplan shook his head.

"Its most prevalent in Oklahoma, Texas, and Arkansas. Its fruit, the horse apple, is about the size of a softball. It's filled with a sticky latex substance. Nothing eats it. Which is odd because that's the whole point of fruit. Trees produce it in order to attract animals. The animals eat it and expel it with their own version of fertilizer, usually at some distance from the tree's roots and shade. But since nothing eats horse apples, they just fall to the ground and rot away."

"What's your point?"

"The horse apple tree is an ecological anachronism. Simply put, it doesn't belong to this time. It belongs to the past, to the Pleistocene epoch."

His curiosity piqued, Caplan leaned forward.

"Thousands of years ago, megafauna—giant animals— roamed the world. Mastodons, mammoths, elephants, short-faced bears, bison, and eight-foot long beavers were plentiful in these parts. Some of those animals consumed the horse apples, spreading the seeds far and wide. And then everything changed." Corbotch paused. "Some ten to 11,000 years ago, megafauna went extinct throughout the world and especially in the Americas. This was part of the Quaternary extinction event. With no one left to eat the horse apples, the tree's natural range shrunk to the Red River region. The only reason it exists elsewhere today is because of human intervention. But it's a doomed species. Unless something changes, it will eventually go extinct. And it's not the only species in danger. The Quaternary extinction event has had a ripple effect, leading to large-scale extinctions of flora and fauna in the modern era. My experts call this the Holocene, or Sixth extinction."

Caplan arched an eyebrow.

"It might not look this way, but nature is inching toward oblivion," Corbotch continued. "Entire ecosystems were built upon the presence and influence of megafauna. Without them, things have run amok. The horse apple tree is just one example. The extinction of predators, for instance, has caused the elk population to explode in certain parts of this country. The elk feed on aspen trees, reducing seed production. Fewer aspen trees hurts other species that depend on them. And so on and so forth down the food chain. Now, the Vallerio—"

"Hang on a second," Caplan said. "Why'd so many megafauna die in the first place?"

"It's one of history's greatest mysteries. Some experts believe in the Overkill Hypothesis. That is, the first people to reach this continent hunted them to extinction. Others blame climate change. And still others blame disease, a comet swarm, any number of things. Regardless of the cause, just one thing can cure it."

"Rewilding?"

Corbotch nodded. "In most places, rewilding is a three-step process. First, the setting aside of protected wilderness areas, large enough to accommodate foraging and seasonal movements. Second, the linking of those areas together with corridors to allow for a greater range of movement. And finally, the reintroduction of megafauna ... keystone species, carnivores, and apex predators." He shrugged. "Obviously, we have much greater maneuverability, given the Vallerio's size and wealth of ecosystems."

Caplan's brow scrunched up. "So, the creatures you've brought to the Vallerio are meant to replace the original megafauna?"

"That's right. Since North America's original megafauna is largely extinct, we imported proxies. Sumatran elephants in place of American mastodons. Asiatic cheetahs for American cheetahs. And Asiatic and African lions to fill the gaps left by American lions and saber-toothed tigers."

Caplan thought for a moment. "You said nature is inching toward oblivion. How close are we to reaching that point?"

"We've got another generation or two before things spin out of control. But make no mistake about it. The Holocene extinction will not resolve itself. If rewilding isn't implemented on a worldwide scale in the near future, entire ecosystems will collapse."

"So, why are you so secretive about your little free-range zoo?" Caplan asked. "You should be shouting about it on the rooftops."

"Bureaucracy has its benefits, but dealing with revolutionary ideas isn't one of them. If the authorities discover the truth about the Vallerio, they'll shut me down. They'll seize the animals, maybe even the whole forest." Corbotch looked out the window. "No, I need to keep this under wraps. At least for the time being."

Caplan sensed a note of finality in Corbotch's tone. Just then a tiny airborne object outside the front windshield caught his eye. It was a cargo helicopter, built for utility rather than comfort. Small letters etched upon its side read, *Blaze*.

Caplan nodded at it. "How many people are in there?"

"Twelve," Corbotch replied. "Actually, thirteen with Cam Moline."

Cam Moline was the real name for the baller from the alley. Although he'd sustained a multitude of cuts and bruises, Moline had quickly recovered from the fire escape fall as well as from the beating Caplan had dished out to him.

Caplan shook his head. "That's too many people."

"Don't worry. They'll remain out of sight until you've secured entry into Hatcher and gotten a chance to assess the situation."

"So, I'll be alone?"

"No. Julius will accompany you."

"But—"

A blaring noise, akin to a billion sirens sounding off in unison, filled the air. It flooded Caplan's head, turning his brain to instant jelly. He clutched his ears, but it didn't help. The noise was everywhere, inescapable.

"Derek," Corbotch shouted. "What is that?"

There was no response from the cockpit. Or maybe there was, but the blaring noise had drowned it out.

Tremendous heat, hotter than fire, engulfed the cabin. Sweat beaded up on Caplan's face, his chest, and his legs. It poured down his body, soaking his clothes and the seat beneath him. He tried to breathe. But the air was thick and he had trouble getting oxygen into his lungs.

A brilliant light flashed to the north. A cold shiver ran down Caplan's back as he stared out the side window. Just a few minutes earlier, he'd marveled at the Vallerio's darkness. But now, that had changed.

Raging flames engulfed the forest. And yet, the flames didn't burn. Instead, they cast an eerie glow, pulsing in perfect rhythm with the blaring sirens.

"What the hell …?" he muttered under his breath.

The glow appeared to originate from the north, growing lighter with distance. It was fairly bright under the *Blaze*, less so under the Rexto 419R3.

Sweat dripped down Caplan's forehead. It oozed past his lashes, stinging his eyeballs. It slipped into his mouth and he tasted salt on his tongue.

"Are you seeing …?" His voice trailed off as he looked at Corbotch. The man twisted in awkward fashion, moving in time with the fluctuations of the strange blaring noise. His hands covered his ears. His eyes were clenched shut. His teeth ground against each other.

But Caplan barely noticed those things. What really captivated his attention was the man's body.

It was glowing.

He blinked, just in case his eyes were playing tricks on him. But when he took another look, he still saw the pulsing orangish light surrounding Corbotch's body. The guy looked like a phantom. A burning phantom. And he wasn't unique in that respect. Quick glimpses at Pearson, Perkins, and himself confirmed that all of them had been transformed into glowing flame-like creatures.

The air morphed around Caplan, growing freakishly solid. The odors of chemicals and metals filtered into his nostrils. Streaking bolts of electric icicles jabbed at him, jolting him over and over again.

Caplan released his ears. The blaring noise continued to assault him. How much time had passed since he'd first heard it? Ten seconds? Ten minutes?

The sirens continued without fail, pounding at his eardrums, his skull. His gaze shot back to the window. The strange non-burning flames continued to pulse through the forest. Glowing lights shot across the sky, stabbing the darkness, retracting, and then stabbing it again. The ample light provided Caplan with a view that seemed to stretch for miles. But his eyes remained glued to a specific spot in the sky.

"What the hell are you doing?" he whispered through clenched teeth. "Get higher, damn it."

But the *Blaze*, surrounded by intense light, continued to descend at an alarming rate.

Out of the corner of his eye, he saw his watch. Took note of the time. Seventeen seconds past 1:27 p.m.

Abruptly, darkness swirled around him, clutching him in its cold embrace. He had no time to think, to consider what was about to happen. One moment, he was wide-awake.

The next, he was out cold.

CHAPTER 15

His eyelids fluttered open. His drooped head stared directly at his lap. He saw his watch. Read the face. Nine seconds past 1:29 p.m. He'd been unconscious for a full one minute and fifty-two seconds. Just a blip of time in the big scheme of things.

But to Caplan, it was everything.

Blinking, he looked across the aisle. Saw Corbotch. The man's head was drooped as well. His eyes were open, however, and he seemed to be in the process of waking up.

Caplan's brow furrowed. Evidently, he hadn't been the only one to pass out. But that thought was forgotten as he realized something else. The blaring noise had vanished. Almost as if it had never happened.

The air felt cool against his skin. It was no longer solid. He smelled the now-familiar odors of oil and Corbotch's expensive cologne. The shooting electric icicles were gone, too.

Looking around, he saw no traces of the phantom glow that had engulfed Corbotch, Pearson, Perkins, and himself. The non-burning flames, both in the sky and in the forest, were gone as well.

His eyes shot to the window as he recalled the downward trajectory of the second chopper. But the sky, growing darker and stormier by the second, kept him from seeing much.

He shifted his gaze. His eyes bulged as he caught a glimpse of distant forest, far from where he'd last seen the *Blaze*. Just a short while ago, non-burning flames had plagued it.

Now, real ones had taken their place.

CHAPTER 16

Date: June 19, 2016, 1:30 p.m.; Location: Prohibited Airspace, Vallerio Forest, NH

The helicopter jolted severely to the right. Caplan realized the odd events had disoriented Perkins. Conditions were ripe for a second crash.

Ripe for death.

He reached for his seatbelt. Fumbled with it for a moment. Finally, he managed to release the buckle. Inhaling a long breath, he rose to his feet. The chopper jolted again, this time to the left. Caplan's balance failed him and he fell back into his seat. His back hit the cushion hard and the impact emptied his lungs. He gasped at the air, taking a few quick breaths. Then he lunged forward.

His momentum carried him all the way to the opposite row. He nearly crashed into Corbotch, but swerved at the last second. Reaching into the cockpit, he grabbed Perkins' shoulder.

Perkins turned around. His mouth hung agape. His eyes were dull, unfocused. His short black hair stood on end. His mocha-colored face looked strangely ashen. "I was out," he muttered. "For almost two minutes."

Caplan's eyes widened. But he managed to keep his brain on the task at hand. "Find a clearing," he said. "And take us down."

"Almost two minutes ..."

Caplan looked into Perkins' eyes. Saw the cloudiness in the man's once-fierce pupils. "What's your name?"

"My name ..." Perkins blinked. The cloudiness faded away. "Derek. Derek Perkins."

"I need you to take us down, Derek. Can you do that?"

Perkins swallowed. "Did you see the *Blaze*? I think it crashed."

"We'll worry about that later. Just get us on the ground."

A bit of color returned to the man's visage. He grabbed the controls and the helicopter began a slow descent toward the forest.

Caplan propelled himself backward. Flopped into his seat. Grabbed his seatbelt and got it buckled.

He wiped his face, clearing away a mask of sweat. A feeling of pleasant nothingness floated through him. He felt no panic, no need to ask questions. Shock had seemingly stilled his brain.

But on a much deeper level, he felt something else. A small dark spot on the very edge of his soul. Something had happened to them. Something he couldn't explain. But he knew he'd carry the memories of the last few minutes for the rest of his life.

Maybe even into the afterlife.

Abruptly, a flood of conflicting emotions wiped away his pleasant nothingness. Amazement and horror. Hope and despair. Elation at being alive. Fear at what had happened to the *Blaze*.

He looked out the window and gazed upon the forest. It looked different than he remembered. He couldn't put his finger on it. It just looked ... different.

He shifted his gaze to the distant flames. They were so far away. The *Blaze* must've swerved farther northward while he'd been unconscious. There was a slight possibility the occupants had survived the crash.

But could they survive the flames?

One by one, his positive emotions vacated him. Five months ago, a man had died because of him. He'd be damned if he let that happen again.

He was tempted to call to Perkins, to demand a closer landing point to the fire. But the pilot already had his hands full trying to locate a clearing in the dense forest. And what if the blaring noise struck again while they were airborne? What if Perkins lost consciousness for a second time? No, the smart move was to land as quickly as possible. Then he could figure out his next move.

He pushed his face against the window, so hard that his forehead began to hurt. Images of Tony Morgan flashed through his mind. Traces of survivor's guilt began to creep through his veins all over again.

"Hold on," Caplan whispered as he stared at the flames. "Just hold on."

CHAPTER 17

Date: June 19, 2016, 1:38 p.m.; Location: Unknown Sector, Vallerio Forest, NH

Metal squealed loudly as the landing skids touched the ground. A harsh snapping noise filled the air.

"Shit," Perkins shouted. "Just … shit!"

Corbotch looked over his shoulder. "What now?"

Perkins fiddled with the controls. The rotors slowed to a halt. "It's fine, sir. I'm sure it's fine." He took a deep breath. "I just need to check something."

"What … was … that?" Pearson's voice, formerly solid as steel, wavered like thin leaves in a gust of wind.

Try as he might, Caplan couldn't think of a single rational explanation for all that had happened. "When that Blare hit—"

"Blare?" Corbotch asked, interrupting him.

"You've got a better name?"

"No …"

"Good." Caplan ran a hand through his hair. "When the Blare hit, the air changed. It got real hot, real thick. And I kept feeling these pricks, like someone was stabbing me with little icicles. Everything started to glow. And then …"

Pearson leaned forward. "Yeah?"

"I passed out."

Pearson gaped at him. "You too?"

"You lost consciousness?"

"Sure as hell did."

Caplan's brow scrunched up in thought. "I saw my watch before and after it happened. I was out for a minute and fifty-two seconds."

"Same here," Perkins called out. "Last thing I recall, the dashboard clock read 1:27 p.m. When I opened my eyes, it was 1:29 p.m."

"How about you?" Caplan asked Corbotch. "How long were you out?"

"I don't know." Corbotch checked his limbs for injuries. "But it could've been two minutes."

"Did anyone else see that fire?" Perkins winced. "I mean the real one."

"Hopefully, the others got out before the flames started." Caplan stared into Perkins' eyes and felt a sudden kinship with the man. Any enmity between them was—at least for the moment—gone, erased by their shared predicament. "Doesn't this bird have a voice?"

"Sure does." Perkins reached for the radio.

"Stop," Corbotch said.

Pearson shot him an uncertain look. "Sir?"

"No radio."

"Are you crazy?" Caplan's eyes bulged. "The *Blaze* needs help."

Corbotch stared into Caplan's eyes. "What if the terrorists pick up the radio traffic? We'll lose the element of surprise."

"What surprise?"

Corbotch hesitated. Then he nodded at Perkins.

Turning around, Perkins reached for the radio. Quickly, he fiddled with some dials.

Static.

Frowning, he fiddled some more. But the radio just spat more static into the helicopter.

Caplan massaged his temples. "Does anyone have a phone?"

No one replied.

"Anyone?"

"No," Corbotch said at last. "And you know why."

Caplan cursed under his breath. Corbotch had insisted on leaving all electronic equipment, including phones, back in New York. It was a necessary precaution, he'd said, since even a single call could give away their presence in the Vallerio.

"Where's my gear?" Caplan asked.

"I stowed it behind your seat," Perkins said. "Next to the HA-78 antibiotics."

Leaning over his seat, Caplan opened a small cargo bin. Then he took out his backpack and a small flexible cooler full of syringes and sealed vials. Carefully, he placed the cooler into his backpack.

Perkins looked out the front window. "As near as I can tell, we're about seven miles from Hatcher, sir."

Corbotch glanced at Caplan. "Got a compass in there?"

"Don't need one."

"Good, because time is short." Exhaling, he checked his watch. "I need you and Julius to head to Hatcher. You'll pass by that fire on the way. Hopefully, it's burnt itself out by now. If you can, look for the *Blaze*. But don't take long. I need you to secure entry into Hatcher and find a way to distribute those antibiotics to station personnel as soon as possible."

Caplan frowned. If the *Blaze* had indeed crashed, then he and Pearson were on their own. "What about the terrorists?" he asked.

Corbotch looked at Pearson. "Think you can handle this?"

Pearson's gaze tightened. Then he nodded and made a move toward the cabin door.

"Wait." Caplan searched his pack. Pulled out a can of insect repellant. Closing his eyes, he aimed the nozzle at his body. One second later, the cool spray hit his exposed face and cheeks.

Caplan tossed the can to Perkins. Perkins doused his body and passed it on to Corbotch. Then he opened his door and climbed out of the chopper.

Corbotch and Pearson covered themselves liberally with the repellant. Then Caplan returned the can to his pack. Shouldering the heavy bag, he opened the cabin door. A breath of fresh forest air, stuffed with flies, wafted into his mouth. He nearly choked on it.

He jumped to the ground. The soil was muddy, a direct result of a recent storm. Wet grass, standing tall, reached his waist. The cabin light shone on it, causing the stalks to shine brighter than Christmas lights.

He trudged away from the helicopter, his shoes squelching in and out of the dark muck. His eyes searched the nearby trees for cameras, but saw nothing.

Holy shit, he thought. *I think … yes, this is 48A.*

He tensed up as horrible memories rushed through him. Then he shot a glance at Corbotch, who was still situated in the cabin. Did the old man know about Sector 48A and the electric fence surrounding it? Unfortunately, there was no way to be certain.

Looking around, he saw the chopper had landed in a small clearing, one ringed by towering trees. The trunks, thanks in part to the growing cloud cover, looked like dark columns. The spaces between them, pitch black, looked like long-forgotten corridors. His spine tingled. He'd forgotten how much the Vallerio reminded him of an ancient city, full of lost ruins and mystical, evil energy.

Soft curse words filled the air. Ignoring them, Caplan turned his attention to the north. He heard plenty of sounds—rustling branches and wet leaves, dripping water, buzzing flies—but nothing unsettling. No snarling, no frenzied movements.

He took a deep breath, forced himself to listen for other sounds. Fortunately, he heard no crackling flames, no distant cries for help. Peering hard, he looked for signs of the fire. But the Vallerio hid its secrets well.

More curse words rang out. Spinning around, Caplan spotted a section of bent grass near the chopper. "What's wrong?" he called out.

"We hit a rock." The grass rustled and Perkins' head and shoulders appeared above the tall stalks. The man's face, illuminated by the cabin light, appeared red. "I couldn't see it in all this damn grass."

"What's the damage?" Corbotch asked as he climbed out of the cabin.

Perkins scowled. "A busted landing skid."

"Is that a problem?"

"Hell yeah, it's a problem."

"We can still fly, right?"

Perkins' head bobbed. "Sure, but we can't take-off or land. At least not safely."

"Can you fix it?"

"I think so. But it'll take time."

Caplan inhaled a long breath through his nostrils. He could scarcely believe how much had transpired in such a short time. The fake mugging. Learning about the terrorists, about HA-78. Flying to the Vallerio. The Blare. The *Blaze* crashing into the forest. Their helicopter landing safely, only to be rendered useless. No radio, no phones, no working communications. And now, Sector 48A.

What a day, he thought, shaking his head. *What a hell of a day*.

CHAPTER 18

Date: Unknown; Location: Unknown

Bailey Mills swallowed and a large slug of mud slid down her throat. She gagged on it. Her eyes snapped open. Immediately, she lifted her face off the wet muck. Coughing and choking, she swallowed down the disgusting hunk of soggy dirt, earthworms, and blades of crushed grass.

She sank her palms into the mud until they struck a firm surface. Then she curled her outstretched legs beneath her. Pushing upward, she lifted her torso off the ground.

"Welcome back." The hipster's voice, soft and frazzled, rang softly in the damp, still air.

Her head rotated to the right. The hipster sat on his rear, knees propped up and arms circled loosely around them. "Where …?" She sputtered, choking out more mud. "Where …?"

"If you're asking about the saber, I don't have a clue. If you're asking about the others, well, that's easy enough."

Following his waving hand, Mills twisted her neck to the left. Brian Toland lay on his back, staring sullenly at the sky. Mud coated his gray beard. More mud was smeared across the lenses of his thick glasses.

A few feet away, Tricia Elliott lay in a crumpled heap with knees close to her chest. Grass stains covered her loose-fitting jeans. Her green sweatshirt dripped with muck.

Despite her yellow dye-job, all the mud in her hair made her look like a brunette.

"By the way, I'm Travis," the hipster said. "Travis Renjel."

"Bailey Mills."

"I know." He smiled. "I see your picture everyday."

Great, she thought. *A perv*. Guys were sooo predictable. Most wanted to romance her, sweep her off her feet. As if she cared about some stupid flowers or fancy meals. But a decent-sized minority—the perverts—preferred to gross her out, to tell her they stared at her picture when they did … well, themselves. Men—boys, actually—who needed them?

"Wow, I've never heard that one before," she retorted. "You must be a real hit with the ladies."

His smile faded. "Wait—"

"No, you wait. People like you make me sick. I get it. I'm beautiful. Lots of guys want me. But that doesn't give you the right to—"

"I'm a reporter."

She blinked. "What?"

"I'm a journalist with the *New Yorker Chronicles*." His smile came back at full wattage. "You know, the paper that practically stalks you."

She blinked again. "But you said—"

"I said I see your picture everyday. And I do. You're a fixture in our pages."

Mills' face heated up. She gave Renjel another look. Mud splatter covered his unadorned face. Same with his skinny jeans. His t-shirt, the one with the cartoon T-Rex, had been ripped and shredded, giving her a good look at his well-toned abs. "What happened to your glasses?" she asked.

"I ditched them," he replied.

Her eyes widened.

"Don't worry." His smile transformed into a wry grin. "They weren't exactly prescription."

She nodded in understanding. "So, you're a journalist, huh? Then you must know Brian."

"Don't insult me," Toland said. "I'm a writer. Not a journalist."

"What's the difference?" Mills asked.

He sat up. Glared at her. "I'm an author, you dolt. I write books. You know. Those things with spines."

Tricia Elliott stirred. Groggily, she sat up. "What ... what happened?"

"We passed out," Renjel said.

"At the same time?"

Uncomfortable silence greeted her. A few seconds later, Elliott clapped a hand over her mouth. "Randi!" She struggled to stand up. But her knees wobbled and she sank back into the mud.

"Don't be stupid," Toland said. "It's not like you can help her."

Tears eased out of Elliott's eyelids as she assumed a sitting position. Carefully, she wiped them away with her palms. "Ohmigod, ohmigod, ohmigod ... this isn't happening ... it can't be happening."

Mills detected a distinct note in the woman's tone. "You knew her?"

Elliott managed a nod.

"How?"

"We ... we worked together." Elliott's shoulders quivered. Lowering her head, she began to sob softly.

A blurting noise, full of force and energy, trumpeted across the clearing. It sounded familiar to Mills, but she couldn't quite place it.

Toland turned his head, locating the sound. "What the hell was that?"

"Don't know, but it came from the northwest." Renjel gained his footing. "I'll check it out."

"Wait for me." Rising unsteadily to her feet, Mills followed Renjel into the ancient forest.

The trees were thick and packed closed together. Coupled with the darkness, her visibility was limited to a few feet at a time. But her sense of touch had no limitations. Each step was like a journey into hell. Her heels ached. The soles of her feet felt like someone had jabbed them full of needles. And her toes hurt so badly, she couldn't put her full weight on them.

Renjel glided to a tree trunk. Then he worked his way forward. After a short walk, he stopped behind a tall, curving tree. Peeked out.

And froze in place.

Mills stayed back and waited for him to move, to say something. But he just stood there, still as a statue. Finally, she couldn't take it any longer.

Her sore feet squelched across the muddy terrain as she half-limped, half-ran from tree to tree. Along the way, she glimpsed hints of a field. Tall grass. A gurgling stream. Plenty of flies.

She pulled to a stop behind Renjel. Listened to his rapid and shallow breaths. Then she leaned out.

And saw them.

Six four-legged creatures occupied the clearing. They averaged nine to ten feet in height. Broad tusks curved out from either side of their single-domed heads. Their long trunks, the likely source of the blurting noise, waved in the air. Thick fur covered almost every inch of their bodies.

Mills swallowed thickly as she watched the creatures. They looked a little like elephants. But unlike elephants, these giants didn't project an aura of gentleness. Instead, they swarmed in a tight gathering, interlocking trunks and using their bodies, heads, and tusks to deliver ferocious strikes upon one another.

Mills winced as she turned her attention to their old scars, their fresh gashes, their bloodstained fur. All six creatures had suffered tremendous battle wounds. And yet, none of them showed even the slightest interest in backing down. Instead, they continued to fight with a frenzied bloodlust that frightened the hell out of her.

"Woolly mammoths," Renjel said with awe in his voice. "Goddamned woolly mammoths."

The name triggered a memory in Mills' head. "They're extinct, right?"

He nodded. "They vanished from the Americas some 11,000 years ago. Right at the end of the Pleistocene epoch."

"Isn't that when sabers supposedly went extinct?"

He exhaled, then nodded again.

She grabbed his arm and gently pulled him away from the field. "Why are they fighting like that?"

"Maybe that's what they do. Maybe that's why they died out in the first place. Maybe ... I don't know." Pausing, he stared hard at the woolly mammoths. "I don't even know where we are."

Mills inhaled some damp forest air. It smelled of blood and sweat. But underneath that, she detected a certain freshness. Even fresher than her collection of Morning Forest scented products from Cander Luxuries.

Blocking out the sounds of animal warfare, she heard other noises. Running water, blowing leaves, chirping birds, warbling frogs. It was nature at its most pure, without the constant interference of man.

An idea popped into her brain. It was one she'd been playing with ever since she'd seen the saber. "Maybe we should forget about the *where*," she replied tightly. "And start thinking about the *when*."

CHAPTER 19

Date: June 19, 2016, 1:52 p.m.; Location: Hatcher Station, Vallerio Forest, NH

Bullets ripped through the open entranceway, chewing up tattered plastic sheets, metal desks, and computer monitors. Morgan pressed her back against the wall. Although the thick concrete protected her from harm, she couldn't help but flinch each time the Lab's guards opened fire.

Sweat oozed past her eyelashes, turning her vision into a blur of dull, textured colors. Still clutching her rifle in both hands, she wiped her face with the crook of her left arm.

Five hours, she thought. Five hours since Codd and Issova had cracked open the hatch. Five hours since she'd led a small group of scientists into Hatcher's basement. Five hours since she'd initiated an assault on the Lab's guard contingent.

She had no desire to kill or be killed. Plus, her side controlled the Warehouse and its small supply of weapons and ammunition. So, she'd implemented a careful attrition strategy, hoping to drain the guards' resources and force them to surrender. But after five hours and countless bullets, she was starting to rethink things.

What if she'd read the situation wrong? What if the guards were better supplied than her side? What if they were slowly draining her and her fellow scientists of *their* ammunition and resources?

As the sound of gunfire faded away, Morgan stared at the floor, at the shards of glass and bullet-ridden equipment. The air sizzled with heat and smelled strongly of electricity.

She stood inside the shattered remains of an air shower, which separated the security checkpoint from the Lab. The checkpoint consisted of four metal desks bolted to the floor. The bullet-riddled remains of monitors, iris recognition devices, and other high-tech equipment were strewn between the desks.

On a normal day, Morgan would slip through the hatch and descend the metal ladder to the checkpoint. After clearing security, she'd enter the brightly lit air shower via a heavy glass door. Stainless steel nozzles, lining both sides of the shower as well as the roof, would douse her with high-speed winds. Heavy particles, dust and dirt, would drift downward and be sucked out of the room via vents. Only then could she exit the shower, walk through the entranceway, and enter the much larger Lab.

She peered at her fellow scientists, all eight of them. Three scientists, like her, were situated inside the remains of the air shower. They were hunkered down behind the concrete walls lining either side of the entranceway. The others were farther back, in the checkpoint area, crouched behind pillars, desks, and anything else that could protect them from gunfire.

She waved at the scientists in the checkpoint area. One by one, they darted to the concrete walls, under the protection of cover fire. "We can't wait any longer," she whispered. "We have to end this."

"Agreed." Amy Carson, an evolutionary geneticist from Toronto, wiped her sweaty hands on her pants before regripping her pistol. "But how?"

"We need to go on the offensive."

Nervous sighs rang out alongside disgruntled groans.

Morgan held up a hand for silence. "They're better supplied than we expected," she said. "For all we know, they're the ones wearing us down, not the other way around. I say we get in there and force them to surrender. How does that sound?"

"Like a death sentence." Alexander Gruzinov, a Russian expert in bioinformatics, glanced distastefully at his rifle. "I barely know how to use this thing."

"Amy and I are experienced shooters. We'll lay down cover fire while you get into position."

"What if they don't surrender?" Theodor Karlfeldt, a Swedish geneticist, arched an eyebrow. "You don't want us to ... you know ...?"

"Yes," Morgan replied. "I do."

A dark mood spread across the air shower as the others realized what she was asking of them.

Morgan gave each of them a final look. Then she slid along the wall to the entranceway. Carson took up position on the other side.

Morgan snuck a glance at the state-of-the-art Lab. Dozens of stations, some of them occupied by giant silken pods, ringed the room. Large skeletons, arranged on pedestals in museum-like exhibits, were interspersed between the stations. A raised platform, roughly ten feet high, occupied the exact middle of the facility. It was built around a load-bearing pillar, one of many dotting the Lab. This was the command post, used to initiate and monitor experiments. It also served as Hatcher's communications hub.

Steel filled Morgan's backbone. Poking her rifle through the entranceway, she squeezed the trigger. The gun reverberated violently in her hands as it spat deadly projectiles into the lab. At the same time, Carson aimed her pistol into the void and squeezed off a couple of well-placed shots.

Crouching down, the other six scientists hustled into the Lab, spreading out and taking cover behind any solid object they could find.

Guards appeared, shifting behind generators, machinery, and the pillars. Despite repeated calls, they showed no interest in surrender.

Soon, guns blazed on both sides. Bodies fell. Gray smoke wafted to the ceiling. Gritting her teeth, Morgan kept up a steady stream of bullets, mowing down guard after guard.

Slowly, the opposing gunfire died out. And two minutes later, Morgan held up a hand. "Ceasefire."

Carson and the other scientists complied. An eerie silence—punctuated only by shattering glass and crackling electricity, spread over the Lab.

Shifting her gaze, Morgan studied the carnage. It nearly took the air out of her lungs. Three scientists, people she'd worked with for years, lay in heaps upon the floor. Blood poured out of their bodies, mixing with that of the slain guards.

Guilt filled her gloomy soul as she stared at the lost lives, the lost potential. The dead scientists might've volunteered their efforts to the battle, but that fact didn't ease her burden.

She and Carson hurried through the entranceway. Then they circled the room, checking the bodies and searching for holdouts. As she felt for pulses, Morgan's heart grew heavier and heavier. There were so many faces. Faces of dead guards, faces of dead scientists.

Too many faces.

After circling the room, she returned to the dimly lit platform. Stairs creaked loudly as she mounted a metal staircase. At the top, she stared at familiar desks, covered with sophisticated computers and devices. Then she knelt next to a grizzled, bearded man. She recognized him as one of the Lab's computer experts. He, along with a small subset of the guard contingent, had been responsible for the Lab's many systems.

Tentatively, she reached out, checked his pulse. Her heart twitched. He was dead, like all the others.

"Amanda?"

Glancing toward the entranceway, Morgan saw Zlata Issova. "Up here."

Issova took a few hesitant steps into the Lab with Codd on her heels. Then she halted. Color drained out of her cheeks as she looked at the corpses.

Keeping her eyes off the bodies, Codd walked past Issova, climbed the staircase, and began to check the platform's equipment.

Morgan watched Issova for a minute. "Zlata?"

Issova shivered, looked up. "Yes?"

"Did you need something?"

She nodded. "About thirty minutes ago, our scanners picked up a bunch of faint activity. Noises, flashing lights, sudden temperature changes, that sort of thing." She paused. "Here's the kicker. I have reason to believe the activity originated in Sector 48A."

Morgan bristled at the mention of 48A. Knowledge of its dark secret flowed through her mind like a raging river. "Are you sure?"

Issova nodded. "Obviously, we don't have feeds of that area. But the activity showed up in all adjoining sectors, as if seeping out from 48A. Plus, I worked the cameras and spotted some gray smoke coming from that general direction. It could be a forest fire."

"In this weather? Not a chance." Morgan tapped a finger against her jaw. "It has to be the Foundation. Do me a favor. Get a team together."

"To visit 48A? That's insane."

"Just do it."

With an audible sigh, Issova spun around and exited the Lab, taking care to avoid the corpses along the way.

"Amanda?"

Stifling an urge to raise her voice, Morgan swung back to the platform. "What now?"

Codd looked up from a computer, pierced by numerous bullets. Little wisps of smoke curled out of its sides. An odd whining noise emanated from within it. "The communications equipment took damage."

Morgan ground her teeth together. "How much?"

"It's difficult to say."

Can't one stupid thing go right today? Morgan wondered. "What do you need?" she said aloud.

As Codd ticked through a list of necessary tools and materials, Morgan swept her gaze across the platform yet again. She saw the corpse of the grizzled, bearded computer expert. But she failed to take notice of the small computer positioned on the table next to him.

If she had seen it, she would've done a double take at its screen. She would've leaned in close and realized that the computer expert had triggered two programs and numerous sub-programs while in his death throes approximately thirty minutes earlier. The first program—*Apex Predator: Stage I Master Controls*—was unknown to her. But the second program—a full expulsion sequence of the 1-Gen and 2-Gen ectogenetic incubators—would've caused alarm bells to clang in her head.

She would've ordered an immediate evacuation of non-essential personnel from the Lab and security checkpoint. Then she would've raced after Issova, praying to every conceivable god that she arrived before the woman had a chance to deploy a team to Sector 48A.

But unfortunately, Morgan, distracted by death and destruction, didn't see the computer. So, she didn't know what was coming.

And therefore, she couldn't stop it.

CHAPTER 20

Date: June 19, 2016, 1:52 p.m.; Location: Sector 48A, Vallerio Forest, NH

"Keep your eyes peeled." Adopting a northern course, Caplan walked across the clearing. Despite the obvious danger posed by his surroundings, he felt strangely bold, almost brash. "This place isn't safe."

"Wait," Pearson called out.

Caplan gritted his teeth. Kept his flashlight aimed to the north, but stopped a few inches short of the tree line. "What—?"

Rough hands grabbed him. Whirled him around in a circle. Then a fist slammed into his jaw, rattling his teeth and sending him veering toward the forest.

Caplan grabbed a tree trunk with both hands, arresting his movement. Inhaled a stiff breath. Spun around and saw another fist heading in his direction. Straightening and stiffening his fingers, he swung his left arm upward and outward. The blocking maneuver stopped Pearson's attack. But just barely and the impact sent a furious jolt through Caplan's body.

Perkins ran across the clearing and jumped between the two men. "Calm down, Julius. You know we have to—"

With a bear-like roar, Pearson swung a right cross, striking Perkins in the right shoulder. Perkins spun in a half-circle and collapsed face first into the mud. Feebly, he tried to get up without success.

Caplan's senses rose to new heights. He saw Pearson, saw the man's height and strength. Saw his fighting stance and how he bounced on the soles of his feet.

Stepping forward, Caplan swung a right cross in a blinding horizontal sweep. Pearson hardened his jaw. Flesh and bone smashed against each other with a sickening crunch.

Explosions went off in Caplan's hand. Stumbling away, he shook his fingers, trying to rid them of the stinging soreness. Then he glanced at Pearson. To Caplan's shock, the man hadn't moved an inch. In fact, only one thing had changed about him.

He was now smiling.

Caplan charged forward. He maneuvered his torso, his arms a whirlwind of activity. But his every cross, every uppercut, every chop was easily dodged or parried.

Caplan stepped back for a breather. With a sudden burst of speed, Pearson dashed ahead. His fists slashed at the air.

Too late, Caplan went into blocking mode. A fist slammed into his right shoulder with inhuman force, nearly knocking it right out of its socket. A piercing blow struck his left side and he gasped. A third fist struck his jaw and sent him hurtling to the earth.

His right side struck the ground, knocking the wind out of him. Mud splashed over his clothes, his face. He tried to wipe it away, to stand up. But his body felt drained of energy.

He stared upward. Through hazy vision, he saw Pearson towering above him. "How about we call this a draw?" he muttered, spitting mud and blood out onto the soil.

Pearson didn't smile. Instead, he knelt down. Grabbed Caplan's shirt and formed his fingers into a massive fist. Rearing back, he prepared to strike the knockout blow.

"That's enough," Corbotch said quietly.

Pearson's fist froze in mid-swing. His face twisted with anger. Then he released Caplan and stood up.

Caplan struggled to his feet. His face felt like hot hamburger meat. His brain ached inside his skull. His ultra-keen senses were dull, diminished. "What the hell was that?" he asked as he massaged his jaw.

"Payback," Pearson replied without emotion. "For sucker-punching me back in New York."

"I thought you were a mugger."

"Don't care. You hit me, you get destroyed."

Perkins rose to all fours. "What the hell is wrong with you?"

Pearson shot him a blazing look.

Perkins held the gaze for less than a second before shifting his face to the ground.

Caplan rubbed his eyes with both hands until his vision cleared. He was halfway tempted to continue the fight, to get a little payback of his own. But time was short, so he glanced at the forest instead.

"No more fighting," Corbotch said. "Both of you need to focus on why we're here."

Putting his anger aside, Caplan gave Pearson a glance. The man was a mountain of flesh and muscle. But that wasn't everything. Stamina, in particular, would be key for trekking across the Vallerio's uneven, hilly terrain. "I'll take him to Hatcher with me. But I'm not holding his hand."

Pearson's eyes narrowed to slits. "You little—"

"That'll do," Corbotch said, cutting him off. "Remember, we're on the same team."

Caplan turned back to the forest. He wasn't thrilled about traveling with Pearson. But he didn't have time to argue.

"Zach." Perkins hiked to Caplan's side. "You look dizzy."

"I'm fine," Caplan replied.

"Sure you are." He lowered his voice, extended a palm. "But if you start, I don't know, foaming at the mouth later, take one of these."

Caplan eyed the amber-colored pill container, complete with child resistant cap. It was unmarked and filled with small white tablets. "You trying to drug me, Derek?"

"It's aspirin," Perkins said, exacerbated. "Just the thing for headaches, muscle aches, ocular problems, breathing issues, and God knows what else. Now, do you want it or not?"

Caplan exhaled. Then he grabbed the container and surreptitiously stuffed it into his pocket.

Turning slightly, he studied the dark forest of Sector 48A. He thought about what had happened in the area five months earlier. And he thought about how it wouldn't happen to him.

Then he shifted his backpack on his shoulders. Checked his bearings.

And strode into the darkness.

CHAPTER 21

Caplan twisted his head to the left. Then to the right. He possessed an excellent internal compass. But the Vallerio was no ordinary forest. It played endless tricks on one's sense of direction. Almost as if it was deliberately trying to lead people astray.

Very faint crackling noises, just a few degrees to his right, caught his ear. A shiver shot down his spine. Shifting his gait, he hiked quickly toward the sounds.

Pearson hurried to keep up. His boots, as well as the rest of his outfit, was soaked with pungent mud. His jaw was a little red from Caplan's punch. But he breathed easily with no signs of injury.

Doing his best to hide his own aches and pains, Caplan swept his beam through the dark woods. He thought back to his childhood, back to his obsession with monsters, myths, and legends. He could still remember walking into the local library. The rich smell of old books. The hushed whispers of elderly patrons. The disapproving looks from bespectacled, stern-faced librarians.

He recalled walking down narrow aisles, sandwiched by massive bookshelves. And he recalled his favorite section, two little shelves of books devoted to the Kraken, Bigfoot, the Loch Ness Monster, and all sorts of other interesting things. It was on those shelves that he'd first learned of the Vallerio

Forest, of the myths, truths, and uncertainty that surrounded it.

Located in northern New Hampshire, the Vallerio covered millions of acres of undeveloped land. Only three scientific studies had been conducted within its limits since it fell into private hands—apparently, those of Corbotch's ancestors—centuries earlier. According to those studies, the Vallerio featured endless trees, grasslands, rock formations, cliffs, lakes, a deep box canyon, streams, floodplains, waterfalls, and a whole host of other natural wonders.

He shifted his beam. His eyes traced a tall pine tree, dripping wet, as it rose into the stormy sky. Pine trees were common inside the forest. A group of scientists and engineers had planted a whole mess of them in 1885, as part of a plan to rebuild the soil. Caplan wondered how that fit into Corbotch's rewilding scheme. Was the point of rewilding to find the right megafauna for the current state of vegetation? Or did Corbotch plan to eventually return the Vallerio to its original, pre-human vegetation?

Pearson grunted. "Why do you keep doing that?"

"Doing what?"

"Turning in circles."

"I'm watching our flanks."

"For what?"

Caplan wasn't sure how to answer the question. Something vicious lived inside 48A. But what? "Lions," Caplan lied. "They roam through this part of the Vallerio from time to time."

Pearson's face tightened. Reaching to his waist, he grabbed hold of a large pistol. Twisting his neck in either direction, he studied the forest. "Animal attacks are rare here, right?"

Tony Morgan's face flashed before Caplan's eyes. "There was one five months ago."

"You're talking about that Morgan guy? I heard he disappeared."

"He did," Caplan lied again. "But we found bloody clothes near his abandoned vehicle. An animal attack is the most likely explanation. You have to remember the creatures that live here have zero human interaction. So, they have no reason to fear people."

"Zero interaction? That's strange. Don't they ever cross paths with Hatcher's scientists?"

Briefly, Caplan wondered about Hatcher Station, about its current status. Was it still operational? Or had the Blare somehow damaged it? If so, how were the terrorists reacting to the sudden change? "Have you ever visited Hatcher?"

Pearson shook his head.

"It might be in the Vallerio, but it's not a part of it. It's surrounded by electric fences. And the employees hardly ever venture outside the concrete walls. They eat there, sleep there. Very few people receive permission to go outside. And when they do, all precautions are taken to avoid wildlife. And with good reason."

"Because that's how James likes it?"

"In part. But also because Tony Morgan wasn't the first person to die here. Three research expeditions have visited the Vallerio over the years and all of them reported incidents involving aggressive animals. The last expedition to come here—the Dasnoe Expedition of 1904—lost six members to a pack of wolves."

The color drained out of Pearson's dark cheeks.

Caplan lifted his nose skyward. Took a quick sniff of the still air. It was a bit warmer than he remembered. But it smelled of fresh rain and was free of cinders. The crackling flames remained at a low volume, giving him some much-needed hope that the fire was contained.

They crossed a small stream, overflowing with water. Climbed over a fallen tree trunk. Weaved in and out of bush-heavy areas. And all the while, Caplan thought about the conversation with Pearson, about what he'd told the man regarding Tony Morgan and the ill-fated Dasnoe Expedition of 1904.

He didn't feel guilty about what he'd said. How could he? Pearson had no business knowing the truth about Tony. Not where he'd died or how it had happened.

And it was better if Pearson didn't know the truth about how the Dasnoe Expedition had really ended. It would just unnerve him. And that was the last thing Caplan needed.

Six people had indeed lost their lives in 1904, but not as he'd described it. After escaping the forest, Joseph Dasnoe spent the rest of his short life begging the U.S. government to send troops into the Vallerio. To seize it. To destroy the creatures that had killed his men. For the creatures weren't mere wolves. They were, he'd claimed, the stuff of myth.

Monsters.

CHAPTER 22

Date: June 19, 2016, 2:16 p.m.; Location: Sector 48A, Vallerio Forest, NH

"What do you think caused that thing?" Pearson inhaled a short breath. Despite the difficult terrain, he held his own with ease. "The Blare, I mean."

Caplan picked his way through some dense thicket. The air wasn't as thick or as hot as he expected, which he took to be a good sign. Maybe the fire had stalled. "Hell if I know," he grunted.

"Do you think—?"

"Less talking, more walking."

Pearson replied with a terse nod.

More minutes passed as they hiked toward the dull sound of crackling flames. The soggy ground made it difficult to walk. Dripping water struck the top of Caplan's head over and over again, as nature subjected him to its own version of Chinese water torture.

As he walked, Caplan sensed something in the air. It was in the giant tree trunks, the ancient mud, and the shifting shadows. It was everywhere.

Dread pitted in his stomach. He'd felt a similar sensation five months earlier, just prior to Tony's death. And it had happened in the same sector as well. Was this some kind of long-dormant sixth sense, reawakened to warn him of impending doom?

Like most casual observers, he'd always treated the Dasnoe Expedition stories with a large grain of salt. They were definitely interesting. And he felt certain *something* had wrecked havoc on Professor Joseph Dasnoe's party. But a monster out of myth? That had been too hard to believe, especially in the absence of physical proof. Even Bigfoot, bolstered by decades of alleged photographs and plaster castings, outranked it on the credibility scale.

But all that had changed on January 6. He'd seen the strange shadows flitting about the Vallerio's ancient corridors. He'd seen them attack Tony, seen them tear the man to shreds. Were these the same creatures Dasnoe had seen way back in 1904? Or something else, something new?

Caplan's dread quickly faded away and he found himself feeling bolder, brasher than ever. He could still hear the faint sound of crackling flames. But he also detected a new sound. An intermittent thumming, thrubbing noise. It came from close by, just ten to twenty yards away.

With speed and silence, Caplan circled a tree trunk. Just ahead, he saw the source of the strange noise. Surprise and confusion charged through him like twin freight trains. He tried to speak, but his jaw refused to operate. All he could do was look. Look at one of the strangest things he'd ever witnessed in a forest. Hell, one of the strangest things he'd ever seen, period.

"What is that thing?" Pearson asked in a hushed tone.

"Spider webbing." Caplan's fingers curled around the flashlight. "I think."

"A spider did that?"

Caplan studied the mess of silk-material. It was attached to one side of a large black box and covered a wide area. It didn't look anything like a typical spider web. Instead, it looked like a spider had spun a large net and proceeded to wrap it around its prey, forming a pod in the process.

Its size was daunting. He estimated its width, which bulged out from either side of the box, at roughly six feet. Its height was just shy of three feet. "You've got another theory?"

"No." Pearson knelt in the soft soil. Aimed a beam at the pod. "Why's it moving around like that?"

"I think there's an animal trapped under the webbing."

"But the whole thing is moving."

"That's because it's a large animal." Caplan inhaled sharply. "A very large animal."

CHAPTER 23

Date: June 19, 2016, 2:23 p.m.; Location: Sector 48A, Vallerio Forest, NH

"What do you think you're doing?" Pearson grabbed Caplan's shoulder, but Caplan shook him off.

Without hesitation, Caplan marched to the pod. Drawing near, he felt its heat, its energy. He could see it vibrate, perfectly in time with a soft, constant noise.

Thrub. Thrub. Thrub.

He aimed his beam at the pod and then shifted it around, trying to find an angle that would allow him to see the shadowy form of whatever poor creature had been trapped inside the silken web. But the threads were too thick, too well woven. Kneeling down, he studied the strange black box. It sparked with electricity and emitted a soft sound of its own.

Thum. Thum. Thum.

Spiders were capable of taking down larger animals. Rodents, frogs, snakes, even birds. But no spider on Earth could capture an animal like the one before him. Even a giant gang of spiders, working in perfect harmony, couldn't do it. No, the webbing hadn't come from spiders. So, maybe it had come from the box. Maybe it was some sort of trap, designed to stun an animal and then shoot webbing all over it. But why would anyone want to do that?

Caplan eased the backpack off his shoulders. Removed a small object—an axe—from the interior and slid off its head cover.

Rising to his feet, he donned the backpack. Gripping the axe tightly in his left palm, he approached the pod. The axe, one of two he carried at all times, weighed in at less than two pounds. But it was sharp as hell.

Pearson shook his head. "Are you out of your mind?"

Caplan had seen—or rather, sensed—the vicious creatures that inhabited 48A. So, he knew the risk of trying to free this particular animal. But he felt no fear, no need to back down. All he felt was a brash certainty that everything would be fine. If the creature turned on him, he'd kill it. If not, he'd be saving its life.

"It needs our help," Caplan said.

"Why? Isn't that the whole point of this place? To be free of people, no matter what the consequences?"

"You think this is nature's work?" He nodded with disgust at the black box. "Guess again."

Pearson studied the box. "What is this thing?"

"I don't know. But it's old and rusted. I'd say it's been here for a long time."

"How'd it get here?"

Caplan spat at the ground. He didn't care about the how or the why. Someone had trapped the animal. And he was going to free it.

Pearson saw the look in Caplan's eye. "Don't do it," he warned. "We've got to—"

Caplan swung the axe. It hurtled downward, just as it had thousands of times before. Its sharp blade crashed against the silk and bounced off it.

Pearson grunted under his breath. Looked away.

Caplan's right hand, still holding the flashlight, shifted to the pod. He saw a shallow cut in the silk-like material. A closer look revealed more layers of intricate, tight webbing. The pod vibrated as if it had a life of its own.

Thrub. Thrub. Thrub.

Aiming for the cut, he swung the axe again and again. Slowly, his blade began to carve through the thick silk-like material, like a much larger axe chopping through a tree trunk.

Thum. Thum. Thum.

He kept up the pressure, timing his cuts with the pod's soft vibrations. His movements, the product of experience, were exacting, precise. But inside, he felt quiet desperation. Desperation to save lives. Desperation to make up for the one he'd lost.

The pod's vibrations sped up. Scraping noises rang out. The silk-like material began to stretch, to pulse with increasing speed.

"Get back," Pearson shouted.

But Caplan didn't hear him. All he heard was the thumming, the thrubbing. He continued to swing his axe, cutting deeper and deeper into the large pod.

The pod trembled violently. The scraping gained volume, drowning out the other noises. And still Caplan kept up his steady assault, slicing deeper and deeper into the pod.

Suddenly, the cut burst like a broken seam. The pod yawned open and a dark, egg-shaped mass appeared.

Pearson took a few steps back. Aimed his gun at the mass.

Caplan swung his beam into the pod, identifying the mass as a large fur-covered creature. Its limbs were pressed tight against its body. Its face, from what he could tell, featured a broad snout, short ears, and long, sharp teeth. Thick hoses connected it to the black box.

The creature winced, turned away from the light. Its coat was golden brown on the sides and streaked with black. Its legs were long, powerful, and covered with black fur.

Slowly, the creature's paws stretched outward. Its limbs unfolded into the void. It began to wiggle about, as if awaking from a long slumber.

Pearson swallowed. "Okay, you saved it. Can we go?"

Caplan studied the animal. Was this one of the creatures that had killed Tony? He wasn't sure.

The creature planted its paws on the bottom of the pod. It rose on all fours, seemingly doubling in size. The hoses ripped away from its body. A low-throated growl rang out.

The creature stood up on its hind legs, stretching the pod and causing the silken strands to *snap, snap, snap*. Finally free, the animal stretched upward. Three … four … no, five feet in length. Its front paws reached for the sky. Its low-throated growl took a turn into the deep-end.

"Zach." Pearson's voice turned urgent.

The creature fell back to the earth, its front paws crashing softly against the pod's tattered remains. It wasn't gigantic. Just five feet long and maybe three feet in shoulder height.

The creature whirled around. Bared its teeth.

And charged Caplan.

Caplan had just enough time to see its savage, orangish eyes before the creature was upon him. He dove to his right. The creature raced straight ahead and slammed into his legs. He felt its fur, felt the power behind it. The glancing blow ripped the axe and flashlight out of his hands. His lower half twisted in a quarter-circle and he slammed face first to the muddy earth.

The creature, clearly some kind of wolf, ground its paws into the muck, sliding to a slippery stop. Twisting around, its paws slapped the ground, finding a footing.

Caplan struggled to his knees. His flashlight lay several feet away, its dull beam glinting along the mud-soaked ground. His axe was a little closer, but still out of reach.

Growling, the wolf charged again.

Pearson planted his legs. Taking careful aim, he squeezed his hand cannon's trigger. Gunfire, suppressed to a dull roar by a silencer, rang out.

The wolf flinched and slid to a halt six or seven feet from Caplan.

Pearson squeezed the trigger again. The pistol reverberated in his hands.

The wolf twisted as a bullet crunched into its hide, just above its right shoulder blade. Snarling loudly, it backed up a few steps, mud slurping under its heavy paws. Its orangish eyes flashed in the dim light. As it backed up into one of the Vallerio's dark corridors, it howled at the sky. Seconds later, blackness swallowed up the strange beast.

Caplan frowned. The snarls and howl were vicious and bloodthirsty. But they were also unfamiliar to him. Clearly, the wolf wasn't responsible for Tony's death.

He crawled forward, retrieving his axe and flashlight. Twisting the beam, he saw no sign of the animal.

Pearson gave him a sharp look. "You're welcome."

"For what?" Caplan hiked back to the remains of the pod. "I had things under control."

"Sure you did." Pearson's gaze moved to the forest. "So, what was that thing? A gray wolf?"

Kneeling down, Caplan sifted through the tattered silken bonds. In the process, his beam glinted against the black box and he saw a small, heavily varnished plaque. "*Canis dirus*," he read aloud.

"So, we've got a name for it."

"There are just a handful of wolf species in the world," Caplan replied thoughtfully. "And you know what they all have in common?"

"What?"

"None of them are called *Canis dirus*."

CHAPTER 24

Date: June 19, 2016, 2:37 p.m.; Location: Sector 48A, Vallerio Forest, NH

"What's that supposed to mean?" Pearson's eyes cinched tight. "That it doesn't exist or something?"

Caplan stood up and checked his watch. His heart palpitated as he noted the time. Morgan and the others had less than two and a half hours to live.

He reoriented himself toward the heat and crackling flames. He estimated they'd traveled close to three miles prior to finding the strange pod, leaving roughly four miles to go. If they kept up their fast pace of six miles per hour, they'd reach Hatcher by about 3:20 p.m. That would leave them just 100 minutes to infiltrate the station and administer the antibiotics. It was a tight window. Tight, but manageable.

That is, assuming nothing slowed them down.

He set forth again, gliding through the soggy forest. Along the way, he warded off some fresh doubts. Yes, he'd grown increasingly bold ever since meeting Corbotch in that dark alleyway. And yes, maybe that boldness bordered on recklessness from time to time. But at least he wasn't standing around, frozen with fear as others faced imminent death. At least he was trying to help, to do *something*.

Pearson hustled to Caplan's side. "I asked you a question," he said angrily.

"I don't know what it means," Caplan replied after a moment. "It looked a little like a gray wolf. But it was broader, stockier, heavier. I'd say it outweighed even a large gray wolf by some forty to fifty pounds. Plus, its fur was the wrong texture and color."

"So, this *Canis dirus* ... it's some kind of mutant?"

Caplan shrugged.

They continued to walk, tramping softly across the mud. The temperature climbed a few notches. It never got hot, but it was definitely warmer. The crackling rose a few decibels. Shifting his flashlight beam, Caplan saw pieces of metal, maybe 100 yards out. Painted with digital camouflage, they blended well with the greenish needles and brown branches of surrounding pine trees. Flickering streaks of orange and columns of gray smoke surrounded the metal.

Caplan picked up speed, breathing faster and tasting ash in the air. Wet branches, covered with sticky white sap, snagged at his shirt, his arms and hands. It felt like he was walking through an ancient corridor of living skeletons, their bony fingers repeatedly grabbing him, smearing his skin with awful white goo. He tried to wipe the residue onto his jeans, but no matter how hard he tried, he couldn't get rid of it.

Skirting to the left, he entered a tiny clearing filled with tall stalks of grass. His breath caught in his throat as he stared at what remained of the *Blaze*. It lay squashed in the mud, mangled and stripped into so many pieces as if were a child's plaything. Its complete destruction, this mighty instrument of man's ingenuity, unnerved Caplan. If civilization's finest technology couldn't survive the ancient evil that held court in the vast Vallerio, then what hope did he have?

Fires, small to mid-sized, impeded his view of the wreckage. They burned slowly, keeping their heat, in an almost supernatural effort to gain traction on the damp soil and soaked grass blades.

Caplan's eyes teared up from all the smoke, the embers. "Can anyone hear me?" he shouted.

No one responded.

He hiked forward. A wall of sweltering heat, many feet thick, met him head-on. He heard the silent screams of the dead just beyond it. The smell of freshly-charred flesh and well-curdled blood hung heavy in his nostrils.

He plunged into the grassy field and his pores opened wide. Buckets of sweat poured down his body and evaporated before reaching the ground. Wiping the salty liquid from his eyes, he studied the wreckage. The cabin door hung from its hinges, mangled by the crash into a multi-sided shape unrecognizable by modern geometry. Flames roared inside the cabin as well as inside the cockpit. Despite the heat, a shiver ran through him.

Where are they? he wondered.

More sweat poured out of his body and fell prey to the heat, leaving him dizzy and dehydrated. He took a few steps forward, but the heat turned unbearable and he was forced to halt. The clearing felt like a giant grill, dialed up to the highest settings.

Spots of color appeared where none had previously existed. He stumbled backward, sideways. His feet caught on something and he felt himself turning, slipping, sliding.

Falling.

His right side smacked against the mud. Blinking, he stared at a face. The face stared back at him, eye sockets agape as if they had seen things no man should ever see.

Tilting his head, Caplan saw other faces, other bodies. They lay quietly amongst the bent grass and well-trodden mud, their souls long released into the great beyond. His fervent wish to keep others from succumbing to the Vallerio Forest had gone unfulfilled.

Large hands grabbed his armpits. A moment later, he felt himself dragged backward along the rocky, wet soil. "Dead," he muttered. "They're all dead."

CHAPTER 25

Date: January 6, 2016, 3:16 p.m.; Location: Sector 48, Vallerio Forest, NH

"What the …?" Caplan leaned forward until the tip of his nose practically brushed the windshield. "Did you know that was here?"

Tony Morgan didn't reply.

Caplan pressed the brake pedal. The clunky four-wheel drive vehicle, known affectionately throughout Hatcher Station as *Roadster*, slid gently along the snow, coming to a stop halfway up a small hill. Narrowing his eyes, he studied the long metal posts and the thick, sparking wires.

The surrounding forest had been cut back to make space for the curving fence. Metal posts, embedded in concrete blocks and painted to look like trees, rose twelve feet above ground and measured at least a foot in diameter. Thick metal bars, interspersed with wires, connected the posts to each other. There were no safety signs, no warnings to keep back.

Inside the fence, Caplan saw more trees, dripping with the vestiges of the last snowstorm. His subconscious detected something unsettling about the ancient pines, cedars, and hemlock trees. The landscape, although picturesque on the outside, hinted at a great evil. An evil that ran deep in the soil, spoiling all it touched.

"I asked you a question," Caplan said, more firmly this time. "Did you know that fence was here?"

Tony, clad in a bright orange coat, remained still for a moment. Then he nodded.

"I'm your boss," Caplan said. "How come you found out about this before I did?"

"Because I'm unlucky as hell. Listen, I need to do a few things. So, if you'll just—"

"Forget it."

"But—"

"I don't know what this place is, Tony. But I know we're not supposed to be here. If we get caught—"

"We're not going to get caught." Tony's voice rose a few decibels. "Do you want to know how I know that, Zach? Because this area doesn't exist. Oh, it exists in person. Just not in Hatcher's systems."

"I don't understand."

Taking a deep breath, Tony lowered his voice. "A couple of weeks ago, I noticed a little shaft of light while browsing the feeds for this sector. Looking closer, I saw a fence. At first, I thought it was some old relic of the past. But I couldn't stop thinking about it. So, I shifted feeds, hoping to get a better look. But it didn't work. That got me real curious and I started comparing the feeds to each other. And you know what I learned?"

"What?"

"The feeds and our instruments only cover part of this sector, even though our systems say otherwise. In other words, there's a gap in our coverage of 48. I call that area— which you see before you—48A."

Caplan stared at him, then at the fence.

"All those times I borrowed *Roadster*, I came here." Tony exhaled. "I've driven and hiked along the fence for miles in each direction. I haven't seen anything yet. Not even animals. But the Foundation has to be hiding something in there."

Caplan's brain swirled with this new information. "I'm sure there's a reasonable explanation for this."

"If you've got one, I'd love to hear it."

Turning his head in either direction, Caplan followed the fence to its vanishing points. It didn't move in a straight line or even close to it. Instead, it curved and angled wildly. Coupled with the paintjob, which also covered the concrete blocks, the fence appeared well disguised from aircraft and satellites. Not that it mattered much since the Vallerio Forest had been designated an official Prohibited Area many years earlier, alongside such well-known places as Camp David, Mount Vernon, and Groom Lake. Other than Corbotch-approved crafts, no flights of any kind were allowed to enter the airspace.

Caplan felt vague hints of curiosity stirring in his joints. But equal amounts of dread stirred with them. Dread of what lay beyond the fence. Dread of getting caught. Dread of losing his job.

"Maybe the Foundation is building a new base of operations." He shrugged. "Regardless, it's none of our business."

"Says you." Grabbing the handle, Tony pushed his door ajar and stepped outside. Hoisting a duffel bag over one shoulder, he shot Caplan a mock salute. "Back in a minute, bro."

"Get back here!" Caplan banged the steering wheel with a frustrated fist as Tony slipped, skidded across the snow-covered earth.

After a short distance, Tony slid down a small hill like a baseball player stealing second. Throwing his bag to the ground, he donned a pair of thick gloves and sorted through it. Selecting an aerosol can, he doused the nearest wires with some kind of foamy, white substance.

Cursing under his breath, Caplan turned off the ignition, jerked his door open, and stepped out into the bitter cold. He lingered for a moment at the open door, soaking up whatever heat he could get from the still-warm car. Then he closed the door. Hunkering down against the biting wind, he hiked across the crunchy, wet snow.

Tony tossed the aerosol can aside and picked up a pair of sharp bolt cutters. Caplan couldn't quite see the handles, but figured they were made of fiberglass or a similar material. He knew he should stop the man, but blazing curiosity kept him from doing so.

Lifting the cutters, Tony attacked the bottom two wires. Sparks flew as he snipped and peeled back four-foot sections of fencing. The gentle buzzing of electricity turned strident. Tossing the cutters aside, Tony flopped onto his belly and crawled under the barrier.

Caplan's heart sank to new depths even as his curiosity soared. "This is stupid," he shouted, emitting tiny clouds of vapor into the icy air. "The interior must be gigantic. You'll never get through it on foot."

"Don't need to." Reaching back, Tony grabbed his bag and pulled it into the gap afforded by the cut wires. "I'm just going to plant a few cameras, set up some instruments. At least we'll have eyes and ears on this place."

"Tony …"

"Give me twenty minutes. That's all I need."

Tony Morgan tossed the heavy bag over his shoulder. After another mock salute, he trudged across the untouched snow, heading to the trees.

Caplan stopped well short of the fence. Clutching his arms across his chest, he shivered. Part of him wished he had Tony's audacity. Part of him wished Tony had his cautiousness.

Darkness swallowed Tony up as the man stepped into the forest. Caplan shivered again as a strange sensation filtered through his blood. Trying to ignore it, he stared at the landscape. The trees floated over the snow banks like ancient pillars of a long-forgotten city. A city abandoned to the elements for reasons modern man would never fully understand.

"Holy—" Tony's shout ceased immediately, like a radio station cut off mid-song.

Caplan cupped his hands around his mouth. "Everything okay?" he called out.

Wet snow crunched like gravel. Tree branches shook violently, sending their snow airborne where it turned into a cloud of thick whiteness.

A roar, not especially loud but full of unearthly evil, rang out. Its sound, fierce and discordant, reached into Caplan's very soul, touching some ancient, instinctual part of him. Vast amounts of fear, fear he'd never felt in his life, sprung up inside his heart.

More roars, the stuff of Caplan's worst nightmares, rang out. Tony's voice lifted above the ruckus, shouting something unintelligible. The dark corridors between the trees started to tremble, to swirl with unseen activity. The darkness expanded, contracted, and expanded again.

Abruptly, two things shot out of the forest at cannon-speed. The first thing—the duffel bag—slammed into the fence and fell to the ground, just a few feet from the gap. The second thing hurtled to the snow several feet in front of the trees and rolled twice. As it came to a halt, Caplan saw sprawled limbs, a ripped-up face, and a sliced and bloodied belly.

Quivering, Tony lifted his head off the blood-splattered snow. He met Caplan's gaze with wild, unfocused eyes. Eyes that had seen too much and might never see again.

The wounds, coupled with the sheer force with which Tony's body had been launched out of the darkness, baffled Caplan. What kind of animal could do such a thing?

Caplan ran toward the fence. Tony's wounds were brutal and deep, but not necessarily deadly. He could still survive the attack, albeit with permanent scars, if he received medical attention.

Caplan slid down the small hill to the fence. As he started to crawl under it, he caught sight of the forest. He could sense its energy, its seething rage. The trees, sturdy columns of nature's most forbidden city, seemed to separate as if inviting him—no, daring him—to enter their presence. He sensed their determination, their steadfast resolve to protect whatever secrets, ancient or otherwise, lay beyond them.

His nerves frizzled like electric wires and he hesitated at the edge of the fence. Only for a minute or so, time which he spent staring into Tony's desperate, horror-stricken eyes.

The dark corridors pulsed and expanded to even larger sizes. The darkness—snarling, frenzied, and very much alive—spread its tentacles across the ground.

Tony's cheeks bulged as it swept over his body. Ungodly fear and clarity filled his eyes. He screamed again and again. Screams not just of pain but also of immeasurable fright. The sort of nightmarish fright one only faced in the darkest of nightmares.

The screams died away. The pulsing blackness retreated back to the tree line, taking Tony's body with it and leaving the duffel bag and bloody scraps of clothing behind.

Sobs tickled Caplan's throat. His body sagged and his eyes closed over. His head lowered to the snow as he relived his moment of hesitation over and over again. Tony was dead.

And it was his fault.

CHAPTER 26

Date: June 19, 2016, 2:56 p.m.; Location: Sector 48A, Vallerio Forest, NH

"It looks like ..." Pearson's face twisted in disgust. "... like something ate him."

Caplan took a few deep breaths, evacuating the last bits of smoke from his aching lungs. Then he paced across the partially scorched field. The various fires, ultimately thwarted by the dampness, had begun to die out. They'd left a variety of corpses—some charred, some mildly burnt, and one totally untouched—in their wake.

He cast a wary eye at the surrounding tree line. The black corridors reminded him of that cold January day five months earlier. He recalled stretching a trembling hand under the fence and grasping Tony's duffel bag. Stretching a little farther, he managed to grasp one of the bloody scraps of clothing. Fortunately, Tony had brought along tools to repair the fence, so fixing the snipped wires only took a few minutes. Then he'd retreated to *Roadster*. For ten minutes, he'd sat alone inside the vehicle, trembling and fighting back tears.

He knew he needed to tell the truth. To reveal the mysterious fence to all of Hatcher and take whatever punishment the Foundation deemed necessary. But was that really the best move? Clearly, someone was hiding something in 48A. What if that person tried to kill him for what he knew? Or worse, what if that person targeted Amanda, figuring Tony might have shared his discovery with his sibling?

And at that moment, racked with grief and uncertainty, he made the first of many decisions that would eventually consume his life. Quickly, he'd driven the vehicle to Sector 84. After parking it in some brush, he planted the blood-soaked piece of fabric nearby. Then he hiked back to Hatcher, manually deactivated the exterior fences, and slipped into the Eye.

By that time, he'd begun to doubt his strategy. But it was too late to back down. So, he accessed and deleted the applicable video feeds, hiding all evidence of the ill-fated trek to 48A. Then he disabled the feeds to make it look like they'd been turned off since early afternoon. Only then did he report *Roadster's* puzzling disappearance.

He'd initiated an investigation and quickly discovered Tony's absence. The other rangers booted up the feeds and soon found the missing *Roadster*. A giant manhunt turned up nothing but the bloody cloth, buried under a couple of inches of newly fallen snow. Everything after that—his resignation, the daylong exit interview and signing of documents, and the flight to Manhattan—had been a blur.

Sighing wearily, Caplan aimed his flashlight beam at the body, identifying it as the baller from the alley. What was his name again? Oh yeah, Cam … Cam Moline.

The twenty-something's mouth was wide open and it looked like he'd died in mid-scream. His eyes, unfocused and bloodshot like a junkie's, stared lifelessly at the sky. They reminded Caplan of the look he'd seen in Tony's eyes just prior to the end.

Caplan tried to close the man's eyelids, but they wouldn't budge. Giving up, he touched the man's cheek with the back of his hand. The skin felt cold and rubbery.

"That's Cam," Pearson said tightly. "He served in the U.S. Army Rangers."

Holding his breath, Caplan lifted Moline's shredded shirt. Something sharp and curved—a claw?—had carved the man's torso up like a Thanksgiving turkey. His organs, the ones that were left anyway—had been chewed into brownish, blackish pulp.

Bile rose in Caplan's throat. "Looks like a cat attack," he said slowly. "Maybe a lion, maybe a tiger."

For a solitary moment, Caplan knelt in the clearing, listening to the dying flames, the buzzing flies, and the *drip-drip-drip* of water. Then he saw a glint of metal just past Moline's body. Standing up, he retrieved a standard-issue U.S. Army 9mm pistol from the mud. Lifting the silenced barrel to his nose, he took a whiff. Then he checked the box magazine. "I can't tell if it's been fired recently," he said. "But it's missing a few rounds."

"Moline was a tough sonofabitch. He must've seen the cat coming and gotten a few shots off." Pearson nodded at the flashlight. "Are you sure we should have that on?"

Caplan gave him a questioning look.

"What if that cat is still hanging around? It might see the light."

"I hope it does," Caplan replied. "You know how it feels to get walloped with a blinding light, right? Well, animals don't like it anymore than we do."

Exhaustion crisscrossed Caplan's brain and body as he walked to the smoldering wreckage. He felt slow, sluggish. God, he wished he could sleep. Sleep until the sun rose, fell, and then rose again.

He aimed his beam into the cabin, sweeping it across the long metal benches, the burnt bags of equipment. He saw plenty of blood, much of it blackened by the fire, but no bodies. Most likely, a few people were injured or died in the crash. The healthy ones evacuated them and started to make their way across the clearing. But a large cat—or maybe several of them—had other ideas.

"I count thirteen corpses." Pearson shook his head. "You know what that means, don't you? They're dead. They're all dead."

Caplan swept his beam in a circle, passing over the gruesome baker's dozen. When it reached a western heading, another glint caught his eye. What was that? Another gun? A piece of the helicopter? Something else?

Caplan hiked to the edge of the clearing, slipped under the overhanging canopy, and entered one of the Vallerio's dark corridors. The ancient city of nature, constructed long ago by sheer chance and evolution, stretched before him. But although he could run its streets and scale its pillars, he knew he'd never truly be one with it. For this, he felt eternally thankful.

Stepping carefully, he entered another dark corridor and hiked past several sky-high pillars of gnarled, damp wood. Before long, he caught sight of what had caused the glinting. He wrenched to a halt. His eyeballs trembled in his head and jolts of electricity shot through his veins.

A large amount of webbing-like material, ten feet end to end, eight feet top to bottom, sat on a small pile of rocks. A pulsing black box, exactly the same as the other one, rested beneath it. Like before, it looked like the box had somehow captured a large animal and encased it in silk strands.

Thrub. Thrub. Thrub.

Thum. Thum. Thum.

Sweat beaded up on his palms. The previous box and pod, isolated and alone, meant one thing. This second set meant something else.

Once is a mere occurrence, he thought. *But twice is a disturbance.*

He hiked to the pod. Shifting the beam, he aimed it at the box's label. *Castoroides ohioensis*, he read quietly.

Canis dirus? *Castoroides ohioensis*? What were these strange creatures? Caplan was a wilderness survival expert, not a zoologist. But he'd worked in the Vallerio long enough to memorize the scientific names of many animals. So, the fact that he didn't recognize either was cause for concern.

Light breaths and faint footfalls sounded out. Moments later, Pearson appeared. He scanned the pod with furrowed brow before lifting his gaze. "Zach." He nodded farther to the west. "Over there."

Caplan followed the man's gaze with his beam. A soft gasp escaped his lips.

Once is an occurrence and twice is a disturbance, he thought. *But this … this is an abhorrence.*

Giant silk-like pods, dozens of them, dotted the forest. Some of the boxes and pods throbbed gently, beating in time to a rhythm he didn't understand. But most of the pods had been clawed open and he saw no sign of their former occupants.

A puttering noise, barely audible, arose abruptly from the north. Caplan's neck prickled. Dousing the flashlight, he turned toward the clearing. Light flames continued to tickle the edges of the wreckage, adding a faint glow to the burnt grass.

Pearson frowned, glanced at Caplan. "What is it?"

Caplan closed his eyes. Lifted his chin and let his senses run free.

"Did you hear me? I said what—?"

Caplan opened his eyes. "It's *Roadster*."

"*Roadster*?"

"Hatcher's ground transport vehicle. The terrorists must've sent it to investigate the crash." His lips moved silently. "In other words, they know we're here."

CHAPTER 27

Date: June 19, 2016, 3:04 p.m.; Location: Sector 48A, Vallerio Forest, NH

The overhanging clouds opened up in unison, releasing their liquid cargo in a fierce torrent. The rain, pent up for far too long, fell hard and fast, eager to complete its journey to the earth. Within seconds, the storm had transformed the clearing's burnt stalks and wet mud into a small swamp.

Bright headlights flashed. But the darkness, thick as sludge, and the never-ending sheets of rain combined to limit their reach.

Caplan cut through the forest like a finely honed machete. Sticking to the shadows, he saw a tall cedar tree. The end of a broken rotor blade stuck out of its trunk, wobbling gently in the breeze. He crept behind the tree and chanced a look to the north.

The fence, he thought. *Finally!*

The fence, with its forest-like paintjob, was barely visible amidst the downpour. But he would've recognized it anywhere.

He tensed up, all-too aware of how Tony had died just inside the fence line. Coupled with the dead bodies outside the *Blaze*, he knew danger couldn't be far off.

The engine grew louder and louder. Then a giant shadow slid into view. There it was, his *Roadster*! The beat-up old SUV came to a stop just outside the fence, up to its rusty axels in swampy soil. His heart thumped as he studied its scrapes, dings, and dents. What a beat-up piece of junk. But damn, how he'd missed it.

The driver cut the engine, but left the beams on at full-blast. Silently, Caplan stowed the flashlight in his pocket. Then he removed the axe and its twin from his backpack and shook off their coverings. The axes had been forged with fine materials and great care. In the right hands, they weren't just tools. They were fearsome weapons, capable of long-distance attacks as well as close-quarters combat. Each axe possessed a foot-long handle, topped off by a curved metal head. Their blades were sleek with v-shaped notches. At the back of each head, the metal tapered off to form a vicious spike.

Rain struck the axes and rolled down their blades, notches, and handles, cleansing the tools of dirt and blood. Caplan felt no fear, no anxiety as he brandished the axes. He felt nothing but cold, bottled-up rage.

"A fence?" Pearson frowned. "I didn't realize we were so close to Hatcher."

"We're not," Caplan replied.

Pearson started to respond. But a single look at Caplan's axes distracted him. "What do you think you're doing?" he whispered.

What's it look like I'm doing? Caplan thought. *Baking a cake?* Hell, he was ecstatic at this turn of events. After defeating the terrorists, *Roadster* would be his for the taking. He could use it to cut precious minutes off their travel time. Even better, he'd strike a blow against the terrorists and get some revenge on behalf of Morgan.

Finally, he could start to earn her forgiveness.

"Put those away," Pearson said. "We can't let them see us."

"Hide if you want." Caplan maneuvered the blades in sweeping circles, warming up his tired arms. "But I'm staying."

"Haven't you screwed up enough already?"

Pearson's words sent shockwaves through Caplan's fragile ego. In an instant, everything he thought he knew about himself, every decision he'd made these last five months, came under question.

"You plunge headfirst into every situation," Pearson continued. "And you keep getting burned for it. So, use your head for once and come with me." Hunching down, Pearson retreated back toward the pods.

Caplan watched him go. But the sound of car doors shutting drew his attention back to the clearing.

His doubts washed away along with the furious rain. Sure, he'd had a little bad luck. But this time would be different.

This time, nothing would go wrong.

CHAPTER 28

Date: June 19, 2016, 3:07 p.m.; Location: Sector 48A, Vallerio Forest, NH

A trio of men, clad in hooded raincoats and carrying rifles, gathered around *Roadster*. They fumbled with their guns but were unable to activate the mounted LED spotlights. Giving up, they walked to the fence.

Caplan held his breath as one of the men reached for the wires. But the man grabbed it with ease and Caplan realized electricity was no longer flowing through the fence. *The Blare must've knocked it out,* he thought. *Maybe it knocked out Hatcher's fences, too.*

Carefully, the men climbed through the horizontal wires. Then they fanned out and strode into the clearing.

Caplan squinted through the slashing rain. The easternmost man walked with a mild limp. The second man, positioned in the middle, was gaunt and continuously flicking his tongue across his lips. The last man, a trembler with a hunched back, occupied the western end of the clearing. He stood closest to Caplan, making him the obvious—but not necessarily the best—target for attack.

The easternmost man, the limper, trudged slowly through the swamp. He made plenty of noise and commotion, causing Caplan to suspect he wasn't trained in the art of warfare.

Seconds later, the man tripped, proving Caplan right. Arms waving like a windmill, he pitched forward into the swamp. The other two shot him nervous glances.

The man lifted a hand, signaling he was okay. Holding his rifle aloft, he let the rain wash away some sludge. Then he backtracked to where he'd tripped and started to fish through the mud.

What he saw—one of the dead bodies, no doubt— startled him and he reared backward, limping awkwardly along the way. The others raced to his side, catching him before he could fall. Then they gathered together and examined the swamp.

After a minute, the men broke apart and returned to their former positions. Stepping far more carefully now, the limper approached the wreckage and aimed his rifle into the interior. Then he lowered it. Twisted toward the second man—the tongue-flicker—and shrugged.

The tongue-flicker, clearly the leader, snapped his fingers. He pointed at the swamp and the other two men began to hike loudly through the mud, evidently searching for more bodies.

Caplan's senses surged to full height as he slid into the swamp. He saw the way the trio moved, the way they shifted their bodies in response to noise. He saw their range of movement, their lack of body armor. He smelled burnt wood and grass along with body odor. He heard a resurgence of crackling flames alongside heavy rain, squelching mud, and buzzing flies.

Wading forward, he approached the trio in relative silence. Yes, he was outnumbered. And yes, his two axes, at least on paper, were no match for rifles. But he didn't doubt his victory, not even for a second.

The key to taking out a small group was to strike fast and hard. First, eliminate the leader. Second, take out the others before they could regroup and find new leadership.

Still crouching, he waded quietly toward tongue-flicker, shifting his legs one at a time. Then he rose upward like an ethereal being, gripped his left axe and swung it like a tennis racket.

Tongue-flicker grunted as the tip of the handle struck the back of his head. He dropped his rifle and only the shoulder strap kept it from hitting the ground. Reaching backward, he felt his skull. Then he went limp and sagged into the muck.

The limper and the trembling man spun toward the noise, guns at the ready. A mixture of fear and confusion crossed their visages as they laid eyes upon tongue-flicker's still body. Immediately, they shifted their weapons, searching for the mysterious attacker.

But he was nowhere to be seen.

An axe handle slammed into trembler's skull. He was unconscious before he hit the ground.

Sensing movement, the limper spun westward, his gun moving toward Caplan's position. Caplan knocked the barrel with his left axe, propelling it away from him.

The air boomed. The rifle recoiled in the limper's hands. A bullet exited the chamber and soared toward the wreckage. It slammed into the *Blaze*'s still-intact gas tank. The tank began sputtering fuel, spitting it out like a fountain.

Time slowed down for Caplan. He tasted smoke and cinders. Felt warm heat. Smelled the pungent fuel.

Flames roared with renewed intensity. Glancing over his shoulder, Caplan saw the flames, orange and hot, licking at the gas.

A massive explosion pierced the air and a shock wave stretched outward. Caplan went airborne before crashing back to the swamp, rolling and flopping around until he came to a halt.

A full minute passed. Groggily, he sat up, covered in muck. Miraculously, the axes were still in his grip.

He twisted his neck. Wrenching his eyes open, he tried to focus his blurry vision. A giant fire engulfed the wreckage. Pieces of blackened metal, expelled outward by the explosion, were strewn across the swamp.

Caplan tried to get up, only to collapse back to the earth. He tried again, but couldn't even reach his knees. Physically, he was spent.

Vaguely, he heard *Roadster*'s engine ignite. It puttered softly for a minute or so before receding into silence.

Caplan dug deep, found a little energy in his reserves. Slowly, painfully, he stood up.

Pearson snaked out of the forest and waded into the swamp. "What happened?"

"One of them got off a lucky shot. Blew up the wreckage all over again." Caplan bent over, chest heaving for air. He searched the clearing for signs of the trio. But they were gone. "They got away."

"Damn it, Zach. I told you this was a bad idea."

Caplan winced. "We can fix this."

"You don't get it." Pearson shook his head. "If you'd kept quiet, those guys would've thought everyone was dead. Now, they know otherwise."

CHAPTER 29

Date: Unknown; Location: Unknown

"Lost in time?" Pressing his back against rough schist, Brian Toland managed an exaggerated eye roll. "Well, that's ... interesting. Does anyone else have an idea? A real one?"

Her face warm with shame, Bailey Mills dipped her head to her lap. "It was just a thought," she muttered softly.

"Yeah, a stupid one." Toland gave her a withering look from the opposite side of the thin cave. "I can't believe an entire generation of women look up to you. Oh, how I weep for the future."

"How about you?" Tricia Elliott interjected.

Toland blinked. "Me?"

"At least she's trying. So far, you've been nothing but dead weight."

"Oh, I see. You're one of those solidarity types. Feminism and girl power, right?" He smirked. "How droll."

"You don't know anything about me, old man."

"Oh, an age joke! So original. Well, I may be older than you, my dear, but at least my entire personality isn't wrapped up in my hair."

Elliott's eyes flashed. "Why you—"

"Stop it." Travis Renjel's voice rumbled through the semi-enclosed space. "Both of you."

Mills leaned back, pressing her shoulder blades against the rock wall. After skirting around the woolly mammoths, their little group had followed the running water upstream, hoping to find some kind of village or encampment. Although they came up short, they'd ventured upon a grassy hillside, partially shaded by pines and spruces, cedars and Douglas-firs. The hill, which rose several hundred feet above ground, promised a much easier way of locating the nearest town. They'd started to climb it, but a sudden outburst of rain turned the ground into a sloppy mess. And so, the group had sought out shelter instead, eventually locating a tight but deep cave a quarter up the hillside.

Peering outside, Mills watched the rain. It was a mesmerizing rain, full of ancient mysticism and strange vibrations. But unfortunately, this was no cleansing storm from a generous higher power, capable of erasing everything that had transpired and spiriting her back to New York City. Rather, it was a force of pure isolation, one that made her feel lonelier by the second.

"I wish I'd never agreed to go to that stupid ball." Tearing her gaze from the rain, she stared at a spot of rock wall between Toland and Renjel. "I wish I'd just stayed home."

Toland cocked an eyebrow. "Ball?"

"Yes, a charity ball." All her anger, all her frustration came out in a sudden spurt of emotions. How dare this man continue to sit in judgment of her? How would he like it if she mocked every aspect of his life? "What about you? What were you doing before you woke up here? Harassing innocent women, I assume?"

"Writing, actually," he said with an air of superiority. "You see, I'm working on a new book."

"Fiction?" Renjel asked.

"As if I'd waste my time on that nonsense. No, it's a generational study, fully and gloriously unauthorized, of the Corbotch family."

Mills' eyes widened.

Elliott's jaw fell agape. "You too?"

He eyed her with disdain. "Are we supposed to believe that you, my yellow-haired friend, are writing a book?"

"Not a book, no. But I've spent the last two years fighting the Corbotch Empire on behalf of northern New Hampshire communities." She looked upon him with fierce interest. "Tell me about this book of yours."

"For centuries, conspiracy theorists have accused the Corbotch family of assassinating leaders, arming terrorist groups, toppling governments, and inciting wars. But no one has ever been able to prove anything. My book will change that." He eyed her with curiosity. "Your turn. Why are you fighting the evil empire?"

Elliott winced slightly. "Before ... all this, Randi and I worked at Scrutiny. She is—was—the executive director and I serve as president."

"With that hair?" Toland asked.

"Yes, with this hair." Elliott rubbed a thin hand through her close-clipped, yellow hair. "Appearances are everything and me being a so-called wild child helped bring a certain class of donors aboard."

"What's Scrutiny?" Renjel asked.

"A global non-profit organization based out of Chicago. Our mission is to shed sunshine on corporate misconduct. You know, scandals, crimes, illegal deals. Stuff like that. So, about two years ago, we stumbled upon something strange." She paused. "Has anyone ever heard of the Vallerio Forest? It's a Corbotch holding."

Toland nodded. "I have."

Mills felt like she was coming out of a drunken stupor. "Me too."

"Then you know it's almost completely cut off from the outside world. A giant fence surrounds it and the U.S.

government has designated it and its airspace as an official Prohibited Area. The only known residents work out of an isolated building called Hatcher Station. Supposedly, it's some kind of observation center. Anyway local residents have registered all sorts of complaints about the forest. Strange sounds, missing pets, even missing people. The Vallerio Foundation, which Corbotch owns, refuses to listen to them. So, Randi and I have been helping them prepare a lawsuit to open up the Vallerio as well as its records for inspection."

"Any luck?" Renjel asked.

"Not really," she admitted. "But we have uncovered documents hinting at a weird project in the Vallerio. It's called *Apex Predator*."

"Weird how?"

"Mind you, this is mostly speculation. But we have reason to believe it involves the illegal importation of large predators to the Vallerio. Bears, lions, tigers … you get the picture."

"Why would Corbotch do that?"

"From all appearances, he believes the world is in imminent danger of a systemic ecological collapse. He thinks this is because we've killed off too many predators. If they aren't replaced soon, ecosystems will fail."

"That's crazy," Mills said.

"Don't be so quick to judge. I've read up on the subject and there seems to be a lot of truth to it. One example I remember dealt with large pieces of grassland in Australia. After predators died out, grass and shrubs grew faster and the soil received far less compaction. Seeds and shelter became more available. Rodent populations took advantage and doubled in size. The diseases they carried doubled with them." Elliott shrugged. "Make no mistake about it. A kink at the top of the food chain can have disastrous consequences all the way down the line."

"You make it sound like Corbotch is doing God's work," Renjel remarked. "So, why the lawsuit?"

"I'll tell you why," Toland said before Elliott could respond. "Because James is a veritable snake of a human being. Everything he does looks positive on the surface. But if you dig a little, you'll find a whole rotten core on the inside."

Renjel nodded and turned his attention to Mills. "So, you've heard of this Vallerio place, too?"

"Tricia isn't the only one with a pending lawsuit." Sighing, Mills stared at the schist ceiling. "You see, I rightfully own the Vallerio, or at least a part of it."

"Impossible." Toland gawked at her. "I would've known."

"Back in the late 1700s, Alexander Corbotch sold part of the Vallerio to my ancestor, Thomas Mills. Thomas died shortly thereafter, willing everything to his sole heir, Daniel Mills. It appears Daniel never knew about the Vallerio transaction. He filed away the paperwork and it went unread until my lawyers discovered it last year."

"And you're suing to get the land back? Centuries later? Wow, I thought you were greedy before, but this—"

"I'm suing because it's not right." She brushed strands of damp, dirty hair back from her face. "The Corbotch family can't just take things that don't belong to them."

"Curious." Renjel turned to Toland. "Does your book deal with the Vallerio?"

"Not really," Toland replied. "There's not much material on it. Just stories of strange experiments and even stranger animals."

Elliott perked up at the words, *stranger animals*. "Like sabers and woolly mammoths?"

"Unfortunately, the specifics are a little murky. For example, back in 1904, Miles Corbotch invited a famous zoologist named Professor Dasnoe to study the Vallerio

Forest. All went well until a sudden attack—wolves, according to newspapers of the time—killed six expedition members. However, Dasnoe went to his grave—an unexpectedly early grave, by the way—trumpeting a different story. They weren't wolves, he said, but rather mythical four-legged monsters of Abenaki lore." Toland shrugged. "There are other stories like that one. Suffice it to say, the Vallerio has earned its reputation as one of the most mysterious places on Earth."

"How about you?" Mills looked at Renjel. "Are you connected to the Vallerio?"

He paused, then nodded.

Her heart skipped a beat. "How so?"

"The *New Yorker Chronicles* is a tabloid paper. But we do a lot of investigative reporting, too. That's my area of expertise." He paused. "For the last four months, I've been researching a story on the Vallerio Foundation. Officially, the Foundation owns the Vallerio. But as most of you probably know, it's really just a front for the Corbotch Empire."

Mills flicked some dried dirt off her legs. "What's the story about?"

"This probably won't sound like a big deal," he replied. "But over the last few years, dozens of the world's top scientists have disappeared from the public eye. They've quit their posts at top universities and companies, stopped publishing research, and basically vanished into the ether. From what I've been able to gather, they took secret assignments with the Vallerio Foundation."

Toland grunted. "Doesn't sound like much of a story to me."

Renjel took a deep breath. "The Foundation doesn't produce anything. No research, no products. Its sole purpose is to manage the Vallerio Forest. So, why would James Corbotch, acting through the Foundation, recruit some of the world's most brilliant scientific minds? What's he really up to?"

"Do you have any theories?" Elliott asked.

"Not yet. But I have reason to believe the scientists work out of Hatcher Station. Which, of course, is located in the Vallerio."

A moment of silence passed over the small group.

"So, we all have something in common." Mills' gaze hardened. "We were all, in one way or another, a potential threat to James Corbotch."

CHAPTER 30

"I hate this thing." Jermain Bernier, a biochemist and geneticist with four years experience at Hatcher Station, shook his head. "It always plays tricks with my brain. I mean, I know it's a marsupial, but look at it. It practically screams *rhino*."

Amanda Morgan glanced at the skeleton, mounted exhibit-style on top of a sturdy platform. Indeed, it looked a little like a rhinoceros. A rhinoceros, sans horn, to be specific.

But the skeleton, nine feet end-to-end and possessing a shoulder height of six feet, was actually that of a *Diprotodon*. The largest marsupial of all time, the *Diprotodon* was just one of many strange megafauna that had once roamed Australia. Related to the modern koala and wombat, it had died out approximately 40,000 years ago during a still-unexplained mass extinction of Australian megafauna.

She moved on, wincing as stabbing pain erupted from her side. Clutching her waist, she squeezed the pain, forcing it to subside a bit.

She walked past numerous exhibits, all devoted to skeletons of long-extinct megafauna. *Miracinonyx inexpectatus*, or the American cheetah, which had sported retractable claws and outran cougars. *Canis dirus*, also known as the dire wolf, a fearsome predator with powerful jaws and pack-hunting skills. *Megalania prisca*, or Megalania, the largest terrestrial lizard known to mankind. And many others. It was a fine collection, rivaling that of the world's best-known museums.

She passed a pair of technicians who were cleaning blood and gore from the floor, utterly oblivious to the partial ten-foot tall skeleton of *Gigantopithecus blacki*—the only one known in existence—towering behind them.

She reached the central platform and climbed the stairs, pausing for a short respite at the halfway point. She found Bonnie Codd and Zlata Issova sitting in swivel chairs and fixated on computer screens. "What have you got for me?" she asked.

"We're making progress," Codd replied. "It shouldn't be—"

Yells and shouts for help rang out from the entranceway. Swiveling her head, Morgan saw a trio of men limping across the slip-resistant vinyl floor. Covered in soil and uprooted foliage, the men looked in desperate need of baths. "What happened to them?" she asked.

Codd didn't look up. "Who?"

"Page, Rice, and Sherman."

Codd lifted her gaze and studied the men. "I sent them to check on 48A," she said, a hint of concern in her voice. "I hope they didn't run into trouble."

"Okay, I'm going to talk to them. Keep me—"

"Amanda!" Bernier raced onto the platform. Lungs heaving, he bent down, hands on knees. "The ... the incubators..."

Morgan swiveled to face him. She saw the redness in his cheeks, the urgency in his eyes. "What about them?"

"They're ..." He gasped. "They're undergoing expulsion."

Unimaginable horror filled Morgan's heart. Turning in a slow circle, she spied eight silken ectogenetic incubators, part of Hatcher's 2-Gen initiative. All of them trembled, quivered, and vibrated with quiet force. Two or three of them showed signs of cracking.

A dizzy spell assaulted Morgan's brain, engulfing it in silken threads of haziness. A full expulsion sequence? How was that even possible?

Morgan snapped out of her haze. Her brain began to work, to plan. Hatcher had protocols for any number of lab-related emergencies, everything from a chemical spill to a full-on incubator failure. But a mass expulsion? Until that very minute, it had been an unthinkable prospect.

Unfortunately, it was now a reality.

She had to figure this out. Otherwise, she'd be forced to evacuate all personnel from the Lab and security checkpoint. Codd and Issova would have to cease work on the communications. All of her plans to stop the Foundation would come to a screeching halt.

Her eyes traced the array of computers and mechanical devices scattered about the platform. The trick to handling the situation, she decided, was to build upon existing protocols. "Bonnie, Zlata," she said. "We've got a full expulsion sequence underway."

Codd froze, the tips of her fingers hardening just above her keyboard. "Does that mean what I think it means?"

"Yes."

Codd and Issova stood up. Moving as if in one body, they turned in tight circles, taking in the entire facility.

"They're not even fully cooked yet," Morgan said in a voice full of equal parts awe and terror. "This could be 1-Gen all over again."

Issova and Codd gave her wide-eyed looks. They hadn't been in the Lab during the 1-Gen debacle. But she'd told them all about it while recruiting them to her cause.

"That bad?" Issova asked.

"Maybe worse." Morgan's heart palpitated. "Speaking of 1-Gen, can you see if we have access to the incubators in Sector 48A?"

Issova hurried to a large monitor. For a few seconds, she pounded on the keyboard. "Okay, the system's working fine." She paused to check the screen. "I can't access the wireless network. But it looks like a general expulsion frequency was sent out to all incubators within twenty miles of this station."

"Oh, wow," Codd whispered. "We're dead. We're so dead."

Morgan exhaled a long breath. If Issova was right, then every single incubator in 48A had been activated at the same time. And in an unprotected setting, with nothing to quell the enormous energy outburst. What would that look like? Sound like? Feel like? She could scarcely imagine it.

Morgan steeled her gaze. "Zlata, how long will it take to deploy the isolation chambers?"

Issova gawked at her.

"How long?" Morgan repeated.

Issova's fingers flew across the keyboard. "Five or six minutes apiece from the looks of it."

"Can you deploy them en mass?"

"Probably. But I'd need to figure it out. If I had an hour—"

"You don't." Morgan scanned the incubators, taking note of their movement and relative cracking. "Okay, we'll do one at a time. Start with the *Arctodus simus*. It's the closest to expulsion."

While Issova worked the keyboard, Morgan turned to Codd. "Can you initiate a general shutdown of the expulsion sequence?"

Codd's face twisted with doubt. "These programs are brand new to me. And even if I figure them out, it could be too late to stop the expulsions."

"Just try."

Codd flung herself into the swivel chair and zoomed across the platform to a mid-sized monitor. Quickly, she got to work, pecking keys with fierce intensity.

Morgan walked quickly to Bernier, who was still trying to catch his breath. Looking toward the entranceway, she saw a group of people gathered around Page, Rice, and Sherman, offering assistance to the beleaguered men.

Cupping her hands around her mouth, she lifted her voice to a shout. "Attention, everyone." She paused as all eyes shifted to her. "The ectogenetic incubators are undergoing a simultaneous expulsion. We are doing everything in our power to stop it, or at least contain it. But to be on the safe side, I need all of you to evacuate this floor in an orderly manner."

Scientists, technicians, and rangers exchanged frightened looks. Then they hurried through the entranceway, with Bernier hot on their heels. Seconds later, rubber thudded against metal as they raced up the waiting ladder.

"No, no, no, no, no!" Issova slammed her fists against the table, sending her monitor into a brief wobbling spell.

What now? Morgan thought as she twisted toward the woman.

"The deployment sequence won't activate," Issova said.

Morgan winced. "Then try another one."

"You don't understand. I tried the *Arctodus simus*, the *Panthera onca augusta*, the *Mammut americanum* ... none of them work."

"Can you fix them?"

"Not easily. Someone, I'm guessing whoever initiated the full expulsion sequence, disabled access to the chambers."

Terrific, Morgan thought. *Just terrific.*

"I've got the same problem," Codd called out. "I can't access the incubators. The connection's been completely sheared."

Morgan felt the weight of all her plans crashing down upon her. The Lab was lost and with it, her ability to communicate with the outside world. Everything—the long hours of preparation, the incredible stress, the battles, the deaths—had all been for naught.

Part of her wanted to fight the truth, to keep working on a solution. But deep down, she knew it was hopeless. Nothing could stop the hell that was about to be unleashed.

Nothing.

"That's it then." Morgan cast a wary eye at the silken ectogenetic incubators. The *Arctodus simus* appeared particularly close to expulsion. "Time to go."

Codd and Issova didn't argue. Rising up, they gathered their laptops and everything else they'd brought into the Lab. Then they booked it down the staircase at top speed.

Morgan stood atop the platform a little longer, the vanquished queen of a kingdom she'd just conquered. For the first time in ages, she had no plan, no way forward. She couldn't access the communications equipment. And she couldn't exactly flee Hatcher Station. There was nowhere to go, nowhere except into the Vallerio's clutches. And that was a non-starter, especially if the 1-Gen incubators in Sector 48A were indeed undergoing expulsion processes.

Morgan darted down the stairs, two at a time. As she leapt to the floor, a distinct tearing noise rang out. Like the ripping of a silk cloth. Recognizing it immediately, she twisted her head and laid eyes upon the torn and tattered remains of an incubator. Its occupant, however, was nowhere to be seen.

A brutal roar rang out. Morgan, still running, glanced back at the entranceway just as a massive ball of black wiry fur smashed into Issova. The impact sent the woman reeling into the wall. Her skull cracked against concrete. Blood spurted everywhere and her dead body sank to the floor.

The creature—a living, breathing *Arctodus simus*—raced toward her on all fours. Even like that, it was easily the height of a person.

It paused above Issova. Lifted its jaw and issued a defiant roar.

Codd tried to circle the creature, to escape through the entranceway. The creature anticipated her move and made to block her. But it overshot its mark and slid into one of the generators. Loud pops rang out. The overhead lights started to fizzle.

Codd gasped. Whirled around and looked at Morgan with wild, frightened eyes. But Morgan couldn't return the stare. She was too busy watching the creature rise up on its hind legs. Watching it rise up to its full height. Ten feet, eleven feet, no ... twelve feet tall.

The lights fizzled again, dimming to a few notches above blackness. The creature's gaze shifted to Morgan. It stared directly into her eyes. Its lips curled back into a snarl. It roared again as it started forward.

And then the lights went out.

CHAPTER 31

Date: June 19, 2016, 3:42 p.m.; Location: Hatcher Station, Vallerio Forest, NH

Hatcher Station, from a distance, looked an awful lot like an abandoned pillbox from the Second World War. Soil, mixed with a sprinkling of dead grass, topped its concrete roof. Long, twisting vines clung to its wet walls. The surrounding area was cleared of foliage and surrounded by several layers of fencing.

As Caplan drew closer, he saw light sparks spurting out of the first fence. Dull buzzing noises filled his ears. His brow furrowed into a hard ridge. The fence, grounded in concrete, was as sturdy as the one dividing Sector 48 from 48A. The only difference was that this fence was still electrified. It would fry him to a crisp and unlike his days as Chief Ranger, he didn't possess the means to bypass it.

He glanced at the building. It morphed before his eyes, seemingly expanding in size. He could see how much ground it covered. And he noticed distinct areas. Areas that made up the entranceway, the Eye, and the Warehouse.

For a long moment, he studied the seven-tentacled structure. Morgan existed somewhere within its sprawling concrete walls. She was so close; he could almost hear the steady rhythmic beating of her heart. All that had happened, all that he'd lost, came back to him in a flood of unwelcome emotions.

Keep your cool, Caplan thought. *You've only got seventy-eight minutes before everyone's dead.*

"I assume that's *Roadster*," Pearson whispered.

Following the man's gaze, Caplan saw the familiar vehicle, stowed under a thin sheet of metal propped up by wooden beams. Old and rusty and held together by years of faded duct tape, he doubted *Roadster* could ever pass inspection out in the civilized world. "Sure is."

"So, the others know we're here."

Caplan scanned the grounds and spotted four—no, five—separate people. They carried rifles and wore dark clothing, blending in well with the soil and grass. He squinted, but was unable to make out their faces in the relative darkness. "I'd say that's a safe bet."

Pearson grunted. "Even if they didn't, this would be a tough nut to crack. No windows. Three fences, each taller than the last. Plenty of cameras and sensors, too. And is that the only entrance?"

Caplan turned his attention from the makeshift garage to three of the tentacles. Two of them led to circular areas. The third one shot straight out, tunnel fashion, and ended in a giant metal door. "That's the only ground entrance," he clarified. "But there's a locked vent system accessible from the roof. The Operations team used to clean it once a week."

"So, we have to breach three layers of electric fencing, sneak past those guards, scale a fifteen-foot wall, and penetrate a locked vent?" Pearson frowned. "All without triggering an alarm?"

"When you put it that way, it sounds easy."

Pearson gave Caplan a disdainful look. "You should—"

Рииисс, рииисс, рииисс!

The sounds, like grenades exploding in rapid succession, took Caplan by surprise. Dodging back into the forest, he took cover behind a tree trunk.

Рииисс, рииисс, рииисс!

The explosions, strangely enough, didn't sound close and concentrated. Instead, they came from all over the clearing.

Рииисс, рииисс, рииисс!

The explosions died away. Taking a deep breath, Caplan chanced a look at the guards. They stood in a small half-circle. They shifted their rifles back and forth, seemingly searching for an invisible assailant.

"What was that?" Pearson whispered.

Caplan focused his attention on his ears. Something had changed. He was sure of it. But what? "The buzzing," he realized at last. "It's gone."

"What buzzing? What the hell are you talking about?"

"The fences were buzzing like bees when we got here. Sparking, too. But no more."

"The fences shorted out?" Pearson's face twisted with disbelief. "But how?"

Caplan grinned. "Maybe our luck is starting to change."

"Don't get cocky."

The front door swung open. A couple of people, some clad in white lab coats, ran outside. They conferred with the gun-wielding guards. Within moments, all of them were on their feet, running toward the open door and disappearing into Hatcher Station. The last person to enter left the door wide open, swinging gently on its hinges.

Pearson arched an eyebrow. "Was it something I said?"

Caplan scanned the area again, paying close attention to the cameras and sensors. On a typical day, they were used to keep an eye out for too-clever-for-their-own-good animals. The ones that somehow eluded Hatcher's security only to find themselves trapped behind the electric fences with nothing to eat or drink.

He was pleased to see the little red lights mounted on each device had gone dark. Whatever had shut down the electric fences had apparently shut down the cameras and sensors as well.

Caplan shrugged off his backpack. Reaching inside, he extracted the small cooler he'd procured from the helicopter bin. He cracked it open and checked the syringes and vials. Satisfied they were in good order, he resealed the cooler and stuck it back into his bag. Then he hoisted the pack onto his shoulders. "Let's go," he said.

"You go. I'll keep a lookout."

Caplan shot him a look. "We don't have time to mess around."

"And we don't have time to depend on luck either. Now, go." Pearson brandished his pistol. "I'll make sure no one gets in your way."

Exhaling softly, Caplan stared at Hatcher. Once upon a time, he'd looked upon the building and the Vallerio with childlike wonder. But now, he saw things differently. He saw the forest for what it really was, namely a bastion of ancient evil. A cursed city out of myth and legend, one of gnarled, twisting towers, torn-up streets, the blackest of corridors, and otherworldly inhabitants. And he saw Hatcher for what it was, too. A foolish outpost of civilization smack dab in the midst of depravity. A place no man, no woman should've ever set foot into, let alone call home.

Sweeping his gaze from left to right, he searched for terrorists. Seeing none, he made a beeline for the fence. As he drew near, his senses perked. The air was free of electric charge. The fence was quiet, still.

Bracing himself, he closed his fingers around a length of wire. His teeth gritted in anticipation of a gigantic shock.

But it didn't happen.

Emboldened, he climbed the first fence. The second fence. But as he darted to the third fence, a change came over the area. Gone was the silence, the stillness. In its place, he heard shouting, felt frenzied energy. It reminded him of helpless prey fleeing from much larger predators.

He climbed the third fence and stepped quietly onto a patch of damp grass. The shouting—although reduced to half the decibels—continued unabated. He smelled coppery blood in the air, enough of it to make his insides queasy. Sweat beaded up on his shoulders and trickled down his arms, a product of the strange heat emanating from the open door.

Caplan shot a quick glance at the forest. Saw Pearson and gave the man a nod.

Pearson flashed a thumbs-up in response.

Senses still perked, Caplan crept toward Hatcher. He could feel a great and mysterious struggle taking place within it. One of those struggles that was somehow about more than life and death. A struggle of ideals, of competing dreams. But the building's exterior reflected none of that. Its concrete walls remained dull and lifeless. Completely unchanged from when he'd last seen them all those months ago.

He studied the nearest wall, taking note of its cracks and indentations. He needed to climb it, to break into the vent system. Then he could focus on delivering the antibiotics. But as he started forward, he heard more shouts, more screams.

What the hell is going on in there? he wondered.

He ran to the doorway. The temperature grew to sauna-levels and his pores worked even faster to distribute sweat to his body.

Carefully, he peeked through the open door. The overhead light fixtures were dark. However, a few rays of sunlight managed to penetrate the storm clouds, shedding a bit of light on the adjoining corridor. To his surprise, it was completely empty.

Rotating his neck, Caplan saw familiar maintenance equipment—lawn mowers, rakes, clippers, shovels, sturdy gloves, and safety glasses—lined up along the right side wall. On the opposite wall, he saw posters and signs, laying out Hatcher's rules for landscape work.

The shouts and screams grew louder, more terrified. The temperature warmed a few more degrees and he sensed feverish, almost frantic activity.

The vent forgotten, he stepped into the corridor. He took a moment to let his eyes adjust to the change in light. Then he pulled out his twin axes. Said a silent prayer.

And headed into the darkness.

CHAPTER 32

Date: June 19, 2016, 3:49 p.m.; Location: Hatcher Station, Vallerio Forest, NH

GRRAWRRR!

The massive roar, softened by distance, forced Caplan to a halt. Weird and conflicting emotions—perplexity, revulsion, and intense curiosity, among others—weaved through his heart. *That came from inside*, he thought. *Inside!*

Somehow a large animal had gotten into Hatcher Station. But how? Until just a few minutes ago, the fences had been fully electrified and guarded. Plus, he'd seen no signs of breakage or forced entry. Nothing about this made sense.

GRRAWWRRR!

The floor trembled ever so slightly under Caplan's feet. He sensed the beast's confusion, its rage. It was angry. Angry and hell-bent on destruction.

He thought about Morgan, about her propensity to put other people first. If this beast was on the rampage, he had little doubt she was in the thick of things, trying to slow it down or even stop it.

Throwing caution to the wind, he sprinted down the corridor. The mighty roars grew louder, angrier with every step. But they also remained strangely muted.

He slowed his pace as he entered the Heptagon, the informal name for Hatcher's central core. Although the overheard fixtures were dark, a few flashlights provided some light to the area. Skirting clear of the beams, he snuck along the walls.

A small group of people, tightly bound, sat in the middle of the room. They faced outward and Caplan recognized a few faces. They belonged to long-time Hatcher guards. He didn't know them all that well—the guards tended to stick to themselves—but he figured they'd make valuable allies in the very near future.

Six people, dressed in jeans and t-shirts, surrounded the prisoners. The closest ones had their backs to Caplan, so he was unable to see their faces. But the rifles clutched in their hands spoke volumes about their identities.

They were terrorists.

At least two-dozen other gun-toting people were scattered about the Heptagon. Some wore lab coats, which he didn't quite understand. Was that how the terrorists had entered Hatcher? By impersonating scientists? How would that even work?

Distraught whispers and frazzled murmurs filled Caplan's ears. The words mixed together, forming a tangled web of indiscernible din.

He felt energy surging, flowing all around him. But it didn't come from the room itself. Indeed, the people inside the Heptagon barely moved. Watching their eyes, he saw they all stared at the closed Research door and its, *Stop: Restricted Access, Research Only* sign.

He studied the door, studied the area around it. Yes, that was it. That was the source of the frenzied energy.

GRRAWWRRR!

He flinched at the sudden roar. It had definitely come from Research, but not on this level. Corbotch's remarks about how the terrorists had broken into the secured Lab came to mind. He'd caught a few glimpses of Research before. He'd seen people working. He's seen the bright lights, the computers, the lab stations. But he'd never seen even a hint of the lower level.

Did that explain the roars? Did Research keep some kind of wild beast in the Lab? If so, why? Were they experimenting on it?

No. No way in hell. Morgan would never participate in such a monstrous thing. And yet, he couldn't escape the facts. A wild beast roamed the lower level. And there were no signs it had forced its way in there. So, either the terrorists brought it with them.

Or it had been there all along.

As the roar died away, the whispers started up again. Rotating his head, Caplan glanced at the entrance corridor. Where, he wondered, was Pearson? Still at the edge of the clearing, watching over the area? Or had he moved closer in order to keep an eye on things?

Caplan replaced the axe covers and stowed the tools in his belt. Then he rescanned the room, counting the terrorists and noting their positions. A large part of him desired a direct fight. But ultimately, he ruled that out. The smart move was to take advantage of the situation. With the terrorists focused on Research, he could sneak into Hatcher's other wings. He could look for prisoners, distribute the antibiotics, and secure weapons.

Then he'd make his move.

A thick-bearded man with bronzed complexion crossed the Heptagon. He knelt close to Caplan and began sorting through a small duffel bag.

Caplan squinted. Was that …? Yes. Yes, it was Dr. Adnan. Quickly, he considered his options. He could keep a low profile and sneak into the other wings as planned. Or he could reach out to the good doctor, but possibly risk discovery in the process.

It only took him a second to make up his mind. With soft, fluid movements he slid along the wall until he reached the man. "Dr. Adnan?"

Dr. Ankur Adnan, Hatcher's primary physician, didn't look up. "What do you need?"

"It's me, doc. Zach Caplan."

"Zach?" Glancing up, Dr. Adnan studied Caplan's features with a pair of sharp, hazel eyes. "But ... but you left."

"Yeah. And now, I'm back. Listen—"

"Traitor!" Dr. Adnan reeled backward, lost his balance, and fell. His body splayed out across the floor. "Here! Over here!"

Caplan didn't have time to move or even think. In a fraction of a second, over a dozen flashlights lit him up like a prisoner caught in a late night jailbreak. He saw confused expressions. Shocked ones, too.

His cheeks scrunched. His eyes narrowed. Wait. He knew these faces. Knew them well. For the most part, they belonged to Hatcher's brainiac scientists. But that didn't make sense. Unless ...

His jaw hardened into rock.

Unless *they* were the terrorists.

CHAPTER 33

Date: June 19, 2016, 3:52 p.m.; Location: Hatcher Station, Vallerio Forest, NH

"Zach?" someone said in disbelief. "Zach Caplan?"

"What is he doing here?" another voice called out.

More questions rang out. But they soon gave way to a sea of angry shouts and accusations.

"He's with Corbotch!"

"He's one of them!"

"Kill him!"

And so on and so forth. For almost thirty seconds, the scientists squabbled amongst themselves. Caplan found it almost amusing, watching these grown-up brainiacs playing at professional terrorists. They looked so eager, so willing, yet so pathetically out of place. Sort of like a terrorist B-team. Or C-team. Hell, make it the Z-team.

Still, they had guns aimed at every inch of his body. And their trigger fingers had all the steadiness of a junkie going through withdrawal. So, he made no sudden moves, silently praying they didn't accidentally turn him into Swiss cheese.

GRRAAWWRRR!

The roar, the most massive one yet, sent a stunned silence through the crowd. Gritting his teeth, Caplan watched the trigger fingers. They flinched, but not quite hard enough to send steaming hot bullets spiraling through his guts.

Heads swiveled back to Research. Eyes focused on the door, the warning sign. Caplan saw his opportunity.

Scanning the room, he focused on another door, the one marked *Operations*, and prepped for escape.

"Don't even think about it." Amy Carson, a redhead with a thick Canadian accent, slid in front of Caplan, blocking his path. She was a tough old vixen with a triangular face and hollow eyes. "How'd you get in here?"

Caplan tried his most winning smile. But sheer exhaustion left him looking like a deranged clown. "You left the door open."

"Sutter," Carson called out. "Secure the entranceway."

Jillian Sutter, a pretty genetics expert with the personality of a wet tennis ball, gathered up her rifle and slid into the corridor.

Carson glanced at Caplan. Her mouth worked in overdrive, chewing every bit of flavor out of a wad of bubble gum. Her pistol, sized just right for her claw-like appendage, was aimed directly at his crotch. "Are you working for Corbotch?"

He nodded at the pistol. "Could you point that somewhere else?"

She flicked her wrist and the barrel slammed into Caplan's right cheek. His head exploded in pain as it whipped to the side.

"Let's try that again." She shifted her aim. "Are you working for Corbotch?"

So, they knew Corbotch owned the Vallerio Foundation. He found that surprising. Carefully, he touched his jaw. Tasted blood on his tongue. Then he nodded at her pistol, which was now aimed at his eyeballs. "Thanks," he said. "That's much better."

Her finger started to squeeze the trigger.

"Okay, okay." He stretched his aching jaw. "Yeah, I'm working for him. So what? Last I checked, he signs your paychecks, too."

Her eye sockets sunk into her head. "Why'd he send you here?"

Caplan thought about HA-78 and the antibiotics in his bag. He needed to distribute them as quickly as possible. But to whom? What was going on here anyway? Why had this collection of eggheads turned on their employer? "He received garbled transmissions about a terrorist attack," he said, deliberately staying as vague as possible. "He asked me to lend a helping hand."

"Like the one he offers his enemies?" She sneered. "No thanks."

GRRAAWWRRR!

"What the hell is that?" Caplan glanced at the Research door. "A bear on steroids?"

"None of your business," Carson replied.

Metallic crashes, distant but still loud, wafted into the Heptagon. Whispers and murmurs died away as the brainiacs cast petrified, guilt-ridden looks at one another.

"We can't just leave them down there." Jermain Bernier, an oily little guy with a creepy mustache, swallowed hard. "We have to help them."

"Who?" Caplan knew the answer even as he asked the question. "Who needs help?"

"Amanda Morgan. Bonnie Codd and Zlata Issova, too, although we think Zlata might be ..." Bernier trailed off, a look of profound sadness upon his visage.

Caplan clenched his jaw. Cowards, all of them. Standing around like idiots, wringing their hands about whether or not to do something. Well, not him. Shoving some gawkers out of the way, he strode toward Research.

"Hold it," Carson called out.

Ignoring her, Caplan twisted the knob and opened the door. Inside, he saw more gawkers, their flashlight beams aimed at the far side. Annoyed grunts and surprised gasps rang out as he pushed his way through them.

He stopped in front of a metal hatch, hinged on one side. Although it lacked handles, it was ajar a couple of inches. He recalled what Corbotch had told him about the hatch, about how the terrorists had hacked into its security program. That was how HA-78 had been released in the first place.

He studied the hatch for a moment. Obviously, it required electricity to open and close. But since it was already open, he figured maybe it could open a little farther.

He reached out. Grabbed the hatch's open side with both hands. Metal groaning, he began to pull it upward.

"Stop, Zach." Gun at the ready, Carson ran to the hatch. "I mean it."

Caplan shot a withering look at the triangular-faced vixen.

She licked her lips. Inhaled, exhaled. Then she lowered her pistol.

Caplan waved at her gun. "Give me that."

"Do I look stupid to you?"

"Do you really want me to answer that?"

While she glowered at him, Caplan turned toward the crowd. He saw plenty of familiar faces. "I need a gun."

He heard some shuffling sounds. A few whispers. But no one stepped forward. Looking down, he eyed his axes. *Guess it's just us*, he thought.

GRRRAAAWWWRRRR!

The sound shocked Caplan into action. Gripping the ladder, he climbed into the shaft. Almost immediately, a strong smell of wet fur accosted him and he wrinkled his nostrils in disgust. He'd smelled fur before, but nothing quite this gunky and greasy. "What's down there?" he asked.

Carson's eyes bored holes into his. "Your worst nightmare."

CHAPTER 34

Date: June 19, 2016, 4:02 p.m.; Location: Hatcher Station, Vallerio Forest, NH

Caplan clambered down the ladder, Carson's cryptic words still ringing in his ears. His worst nightmare? What the hell was that supposed to mean?

Deeper and deeper he spiraled into the shaft. His throat clenched up involuntarily with every roar, every inhuman grunt. And still, he went on, driven by memories of Tony's fate. By an overwhelming desire to save Amanda Morgan.

By a soul-deep need to earn her forgiveness.

Light from the overhead flashlight beams began to fade. He glanced at his watch. His spine iced over as he noted the time. 4:02 p.m. Less than one hour to go.

Less than one hour until Hatcher became a cemetery.

As he descended, he thought about the antibiotics stored carefully in his backpack. What should he do with them when he returned to the upper floor? Should he hand them out to the brainiacs, even though they were behind the attack on Hatcher? Or should he focus on getting them to the dignitaries and trussed-up guards, thus dooming the brainiacs to certain death?

He maintained an even pace, the soles of his trail-runners scuffing gently against each metal rung. Why had the eggheads revolted in the first place? What was their grievance against Corbotch? Was it possible they were the good guys in all this?

Another roar knocked that thought right out of his head. He chanced a look at the ground. It was too dark to see anything, but he could still sense the creature. He could feel its heat, its energy. He could hear its rapid breathing, deep-throated grunts, and heavy paws slapping against the tough floor. And he could smell its greasy fur, its feces, its ripe body odor.

He resumed his descent and didn't stop until he reached the floor. Then he shrugged off his pack and set it next to the ladder. Hopefully, the syringes would be safe there.

Reaching to his belt, he drew his twin axes and peeled off their covers. The axes felt like kid's toys in his hands. But they were all he had, so he clung fast to them.

He looked around the dark, shadowy room. It was difficult to see much. His eyes quickly adjusted, however, and he noticed broken tables, busted machines, shattered glass, blood smears, and bullet-ridden concrete pillars. It looked like a security checkpoint, albeit one ravaged by gunfire. *Still beats the Bronx*, he thought.

Clanging pipes and growls drew his attention to the opposite side of the room. He noticed an entranceway, surrounded by shards of glass. It led to a dark void, dimly illuminated by scattered sparks and flickering flames.

He slid along the floor, inch by inch, carefully avoiding the glass. And all the while, he listened to sounds of rampage coming from the void. He heard hollow metal pipes banging against solid metal objects. Heavy machines slamming into the floor and breaking into millions of pieces. Furious bellows followed by paws thumping against the floor.

His adrenaline went through the roof. He itched to rush into the void, to take down the creature and get Morgan to safety. But the growls gave him pause. They reminded Caplan of a full-size bear. Which was a bit of a problem. How was he supposed to battle a creature that could rip him in half? And it wasn't like he could lead it away, giving Morgan a chance to escape. A grizzly, capable of speeds up to thirty miles per hour, would chase him down with ease.

He paused at the entranceway. Up close, he saw the void was really a gigantic room filled with pillars, oddities, and gizmos. Smashed generators, stricken with fire, were positioned near the walls. Strange skeletons, mounted on platforms, occupied much of the floor space. They were large, almost dino-sized. But they looked more like ... well, like nothing he'd ever seen before.

He noticed individual stations, hooked up to machines and monitors, positioned between the skeletons. Most of them looked empty, like a bedroom without a bed. But a few of them held giant silken pods, reminiscent of the ones he'd seen in the Vallerio. *Great*, he thought. *As if things weren't already creepy enough down here.*

A hulking shadow, black and covered with fur, shot across his line of sight. Speedily, it clambered up a staircase onto a ten-foot tall platform in the middle of the room. It rose up on its hind legs before flinging itself onto some wooden tables, dashing them to smithereens.

Caplan's eyes widened. *No way I'm arm barring that thing into submission*, he thought.

The creature twisted in a half-circle. Then it twisted back again. Slowly, its body unfolded, growing taller and taller. It didn't stop until it had reached its full height for a second time.

GRRRRAAAWWWWRRRRR!

It's been supersized, Caplan thought, recoiling in shock. The creature definitely moved with the grace and power of a grizzly. But while the largest grizzlies topped out at about ten feet on hind legs, this thing was closer to twelve feet at full height. And while giant grizzlies might tip the scale at 1,500 pounds, this particular creature looked to be some 500 pounds heavier.

The creature fell to all fours. Tipped its head to the roof and sniffed the air. Then it slipped off the back end of the platform. Its paws slapped the floor.

Caplan waited for more sounds of movement. But instead, an eerie silence fell over the room. His eyes flitted from left to right. His breath caught in his throat as he laid eyes upon two bloodied and mangled bodies. They belonged to Bonnie Codd and Zlata Issova, both of whom had worked in Operations. He considered them friends and their deaths hit him hard.

Caplan gripped and regripped the axes. He was sorely tempted to race into the room, to find the creature and ravage it with his blades. But he forced himself to stay cool, focused. Morgan was still alive. He couldn't see her or hear her. But he could feel her. He could feel her adrenaline, her beating heart. She—not vengeance—was all that mattered now.

GRRRRAAAWWWWRRRRR!

A giant black mass slammed into the entranceway. Startled, Caplan reared back and fell on the floor, crunching glass beneath him. Wide-eyed, he watched the creature press against the frame. Its left arm, covered with wiry black fur, reached into the security area. It swiped at Caplan, stabbing its long claws at empty air.

Caplan backed up a few inches. The creature looked even bigger from close-up. His original guess as to its identity—a bear on steroids—seemed particularly fitting. But why would Morgan and her fellow brainiacs—a hodgepodge collection of geneticists, biologists, and other -ists—want to do such a thing? What purpose did it serve?

The giant bear strained at the entranceway for several seconds. Then it withdrew its arm and vanished from sight.

Caplan exhaled a sigh of relief.

Abruptly, the creature's massive head poked through the entranceway. Its eyes, fluid and lava orange, bored holes in Caplan's forehead. Slowly, it bared its teeth, spitting and drooling on the floor. Then it roared again.

Caplan's brain tried to come up with a little quip, a joke. Anything to break the wall-thick tension. But he was too terrified to think straight.

The giant bear rammed its left shoulder into the entranceway, squeezing partway into the security area. It strained for a couple of seconds, kicking dust and debris into the air. Then it backed away, only to slam into the entranceway yet again.

Caplan scrabbled backward like a crab. He'd never felt more outmatched in his life. Forget his axes, forget guns. He'd need a damn missile to take out a creature of that size.

Again, the creature backed away. And again, it rushed forward on all fours, crashing into the entranceway and sending sharp vibrations through the surrounding walls.

Think, Caplan thought. *Think!*

The creature's rear left paw scratched against the ground, searching for purchase. Its front left arm pressed against the entranceway as it tried to force itself through the too-narrow gap.

"Hey!" A voice, one Caplan hadn't heard in many months, rang out. It was licorice-sweet, but full of menace. "Over here!"

Caplan perked up at the voice. It gave him meaning, purpose. But it also filled him with anger. *Damn it, Amanda*, he thought. *You're going to get yourself killed.*

The bear's front and rear paws froze in place. Its torso twisted toward the room's center.

Seizing his opportunity, Caplan leapt to his feet. Racing forward, he plunged both blades into the creature's front left arm. Blood spurted out, wetting the creature's wiry fur.

Roaring with pain, the bear lashed out. Its left arm smacked into Caplan. Stunned, Caplan fell to the floor. Then the creature yanked itself out of the entranceway and raced toward Morgan's voice.

Caplan touched his chest and winced. No broken ribs, but he'd have a nice bruise by morning.

Assuming he lived that long.

Still clutching the axes, he struggled to his feet. He felt faint, woozy. Shaking it off, he looked into the large room. The creature bounded onto the platform, bellowing with fury. It knocked over a bunch of tables, scattering them to the lower floor. Then it began slamming its paws into the platform.

Caplan snuck into the room, taking cover behind one of the skeleton exhibits. Peeking out, he watched the giant bear rip a piece of metal away from the platform and knock it in Caplan's general direction. The metal hit the floor and bounced a few times. Squinting, Caplan saw copious amounts of blood on the metal. *Amanda's blood?* he wondered. *Or the creature's?*

There was no time for a blood test. Obviously, Morgan was hiding underneath the platform. A platform that was seconds away from being completely dismantled.

"Hey, furball," Caplan shouted, holding his axes aloft. "How's your arm?"

The creature's head spun toward Caplan. And suddenly, Caplan felt very small and insignificant. *Probably should've thought this one through*, he ruminated. And then he was running for his life.

With a mighty roar, the creature leapt off the platform. It smashed into the skeleton, knocking over the metal support structure. Bones launched into the air, spinning like so many Frisbees.

With the bear in hot pursuit, Caplan retreated toward one of the many stations. He darted around a giant silk pod, eight feet wide and four feet tall. It was connected to a black box and looked similar to the ones he'd seen in the Vallerio. But he heard no thumming or thrubbing. Instead, his ears detected soft cracking noises and he felt vibrations coming from within the silken strands.

"Run, Amanda," he screamed as he passed the pod and hurtled a pair of waist-high machines. "Get out of here."

The creature veered off path, scampered across the floor and threw itself into the next station.

Arms flailing, Caplan slid to a halt just a few feet from the bear. He stared dumbly at its lava eyes, its bloody paws. Then he shifted his gaze to the creature's wounded arm. "There's more where that came from," he said in the toughest voice he could manage.

Snarling, the creature advanced a few inches.

You're talking trash to a bear, Zach, Caplan thought. *Guess that means you've finally lost it.* Slowly, he backed up, keeping the axes in front of him.

"Hey!" Morgan's shout echoed in the room. "Did you forget about me?"

Her voice sent a shiver down Caplan's spine. Obviously, she had no intention of leaving him to face the creature alone. That left him with two options. Defeat it or find a way for both of them to escape.

The creature shifted its gaze to the platform. Caplan did the same and saw Morgan. Her entire body, from her sweaty, bedraggled hair to her trembling legs, looked exhausted. But her gaze was one of pure defiance.

The bear started toward her, moving with great deliberation.

Caplan opened his mouth to yell at it, to goad it back in his direction. But that wouldn't solve his problem. So, he raced back to the station. Muscles tense, he swung his axes at the pod. The silk-like strands vibrated, trembled. New cracks appeared and Caplan attacked with them with ferocity.

The pod yawned open and Caplan ducked behind it. He caught a glimpse of the black box's small plaque. It read, *Megalonyx jeffersonii*. The name, which he assumed to be a combination of genus and species, meant nothing to him.

The pod rustled and stretched. Then a large beast, covered in brown fur and a thick mucus-like substance, slid out of it. It shook itself, as if arising from a deep slumber, and rose on all fours. With a strident screech—*AHHEEEEE*—it shuffled away from the pod.

The bear twisted around. Catching sight of the beast, it rose to its full height and clawed viciously at the air.

The beast, not to be outdone, rose upon its hind legs as well. It was shorter than the bear by a foot or two, but outweighed it thanks in part to a short, powerful tail. It possessed a rodent-like snout and a strange jaw filled with oversized teeth.

The bear strode forward on its hind legs. Then it threw itself at the beast. Snarling, the beast fought back, snapping at the creature's visage and clawing at its chest. They tussled for several seconds, broke apart, and then slammed into each other again.

Caplan took his gaze off the titanic struggle and locked eyes with Morgan. Her brow tightened. Then she hurried toward the staircase.

Caplan slipped away from the pod and melted into the shadows. Slinking along the wall, he made his way back to the entranceway where he found Morgan waiting for him. She frowned, gave him a quick once-over. Then she led him into the checkpoint area.

High-pitched screeches and furious roars rang in Caplan's ears. Turning around, he cast one last look at the epic struggle. The giant bear held the beast down with one front paw and wailed at it with the other one. Blood was everywhere.

Caplan picked up his backpack and donned it. Then he glanced at Morgan. Oh, how he'd waited for this moment. A moment to apologize, to tell her the full truth of her brother's horrible death.

"Are you, uh, okay?" he asked.

Smooth one, Zach, Caplan thought. *Real smooth.*

Morgan stared at him. "You shouldn't have come here, Zach."

"Why not?"

She didn't reply. Instead, she reached for a rung and hoisted herself onto the ladder. Then she began to ascend the shaft.

Caplan grabbed a rung and took one last look at the battle. The beast lay dead on the ground, its head twisted in an awkward direction. The giant bear towered over it, continuously pounding the corpse into fleshy pulp. "What is this place?" he called out as he started to climb.

"It was supposed to be Eden," Morgan said without looking down. "But it turned out to be hell instead."

CHAPTER 35

Date: Unknown; Location: Unknown

"Come on," Renjel called over his shoulder. "We're almost there."

"Would you shut up already?" Toland snapped between breaths. "We're going as fast as we can."

For once, Mills agreed with Toland. While Renjel seemed to have no problem scaling the slippery hillside, she found it far more challenging. Her body begged for rest. And she hurt all over, from her cut-up feet to the tangled mess of hair lumped atop her head. Worst of all, she was positively ravenous. Her stomach ached for food, specifically Sake and Sushi's Furious Dragon Rolls. Oh, how she loved those rolls. Her mouth watered just thinking about the tender white rice, the not-too-crunchy shrimp tempura, the oh-so-succulent avocado, the spicy sauce, the fresh jalapeno, and the rich, smoky eel. Given the chance, she would've gladly traded her convertible for a couple of rolls. Or even just one roll. Or maybe even just a bite.

"I'm so hungry." Elliott's voice was whisper-like. "If we don't find food soon, I'm going to eat worms."

The word *gross* came to mind. But it died in Mills' throat. Truth be told, she was of a similar opinion. Forget the Furious Dragon Rolls. She'd eat worms, bugs, mud, bark, whatever … anything to fill her belly. "I don't suppose you know how to hunt," she said.

Elliott shook her head.

"I do," Brian Toland said. "I've hunted all over the world and I've got the trophies to prove it."

Elliott's face reflected disgust. "Hunting should be outlawed."

"You eat meat?" he asked.

"As if. I'm a strict vegetarian."

"So, you're a plant killer."

"If you think that's the same thing as murdering an animal, then you're dumber than I thought."

"Plants might not have central nervous systems," he retorted. "But they're still living entities."

Mills arched an eyebrow. "Are you really trying to tell us you care about the plight of plants?"

"Wow," he said in a mocking tone. "I didn't think your vocabulary was broad enough for a word like *plight*."

Mills' fingers curled into fists. Being stuck in this place, this time was hard enough. But being saddled with a self-important windbag to boot? That was sheer torture.

While Toland and Elliott continued to bicker over food ethics, Mills focused on walking. Soon, the pines and spruces began to thin. Then they gave way altogether.

The air smelled of fresh dew. The wind, a little stronger now, felt hot against her bare skin. Glancing up, Mills saw a thick array of dark clouds. A few raindrops fell here and there, hinting that the storm had another chapter left to write.

The hill steepened. Her leg muscles groaned as they adjusted to the new reality. She continued onward, barely keeping her footing in the wet grass.

Renjel offered her a half-hearted smile as she and the others joined him at the highest part of the hill. "Nice work."

"Yeah, yeah." Toland, breathing heavily, bent over at the waist. "So, how's the view?"

Telling," replied Renjel in a defeated tone.

Mills turned in a slow circle and saw what he meant. Close up, she noticed coniferous forests of pines, spruces and larches. Farther back, she observed a section of temperate broad-leaf woods full of beeches, elms, maples, and oaks. And she saw temperate grasslands as well as something that looked like tundra in the distance. But there was one thing she didn't see.

Civilization.

Nature, as pure and pristine as she'd ever seen, surrounded her on all sides. It took her breath away.

But it took her last shred of hope, too.

"Damn," Toland said, summing up their thoughts quite nicely. "I mean … well, damn."

"No, no, no," Elliott's voice lifted to a scream. "No!"

"Keep it down," Renjel cautioned. "We need to—"

"We need to what?" Her eyes flashed. "We've got no supplies, no food, no way out. Might as well bring on the animals. Let's put an end to this once and for all."

"If you want to kill yourself, go right ahead," Toland said. "But do it somewhere else."

She glared at him. "I hate you."

"Oh, no." His hands flew to his cheeks in mock horror. "Whatever will I do?"

"Listen," Renjel said, desperation evident in his voice. "Does anyone have any experience in the outdoors? Hunting, fishing, camping? Anything like that?"

"He knows how to hunt," Mills said with a nod at Toland.

Renjel gave him a hopeful look. "Is that right?"

"Yes," Toland replied. "With a gun. But as you can see, I'm lacking in that department."

"That's not the only department you're lacking in," Elliott muttered under her breath.

"Stop it," Renjel said. "Both of you. We need to work together if we're going to make it through this."

Toland crossed his arms and Elliott looked away. Meanwhile, Mills turned in another circle. She grieved for her former life. For the cocktails, the parties, the boys. And most of all, for the fame. Like all self-respecting celebrities, she claimed to hate fame. But if she was completely honest with herself, she secretly loved it. She loved it when people did a double take as they recognized her in passing. She loved the endless stream of smooth-tongued men who accosted her at every turn. And she loved teenage girls running up to her on the street, saying they adored her and oh, could she please pose for a selfie?

Her mind worked in overdrive as she processed her new reality. How was she going to live without fame? Without the lovers, the clothes, and the lavish getaways?

"What's the point?" Elliott said. "Work together, don't work together … either way, we die."

"Not if I have anything to say about it." Renjel's visage twisted in thought. "We'll use the cave as shelter. We can stack wood in front of it to keep out the animals. And we can make beds out of dirt and leaves."

"That could work." Toland nodded slowly. "And we've got the stream for water."

"Exactly," Renjel said. "For food, we'll eat berries and leaves. Animals too, if we can figure out how to catch them."

Mills' gaze focused in on Renjel. She studied his face, his five o'clock shadow. It was a handsome face, she realized, chock-full of self-assurance. Back home, she wouldn't have given him the time of day. Not because he was ugly, but because he was beneath her station. And dating beneath one's station was the kiss of death in her world. But out here, out in the middle of nowhere, things were different. Those old rules no longer applied. And even if they had, who cared?

A small part of her was starting to realize the emptiness inherent in her old life. For the first time, she found herself craving something else, something deeper and more meaningful. *Christ, Bailey*, she thought. *Get your head out of the clouds.*

"We still need fire," Toland said.

"For what?" Elliott asked.

"To keep predators at bay, you dolt."

"But he—" She nodded at Renjel. "—said we'd stack wood to keep them out of the cave."

"You really think some measly tree branches are going to keep that saber from chowing down on us?" He gave her a scathing look. "Anyway how do you expect to keep warm without fire? Or cook a meal? Or disinfect water? Or—?"

"You made your point." Renjel looked around. "Anyone have a lighter or matches?"

Heads shook back and forth.

"What if we scraped rocks?" Mills asked, breaking the silence. "Doesn't that produce sparks?"

"Only if you've got high carbon steel and the right rock." Toland arched a superior eyebrow. "And this is just a guess, but I'm willing to bet you couldn't tell flint from slate."

"No, but I've got plenty of time to figure it out," she replied evenly.

Renjel adopting a calming tone. "Okay, Bailey will work on fire. Now, let's—"

"Wait." Mills' gaze flicked to the side, to a spot just above Renjel's ear. "Speaking of fire, I think I see one."

The others turned around and focused their attention on a section of coniferous treetops. Thin wisps of grayish smoke floated above them before disappearing into the stormy sky.

"A campfire." Elliott smiled broadly. "Thank God."

"Or a forest fire," Toland remarked. "If you—"

Mills was first to hear the snarl. Whirling around, she saw a black and orange streak racing up the hillside. She tried to scream, but it struck her side. She twisted, fell to the ground.

The streak continued without pause, racing across the hilltop. Moments later, it smacked into something. Bones cracked. A wail of agony rang out. Then claws sliced into flesh, spilling blood and organs onto the wet grass.

Shaking off the cobwebs, Mills struggled to a sitting position. Ten feet away, she saw the saber, snarling and drooling. It looked taller than she remembered by at least a foot. Meaner, too.

Shifting her gaze, she saw a writhing body underneath its heavy paws. Horror swept through her. *No, no, no*, she thought, her mind reeling in shock. *Not him ... not Travis!*

CHAPTER 36

Date: June 19, 2016, 4:24 p.m.; Location: Hatcher Station, Vallerio Forest, NH

"Well, that was interesting." Caplan, still shouldering his backpack, hoisted himself out of the shaft. "Let's never do it again."

Morgan said nothing. But her look spoke volumes about her inner pain, her deep sadness. With a deep sigh, she turned to the gathered brainiacs, technicians and rangers. "Bonnie and Zlata are dead," she said. "But mourning will have to wait. We've got a full expulsion sequence on our hands. And the 2-Gens are just as brutal as the 1-Gens. Maybe more so."

Faces tensed up throughout the room.

"What about the *Arctodus simus*?" Amy Carson nervously licked her lips. "Is it—?"

"It's loose," Morgan replied to gasps of horror. "It already killed the *Megalonyx jeffersonii*."

"Then I say we kill it." Carson lifted her pistol for all to see.

A few weak cheers rang out and Morgan waited for them to die down. "You know how hard it is to kill those things," she said. "Anyway we've still got six incubators to go. Better to let them reach expulsion. The 2-Gens will kill each other and we can retake the Lab."

"What if they don't?" Carson retorted. "What if the *Arctodus simus* survives? What if it tries to come up here? With those semi-opposable thumbs, it—"

"We don't have to worry about that. Fortunately, it's too big to squeeze into the checkpoint area." Morgan paused. "Look, we've obviously got to get back down there to access the communications systems. But in the meantime, let's play it safe. Get a team together and watch the shaft. If you see anything, start shooting."

"What if it keeps coming?"

"Then we'll close and seal the hatch until we can figure out an alternative plan."

"Easier said than done." Gino Suarez, one of Hatcher's brightest technicians, coughed. "Without power, we can't seal the locks."

"And the generators are in the Lab." Morgan rubbed her temples. "Christ, can this get any worse?"

"I've got a team working on it," Suarez said. "We should be able to whip up a new power source, but it could take a while."

"Amanda." Caplan opened his pack. "I know you're busy, but I really need to—"

She gave him a fierce look. "Be quiet."

"But—"

"I said, be quiet."

Caplan glanced at his watch and realized he had more than thirty minutes before the full effects of HA-78 began to kick in. It wasn't a ton of time, but he could afford a few minutes.

"Okay," Morgan said after a moment. "Suarez, get me that power source. Amy, guard the shaft but be ready to move into the Heptagon if something goes wrong. Everyone else, get your stuff together. If a 2-Gen somehow breaches the hatch, we may need to move outdoors."

"What should we do with the prisoners?" a voice called out.

"Keep watching them. And be ready to transport them outside at a moment's notice."

"What about Zach?" another voice shouted. "He told us he's working for James."

"Let me worry about him." Her eyes flitted to Caplan. "By the time I'm done, he'll wish he never came back."

CHAPTER 37

Date: June 19, 2016, 4:29 p.m.; Location: Hatcher Station, Vallerio Forest, NH

"That's far enough." Morgan swung a pistol like a whip, cracking it against Caplan's head. Dazed, he sank to his knees in a small pool of his own blood. "Why'd you come here?"

Caplan winced as the gun barrel dug into the back of his pounding skull. He'd been relieved of his pack and axes. And none of his skills, none of his tricks could help him now. "I missed the hospitality," he replied.

Morgan jabbed the barrel against his head. "You've still got a smart mouth."

"And you've still got a temper." He scanned the Galley. Thanks to a couple of battery-powered lamps, he could see a salad bar, empty at the moment, to his right. A coffee station, normally manned by a friendly barista, sat to his left. Numerous long tables, surrounded by metal chairs and outfitted with napkin dispensers and bottles of condiments, ran zigzag along the floor.

"Why'd you come here?" she repeated.

"To save you. Or maybe to stop you." He frowned. "To be honest, it's kind of confusing."

The air whistled. The gun cracked against Caplan's skull for a second time. Clutching his head in pain, he slumped to the ground.

"I'm only going to ask you one more time," she said. "Why'd you come here?"

"Okay, okay." He climbed back to his knees. Gently, he rubbed his throbbing scalp. "This morning, a guy came to see me. He said his name was James Corbotch and that he owned the Vallerio. That was news to me."

She nodded. "That's because you worked in the Eye. Only people in Research were authorized to know about James."

"It took some convincing, but I ended up believing him. He said terrorists had seized Hatcher. He wanted my help to take it back."

"Why you?"

"He needed someone who knew the area."

"Very good." She pushed the barrel into the back of his neck. "Now, where's your back-up?"

He wanted to tell her everything. God, he wanted to. But he hesitated. This wasn't the same girl he'd flirted with all those months ago. She was different now. Colder, harder. What would she do if she found out Pearson, Corbotch, and Perkins were still alive? Would she send a squad of brainiacs to hunt them down?

Would she kill them?

"They're dead," he lied.

"Try again."

"Okay. They're dead." A pause. "How's that?"

Morgan clucked her tongue against the roof of her mouth. "How'd they die?"

"Helicopter crash."

"You really expect me to believe that?"

"Only if you've got a brain. Ask the guys who came looking for it. That is, unless they're too embarrassed by the beating I gave them."

"Beating?" Her eyes flashed with sudden understanding. "So, that's why they looked like mud wrestlers."

Caplan smirked.

"Fine," Morgan said. "What caused the crash?"

"We were flying here when the Blare—"

"Blare?"

"That weird phenomena three hours ago." He searched her face, but saw no sign of recognition. "You didn't experience it?"

She shook her head.

"Consider yourself lucky. It sounded like blaring horns. The air got hot and thick. I felt these sharp pinpricks of ice. This weird glow covered everything. And then I passed out. When I woke up, I was surrounded by wreckage and dead bodies."

"Oh my God, the 1-Gens." Her eyes widened. "The full expulsion sequence must've created some kind of, I don't know, weird energy."

"The 1-Gens?"

"Never mind." She paused. "So, you came here after the crash?"

"Where else was I going to go?"

A long pause followed. Finally, Morgan sighed. "What did Corbotch tell you about us?"

"Can I just …?" Prepping for another blow, Caplan slowly swiveled his head. But this time, Morgan didn't strike him. Emboldened, he twisted all the way around on his knees and gave her a good look.

A tattered lab coat, soaked with blood on one side, covered her gaunt, sweaty frame. Underneath it, he saw hints of a tight crimson shirt and black yoga pants. "You're hurt," he said.

She aimed her pistol between his eyes. "I can still shoot."

"Let me help you."

"Not a chance. Now, answer the question."

Caplan sighed. "It's like I told you. He said terrorists seized Hatcher and a bunch of dignitaries. You and the others were in danger."

"So, he lied." She exhaled. "Typical James."

Thoughts of Tony swirled inside Caplan's head. He still didn't know what was going on. Nor did he understand her motives. But one thing was certain.

It was time to start making things right.

"It's no lie," he replied. "Tell me something. Did you have to hack your way through that hatch to enter the Lab?"

Her eyes glittered with suspicion. "What's your point?"

"And when you entered the shaft, did you feel a rush of air?"

"Of course. It happens every time the hatch is opened. That's part of how we keep the Lab free of contaminants." Her gaze narrowed. "What's this got to do with anything?"

"Everything. The hack triggered a gas switch. So, that wasn't air you released into the shaft." He paused. "It was HA-78."

"HA-78?"

"James told me all about it. But don't worry. He gave me enough antibiotics for everyone. They're in my backpack along with a whole mess of syringes."

She stared at him.

"Once his people took out the terrorists, he wanted me to distribute the treatments to all of you. Of course, he never realized you were the terrorists. You'll have to explain that one to me." Caplan paused. "But not now. We only have until five o'clock. After that, people start dying."

"Let me get this straight. You came here to stop us. But now, you want to help us?"

"Just distribute the antibiotics. Then we'll sit down and figure this out."

Morgan paced to the door. Cracked it open and leaned her head out. Occasionally glancing at Caplan, she chatted quietly with someone in the Heptagon. Then she took hold of a small cooler and turned back to the Galley. "Is this it?" she asked.

His eyes brightened at the sight of the familiar container. "The syringes are inside. You just have to—"

She opened the cooler and turned it upside down. Syringes and vials plunged to the ground. The syringes bounced harmlessly against the beige vinyl flooring. But the vials shattered upon impact, spilling liquid everywhere.

Caplan gaped at the vials, then at her. "Are you crazy?" he said. "Do you know what you just did?"

"Yes." Her eyes were dark, unreadable. "I spilled water."

"No." A cloud of confusion passed over his brain. "Those vials held antibiotics."

"Not according to the people who just analyzed them." She sighed. "This isn't a BSL-4 lab, Zach. Not even close. There are no deadly biological agents on the premises."

"But James said—"

"James lied to you. He must've told you that story so you'd agree to lead his people here. But don't feel bad about it. He lied to all of us too. That's why we took over Hatcher. We're going to stop him, expose him." She extended a hand to Caplan. He took it and she helped him to his feet. "Or die trying."

CHAPTER 38

Date: June 19, 2016, 4:37 p.m.; Location: Hatcher Station, Vallerio Forest, NH

There's your life lesson for the day, Caplan thought. *Never trust a guy who fakes his own kidnapping.*

Pain exploded inside Caplan as he dragged his exhausted body across the room. Aches ripped through his back and shoulders, his calves and thighs. It felt like he'd played a few games of pinball … from inside the machine.

Amanda Morgan made her way to the nearest table. Her eyes glassed over as she eased her body into a metal chair and began to pull off her lab coat.

Caplan frowned. "Hey, are you alright?"

The tattered and bloodied lab coat fell to the floor. She lifted her crimson t-shirt a few inches, exposing some blood-soaked bandages. "I'll live," she replied in a faint voice.

"That doesn't look so good." Shifting course, he doubled back to the door. "I'll get the doc."

"No, no." She nodded to her right. "Check the cabinets. There should be first-aid kits in one of them."

Caplan grabbed one of the battery-powered lamps and hurried to a stretch of countertop. It held drink-serving machines—coffee, espresso, soda—along with several large sinks, interspersed by paper cups, lids, sugar packets, straws, and other items. Underneath, he saw a series of unmarked cabinets.

Quickly, he filtered through the cabinets, taking a few first-aid kits along with some spare linens. Then he filled a paper cup with water from the sink, helped himself to a straw, and returned to the table.

Morgan held out her hand, fingers relaxed but wrist cocked. "I'll take it from here."

Caplan placed the lamp and items on the table. Then he opened the first-aid kits and pulled out some large bandages. "Yeah, because you've done such a good job of taking care of yourself."

"I'll have you know—"

"Just shut up and sit still."

Morgan moaned as Caplan peeled off the bandages. Underneath, he saw a deep wound zigzagging across her smooth skin. He poured a bit of water on her waist, clearing away the blood. Then he watched as more blood slowly oozed out of the gash.

He grabbed a saltshaker from the table and twisted off the top. Then he dumped the contents into the cup.

Morgan cast him a wide-eyed look. "Uh, on second thought, maybe you should get Dr. Adnan."

"What's wrong?" Using the straw, Caplan stirred the salt into the water. Then he poured the mixture onto a fresh linen, completely saturating the cloth. "Don't you trust me?"

"Do you really want me to—?"

Caplan pressed the saturated cloth against her wound.

Her teeth ground together. "Ahh!"

"Does that hurt?"

"What do you think?"

"I think it's better than bleeding to death." For the next three minutes, Caplan held the cloth against her waist, occasionally lifting it to take a look at the gash. Then he repeated the process with a separate linen, also soaked in salt water. Afterward, he studied her skin. "You could probably use a few stitches. But at least it's stopped bleeding. Plus, the salt should act as a disinfectant."

Eyes still glassy, she gazed at her waist. "Where …?"

"It's just an old home remedy." He grinned wistfully. "Courtesy of Grandma Caplan."

Morgan saw the look in his face. "When she'd die?"

"Almost ten years ago." He got some fresh water and poured it over the wound. Then he patted it dry and rebandaged it.

"I'm sorry."

"So am I."

"About what?"

Tony Morgan's face flashed before his eyes. "More like who."

Her warm gaze chilled over. She pulled her tee back over the wound and started to stand up. But Caplan grabbed her shoulders and pushed her firmly back into the seat.

"I need to get out there," she protested.

"Do you want to start bleeding all over again?" He cocked an eyebrow. "I didn't think so."

She crossed her arms. Looked away.

Caplan wanted to tell her about Tony, about how the man had really died. And he needed to apologize for freezing up, for not helping Tony escape those vicious creatures. But he knew it wasn't the right place or the right time. So, he switched gears. "What happened here?" he asked. "Why are you doing all this?"

She snorted like he was some comedian. Not a great comedian. But still, a comedian. "I don't know where to begin."

"At the beginning?

"Always the wise ass." She exhaled. "The Vallerio Forest, as you probably remember, is a rewilding sanctuary. Over the years, James Corbotch and his minions at the Vallerio

Foundation have gathered an array of megafauna—elephants, lions, and others—within its boundaries. Those megafauna roam millions of acres as they please, held back only by the exterior fences."

Caplan recalled his conversation with Corbotch aboard the helicopter. "Go on."

"Obviously, rewilding isn't just some lark. It has a purpose. The last 60,000 years saw thirty-three genera of North American megafauna, keystone species, and apex predators go extinct. At least fifteen of those genera—and possibly more—died out some 11,000 years ago. They left behind a severely damaged food chain. To this day, that food chain continues to unravel, driving countless plant and animal species to extinction."

"You're talking about the ... the ..." He snapped his fingers. "... the Holocene extinction."

"That's right. Or the sixth extinction, if you prefer. Theoretically, rewilding will put an end to all the deaths. Patch up the top of the food chain and everything else will fall into line. There's just one problem." She took a deep breath. "It doesn't work."

Caplan arched an eyebrow.

"Thousands of years ago, American mastodons, Columbian mammoths, woolly mammoths, and imperial mammoths roamed North America. Since those species no longer exist, James tried to fill their place with proxies. For example, he used Asian elephants in place of mammoths. He placed the elephants into open grassland, reminiscent of the landscape occupied by mammoths during the Pleistocene epoch. Then he sat back, and waited for the Vallerio to respond. But the soil didn't regenerate as expected. The forest continued to spread into non-forest areas. The elephants started to die. And so on. So, he went back to the drawing board."

"And?"

"And he came to a realization. The elephants were the problem. Simply put, they couldn't fully fill the gap left behind by mammoths. So, that left him with two options." Gingerly, she touched her waist and winced. "First, he could wait for the situation to reach a new equilibrium. But his inner circle calculated that could take years. And besides, the elephants were dying too quickly to get a foothold. So, he chose the second option."

"Which was?"

"He'd forget the proxies and instead, use the real deal."

"I can see one major flaw in that idea." Caplan grinned. "In case you forgot, mammoths are dead."

"That's why he hired me." She inhaled a mouthful of air. "To bring them back to life."

CHAPTER 39

Date: June 19, 2016, 4:49 p.m.; Location: Hatcher Station, Vallerio Forest, NH

"Come again?" Caplan held a hand to his ear. "Because it sounded like you said you'd brought dead creatures back to life."

If she heard the incredulity in his voice, she didn't let on. "It took years of painstaking work to revive saber-toothed cats and woolly mammoths. Since then, things have moved very fast."

Zombie mammoths was Caplan's first thought followed by: *Someone should really make that into a movie.* But he knew that wasn't what she meant. Morgan and her fellow brainiacs hadn't raised the dead. Instead, they'd breathed new life into long-extinct species.

"Speechless, huh?" Morgan arched an eyebrow. "That's a first."

"I just, well … how come you never told me about this?"

"All Research employees are required to sign strict non-disclosures with stiff penalties for non-compliance." A hint of a smile crossed her lips. "We always wondered how much the rest of you knew about our work. Didn't you ever wonder why Hatcher employed so many geneticists and biologists?"

"Not really," he admitted. "So, that creature in the Lab … that was one of yours?"

She nodded. "It's an *Arctodus simus*, or short-faced bear. It's one of the largest mammalian carnivores to ever walk on land and one of our 2-Gen prototypes. The fossil record is a bit sketchy, but we think the species died out about 11,000 years ago."

"How'd you do it? How'd you bring the dead back to life?"

"It would take hours to explain the entire process for each animal. But here's the basic gist for how we created our first woolly mammoth. James, acting through the Foundation, sent teams across the globe in search of frozen soft tissue samples. We used those tissues for a massively parallel genomic study to fully sequence the woolly mammoth's DNA. Afterward, we extracted the egg cell from a female Asian elephant and replaced its nucleus with one we'd created using our sequence."

"I see," Caplan replied thoughtfully. "You induced the cell into dividing and then inserted it back into the elephant. That elephant carried the cell to term and—presto chango— you had yourself a baby woolly mammoth."

"I wish it were that easy. We tried that method on seven separate eggs, but none of the calves survived birth. Someone—I forget who—finally figured out the problem. We were trying to grow a woolly mammoth inside the fetal environment of an Asian elephant. That's like trying to grow a Neanderthal baby inside a person."

"Thanks." Caplan made a face. "That thought should feed my nightmares for at least a month."

Her eyes flashed.

"Wait a second," he said slowly. "Did you actually do that? Did you grow little bundles of Neanderthal joy?"

"Not us, no." She brushed her hair back. "Anyway we needed a womb that could accommodate the needs of a woolly mammoth. And since nature couldn't provide one for us, we turned to science."

"You made your own wombs." A thought occurred to him. "Those silk pod things?"

"We call them ectogenetic incubators. But yes, those are artificial wombs. Each one is specifically designed to meet the needs of a particular species. It took months of extensive research and planning to build them." She exhaled. "The one you cut open held a *Megalonyx jeffersonii*, also known as a giant ground sloth. They once ranged over much of North and Central America. They were largely forgotten until Thomas Jefferson used their fossils to support his completeness of nature theory."

"His what?"

"Jefferson didn't believe in evolution. As part of that, he didn't believe species could go extinct via natural means. When bones of a *Megalonyx jeffersonii* came to his attention, he argued they belonged to an unknown species of lion. If that lion could be found, he thought it would help support his theory."

"Let me guess. Old T.J. wound up with egg on his face."

"Smart ass." Despite her words, Morgan smiled a bit. "T.J. might've been wrong, but his work helped to kickstart the study of vertebrate paleontology in this country."

Caplan rubbed his jaw. "How large do giant ground sloths get?"

"They max out at about ten feet from end-to-end. At that size, they tip the scales at roughly a ton."

"But that one we saw—"

"—had already reached full-size. Yes, I know." She shrugged. "Unfortunately, we didn't have time to grow baby woolly mammoths, baby ground sloths, and the like. We needed full-size ones. Ones we could insert into the wild as soon as possible."

Caplan's gaze narrowed. "What's the rush?"

"It took thousands of years, but the loss of megafauna during the Pleistocene epoch has finally caught up to us. Ecosystems across the globe are in a state of near-collapse. According to studies conducted by the Vallerio Foundation, we've got twenty to thirty years to turn things around. Otherwise, the Sixth extinction will go full tilt. And if it's anything like the previous five, at least seventy percent of all species—and that includes humans, by the way—will die out."

"It can't be that bad."

"Believe me, I wish it weren't. But the research says otherwise."

"This doesn't make sense," Caplan said. "If we need those extinct mammals so badly, then why are you trying to shut this place down?"

"We're not trying to shut it down. We're trying to shut the Foundation—specifically, James Corbotch—down."

"But why? He built this place. Without him, your little de-extinction program wouldn't even exist."

"That might be true. But it doesn't excuse his crimes."

"What crimes?"

"Those incubators you saw in the Lab are classified 2-Gen, or second generation. The preceding generation of animals, 1-Gen, was born into this world with unexpected genetic mutations. Mutations that left them ultra-violent and, well, bloodthirsty. All they did was kill each other, making them completely useless for our purposes. We decided to destroy the surviving animals, along with the unopened incubators. James agreed with our decision. But secretly, he took them to an uncharted area of the Vallerio."

Caplan recalled the clandestine fence. He recalled Tony Morgan slipping beneath it and dying at the hands of vicious animals. He remembered the strange wolf, the other silk pods, and how unknown animals had killed the survivors from the *Blaze*. At long last, everything made sense. "Sector 48A?" he asked.

"How'd ...?" Her eyes bugged out. "Tony told you?"

Caplan didn't respond.

She stared into his eyes for a long moment. "Yes, he took them to 48A. But that wasn't the end of it. James had plans for our creations. He used them to create something evil."

"What?"

"A killing ground."

CHAPTER 40

Date: Unknown; Location: Unknown

With a pathetic whimper, Brian Toland flopped face first onto the ground. He slid across a patch of mud, scraping his belly against tiny pebbles and twigs. When he came to a stop, he didn't bother rising to his feet. Instead, he just lay there, spread-eagled.

Mills whirled around in mid-step. Her lips curled in anger as she laid eyes upon the older man. She was tempted to keep going, to leave him behind. It would serve him right for all his snippy comments.

But she retraced her steps anyway. After Renjel's untimely death, she, Elliott, and Toland had hightailed it down the hillside. They'd proceeded to cut through the forest, utilizing brief sprints interspersed with fast walks. She wasn't sure how long they'd been running and walking. But it felt like hours.

She ground to a halt a few inches from Toland's head. A burning sensation appeared at the tips of her bruised toes. It extended down the soles of her stinging bare feet. It reached up her calves, her thighs. And it didn't stop there. Within seconds, her whole body felt like it was on fire. Was this what athletes meant by feeling the burn? If so, she didn't want to feel it. Not ever again.

Elliott appeared, sliding between two tree trunks and pacing to Mills' side. Thick mud covered her sweatshirt and jeans. More mud was smeared across her face, her neck, her head. All told, she looked more like a walking swamp than a person.

Breathing heavily, Elliott wiped a muddy hand across her muddy face, with predictable results. "Man up, Brian." Her free hand clutched her waist in a firm grip. "We don't have time for this."

"Screw you." Toland rolled onto his back. Despite his obvious exhaustion, he still managed a look of complete disdain. "I'd like to see you run this much when you're my age."

"If we don't keep running, I might not reach your age."

"Quiet." Mills tilted an ear to the forest and listened hard. "I don't hear anything. Maybe we're okay."

"That doesn't mean anything," Elliott retorted. "We didn't hear that saber until it … you know."

Mills knew. She knew it well. One moment, she was staring at Renjel, nursing ridiculous fantasies about romance in the wild. The next, she was watching that saber tear apart his organs.

Her shoulders quivered and tears splashed down her cheeks. Quickly, she turned away, coughing to cover up the faint sobs emanating from her throat.

"What's the matter with you?" Toland asked.

"Just … just got something in my throat," she managed between sobs.

He snorted.

This was stupid, so stupid. Randi Skolnick had died. Now, Renjel—the closest thing she had to a friend in this sad group—had followed the woman to an early grave. On top of all that, she was exhausted, hungry, and scared witless by her surroundings. In short, she had every reason in the world to cry. So, why was she so afraid of showing it?

The thought distracted her long enough for her eye faucets to slow to mere trickles. She recalled many other times—break-ups, betrayals, and nasty rumors about her personal life—when she'd hid her emotions. And she realized something as she stood there in that strange and ancient forest. She wasn't allowed to have negative emotions. Not without serious repercussions anyway.

After all, she was Bailey Mills! The rich and beautiful party girl with the perfect life. She could buy anything, go anywhere, date anyone. She didn't have to worry about the glass ceiling or whether or not she could pay her rent on time. No, her problems were strictly of the first-world variety. Heck, they weren't even that important.

One particular memory from 2013 came to mind. During an interview, she'd expressed annoyance that her one-of-a-kind convertible, which had set her back nearly a million dollars, had been sidelined with engine issues. Within minutes, social media users were on the warpath. They raked her over the coals, calling her a spoiled brat who didn't appreciate the silver spoon from which she'd been fed. Internet memes popped up, contrasting her situation with that of the billions of people who couldn't even afford a car.

The worst part was that she agreed with them. She was, indeed, a rich bitch. Plagued with guilt, she made a series of public apologies and hit up the charity circuit with renewed vigor. Afterward, she did her best to appreciate the magnificent life she'd been given. Even so, she still felt occasional sadness, annoyance, and discontentment. She did everything in her power to keep those feelings to herself. It wasn't easy, especially since she lived much of her life in the public sphere. But she soon learned to control those negative emotions, to lock them away in the pit of her soul.

Now, all that stored negativity came flooding out of her in a deluge of fury. She was a human being, damn it! She felt the same emotions—good and bad—as anyone else. But noooo. The public and media didn't see it that way. How dare she complain about a busted engine! How dare she show anything other than gratefulness every second of her life!

Well, no more. She was going to be herself—whoever that was—whether people liked it or not.

"I'm crying." Spinning around, she looked Toland straight in the eyes. "Got a problem with that?"

He blinked, momentarily stunned by her forceful response.

Elliott arched an eyebrow at Mills. A faint smile creased her visage. Then she knelt down and helped Toland to a sitting position. "I know you're tired," she said in a voice laced with venom. "But we need to keep going."

Toland rested for a moment. Then he stood up and stretched his muscles. "I'm not taking another step," he said, recovering his bravado. "Not until we stop acting like morons and start using our brains."

"But—"

"Wait." Mills held up a hand. "I hate to admit it, but Brian's right. I'm almost positive the saber that killed Travis was the same one that attacked Randi. It's stalking us. If we keep running, it'll just keep coming."

Elliott exhaled softly. "So, what do we do?"

"We've been running blind, taking the path of least resistance. I think we have to reset, focus on a specific destination."

"You mean the smoke?"

"Exactly."

"Yes." Toland clapped his hands together. "I'm glad to see that one of you is finally showing a bit of sense."

"Shut up, Brian." Mills turned in an arc. "Okay, I think I see it. Over there. There must be a camp nearby."

"A camp?" Toland shot Mills a crafty look. "I'm confused. I thought you said we were lost in time. Sent back to the ancient days by forces beyond our control."

Mills sighed. "It was just a theory."

"An incredibly stupid one."

"Do you ever stop talking?"

"Oh, that's real—"

"What if it's not a campfire?" Elliott asked, interrupting the argument. "What if it's a forest fire?"

"Yeah." Toland smirked at Mills. "What then?"

"Then we'll burn to a crisp." Mills started forward, stepping carefully so as to avoid some wet pine cones. "Look on the bright side. At least the saber won't enjoy its meal."

"Eww," Elliott replied.

The trio strode forward with Mills in the middle and Toland and Elliott at her flanks. The temperature warmed and before long, beads of sweat began to roll down Mills' face, washing the mud streaks away.

Flames crackled softly in the distance. Rainwater dripped from the trees, splashing against the wet ground. But other than that, the forest was eerily quiet. More than once, Mills turned her head around, checking their rear. Although she didn't see the saber, she knew it was out there somewhere.

"I see flames." Toland huffed and puffed his way over a small hill. "Lots of them."

"Agreed." Elliott slowed her pace a bit.

Mills didn't break speed. Instead, she continued to march forward, all the while keeping an eye out for the saber. Thirty seconds later, she pulled to a stop. Her heart pounded ferociously against her chest.

Just ahead, she saw a clearing and a long barn-like building, painted camouflage-style. Flames, a striking mixture of orange and red, engulfed one end of the building.

Gray smoke rose above the flames, curling into the dark sky. A fence, constructed from tall metal posts sunk into large concrete blocks, surrounded the area.

"Well, there you go," Toland said, triumphantly. "What do you think of your time travel theory now?"

Mills ignored him.

"Did you hear me?" he asked. "I said—"

Mills lifted a finger to her lips and shushed him.

Toland arched an eyebrow. But he kept quiet.

"What's wrong?" Elliott whispered.

"That's an electric fence, probably designed to keep out animals," Mills replied. "Only the electricity isn't working."

"And that's important?"

"See how that post has been ripped out of its concrete block?" She waved her hand at the fence. "I think something took advantage of the power outage. And for all we know, it's still in the area."

Elliott bit her lip. "Another saber?"

"No. Something bigger. A lot bigger." Twisting her hips, Mills hiked alongside the fence. The mud-soaked needles acted as a carpet, cushioning her bare feet and allowing her to stay quiet.

She walked to the opposite side of the clearing. She could see the fire clearly now. It slowly chewed away at the building, working its way along the wall and deeper into the seemingly hollow interior. She shifted her gaze to a large concrete block. A jagged hole indicated where its metal post had once stood.

She looked at the fallen post. It lay inside the fence's perimeter, partially embedded in the soil, and still attached to surrounding posts via wires. Clearly, a powerful force had smashed into it, ripping it out of its concrete casing. The impact drove the post into the soil, taking the wires with it.

Moving forward, she studied the ground inside the fence and saw big, cabbage-shaped footprints going in either direction. She knew nothing about animal footprints. But they looked large enough to belong to one of the woolly mammoths.

A few tears sprung up in her eyes again. She remembered standing next to Renjel as they watched the group of mammoths tear into each other. She missed him, missed his strength.

She took a deep breath, allowing herself a few seconds to grieve. Then she reassessed the situation. The tracks indicated that whatever had knocked the post down had already left the area. And she didn't see any other tracks in the vicinity. So, she slid past the concrete block, stepped carefully over the wires, and made her way to the burning building.

"Wait," Elliott whispered loudly from just outside the fence. "We need to think about this."

Mills retreated to the concrete block. "What's there to think about? I don't see any animals. And there could be people in there. Plus, food and water. Maybe even a way to get help."

"What about the fire?" Toland frowned. "Sure, it looks contained. But any minute now, that whole place could go up in flames."

"All the more reason to hurry." Mills' eyes bored into his like drills. "That place is our best shot at survival. You know it, I know it. So, be quiet for once and help me save it before it's too late."

Spinning around, Mills hightailed it across the close-cut grass. The temperature jumped a few notches and she tasted cinders on her tongue. Trails of smoke curled into her nose, nearly sending her into a coughing fit.

She turned, adjusting course. In the process, she noticed several charred objects—bodies, from the looks of it—

amongst the flames and smoke. Fury engulfed her heart. She'd finally stumbled upon a modicum of civilization, only to have it burn before her eyes.

Skirting around the fire, she raced parallel to the building, eventually reaching a small door. She paused for a moment to touch the smooth metal. It felt cool. Turning the knob, she thrust the door open and hurried into the structure.

A mind-numbing wave of heat washed over her. She swooned, but still managed to maintain consciousness. Ducking beneath the smoke, she noticed the interior was hollowed out just like a barn. But there were no haystacks, stalls, or tools. Instead, machines of all shapes and sizes covered the vinyl flooring.

She stared at the machines in awe, feeling a little like a visitor to some far-off alien world. Style, fashion, drinking, parties ... those were her strong suits. But this ... this warehouse of strange machines ... well, it was way beyond her comprehension. *What is this place?* she wondered. *Why is it here?*

A machine, engulfed in flames, exploded into a million pieces. The noise deafened Mills and an accompanying shockwave sent her to the floor. She landed hard, hammering her nose against the surface.

Elliott grabbed Mills' arm, pulled her to her feet. "Are you okay?"

"I'm fine." Mills rubbed her nose and turned to look at the fire. The flames were longer now. Hotter, too. It felt like her core temperature was about to go through the roof. "Help me find the fire extinguishers."

She nodded at the far wall. "Over there."

Swiveling her neck, Mills saw red extinguishers mounted on the wall. She grabbed one and fiddled with it, causing a white stream of foam to shoot onto the floor.

Satisfied, she stumbled toward the fire and began to douse the nearest flames with chemical foam.

Elliott joined her and together, they attacked the fire. The flames fought back, showering them with sparks.

Extinguisher in hand, Toland raced into the fray. With his help, they turned the tide. Inch by inch, they advanced through the structure, covering the machines and walls with thick layers of chemical foam. In the process, Mills saw numerous corpses, burnt to a crisp.

Despite that, she felt a bit of hope inside her chest. Maybe they could do this after all. Maybe they could save the building and patch up the fire-damaged wall. Maybe they could even fix the fence and figure out a way to restore the power. Sure, they'd have to bury the bodies. And they'd have to figure out how to procure supplies. But at least they'd be safe. At least they could live here for a spell while they figured out their next move.

She lingered for a few seconds, directing extra spray at some particularly stubborn flames. When they'd finally blinked out, she took a closer look to see what had fueled them.

A pile of charred logbooks lay smoldering in a neat pile. She brushed the bottom edge of the extinguisher against the pile, reducing it to ash. Sweeping aside the debris, she focused her attention on a slab of smooth metal, with hinges and a handle on opposing sides.

She returned to the fire and within a few minutes, the last of the flames had been turned into smoke. Elliott added a few extra squirts of her extinguisher for good measure.

"That wasn't the worst effort I've ever seen," Toland said. "But next time, the two of you should …"

Blocking out his voice, Mills hiked back to the metal slab. It was square-shaped, measuring about three feet on each side. A tiny monitor, black as night, had been sunk into the metal.

Elliott appeared and knelt next to the slab. "What do you make of it?" she asked Mills.

"It looks like ..." Mills paused, searching for the right word. "... a hatch."

"Where's it lead?"

"How should I know?"

"What the hell is wrong with you two?" Toland asked angrily. "Here I am offering a little advice and—"

"Yeah, yeah," Mills said, dismissively, her gaze locked on the hatch. "Whatever you say, Brian."

Grunting in displeasure, Toland hiked across the floor. But his anger melted away when he saw the hatch. "Open it," he said, his tone full of undeserved authority.

Mills glared at him. Of course, she was going to open the stupid hatch. Not because he told her to, but because it was the obvious move. She nearly said something to that effect, but ultimately decided against it. Toland wouldn't have believed her anyway.

She gripped the handle with both hands. Straining, she lifted the hatch a few inches. Elliott joined her and together, they pulled it all the way open. A shaft and metal ladder appeared. Mills squinted into the bowels of the shaft, but it was too dark to see anything.

"What are you waiting for?" Toland asked. "Get down there."

"But you're a man." Mills gave him a sweet, innocent look. "Shouldn't you go first?"

"And violate one of the core tenets of feminism? I wouldn't dream of it. Besides, someone needs to keep an eye out for that saber."

David Meyer

Shaking her head, Mills sat down. She kicked her legs into the shaft and felt around for the rungs. They were warm against her bare feet.

She found her footing. Then she twisted around. Grabbed onto the top rung. Took a deep breath.

And descended into the darkness.

CHAPTER 41

Date: June 19, 2016, 4:57 p.m.; Location: Hatcher Station, Vallerio Forest, NH

"A killing ground?" Caplan shook his head. "Why would James need something like that?"

"He doesn't need it." Morgan sagged a little deeper into her chair. "He wants it."

"James isn't a killer." But even as he spoke, Caplan questioned his words. How well, after all, did he really know Corbotch?

"He might not be doing the actual killing, but he's responsible all the same. You see, there's a certain clearing in 48A favored by 1-Gen saber-toothed cats. It, along with the surrounding area, is monitored by closed-circuit video cameras. The feeds are hidden and well-secured, but accessible from Hatcher's private network. Bonnie and Zlata …" Her eyes turned misty. "… managed to hack them."

"And?"

"Every now and then, James' private helicopter would fly to the clearing. It hovered a few feet above ground and a couple of people—almost certainly drugged—were dumped overboard. The cats prefer to stalk their prey. So, they always kept their distance until the helicopter flew away and the people woke up. Then the hunt would begin."

Caplan's eyes bulged. "You've actually seen one of these hunts?"

She didn't respond. She didn't have to. The haunted look in her eyes said everything.

"I don't get it," Caplan said after a moment. "Why would James want to kill anyone?"

"I don't know," Morgan said, finding her tongue. "But I always see him in the feeds, sitting quietly in the helicopter. He and the pilot never get their hands dirty. Instead, two goons handle the actual drop-off. I can't be certain, but I suspect James watches the feeds later, from a remote location. Somewhere close enough to access Hatcher's network."

"How do you know all this?" Caplan asked. "And how'd you know to look for feeds in the first place?"

"The same way you know about 48A ... Tony told me, at least in a manner of speaking."

Caplan's chest tightened. He ached to tell her the truth. To tell her that her brother had died while investigating 48A. To tell her how he'd failed to help the man in his time of need. And to tell her how he'd panicked and covered up the truth, partly out of self-preservation but mostly because of her. Because he feared the people behind 48A might see her as a potential liability. "We should talk about him."

She wiped her eyes with the palms of her hands. "Not now."

"But—"

"Not now," she repeated. "After he died, I found Tony's notes, his journals. He wrote about a place he called Sector 48A. It was a good distance from Hatcher's primary cameras and sealed off by an electric fence. He never saw anything, but he was absolutely certain something lived there. Right away, I thought of 1-Gen animals."

"Didn't you say James agreed to destroy the 1-Gens?"

"Yes. And the unopened incubators, too. But a small part of me had always doubted he'd do it." She exhaled. "After Tony's death, the Foundation clamped down on *Roadster* trips. Since I couldn't see 48A for myself, I did the next best thing. I brought Bonnie and Zlata into the fold and convinced them to reprogram Hatcher's primary cameras. While they were trying to get a better look at the area, they accidentally stumbled on the secret feeds."

Caplan beckoned at her to continue.

"I still remember watching one of those feeds. The helicopter hovering above the clearing, swinging in a slow circle. Those two goons rolling people out the cabin door. The helicopter taking off. And then stillness." She shuddered. "At first, I thought James was disposing of corpses. And that was horrible enough. But when those people started to move, my jaw hit the floor. And when the saber-toothed cats—the same ones I'd help create—closed in for the kill, I lost it." Her eyes glittered with anger. "My work, Zach. He used my work to kill people. I couldn't let that stand."

"But why this?" Caplan waved his hand in an effort to encompass the rebellion. "Why not just go public?"

"What do you think we're trying to do? You know as well as anyone how tight security is around here. Nothing— and I mean nothing—is allowed to leave the premises. So, I had no way of sneaking those feeds out of Hatcher. And without evidence, it would just be my word against the entire Corbotch Empire."

"I see," he said slowly. "So, the only way to reach the public was through the Lab's communications equipment."

She nodded. "Bonnie, Zlata, and I brought others into the fold, one at a time. We decided to make our move on June 18 and began prepping for it."

"Why June 18? Because of the dignitaries?"

"You know about them?" Morgan frowned, then nodded. "Of course. James told you. Yes, they had something to do with it. We knew he'd do just about anything to end our little revolt. But we figured a few high-value hostages might give us a little bargaining power."

"Who are the dignitaries anyway? Why are they here?"

"Honestly, I don't know." She shrugged. "Nor do I care."

Caplan considered everything she'd told him for a moment. "Aren't you afraid of what might happen to this place once you go public? Aren't you worried the authorities will shut you down, confiscate your research?"

"Yes," she admitted. "Especially with mass extinction so close at hand. That's why my colleagues and I have decided to take our knowledge elsewhere, to anyone who will listen. We'll even pool our resources and go it alone if necessary."

"There's one thing I don't understand." Caplan's brain worked in overdrive as he tried to connect Morgan's version of Corbotch with the man he knew. "Why bother with a killing field? If he's got enemies, why not just hire assassins? Or better yet, why not just bury them under mountains of lawsuits and bad publicity? Isn't that how the super-wealthy usually settle their grudges?"

"Because he's a sick bastard?" She shrugged. "I really don't know."

Caplan wondered about it for a moment. But ultimately, he decided he didn't need an answer. He could see the truth now. He could see how Corbotch had hoodwinked him into coming to Hatcher on false pretenses. "There's something you need to know," he said. "I lied before."

She frowned. "About what?"

"We didn't come in one helicopter. We came in two. The *Blaze* crashed in 48A. Everyone died, either from the impact or from animal attacks. Probably 1-Gens, now that I think about it. But the second chopper—the one I flew in—landed safely." He thought about Corbotch and Perkins, about how they were probably surrounded by ferocious 1-Gen animals at that very moment. Unless, that is, they were already dead.

"Three people landed with me. I lost track of Julius Pearson outside Hatcher. The other two—Derek Perkins and James Corbotch—stayed with the chopper."

"James is here?" Her eyes cinched to slits. "Why didn't you tell me before?"

"You mean while you were pistol-whipping me?"

Her gaze softened and she took a deep breath. Then she clutched her waist and rose slowly, painfully to her feet.

Caplan stood up, ignoring his burning joints and bones. Walking around the table, he helped steady her. "You need more rest."

"What I need is to tell the others about James. If we catch him, maybe we can end this." Turning around, she limped toward the door.

Caplan slipped his right shoulder under her left one. His right hand snaked around her waist, taking care not to touch her wound. "Those incubators in the Lab—I saw a whole bunch just like them on my way here."

"I'm not surprised. For reasons I still don't understand, James took the unopened 1-Gens to 48A."

"How many did you originally make?"

"Dozens. We only initiated expulsion sequences on fourteen of them, mostly saber-toothed cats and woolly mammoths. After seeing how violent they were, we wrote off the rest of 1-Gen."

"Did you make something called *Canis dirus*?"

She nodded. "Why?"

"I, uh, sort of cut one free."

"And you survived?"

"Not without help." He wondered about that, wondered why Pearson had saved him from the creature.

"*Canis dirus* is the scientific name for dire wolf. It was one of the fiercest predators in history until it died out some ten to 11,000 years ago." Morgan's eyes turned hazy and unclear. "What was the incubator like when you found it?"

"I already told you. It looked like the ones in the Lab."

"I mean what was it doing? Was it still? Quiet?"

He shook his head. "It was quaking and throbbing like a virgin on prom night. And the little black box beneath it was making noise too. This weird thumming sound."

"The other incubators ... were they acting the same way?"

He nodded.

Her eyes closed, then reopened. "One of the guards initiated a full expulsion sequence. I wasn't sure if it reached the unopened 1-Gens. But I guess it did." She paused. "The amount of energy must've been tremendous. Did you notice any weird phenomena?"

Caplan recalled the Blare. "You could say that."

"That's ... ooohhh ..." Morgan's legs crumpled under her. Only Caplan's support kept her from collapsing to the floor. "I don't feel so hot."

"What's the matter?"

"My head ... it's like mush. My skin is burning up." She broke out into shivers. "Can't see real well either."

"It must be that wound." Still propping her up, he hurried to the door. "Help," he shouted. "Get Dr. Adnan."

No one answered his shout and Caplan cursed under his breath. Of course. The stupid walls had blocked his shout. He'd nearly forgotten about Hatcher's extra-thick walls. He'd appreciated them during his tenure. But now, they infuriated him.

With his free hand, he grabbed the knob and twisted it. A hard push sent the door flying on its hinges.

"Dr. Adnan," he yelled. "Where ...?" His voice trailed off. A dumbfounded expression crossed his visage, followed by one of sheer horror.

Two-dozen people lay in the Heptagon, their limbs askew. Flashlights were scattered about the floor, casting light upon the corpses. So, he could see their eyes were moist and glassy. Foam dripped from their purple lips. A few of them clutched their throats with fingers that had grown stiff from rigor mortis.

"They're dead." Caplan winced. The bodies smelled like spoiled meat, laced with cheap perfume. "But you said HA-78 didn't exist. So, how ...?"

"I don't know the how, but I know the who." Morgan's fingers curled into fists. "James did this."

CHAPTER 42

Caplan's eyes took a trip around the room, making short stops at the shadowy faces. He saw scientists, technicians, trussed-up guards, as well as rangers. He knew some better than others, but he'd spent time with each and every one of them. There was Dr. Joy Hopkins, his long-time chess nemesis. Verna Mullins, the beer-guzzling guard who once stripped naked and ran around the Heptagon on a bet. And of course, Andres Sandoval, the cricket-loving ranger who liked nothing better than to fill Caplan's ears with endless stats and factoids during late nights in the Eye.

I failed them, Caplan thought bitterly. *Just like I failed Tony*.

Morgan's legs gave out a second time. Caplan had to act fast to keep her from sagging to the floor. As he propped her back up again, he took a look at her pale face, her bluish lips. Quickly, his eyes shifted between her and the corpses. *Damn it*, he thought. *Same symptoms*.

"Put me down," Morgan whispered.

"I'm not leaving you."

"You … you need to look for survivors."

"But—"

"Please … but be careful … whoever did this …"

She trailed off, but Caplan understood what she was trying to say. One of Corbotch's people—probably Pearson—had somehow poisoned everyone in the Heptagon. That person had most likely moved on to the individual wings in search of others to kill.

But wait. That didn't make sense. Caplan had been with Morgan the whole time. How had she gotten sick?

Gently, he lowered Morgan to the ground, away from the corpses. Then he scanned the floor and caught sight of his backpack. He unzipped it, took his twin axes out.

He'd failed the others and he had serious doubts about finding any survivors. But he saw a small light in the darkness. He could still save Morgan, could still earn a measure of forgiveness for her brother's untimely death. To do that, he needed to know what had happened to her.

He donned the pack and, axes poised for battle, checked the doors. Last he knew, the others were holed up in Research, keeping an eye out for the massive short-faced bear and trying to create enough power to close the hatch. Moving silently, he crossed the Heptagon.

He thought back to his time in the Galley. At one point, Morgan had opened the door to get a report on the so-called antibiotics. Was that when she was poisoned? If so, why hadn't he been poisoned at the same time?

He positioned himself next to Research's doorframe. Taking a deep breath, he twisted the knob and opened the door. His heart fell as he snuck a quick peek.

More corpses.

He slid into Research. Flashlights littered the floor, their beams striking the bodies and casting weird shadows upon the walls. As far as he could tell, the corpses showed the same moist, glassy eyes, the same purplish lips, and the same foam-filled mouths as the bodies in the Heptagon.

He glanced at the hatch. It was propped all the way open. Axes at the ready, he made his way forward, stopping briefly to examine two more corpses, Dr. Amy Carson and the technician Gino Suarez.

Just the way I like my holes, Caplan thought as he peered through the open hatch. *Scary as hell*. Indeed, the bottom of the shaft was blacker than night. He couldn't hear or see anything and he didn't dare shine a light down there lest he attract the bear's attention.

His fingers curled around the edges of the hatch. With a little bit of pushing, he closed it over until it was almost even with the floor. Unfortunately, it wouldn't go any farther. And without power, there was no way to lock it. He looked around for a way to remedy the situation, even though he knew it was hopeless. If a brilliant technician like Suarez couldn't close the hatch, how was Caplan supposed to do it?

Giving up, he left the room as quietly as he'd entered it. Then he returned to the Heptagon and checked on Morgan. Her breathing was more labored; her eyes were full of tears. She tried to speak, but could only make little noises.

Moving faster now, he swiftly checked the Barracks, Operations, and the Warehouse. He found nothing helpful, just a few dead bodies along with fallen guns and flashlights.

Panic gripped his throat as he raced back into the Heptagon. Morgan's eyes were full-on glassy and she was choking as if she couldn't breathe. He tried to help her, but she waved him away.

Feeling helpless, he scanned the remaining doors. One led outside. The other two led to the Galley and the Eye, respectively. He decided not to bother with the Galley. After all, he and Morgan had been the only ones in there. And that isolation, from all appearances, was the only reason they were still alive.

Then again, isolation couldn't be the sole reason for her delayed symptoms. Otherwise, he'd be just as sick as her.

He sprinted to the Eye and cracked the door. His gaze cinched tight. Only two flashlight beams rested on the floor, their beams crisscrossing the wide room. Even so, he could see that the Eye looked more like a fancy ballroom than a wildlife surveillance center. The workstations and desks he remembered so well had been pushed to the walls. In their place, he saw circular tables, covered with white cloth and surrounded by chairs. Gourmet dishes—roast chicken with fennel panzanella, orecchiette bolognese with chestnuts, salt-baked leg of lamb strewn with sea grapes, and others—rested upon the tables, their stunning colors and freshness gone limp with time. Expensive bottles of wine, only partly consumed, were situated between the dishes.

He opened the door a little farther and stepped into the room. Charlie Lodge, a geneticist and five-year resident at Hatcher, lay against the wall to his left. His eyes looked red, but glassy. Foam bubbled in his still mouth.

Caplan's heart grew heavy as he spotted a second body a couple of feet away. It belonged to Fei Nai-Yuan, an expert in Earth's physical processes and properties and one of Caplan's closest friends at Hatcher.

Sighing heavily, he shifted his gaze back to the tables. Clearly, the dignitaries had been having dinner when Morgan staged her rebellion. But where were they now? The only two corpses in the room, as far as he could tell, belonged to Lodge and Nai-Yuan.

"Hello?" A familiar voice rang out like an off-key instrument. "Is someone there?"

A survivor! Caplan thought. Heart thumping against his chest, he glanced to his left. To his amazement, he didn't see just one survivor. Instead, he saw nearly two-dozen people huddled near a bank of dark monitors. He scanned the faces, looking for familiar ones. And oddly enough, many of the faces were familiar. Not familiar like he'd actually met them. But familiar like he'd seen them before, perhaps on television or in Hatcher's collection of old newspapers and magazines.

His gaze settled on a woman and he barely hid a grimace. It was Deborah Keifer, president of the Vallerio Foundation. He'd only spoken to her on a few occasions, including his exit interview. But she gave off nasty vibes, like a raptor toying with its prey.

For a long moment, he stared at Deborah's cohorts, pegging them as bankers, politicians, and CEOs. They exuded wealth and power. But they also seemed rough around the edges. Not so much dignitaries as a collection of blue collar big shots.

"Hey Deborah," Caplan called out. "It's me. Zach Caplan. How are your symptoms? Because—"

"Will someone please take care of him?"

Keifer's question, spoken with casual disdain, chilled Caplan to the bone. As he tried to understand what was happening, an older man stepped forward. Lifting a rifle, he took aim at Caplan's head. His finger squeezed the trigger.

And the Eye exploded with gunfire.

CHAPTER 43

Date: June 19, 2016, 5:24 p.m.; Location: Hatcher Station, Vallerio Forest, NH

Money can buy a lot of things, Caplan thought as he threw open the door and raced into the Heptagon. *Good thing aim isn't one of them.*

Dropping his axes, he scooped a rifle off the floor. Twisting around, he saw the shooter's shadowy figure, doused in flashlight beams, race into view.

Caplan squeezed the trigger and the gun recoiled in his arms. Wine bottles shattered, sending red and white liquid all over the clean table clothes. A bank of monitors cracked and sizzled.

Squealing like a pig, the shooter reversed course. A hail of gunfire crashed into his shoulders, propelling him at high speed back into the Eye where he vanished into the shadows. Caplan wasn't sure whether he'd killed the man or not. But he didn't have time to worry about it.

He closed the door to the Eye and dragged a few bodies in front of it for good measure. Then he gathered up his axes. Covering the blades, he returned them to his belt.

He jogged to Morgan's side. Her glassy eyes refused to focus. Her whole body shook like one of the incubators. The first hints of foam appeared at the corners of her mouth. She needed medical assistance and fast. But how the hell was he supposed to help? He wasn't a doctor. Hell, he didn't even know what was wrong with her. And he couldn't exactly keep looking for answers, not with those big shot pricks trying to kill him.

He wondered about Keifer, wondered why she'd ordered his death. Did she think he was part of Morgan's rebellion? Had she somehow forgotten that he'd left the station five months earlier?

Placing the rifle's strap over his shoulder, he helped Morgan to her feet. *Outside*, he thought. *Maybe fresh air will do her good.* Admittedly, it was a dumb idea. But it was the only option he hadn't tried yet.

Morgan tried to walk on her own without success. It was like she'd experienced almost total muscle failure. "You shouldn't have come here," she whispered.

"Now you tell me." Walking quickly, he dragged her toward the exit. He kept up a string of light banter, hoping to keep her from passing into unconsciousness.

He stopped a few feet from the heavy door. Took a moment to adjust Morgan's weight on his shoulder.

Abruptly, the heavy door flew open. It crashed against the stopper then bounced back a few inches. Time slowed for a split-second and Caplan saw many things. He saw the dark clearing, the quiet fences. He saw flickering flashlight beams shooting across the grass, bathing everything in horrific light. He saw more scientists, technicians, and rangers, splayed out in the field, dead to the world. But most of all, he saw the grin. That nasty, toothy grin he'd first seen in Manhattan. He'd known the grin for less than a day. But it felt more like a lifetime.

"Good, you're still here." Julius Pearson's grin widened as he lifted his rifle. "Enjoy hell, Zach."

CHAPTER 44

Date: June 19, 2016, 5:26 p.m.; Location: Hatcher Station, Vallerio Forest, NH

"Your face," Caplan said, thinking fast. "Does it hurt?"

A confused look crossed Pearson's visage. His finger twitched, then paused on the trigger. "What?"

"Well, it does now." Caplan's foot lashed out, slamming into the heavy door. The hinges squeaked as the door swung toward Pearson. It bashed into the man's face, busting his nose wide open. Blood squirted everywhere and Pearson stumbled backward, clutching his broken proboscis and shouting curses at the sky.

Caplan kicked the door again, shutting it. Then he retreated into the Heptagon, Morgan's limp body still hanging from his shoulder.

Scratching noises caught his attention and he looked at the Eye. The door was cracked a few inches and he could see a middle-aged man shoving it. It opened a little farther, shifting the piled-up corpses with it.

Like all big shots, the guy probably fancied himself a badass. And who could blame him? Undoubtedly, he employed assistants who fawned over him, complimenting his wisdom and dynamism at every turn. Peons most likely begged him for favors and kowtowed to his whims, afraid of incurring his wrath.

Caplan fired a couple of shots at the door. One of the bullets made it through the crack. The man screamed and clutched his side. Then he twisted in a circle and fell to the floor. Invisible hands dragged him away from the crack and the door slammed shut. Despite everything, Caplan grinned. *Everybody's a badass*, he thought, *until the bullets start flying*.

But Caplan's triumph faded fast. Morgan was still dying. Pearson blocked the exit and sooner or later, the big shots would make it into the Heptagon.

He peered at the other doors, finally settling on the one leading to the Barracks. The Barracks was wide open and thus, would be simpler to defend from attack. Plus, the clinic—really just a few beds and some locked cabinets full of supplies and antibiotics—was in there.

He started forward, his shoulder aching under Morgan's dead weight.

"No," Morgan muttered. "Research."

"Barracks has the clinic," he said without breaking stride.

Her eyes focused for a single instant. "Research," she said with near-perfect enunciation.

Caplan grunted, glanced at Research. He remembered the dead bodies strewn about the space. But most of all, he recalled the unlocked hatch, the dark shaft, and the 2-Gen monsters that were probably ravaging the Lab at that very moment.

Acting against almost every bone in his body, he shifted toward Research. He had few, if any, illusions about survival. At this point, it was all about how he wanted to die. And the last thing he wanted was to give that honor to Pearson or a bunch of big shot losers. *There's always the bear*, he thought crazily. *Pyrrhic victory, here I come.*

Caplan opened the door and dragged Morgan to a chair. He quickly closed the door and, ignoring the creeping stench of death, began pushing cabinets, tables, and other heavy items in front of it.

He couldn't hear anything through the thick walls or door. But he knew the big shots and Pearson would soon come face-to-face in the Heptagon. What would they do when they saw each other? Exchange gunfire? Or warm greetings? The latter seemed more likely. After all, the big shots were likely Corbotch's friends.

"You need to go." Morgan's voice sounded faint and ghastly, like her mouth had been sewn-up with needle and thread.

Muscles straining, Caplan pushed a heavy filing cabinet in front of the door. Then he ran to another cabinet and began to push it across the floor as well. "I'm not leaving you."

"Gate ... in the Lab. Leads outside."

Caplan paused. Perspiration trickled down his neck, soaking his sweat-stained shirt all over again. "There's a gate down there?"

She tried to nod, but her neck refused to cooperate. "That's ... that's how we got our equipment into the Lab. And how we were going to get our animals into the Vallerio."

Caplan blinked. Although the revelation surprised him, it made perfect sense. The shaft was an entirely impractical way to move large objects or animals. For one thing, there was no elevator or lifting platform. For another, the entranceway dividing the security checkpoint from the Lab was simply too small to accommodate anything larger than people. And finally, the de-extinction program had been run in complete secrecy. Secrecy that would've been impossible to maintain the second a woolly mammoth tromped out of Research and into the Heptagon.

"Where's the gate lead?" he asked.

"Short tunnel ... to the cliffs ... there's a ... a blind spot in Sector 12 ..."

That too made sense. Sector 12 was located southwest of Hatcher Station. It featured a small ravine lined by steep cliffs. A tunnel would only have to extend 100 yards or so to reach it.

Caplan had plenty of questions. But one rose to the top of the heap. It was a question that, for some reason, filled him with unexplainable horror. "Who knows about the gate?" he asked.

"People who worked in Research," she replied, her voice growing softer with every word.

"What about James?" Working fast, he began to pile smaller items—machines, tables, chairs, anything he could find—on top of the larger ones. "Did he know about it?"

"Of course." She spat foam from her mouth. "That's … how he got the 1-Gens out of the Lab."

So, Corbotch had known about the gate all along. But if that was the case, why hadn't he mentioned it? Why hadn't he sent Caplan and Pearson that way?

Caplan recalled the flight to Hatcher, the immunization shot he'd received at the hands of Pearson. He recalled the water-filled vials, the fabricated danger of HA-78. And he recalled how Pearson had vanished right when Caplan had entered Hatcher.

The answer came to him like a bolt of lightening, sizzling to the deepest recesses of his brain and heart. And then he knew. He knew why Corbotch had recruited him. He knew how everyone had died. He knew everything.

The whole mission was a sham from the beginning. Corbotch hadn't picked him for his knowledge of Hatcher but rather, because he knew Morgan and the others. Because he could get physically close to them.

Ever since he'd first seen the corpses, Caplan had puzzled over the deaths, over what had caused them. And now he knew the truth. HA-78 wasn't fictional. It was a real virus, one that had been carried into the building.

By him.

Chapter 45

The truth was too horrible to contemplate, yet impossible to ignore. Pearson had injected Caplan aboard the helicopter, supposedly to protect him from HA-78. But in reality, the injection had done something else.

It had infected him.

Caplan didn't know the specifics. But he suspected he'd been turned into a modern Typhoid Mary. In other words, he carried a disease, but it didn't affect him.

Corbotch had never intended to raid Hatcher. Instead, he merely planned to use Caplan as a walking, talking biological weapon. Caplan would sneak into the building or perhaps, get caught trying. Either way, he'd eventually spread HA-78 to some of his former co-workers. They, in turn, would spread the disease to others. In Hatcher's closed environment, 100% fatality was a near certainty. Then Corbotch's guards could enter the building, secure the Lab, and get rid of the dead bodies. New scientists would be brought in to continue the research.

The plan had experienced more than its share of hiccups. But Caplan had eventually gotten into the building and, unbeknownst to him, infected the others. Morgan, trapped in the Lab at the time, was the last person to contract the virus. That was why she'd outlived the others. As for Pearson,

Perkins, and Corbotch, they were obviously immunized against the disease. Same with the big shots.

His brow furrowed. But why? Why would Corbotch bother to immunize the big shots from some deadly disease? It wasn't like he knew any of this was going to happen.

A memory nagged in the dark recesses of his mind. Concentrating hard, he managed to grab hold of it. It was from earlier that day, in the clearing just after his fistfight with Pearson. Thinking hard, he slowly wrangled the rest of the memory into the light.

"Zach." Perkins hiked to Caplan's side. "You look dizzy."

"I'm fine," Caplan replied.

"Sure you are." He lowered his voice, extended a palm. "But if you start, I don't know, foaming at the mouth later, take one of these."

Caplan eyed the amber-colored pill container, complete with child resistant cap. It was unmarked and filled with small white tablets. "You trying to drug me, Derek?"

"It's aspirin," Perkins said, exacerbated. "Just the thing for headaches, muscle aches, ocular problems, breathing issues, and God knows what else. Now, do you want it or not?"

Caplan exhaled. Then he grabbed the container and surreptitiously stuffed it into his pocket.

The memory blinked away, returning to the comfortable darkness of Caplan's mind. For a couple of seconds, Caplan mulled over Perkins' words and the surreptitious way in which they'd been spoken. *Foaming at the mouth … ocular problems … breathing issues …* all delivered with a bare whisper.

He reached into his pocket, wrapped his fingers around the cylindrical pill container. Extracting it, he knelt on the floor. Three separate beams of light struck the container, filling it and its white tablets with an almost holy glow. Was this the cure for HA-78? Had he been carrying it with him the entire time?

A storm of new questions rained on his mind. Was this another one of Corbotch's tricks? Or had Perkins broken ranks with Corbotch? If so, why?

Morgan still sat in the chair, but just barely. Quickly, he popped the container open and took out a pill. He hesitated, but only for a second. She was already on death's doorstep. How much worse could things possibly get?

He inserted the tablet into Morgan's foamy mouth. "Swallow," he said.

Foam gurgled in her throat.

"Swallow," he repeated.

Her mouth closed over. Her throat vibrated. Then she went still.

Caplan pried her mouth open, checked it thoroughly.

No tablet.

He watched her for a few seconds, full of hope. But she remained still. Her eyes looked moist and glassy. Her mouth continued to foam up like she had rabies. With a trembling hand, he reached for her pulse.

Abruptly, Morgan twisted up and to the right, screeching at the top of her lungs. The chair slipped out from under her and she sagged onto the floor. Almost immediately, her body began to twitch and flop around like a fish trying to swim on land.

Caplan grabbed her shoulders, tried to hold her down. But she bucked violently, sending him crashing into a table leg. The table jolted. Screws, batteries, pencils, and sketch pads fell to the floor.

A loud crash sounded out. Caplan's gaze shot to his makeshift barricade of cabinets, tables, and machines. He heard a fleshy smack followed by the door crunching against the barricade. One of the tables started to wobble. A box-shaped machine, propped on top of a tall filing cabinet, shifted a few inches to one side. The barricade was solid, but it wouldn't last forever.

"Zach ..."

Caplan looked at Morgan. Her eyes were still moist and glassy, but he saw a spark of life in them. Her lips had lost their bluish hue and her mouth no longer dripped with foam.

His heart leapt to new heights. He wanted to grab her, pull her close, smack her a big wet one on the lips. He didn't even care about the residual foam. "Feeling better?" he asked.

"I nearly died." She blinked a few times. The glassiness faded away. "And all you can say is, 'feeling better?'"

"What do you want? A poem?" He offered his hand. "Come on."

She gripped it. He pulled and she rose to her feet. He held her for a moment, staring deep into her eyes. God, he could swim in those eyes. They were almost enough to make him forget the past.

Almost.

Again, the door crunched against the barricade. Three or four grunts rang out in unison. The door shifted an inch, moving the cabinets and causing the box-shaped machine to tumble to the floor.

Rubbing her eyes, Morgan broke away from his embrace. "Did you find any other survivors?"

"Only ones who want to kill us," Caplan replied.

Morgan didn't scream or break down crying. But the look of dull despair in her features spoke volumes.

"I did this," Caplan said. "I brought the disease here."

Her gaze shifted to him. Her brow furrowed.

"Corbotch's goon injected me aboard the helicopter," Caplan explained. "I thought they were immunizing me against HA-78."

"But instead they infected you," she said, slowly. "And you infected everyone else. So, why am I still alive?"

"Because of this." Caplan held up the pill container. "Corbotch's pilot gave it to me on the sly. I didn't understand why until just now."

"Let me see that." More clashes and clattering rang out. Ignoring the ruckus, she took the pill container, opened it, and studied the tablets. Then she recapped it, handed it back. "Hold on to this."

"You want to study them?"

"Actually, I was thinking about more immediate concerns. Without those tablets, you'll kill everyone you meet."

Caplan's eyes widened.

The grunts grew louder. Flesh and muscle slammed into the door. Metal screeched as the barricade shifted a couple of inches across the vinyl flooring. A hand, clutching a pistol, snaked into the void.

Caplan pushed Morgan to the ground. A couple of gunshots, all wild, streaked overhead. Then the hand disappeared and the assault on the barricade started up again.

Caplan eyed the myriad of weapons littering the floor. "We can hold them off," he said. "But not forever."

"Then it's time we make our exit." Morgan crawled under the nearest table. Caplan followed suit and they made their way to the back of the room. Upon arriving, Morgan rose to her knees and grabbed the hatch's handle.

Caplan frowned. "Are you sure about this?"

"The gate's in the Lab."

"So is the bear."

She gave him a little smirk. "Don't tell me you're scared."

"Let's just say being bear food isn't on my bucket list." Caplan's face twisted in thought. "Will the gate even work without power?"

She nodded. "There's a crank mechanism."

"And after we get through the gate?"

"We enter a short tunnel. It opens up into a natural cave in Sector 12. After that ..." She shrugged.

Due to the steep cliffs, few animals bothered with 12 and thus, it was almost always free of predators. But what would they do when they got there? They couldn't just sit around, twiddling their thumbs. Sooner or later, Pearson would show up, probably with the big shots in tow.

The smart move was to head for the helicopter, to seize it. Yes, that could work. If they were fast, they'd only have to deal with Corbotch and Perkins. And Perkins had already secretly helped Caplan by passing on the pill container.

Caplan grabbed the metal handle and helped Morgan pull. The hatch yawned open. He stepped over to the ladder. Stared into the dark shaft.

I must be out of my mind, he thought.

But he grabbed hold of the ladder anyway.

And slid into the waiting darkness.

CHAPTER 46

Date: Unknown; Location: Unknown

"What's he doing up there?" Mills fixed her gaze on the metal ladder and accompanying shaft. A dull thumping noise, coming from high above, filled her ears. "Running laps?"

Elliott kept her focus locked on a wheel-shaped object. Constructed from a tough, opaque plastic-type material, it measured about four feet thick and roughly twice that in diameter. "Probably seeing how fast he can pat himself on the back."

With a faint smile, Mills turned her attention back to the strange room. Sixteen wheels, identical in shape and size, occupied most of the space. They were positioned in a perfect circle. Thick cables connected them to a centrally located bank of computer monitors and machines.

Shelves, cabinets, metal tables, and other pieces of furniture sat outside the circle of wheels. For nearly an hour, Mills had strained her eyes in the near-blackness, searching for clues to their whereabouts. A small part of her knew it was a foolhardy exercise. Her time would've been better spent fixing up the broken fence and cabin. But still, she continued her search.

Mills snuck a glimpse at Elliott, at a scattered array of tools. The woman sat next to one of the wheels, driven by a seemingly-urgent need to pry one open. Mills understood that need. She felt the exact same thing when it came to the mysteries—how they'd gotten there, the extinct animals, the strange barn-like building and even stranger basement—that surrounded her.

Mills opened the top drawer of a small chest. Swiftly, she searched the contents. They were relatively innocuous—extra file folders, binder clips, packages of light bulbs—until she reached the bottom of the drawer.

Her heart beat a little faster as she pulled a laminated sheet of paper, eleven inches by fourteen inches, out into the open. She squinted at it, barely making out the small printed words. "I got something," she said.

Elliott dropped a flat-head screwdriver, letting it clunk against the floor. Then she picked up a slightly larger one and returned to the wheel. "Yeah?"

"It's a map. Of the Vallerio Forest."

Elliott's grip tightened on the screwdriver. "You sure?"

"That's what it says. The Vallerio Foundation is listed as the author."

"And James Corbotch owns the Foundation. I guess that settles it. We're here because he put us here."

"Yes." Mills scrunched up her brow in thought. "But it doesn't make sense. This can't be the Vallerio."

"Why not?"

"The saber for one thing. The woolly mammoths for another." She shook her head. "The Vallerio isn't some distant jungle, isolated from civilization. It's in the U.S., for cripes sakes."

"Yeah, but in northern New Hampshire," Elliott replied. "It's like America's version of Siberia."

"It's still in the U.S."

"The Corbotch Empire fenced off the Vallerio well over a century ago. They use cameras and armed guards to keep people out. And they paid off bureaucrats to make it an official Prohibited Area, so pilots can't even fly over it. It's the Fort Knox of forests."

"So, what are you saying? That they did all that to protect a few supposedly extinct species?"

"I'm merely saying if sabers or mammoths lived in the Vallerio, it's not inconceivable that James could keep it a secret. Seriously, how could anyone possibly find out?"

"By getting dumped here."

"Good call." Elliott removed a long screw. Abruptly, one side of the wheel came loose. She ducked out of the way, narrowly dodging a piece of heavy plastic as it thudded to the ground. "Ohmigod."

Mills turned around. With the side removed, she could see the wheel's interior. Its core was hollowed out. A lumpy object, shaped like a flattened *S* turned sideways, lay inside it. Shadowy, curvy lines connected the object to areas inside the wheel.

A sweet, sickly scent spread through the basement. Mills' face twisted involuntarily. "Ugh," she said. "What is that?"

"A person," Elliott said, backing away. "A dead person."

The body of a twenty-something year-old man rested on curved cushions, similar to those in a dentist's chair. His back and head were upright. His knees were propped above his rear and feet. His head lolled to one side, mouth ajar as if ready for a bi-annual check-up.

A gray surgical gown rested gently upon the man's body. Wires and tubes snaked out of the back wall and under the gown, presumably connecting the corpse to the wheel.

Mills gazed upon the man's face. It was tanned, clean-shaven, and Hollywood-handsome with all the right angles in all the right places. But his skin was cold, pale. His eyes were dry, lifeless. "He looks ... peaceful."

Elliott reached a tentative hand toward the body. Mills slapped it hard.

"Ouch." Elliott withdrew her hand like a snake had bitten it. "What was that for?"

"Your own good," Mills said. "What if he's got some kind of weird disease? I mean, why else would he be in there?"

"I don't know." Elliott studied the wheel. "It looks like an isolation chamber. Maybe it was some kind of experiment."

"Then why is he dead?"

"We know the exterior fence lost power. So, it stands to reason these wheels lost power, too. Animals overran the fence and whoever was monitoring the experiments went upstairs, got themselves killed." She gazed at the body. "This poor guy was trapped with no food, no water, no oxygen. Death was inevitable."

"Yeah? Then how come he's just lying there, all peaceful-like? How come he didn't try to claw his way to freedom?"

Elliott frowned, but only for a moment. "Maybe you're right about the disease. If so, this thing isn't an isolation chamber. It's a life-support system. And that would explain those wires and tubes. They were used to monitor him, care for him. When the power failed, the system went off-line. People went upstairs to see what had happened. They died before they could restore the electricity."

"And this guy died shortly after," Mills twisted her mouth in thought. "It makes sense. But it doesn't."

"What do you mean?"

"Why build a life support system in the middle of nowhere? Why not just take him to a hospital?"

Elliott shrugged.

On a whim, Mills marched to the central core of monitors and machines. A little browsing turned up a large logbook made of fine leather. Her brow furrowed as she started to crack it open.

"Get your asses up here," Toland shouted from above. "The roof is—"

Cracking and crackling noises drowned him out.

Elliott raced to the ladder. Mills lingered for an extra second, her gaze locked on the logbook. Then, for reasons she couldn't quite fathom, she tucked it into the back of her waistband and darted to the shaft.

As she followed Elliott up the ladder, Mills shifted her gaze skyward and saw streaks of fire zoom across the ceiling like shooting stars. Beams buckled and splintered as the roof disintegrated before her eyes.

Elliott climbed out of the shaft. Then she ran to the door.

Muscles aching, Mills pulled herself up the rest of the way. The logbook slipped as she gained her footing so she took it out of her waistband and clutched it against her chest.

Her bare soles pounded against the floor as she sprinted for the door. She felt heat at her back, at her sides. Flames jumped from machine to machine, chasing her down in relentless fashion.

She reached the doorframe seconds behind the fire. She caught a brief look outside, at Toland and Elliott standing in the clearing. Then more flames sparked up, surrounding the frame on all sides.

The heat drove her back a few feet. Something exploded behind her. Throwing caution to the wind, she ran forward and leapt through the rectangle of fire.

She landed hard on the damp soil, still holding the book to her chest. Elliott and Toland grabbed her elbows, lifted her up, and hustled her away from the building.

Another explosion, the biggest one yet, rang out. The shockwave pushed Mills to run faster and she didn't stop until she reached the fallen metal post.

"That ..." Sucking at air, Elliott hunched down, hands on her knees. "... that sucked."

Mills flopped onto the ground and watched the structure crumble to the earth. She felt dull on the inside. Dull and hopeless. Despite the corpses of its former inhabitants, she'd still viewed the building as a potential refuge. A place to hide from the saber and whatever other horrors awaited them in the forest. But now, it was gone, returned to the earth from whence it came. And she would soon follow suit, she reckoned. Maybe by the saber's claws, maybe not. It didn't really matter. Death was death, right?

"What the hell were you doing down there anyway?" Toland growled under his breath.

"We found something." Quickly, Elliott filled him in on the map of the Vallerio, the strange wheels, and the dead body.

"So, let me get this straight," Toland said as she finished up. "You don't know anything."

Elliott's face flushed. "Weren't you listening? I said—"

He held up a hand. "Do you have the map?"

Elliott glanced at Mills.

Mills shook her head.

"So, all we have is a bunch of useless speculation. We *might* be in the Vallerio. Corbotch *might* have put us here. Those wheels *might* have been life support systems." Brushing soot from his hair, Toland hiked to the concrete block. "Well? Are you two coming or not?"

With a deep breath, Mills pushed away her dark thoughts. She couldn't give up. She had to keep fighting, keep surviving. "We can still stay here." She nodded at the metal post. "We just need to stick that back in its block, cement it somehow. That should keep out smaller animals. And maybe we'll find some supplies or tools once the fire burns out."

"My plan is better."

Elliott rolled her eyes. "Of course it is."

"I found a large whiteboard just before the roof started to cave," he said. "There was a rough map on it."

"What kind of map?" Mills asked.

"Does it really matter?"

"It might."

"There was a small box, surrounded by empty space and a bunch of squiggly lines. Farther back, there were trees. I figure the box was the building."

Elliott smirked. "And you accuse me of speculating?"

"The empty space was shaped like this clearing," he retorted. "And the squiggly lines matched up perfectly with the fence."

"Fine. You *might* have found a map of the clearing." Mills coughed some smoke out of her lungs. "How does that help us?"

"Above and to the left, I saw a large X." He smiled broadly, as if he'd just solved the world's toughest math equation.

"That's it?" Elliott said after a moment. "What's the X?"

"Another building?" He shrugged. "Who cares? At least it's not here."

Elliott rolled her eyes. "Yeah. This is a great plan."

Whistling noises rang out. Turning around, Mills watched as small bits of fire shot into the air like missiles. They rained down on nearby pine trees. The first wave of fire quickly burned itself out on the damp wood and needles. But the second, third, and fourth waves were a different story.

Equal amounts of pain, horror, and helplessness filled Mills' heart as she watched small blazes and gray smoke spring up all around her. A stiff breeze caught hold of burning branches and needles, sending them to new trees and fanning the flames in the process.

Unfortunately, the fire extinguishers were buried in the building's ruins. And even if they had access to more extinguishers, the flames were far too high to reach. The *New Yorker Chronicles* would love this. She could almost imagine the headlines. *Billionaire Bailey Sets Wilderness Ablaze! The Boozing Bad Girl Burns Down Famous Backwoods!*

"Do you think you can lead us to that X?" she asked.

"Do fires like wood?" he asked, his voice dripping with sarcasm. "Yes. Of course, I can lead you there."

Mills shifted her grip on the logbook and stood up. "Then do it."

His eyes scrunched at the corners. "What have you got there?"

"I don't know." Mills blinked as she looked at the book, like she was surprised to see it. "I just grabbed it on the way out of the basement."

"Well?" He stared at her. "What is it?"

She glanced at the sky. It was even darker now and she sensed the approaching cloak of nighttime. But the fire was growing fast, casting wild light throughout the forest. "Later," she said. "We need to go."

He grunted in annoyance. But he turned around anyway and paced over the trampled wires. Mills and Elliott fell in behind him. Just before exiting the clearing, Mills took a quick glimpse at the logbook's leather cover. Squinting hard, she saw two words emblazoned in bronze-colored text.

Apex Predator, she read. *Where have I heard that before?*

CHAPTER 47

Maybe the 2-Gens killed each other, Caplan thought just before a full-bellied roar shattered his hopes and nearly his eardrums. *Or maybe not.*

He descended a few more feet. Then he peered into the dark abyss. The floor, dimly lit by flickering flames, was still some ten to fifteen feet beneath him. He saw no sign of the short-faced bear or any other animal for that matter. But he could hear them. He could hear their screeches, roars, and growls. Scuffling, gnashing teeth, and the crunching of sinew and muscle tissue. At the same time, various odors rose up to greet him. Greasy fur. Sweat and body odor. Plus, blood.

Lots and lots of blood.

It's a promoter's dream, he thought. *An honest-to-goodness Pleistocene death match.*

He shifted his shoulders, adjusting his backpack and the rifle strap. Then he glanced up. Morgan's feet were poised a few rungs above his head. Her eyes, filled with question marks, peered down at him.

His soul longed to dive into those eyes, to unburden itself of the truth behind her brother's death. To admit he'd stood by while beasts had ripped Tony to shreds. But even if he could, he knew it wouldn't have helped. His sin required far more than mere confession.

I'll get you out of here, he thought. *That's a promise.*

He faced forward again. Regripped the ladder with his sweaty palms. Then he finished his descent into the semi-darkness.

His right boot struck the floor and he stepped away from the ladder. Turning in an arc, he swept his rifle across the security checkpoint. Everything—the broken tables and machines, glass shards, blood smears, and pockmarked concrete pillars—was just as he remembered it.

Morgan released the ladder and fell to the floor, landing lightly on her feet. She swung her pistol around, checking the room. Then she exchanged glances with Caplan.

Caplan nodded and turned toward the entranceway. Waves of invisible heat and energy crested over him. His skin grew slick with sweat. His neck flinched at every roar, every snarl, every screech.

He made his way to the left wall and picked his way forward, avoiding the glass. Not that it made much of a difference. The death match had reached a new crescendo and the sounds of violence—chomping teeth, ripping flesh, clicking claws, cracking bones, bodies slamming into each other, into concrete, and into metal—were intense.

The heat thickened and intensified until Caplan found it difficult to breathe. His vision blurred around the edges and he felt none of the adrenaline he'd experienced during his last visit.

He took up position on the entranceway's left side. Air exited his lungs as he scanned the Lab. *Could be worse*, he thought. *At least you don't have to clean all this up.*

The concrete pillars were still in place, thank God. But the rest of the Lab lay in ruins. The central platform had been reduced to a fiery heap of metal and lumber. The giant skeletons, painstakingly reconstructed and mounted, had been knocked off their platforms and ripped to shreds. Pieces of machinery, broken monitors, shards of glass, and bloody carcasses littered the floor.

Two things, more than anything else, caught Caplan's attention. First, the incubators. Every last one had been cracked wide open. Now, they lay quietly in their stations, abandoned like snake skins. And second, a tangled mass of heaving flesh, leathery skin, and fur, which occupied much of the Lab's far right corner.

"I see four animals." Caplan squinted into the darkness. "No, wait. Make that five. The short-faced bear is still going strong. And is that an elephant?"

Morgan, positioned on the opposite side of the entranceway, kept her gaze locked on the pulsing mass. "It's a *Mammut americanum*," she replied. "The others are a *Panthera atrox*, a *Panthera onca augusta*, a—"

"English, please."

She grunted. "That elephant, as you call it, is actually an American mastodon. I also see an American lion, a North American jaguar, an American cheetah, and of course, the short-faced bear."

"I don't suppose any of them are herbivores."

"The mastodon is." She breathed softly. "Although it doesn't look that way right now."

Caplan focused on the mastodon. In the dim light provided by the burning platform, he saw it stood almost ten feet tall. Using its head like a battering ram, it attacked the other animals with quiet fury. The other animals fought back, biting its legs as well as each other.

The American lion and American cheetah broke off and went for each other's throats. The North American jaguar attacked the cheetah while the short-faced bear ripped away at all three of them, its sharp claws drawing blood with every strike.

The mastodon backed away from the frenzied mass. For a moment, Caplan thought it was extracting itself from the fight. But then it lowered its head and charged the pile. Its right tusk cut deep into the American cheetah's belly. The cheetah tried to snarl, but it came out more like a yelp instead. Then its body sagged and it slumped to the ground.

Caplan cocked his head, curious about what the others would do. He didn't have to wait long to find out. In less than a second, the four surviving animals pounced on the cheetah. They tore at its eyes, ripped at its mouth, and stomped on its body. The cheetah, screaming and shrieking, tried to fight back. But its frenzied movements soon ceased under the onslaught.

Immediately, the American lion charged the North American jaguar, slashing its face and biting its shoulder. The short-faced bear rose up on its hind legs, bellowed out a roar, and plowed into the mastodon's front right leg. The mastodon shook off the blow and resumed using its head like a battering ram. But this time, the short-faced bear was ready. It pounced onto the mastodon's head, pinning it to the floor. Its claws swiped at great speed, stabbing the mastodon's eyes and ears.

The mastodon reared up, bellowing fury from its trunk. The short-faced bear, growling and roaring, scrabbled for purchase. It kept its balance long enough to dish out a few more swipes. Then it leapt backward and came crashing down on the North American jaguar.

"Hot damn," Caplan said under his breath. "I didn't know animals were so violent back then."

"They weren't," Morgan said. "At least, there's no evidence to that effect."

"Then what do you make of this?"

"I don't know. But it's 1-Gen all over again. Like a feeding frenzy without any actual feeding."

Caplan's eyes moved from the dead American cheetah to the carcasses of other animals. "Animals kill for sport, right?"

"Sure. But this isn't sport. They're destroying each other."

The faint sound of leather scuffing against metal floated into Caplan's ears. Whirling his head around, he stared at the ladder. "We've got company," he said.

"Then we'd better move fast." Morgan pointed at the back wall. "See those cylindrical things?"

"They look like bars."

"That's because they are bars. They're made of reinforced steel and built directly into the gate."

"Gotcha." Caplan traced the crisscrossing bars from left to right, from top to bottom. All in all, the gate covered an area roughly twenty feet in length and fifteen feet in height. "How do we open it?"

"The crank is left of the gate," she replied. "It was part of the original design."

"Ever used it?"

She shook her head.

The scuffing noises grew louder. Spinning around again, Caplan saw a dress shoe exit the shaft, stepping onto a rung just below the ceiling. He lifted his rifle, took careful aim. Squeezed the trigger.

"You don't want to do that." Reaching across the entranceway, Morgan gently pushed down on the gun.

"Speak for yourself." But Caplan released the trigger anyway. She was right. He would've loved to wing a few of Corbotch's friends. But he couldn't risk attracting the attention of the 2-Gens.

Caplan twisted around just in time to see the short-faced bear sink its teeth into the North American jaguar's right shoulder. At the same time, the American lion clawed the jaguar's belly, carving it open and causing organs and blood to spill to the floor. The jaguar screeched at high decibels before collapsing into a blood-soaked heap.

"Now." Morgan snuck through the entranceway. "While they're distracted."

Shocked by the gore and frenzied violence, Caplan numbly followed her to the left wall. As they slunk alongside it, he kept one eye on the floor, making sure he didn't trip over anything. His other eye, however, remained fixed on the bloodbath.

The American lion leapt on the jaguar's belly, ripping out more organs and callously tossing them to the floor. The American mastodon trampled on the jaguar's hind legs, shattering the bones. And the short-faced bear bit into the jaguar's face, ripping at its eyes and snout. Within seconds, the creature's carcass had been completely dismantled.

As the survivors turned on each other, Caplan's fingers tightened on the rifle. Outside of sharks, he'd never seen such predatory violence before. How had they become like this? Had the process of de-extinction somehow turned them into bloodthirsty monsters?

At the corner, Morgan turned right. Hugging the wall, she made her way past ruined stations, broken equipment, and abandoned incubators. Caplan followed close at her heels, gun at the ready.

Jaws and claws dripping with blood, the short-faced bear rose up to its full height. Its head swiveled and cocked to one side.

Then its eyes bored into Caplan's.

Oh, shit, he thought.

Abruptly, the American lion leapt into the air. It smashed into the bear, knocking the creature to its side. Before the bear could recover, the lion was scrambling on top of it, jaws chomping furiously as it tried to strike a deathblow.

The mastodon lifted its horn, blew out a couple of notes, laced with strange insanity. Then it charged the bear and lion.

The bear swiped its arm like a club, nailing the lion's head. The lion lost its footing and spilt to the floor. The bear rose up, saw the mastodon. Claws clicking loudly, it climbed to its feet. As it dodged the charge, it turned its head again.

And looked at Caplan.

Caplan's heart raced.

The bear turned to the lion. With a mighty roar, it slashed a paw at the creature's skin.

Morgan and Caplan reached the next corner and started forward again, drawing ever closer to the Pleistocene death match. The available light from the flickering flames was exceedingly dim on this side of the facility. But Caplan could still see the beasts continue their relentless assaults on each other. Blood poured freely from their many wounds. But they didn't bother to step back, to take breathers. They just kept biting, stabbing, stomping, and slamming into each other with unimaginable force.

Morgan and Caplan stopped in front of a large crank. It was chest-high and embedded into the concrete. The massive gate stood a few feet away, sandwiched between upper and lower brackets.

Caplan tried to study the crank. But a nearby carcass, that of a giant four-legged creature, distracted him. Against his better judgment, he stared at its bloodied fur, its carved up skin, its empty eye sockets. He didn't recognize it, but it had possessed sharp claws and even sharper teeth. If it couldn't defend itself against the other 2-Gens, what hope did he and Morgan have?

"The gate's on wheels and moves sideways," Morgan whispered. "So, we just need to unlock the crank and give it a few turns. The gate will open and we can make a run for it. Should be easy enough."

Loud blasts pierced the air. Projectiles soared across the Lab, slamming into the gate and chewing up the walls.

Caplan threw Morgan to the ground and dropped on top of her. "You were saying?"

She opened her mouth to retort. But another volley of gunfire caused her to duck.

Anger surged through Caplan as he tried to shield her from the gunfire. He was tempted to grab his rifle, to return fire. To take out a few of Corbotch's allies. But instead, he shifted his gaze along the floor. "Follow me," he whispered.

Crawling quickly, Morgan and Caplan reached the carcass. Then they curled up into little balls, making themselves as small as possible.

A ghastly growl rang out. Lifting his head, Caplan saw the mass of Pleistocene beasts separate. He shot a quick glance at the entranceway and his gaze fell upon a small crowd of armed big shots. A grin curled across his lips. *I hope you liked your little dinner party*, he thought. *Because the menu's about to change.*

With an earsplitting roar, the American lion took off across the basement. Claws clicking, it raced past the burning central platform. It reappeared as a shadowy streak a few seconds later.

More gunshots rang out. Shoes slapped against the floor. Then the horrible screams started. Caplan squinted, trying to make sense of the madness. But all he could see were big shots toppling like dominos.

Morgan pinched Caplan's arm. Cocked her head toward the crank.

Caplan nodded and followed her back to the mechanism. As he grabbed hold of it, she unlatched a small box. A couple of dials and levers sat inside it, along with a key already in its lock. She turned the key. An audible click rang out.

Steeling his muscles, Caplan prepared to turn the crank. But an emphatic trumpeting froze him in place. Glancing up, he saw the American mastodon.

It lowered its trunk. Looked directly at him and Morgan. Its feet rose up and came down again, pounding against the floor.

Then it charged.

Caplan released the crank and grabbed hold of his rifle. It wasn't nearly enough firepower to stop a creature of that size. The best he could hope to do was redirect it.

Morgan turned around and reached for the pistol tucked into her waistband. Before she could draw it, Caplan jumped in front of her. She gave him a dirty look and shoved him out of the way. Then she lifted her gun and took aim at the beast.

Caplan did the same. But before either one could fire, a powerful bellow filled the air. Then the short-faced bear barreled into the mastodon's rear legs. The mastodon stumbled, lost its balance. Its front limbs splayed wildly and it came crashing down upon its knees. Trumpeting angrily, it rose up again and continued forward.

Caplan's finger squeezed the trigger. But a sudden movement gave him pause. Horror filled his soul as he saw the short-faced bear streaking in their direction.

He changed stances, taking aim at the bear's face. Maybe he could sink a bullet into its skull. Maybe even its brain. Then he could whirl back to the mastodon, pump its feet and legs full of bullets. It was a long-shot, but what else could he do?

The bear raced forward, its paws scraping the floor with fury.

Caplan's finger twitched against the trigger. It was only fifty feet out now. He wanted to shoot, but his brain told him to wait, to be patient. He wasn't sure why, but somehow he knew it was the right decision.

Forty feet. Gaining speed, the bear passed the mastodon.

It's a race, Caplan thought. *And we're the prize.*

Thirty feet.

He could smell blood now. Wet fur, leathery skin, and rancid breath, too. The stench was overpowering, but the rising heat was even worse. Sweat dripped from his arms, his hands. He felt light-headed and off-balance.

Twenty feet.

Gritting his teeth, he squeezed the trigger as far as he could without firing the weapon. Then he steeled himself. Even if he managed a kill shot—a very unlikely proposition— the bear's momentum made a collision almost inevitable.

Abruptly, the bear put on the brakes.

Caplan eased up on the trigger. *What the hell is it doing?* he wondered.

The bear leapt in front of the mastodon. With a piercing bellow, it rose up on its hind legs.

It's ... protecting us?

The mastodon blurted out a surprised trumpet. Then it charged the bear. Crashed into it and sent it spinning, rolling into the gate.

The bear flew back to its feet. Blood dripped from its furry chest as it once again rose on its hind legs. It swung its powerful arms, clobbering the mastodon's head and scratching the creature's face.

Caplan raced back to the crank. With the screams of Corbotch's big shots ringing in his ears, he began to turn the mechanism. Slowly, the gate rolled sideways.

A fresh breeze, smelling of leaves and rain, blew through the gap. Feeling renewed, Caplan pushed harder. Morgan joined in to help and the gate rolled open another few inches.

The mastodon trumpeted again. Lowering its head, it swung its trunk at the bear's legs. But the bear pounced on the trunk, forcing it to the ground. As the mastodon bucked like a wild horse, the bear sank its jaws into the creature's neck. Blood spurted out fountain-style. The mastodon continued to thrash about, but with far less strength.

Morgan and Caplan gave the crank another full turn. The gate slid open a few more inches. "There." Morgan released the crank. "That should do it."

Roaring at a deafening volume, the bear opened its jaws for another vicious bite. But at the last second, it spun toward Morgan and Caplan.

And started to run.

The creature's enormous size caused Caplan to do a double-take. It looked even bigger than he remembered. *What the ...?* he thought. *Is it ... bigger?*

Heart pounding, Caplan hoisted his rifle. But before he could aim it, the beast shifted a couple of feet to the side. Still running, it rose up on its hind legs and slipped between the narrow gap afforded by the open gate. Once outside, it dropped to all fours. Its paws pounded against concrete.

And then it was gone.

"It wasn't protecting us," Morgan said, her voice tinged with curiosity. "It was using us. Using us to get outside."

CHAPTER 48

The mastodon was dying, but it sure didn't act like it. Instead, it thrashed weakly about on the floor, bathing itself in its own blood. It tried to regain its footing on numerous occasions and blurted angrily with each failed attempt.

Caplan stared at the creature's face and for the first time, noticed that its bright orange eyes were staring right back at him. They hinted at deep insanity, the sort of insanity that couldn't be reached via natural means.

Lifting his gaze, he stared at the security checkpoint. He heard brutish growls and snarls. But no gunfire.

Squinting, he noticed six or seven big shots on the ground, some moving and some not. The others, he decided, had probably retreated back up the ladder to Research.

"If we wait any longer, we'll be next," Morgan whispered.

Caplan followed her through the open gate. He found himself in a dark concrete passage, supported by the occasional pillar. Although sturdy, the tunnel was in rather dilapidated shape. "This tunnel looks old," he remarked.

"It *is* old," she replied. "According to rumor, it was bored out of the ground by one of James' ancestors."

"Why?"

She shrugged. "Because he liked tunnels?"

They walked a little farther, following the tunnel as it curved to the southwest. A jet of warm wind accosted them, bringing with it the lingering scent of mud and pine needles. The outdoors ... the Vallerio! Ahh, Caplan couldn't remember the last time he'd been so eager to stride into the wild. A load lifted from his chest. His feet felt light in his muddied trail-runners.

But that wonderful feeling lasted mere seconds before reality crashed down upon him. The power was still down, meaning Sector 48A's electric fence was out of commission. 1-Gen animals, newly hatched from their incubators, were probably swarming the Vallerio at that very moment. And of course, there was still the matter of the short-faced bear.

The *growing* short-faced bear.

"We should slow down," Morgan said out of the blue. "The bear could be waiting for us."

"Or the lion could be chasing us," he countered.

Her gait shifted, morphed. She picked up speed, matching his pace. At the same time, she tried to mimic his silent footsteps with mixed results. He watched as she picked her way through the crumbling concrete chunks, dirt, twigs, and other debris. While he admired her effort, he knew it would only go so far. Speed and stealth were second nature to him, thanks to years spent in the wild. A test tube girl like Morgan, on the other hand, was simply out of her element.

Morgan winced as some old leaves crunched under her shoe. "What was that back there?" she whispered.

"You mean the animals? That's your department, not mine."

"I mean you jumping between me and the mastodon." Her tone turned angry. "I can take care of myself, you know."

"I know." He exhaled. For five long months, he'd practiced speeches on the off-chance he'd ever see her again.

But now that the opportunity had arrived, he had no idea what to say. "It's just ... well, I owe you."

"Owe me?"

His face flushed, burning like fire. He tried to look at her, but couldn't quite meet her gaze. "I was there when Tony died."

Her facial muscles stiffened.

"He came to me on January 6," Caplan continued, "and asked to borrow *Roadster*. Long story short, I agreed, but with one condition. I wanted to go with him."

He paused, giving her an opportunity to respond. When she didn't, he dove back into the story. "He directed me to a place he called Sector 48A. I still remember pulling up to it, seeing that electric fence. I asked him how he knew about it. He told me he'd first seen the fence on one of the video feeds."

"And?" Morgan's tone was firm, distant.

"He wanted to plant some cameras. So, he cut through the wires and crawled under the fence. Everything was fine until ..."

"Yes?"

"Until he was attacked." A flood of emotions grabbed hold of Caplan, tossing him to and fro. "These things ... they snatched him away into the darkness. Seconds later, they sent him flying back toward the fence. He was cut up and bleeding like crazy. But he was still alive."

Caplan swallowed hard as he remembered the look in Tony's face. That strange, savage look. Like the man had ventured into some other dimension and seen sights not meant for human eyes. "I ran to the fence. There was still time to help him. But I froze. I can't explain it. I just ... froze." His emotions flooded out of him, gushing through his pores. And then he felt drained. Drained and empty. "The things, I assume they were 1-Gens, swept over him. They killed him, dragged him away. I never saw him again."

"But *Roadster* ... it was in Sector 84 ..."

"Because I put it there." He exhaled. "Truth is, I panicked. I knew something big was happening in 48A. And I was afraid of what would happen if anyone found out I'd been there. I figured they might kill me. You too, seeing as how Tony was your brother. Anyway I couldn't face you after that. So, I resigned and moved as far away from nature as possible, to Manhattan."

She exhaled a long sigh, as if releasing her own pent-up sea of emotions. "So, you're a coward."

"I know."

"I don't mean because you didn't save Tony. Bottom line, Tony was responsible for Tony. He put himself into that situation. And if he were still here, he'd tell you the same thing." She shook her head. "No, you're a coward for one simple reason. You ran away."

New emotions, strange and unexpected, flooded back into Caplan, filling the temporary void in his soul. A deep sense of shame, tempered by the slightest hint of relief. Self-disgust offset by an odd euphoria. And most of all, intense grief mixed with a longing. A longing for normalcy. For the life he'd abandoned. For a life that just might be within his grasp.

The crumbling concrete gave way to crumbling schist, damp moss, and flies. They hiked a little farther and Caplan caught sight of the Vallerio Forest. Ancient pine trees stood firm, impenetrable columns of Mother Nature's most wicked city. Their gnarled branches stretched to the cloud-covered sky, as if preparing an onslaught on the heavens themselves. Black corridors, laced with horrible secrets and desperate monsters, pulsed between the trees. A stream, furious and opaque, twisted in and out of the blackness like a slithering snake.

A familiar energy, malevolent and older than time itself, washed over Caplan. It swept away his newfound emotions, replacing them with anguish, fear, and revulsion.

Morgan stopped on the cusp of the cave. "Where to?" she asked.

Caplan gazed upon the ravine. "48A," he replied.

She gave him a questioning look.

"We have to get to Corbotch's helicopter," he said. "It's the only way out of this hellhole."

She nodded and took a hesitant step into the ravine. She slipped a bit on soft mud, but quickly got control of her footing.

Caplan's gaze drifted to Morgan and he didn't see Tony's sister. Instead, he saw her as a lover, a friend, a heroine, and many other things. Her complexity, like a die with infinite sides, staggered him to the core. His mistake was all too apparent. Five months ago, he'd reduced this outstanding woman to a cardboard cutout. She'd become nothing more than Tony's sister to him, with utterly predictable emotions and thoughts.

Well, no more. He still yearned to protect her, still hoped to earn her forgiveness. But no longer would he view her as a one-dimensional being that, if soothed correctly, could salvage his soul.

A seed sprouted within him. His dark emotions withered a bit, making room for something else. Something new.

Something good.

CHAPTER 49

Date: June 19, 2016, 6:46 p.m.; Location: Sector 48A, Vallerio Forest, NH

Caplan inhaled sharply as he caught sight of the sheared wires, the trampled metal bars and posts, and the crumbling concrete blocks. This particular section of giant fence, once a mighty beacon of man's control over nature, had been reduced to mere rubble and scrap metal.

He walked out of the forest, still recuperating from the difficult trek through Sector 12, and stood before what remained of the curving fence. Two metal posts, fifteen feet long and painted to look like trees, had been heavily scratched and ripped out of their respective concrete blocks. Now, they lay on the mud alongside bent metal bars and long strands of wire.

Looking past the fence, Caplan saw familiar evergreen trees, dripping with rainwater and framed by the inky black sky. The pines, cedars, and hemlocks triggered something in his subconscious and he shuddered. The landscape was just as picturesque as he remembered.

And just as evil as well.

The next few seconds felt like hours. And as he stared at the forest, all the old memories and feelings came rushing back to him. He recalled the crunching snow, the nightmarish roars, the pulsing corridors, and the snarling, frenzied, living darkness. But most of all he remembered the screams. Those ungodly, anguished screams of insanity.

"This is the place," he said softly. "This is where he died."

Morgan looked at him, then at the conifers. "You're sure?"

"Absolutely." Caplan stepped over the mud-embedded posts, bars, and wires. He saw scattered footprints of different sizes. Clearly, numerous creatures had escaped 48A. That fact should've made him feel better, but it had the opposite effect.

He stopped at the edge of the former fence line. Again, he looked at the dense columns of evergreen trees, at the black corridors, at the streets of mud and green needles. Was it sheer coincidence he'd come to this exact spot? Or had his subconscious driven him to it?

Taking a deep breath, he stepped across the fence line. Paranoia hit him hard and he began swinging his rifle in arcs, searching for signs of pulsing blackness.

He made his way to the tree line and checked his heading. Then he slid into one of the dark corridors. For several minutes he hiked, heading deeper and deeper into the bowels of the strange, ancient city.

"Wait." Morgan tugged his arm. "Over there."

Caplan's gaze—and rifle—shot to the southeast. His heart skipped a beat as he caught sight of a large silken mass nestled within a clump of trees. Although the incubator was still in one piece, he noticed numerous cracks lining its dirt-stained side.

"We should destroy it." Morgan's jaw hardened. "Before whatever's in there has a chance to come out."

The proposition would've tempted the Caplan of several hours ago. But that Caplan no longer existed. "Why go to all that trouble? Why not just kill ourselves and be done with it?"

She glared at him. "What's that supposed to mean?"

"It means you'd have to be suicidal to mess with those things." He hiked forward, skirting well clear of the incubator. "Trust me. I should know."

Morgan hesitated for a split-second before hurrying to catch up. For a minute, she tried to match his quick pace and quiet gait. Failing that, she settled for speed over silence. "You don't understand."

"What don't I understand?" He arched an eyebrow. "That you've got a death wish?"

"The gene sequencing, the incubators, the 1- and 2-Gens … I'm responsible for all of it."

"Not by yourself."

"Maybe not, but everyone else is dead." She exhaled. "That makes it—all of it—my responsibility. I have to fix this, Zach."

"Getting yourself killed won't fix anything."

She inhaled a deep breath of air. "What am I supposed to do?" she asked. "How do I make this right?"

Her questions jostled Caplan's brain. He thought back to his own failure all those months ago. He thought about how he'd reacted to Tony's death, then and now. And he thought about what he'd do if he could go back to that moment in time, when the whole world seemed to be crashing down upon him. "First, you forgive yourself and get your head straight," he replied. "Then you go with your gut."

A roar, soft at first, erupted from the southeast. It quickly gained decibels, rising to howler monkey levels. Then lion levels. Blue whale levels.

And beyond.

Ground tremors sprung up under Caplan's shoes, sending tiny vibrations through his body. Reaching out, he grabbed hold of a juniper for support. The ancient wooden column quaked and trembled against his fingertips. Needles and scaly green leaves shook loose and dropped to the earth.

A few seconds later, the disturbance ceased. Releasing the tree, Caplan cast a wary glance at Morgan. "Please tell me you didn't make dinosaurs," he said.

She gazed southeast with wide, confused eyes. "No, just Pleistocene megafauna. James was very strict on that point."

"Then what was that?"

"It definitely wasn't a woolly mammoth. And it was way too loud to come from one of the sabers." Her face twisted in thought. "It must've been one of the newly expelled 1-Gens. Only ..."

"Yeah?"

Tearing her gaze from the forest, she looked at Caplan. "I can't imagine any of them having the vocal chops to pull it off."

Great, just what we need, Caplan thought. *Another mystery to solve.*

Kicking his speed up another gear, Caplan trekked deeper into Sector 48A. The forest thickened. Evergreen branches stretched toward other branches, forming enormous arches and blocking out the inky, cloud-covered sky.

The Vallerio played tricks with Caplan's mind, trying to throw him off course. But his internal compass rose to the occasion. And so he continued onward, hiking toward Corbotch, Perkins, and the Rexto 419R3 corporate helicopter.

With each step, he felt himself drawing closer to ancient and otherworldly evil. At the same time, he felt his true self— the one he'd lost five months ago—shed its shackles and take its rightful place at the forefront of his consciousness.

The archaic columns of gnarled wood began to transform into ordinary evergreen trees. Black corridors morphed into somewhat-welcoming pathways. He spotted footprints and animals trails. Heard quiet chirps and snapping twigs. Felt the breeze and the pulsing of distant creatures. The Vallerio was still ancient, still evil.

But he no longer viewed it solely through lens of fear.

A strange sensation ran through him. He veered off-course, acting solely on instinct. Morgan hurried to keep up with him. As he hiked in this new direction, he observed his surroundings. He smelled feces in the air. He saw scratching posts and drag marks. But that wasn't what drove him onward. It was something else. Something he couldn't quite explain.

He stopped at the foot of a giant pine tree, easily some 200 feet tall. His heart began to pound against his chest. Kneeling down, he studied the soil. Then he swung his rifle to his side and carefully cleared away the top layer of wet dirt. Underneath, he found a bed of brown pine needles and dead grass. And underneath that, he found exactly what he knew he'd find.

Morgan stared at the dirt-smeared objects. "What are those things?"

"Bones." He dug a little deeper, revealing some shredded orange fabric. He touched it and memories flooded through him. "Tony's bones."

CHAPTER 50

Morgan stared at Caplan, her eyes filled with the deepest imaginable horror. "How can you be sure?"

"The bones belong to a man. Plus, they're big." Caplan gently maneuvered the dirt-smeared objects to give her a closer look. "Eyeballing them, I'd say they're a good fit for his frame. But that piece of orange fabric is the kicker. Tony was wearing an orange jacket that day."

"I remember that jacket ..." Her voice, tinged with sadness, trailed off into the night.

"The bones are picked clean." Extending his fingertips, Caplan carefully pried a ribcage out of the soil. He brushed off the ribs, revealing deep puncture marks. "But whatever got him had long, sharp teeth. You know, I saw wounds like these earlier today. On some of the bodies near the *Blaze*'s wreckage."

Morgan inhaled. "Cats made those," she said. "Saber-toothed cats."

"Why do you keep calling them that?"

"Saber-toothed tiger is misleading because they're not closely related to tigers. Though now that I think about it, they're not closely related to modern cats either."

"How can you be sure it's a saber?"

"Because of their long upper canines. From our tests, we know that's how they like to kill. They're ambush predators who hold down prey with their forelimbs. Then they use their neck muscles to drive their upper canines into soft flesh, usually the throat or abdomen." She exhaled. "Besides, it's the only thing that makes sense. We know James took sabers, woolly mammoths, and the incubators here. The incubators didn't start opening until the full expulsion sequence was initiated a few hours ago. And if a woolly mammoth had killed Tony, the bones wouldn't be in such good shape. So, that leaves sabers."

A howl, vicious and bloodthirsty, rose out of the forest. Caplan clenched his jaw. He knew that howl all too well. *Well, well, well,* he thought. *Look who's back for round two.*

A large creature, cloaked in shadows, stepped out from behind a thick cedar trunk. It was over six feet long with shoulders rising more than four feet off the earth. Its right shoulder blade slumped a bit and Caplan saw a small hole, ringed by dried blood and matted fur.

It's the same wolf, he thought, his eyes narrowing to slits. *But it's at least a foot longer and taller. What the hell is going on around here?*

CHAPTER 51

Date: June 19, 2016, 6:54 p.m.; Location: Sector 48A, Vallerio Forest, NH

Caplan felt a twinge of fear pass through him. But this time, it didn't originate from the Vallerio. Instead, it came solely from the strange beast. Not from its existence, but from its unexplained growth. How could any animal grow so much in such a short span of time? It was unthinkable, impossible. And yet, undeniably real.

"That's a dire wolf," Morgan whispered. "It looks exactly like our sketches. All but the coat, that is. We thought its fur would be more like that of a gray wolf."

Caplan studied the dire wolf from afar. Its golden brown coat, streaked with black, shimmered in the dim light. Its savage, orangish eyes flicked back and forth between him and Morgan. Its tongue licked its lips over and over again. All in all, it looked similar to how he remembered it. It was just a taller, longer, and bulkier version of itself.

"That's the one I cut out of the incubator," Caplan said. "See that bullet hole? James' guy shot it when it attacked me. He saved my life."

Morgan lifted her pistol, took aim at the wolf. "This is the same guy that infected you?"

"The very one." Memories of Julius Pearson weighed heavily on Caplan's mind. What had happened to him anyway? Did he venture into the Lab with the big shots? Did he get his comeuppance? Or was he still out there somewhere? "By the way, how big do these wolves get?"

"I don't remember. Why?"

"Because that one's hit a growth spurt since I last saw it. At least a foot in height and even more in length."

Her gaze hardened. "That's impossible."

"Tell me about it." With slow, fluid movements, Caplan placed his rifle and backpack on the ground. Then he grabbed hold of his twin axes and carefully removed their head covers.

Morgan kept her pistol aimed at the dire wolf. Her gaze shifted to him, then back to the wolf. "Are you sure that's a good idea?"

"Let me get back to you on that." He brandished the axes like weapons. Like it or not, the situation called for patience, not power.

He'd fended off wolves in the past. The trick was to establish dominance, usually by yelling, throwing rocks, and making oneself as large as possible. But this wolf, well, it was a different story.

According to Morgan, the 1-Gen sabers and woolly mammoths had come out of their incubators violent and thirsty for blood. And the 2-Gen creatures had shown similar characteristics. With the exception of the short-faced bear, they'd fought almost mindlessly. Like rabid animals, they'd attacked anything with a pulse. So, there was every reason to expect the same thing from the dire wolf.

Last time, Pearson had driven it off with gunfire. But that was right after it came out of the incubator and before its recent growth spurt. This time, Caplan suspected, would be different.

This time it would fight to the death.

And that made it especially hard to forgo his rifle. Unfortunately, gunfire would attract too much attention. The last thing he needed was for the rest of the 1-Gen newborns, drawn by the loud noise, to come sniffing around.

The dire wolf snarled and bared its teeth. Its paws scraped the ground. Then it sprinted forward.

"Zach …" Morgan's gun hand quivered and she took a step backward.

"Don't shoot." Caplan whirled the axes in his hands. "And don't turn your back on it."

The wolf's black legs pumped furiously, blending in and out of the darkness. Its golden coat turned into a blur of shifting, twitching muscles.

Caplan ignored the creature's sharp, gnashing teeth. Instead, he zeroed in on its legs.

Fifteen feet out, the creature's gait began to change. It ran another five feet before launching itself into the air. Its orangish eyes blazed holes in Caplan's face. Its jaws snapped wildly, eager to bite, to kill.

But Caplan was ready and sidestepped the attack. As the wolf hurtled past him, he slashed its side with the left axe. The blade struck hard and unexpected reverberations shot through Caplan's arm. It felt like he'd chopped at concrete rather than flesh and bone. Even worse, the blow did little damage, opening the smallest of slits in the wolf's tough hide.

The wolf twisted in mid-air before smacking to the ground. Its head curled sideways, toward Caplan. Its jaws snapped at him, narrowly missing his legs.

Still clutching his axes, Caplan leapt on top of the creature. The dire wolf squirmed out from under him and bit his leg. Caplan clamped his mouth shut, barely avoiding a scream. *Okay, that does it*, he thought. *You don't mess with the Holocene.*

Caplan adjusted and pinned down the wolf. Then he dropped the axes, pushed its snout to the ground, and wrapped his arms around the creature's head. Leaning back, he squeezed with all his might.

The wolf, snarling and yipping, struggled to escape the headlock. But Caplan maintained a vice-like grip. "The axes." He looked at Morgan. "Kill it."

Morgan stuck the pistol into her waistband and hurried to his side. She picked up the axes and hesitated. "How?"

The dire wolf wriggled and snapped its jaws. It took all of Caplan's strength to hold it down. "Just do it!"

Morgan's right arm reared back. Seconds later, she sent the axe slamming into the creature. The blow opened a small cut on its belly. But it also jolted her and she slipped, falling to the ground.

Frowning, she scrambled back to her feet. Using shorter strokes, she attacked the cut, causing it to widen and deepen.

As its blood began to flow freely, the wolf's movements turned frantic. Caplan, in turn, dug deep into his reserves and managed to keep his grip on the creature's head.

The dire wolf's movements grew even more frantic. But it quickly began to lose energy. And after another two minutes of steady blows, it finally died in Caplan's arms.

Morgan dropped the axes and fell to her knees, physically spent. Caplan released the wolf's limp head and stretched his sore arms. Then he gathered up his axes, rifle, and backpack.

Morgan took a few long breaths of air. Then she stood up again, clutching the bandages on her side. Her blonde hair, soaked with sweat and grime, hung limply from her head. Her eyes looked distant and sad.

"First time?" Caplan asked quietly.

She opened her mouth, but no words came out.

Caplan knew how she felt. He'd killed animals in the past, always for food or to protect himself. But that didn't make it any easier. Every time he took a life, he felt a little piece of himself disappear with it.

But come to think of it, that wasn't entirely true. He had no problem swatting flies or squashing spiders. If he was completely honest with himself, he cared mostly about mammals and maybe birds. Fishes, reptiles, and amphibians were still important, but less so. Invertebrates were at the bottom of his list. Where did the dire wolf, this violent creation of modern science, fit into things? He wasn't sure.

He reached for Morgan. She hesitated for a moment before accepting his embrace. They hugged fiercely, allowing months of frustration, guilt, and anger to melt away. And when they finally parted, Caplan felt renewed, reenergized. As if he could take on the entire Pleistocene epoch by himself.

Morgan approached the carcass with some trepidation. Gently, she kicked its legs with the toe of her shoe, drawing it out to its full length. "Are you sure its larger?" she asked.

Caplan nodded.

"I believe you, but I don't see how it's possible. We programmed all incubators to grow animals to their full sizes. And based on the video feeds, the sabers and mammoths haven't grown a bit since expulsion. Unless ..." She blinked. Her eyes widened as if she were awaking from a deep sleep.

"What?" Caplan asked.

"My colleagues and I developed the science for de-extinction, but we didn't physically control it. For security purposes, the Lab's guard contingent managed all systems, including the ones dealing with expulsion."

"So?"

"So, I always thought it was more of a formality than anything else. But I suppose it's possible they used their position to conduct secret experiments with the incubators. They could've administered hormone injections, maybe even altered genes."

"And you let them get away with that?"

"I didn't let them get away with anything," she retorted. "I'm just saying it could've happened. And come to think of it, it could've happened to the sabers and woolly mammoths, too. The guards inserted various microchips into their bodies. It's possible those chips could be used to stimulate hormones or do any number of things via radio waves."

"So, injections or microchips could explain the growth. Maybe the crazy violence, too." Caplan exhaled. "Theoretically speaking, how large could 1- and 2-Gens grow?"

"Mammals evolved to enormous sizes in order to fill the ecological niche left by dinosaurs. In order words, they didn't stop growing because they reached some kind of biomechanical restraint. They only stopped because of a warming climate and the amount of food available to them. With 1- and 2-Gens, those things might not be a factor, at least not at first." She took a deep breath. "In other words, the sky's the limit."

CHAPTER 52

Date: Unknown; Location: Unknown

The crackling sound, louder than a siren, reverberated through the forest, ping-ponging from tree to tree. Mills winced, but didn't look backward. Instead, she stared straight ahead and kept up a steady pace, wincing every time her bare feet touched the pine needles.

Toland halted. Whirling around, he cast a keen eye on the forest. "It's getting bigger," he said.

Elliott stopped next to him. Her face was tomato-red. Dark bags hung from her eyes. Balancing her hands on her knees, she gulped at the oxygen. "We need to … keep going."

"A lot bigger." Toland said, ignoring her. "This X-thing better be underground."

Bailey Mills, still clutching the strange logbook, dragged herself to the others. Her feet stung so bad it brought tears to her eyes. Her heart pounded away inside her chest, like a hammer on a stubborn nail.

She clutched her waist with both hands, barely keeping stitches at bay. Then she turned around.

She could see nearby objects like rocks and dirt and moss. A little farther back, she saw rows of evergreen trees along with fallen needles and pine cones. Beyond that, the forest was ripe with flames. Seeing the fire—that distant instrument of destruction—set her nerves to the breaking point.

It wasn't the size of the fire, which was difficult to tell at this distance. It was the fact that it appeared *alive*. The flames vibrated and pulsed with intense fury. As if an ancient dragon existed within them, propelling them onward with nothing but sheer will.

Elliott was the last to turn around. Her mouth drooped as she stared at the fire. "Ohmigod."

Toland grunted and twisted away from the fire. Mills chased after him, cutting through pines and spruces, and keeping an eye on the distant flames. Her feet still stung and a splitting headache made it hard for her to think. But her discomfort couldn't compare to the pit of terror embedded deep in her stomach.

Knowledge was a powerful thing. And the possibility that they were in the Vallerio—*her* Vallerio—had wiped some of her fear away. Unanswered questions still abounded, of course. Questions about the saber and woolly mammoths. Questions about why the animals were so violent and why the saber seemed so intent on killing them. But at least she felt like she was starting to get a handle on the situation.

But the wildfire, well, it was a game changer. And as she hurried onward, tripping over roots and rocks, the pit in her stomach blossomed in particularly nasty fashion, sending shoots of fear through her veins.

The soft snapping and cracking of wet wood crested through the forest. The noises caught hold of Mills' sanity, nearly ripping it right out of her body. Then a new sound punctuated the night air. It sounded like ... yes ... it was metal clinking against metal in ferocious fashion. Mills' gaze shot leftward and she noticed faint glimmers of light. "Wait," she whispered through clenched teeth. "I see something."

Toland maintained his pace, but cast a withering look over his shoulder. "Yeah," he said. "We saw it too."

"Not the fire, you idiot." She stopped, pointed to her left. "Over there."

Applying the brakes, he slid to a stop. His neck swiveled to the side. His eyelids cinched into squint position. Then he started toward the glimmers. With a pained groan, Elliott stumbled after him.

Taking her own route, Mills hiked toward the glimmers at a fast clip. Soon, she caught glimpses of a small clearing, surrounded by tall evergreen trees. A large object rested in the middle of it. It looked silky-smooth from a distance and black as night.

Mills slowed her pace a bit, slipping from tree to tree. At the edge of the clearing, she knelt behind some bushes, making herself as small as possible.

The object was a small corporate helicopter, probably a four-seater with all the right luxuries. It reminded her a little of the one her ex-boyfriend owned. She'd flown in it a few times, usually for quick getaways to the Hamptons.

The tiniest smile curled upon her lips. She barely remembered her ex at this point. But riding in his chopper? Ahhh ... that had been divine. Seats as cushy as teddy bears. Succulent dishes prepared in advance by a world-class chef. Windows, clean and free of streaks, offering a portal to the world beyond. And of course, the bottles of expensive liquor. Oh, that liquor ... so delish! She could almost taste it on her tongue.

A snarl, vicious yet soft, screeched into her ears, putting an end to her memories. Alarm bells rang in her head.

The saber!

She tried to place the sound, but the forest threw off her senses. She couldn't tell if it was this way or that, distant or close. The confusion infuriated her and she felt her sanity slip a little closer to a precarious edge.

Footsteps padded over plants and squishy fruit. Heart racing, Mills spun toward the noise. Then she relaxed. It was just Toland and Elliott, slipping out from behind a tree and hurrying to the bushes.

Toland crouched next to her and breathed softly through his mouth. His breath smelled of rotten teeth and garlic and it took all of Mills' self-control to face him. "Did you hear that?" he whispered.

Mills nodded, too terrified to speak.

Moments later, Elliott crawled up on Mills' other side. Wild-eyed and caked with mud and leaves, she looked almost feral. "It's close," she whispered. "I can feel it."

"The only way you'll feel that saber is if it bites you on the ass," Toland said. "Face it, you're not exactly Atalanta."

Elliott gave him a puzzled look.

"Oh, you've never read Greek mythology. How shocking." Toland rolled his eyes and glanced at the chopper. "Expensive bird."

"You've got rich friends, right?" Elliott looked at Mills with pleading eyes. "Maybe it's one of them."

If only, Mills thought. But she was pretty sure she'd been MIA just a day or two. Most likely, people hadn't even noticed her disappearance. But even if they had, she doubted any of her friends, even her besties, would go to much trouble to find her. Sure, they'd make the talk show rounds and have their assistants post moving messages on social media. But that would be the extent of it. She knew that because, quite frankly, she would've done the same thing if the roles had been reversed.

Wow, she thought. *Just … wow.*

"Well?" Toland whispered. "Do you recognize it?"

She shook her head.

The clink-clank of metal brushing up against metal rang out. Mills focused her attention on the waist-deep grass surrounding the helicopter.

The grass shifted a bit and some blades vanished. A head, topped with curly hair, appeared in the clearing. Then it ducked out of view.

Mills shot another glance at the wildfire. It was still distant, but getting closer. She could see red flames. A few orange ones, too. They shot forward and sideways, gradually spreading themselves through the evergreen trees. Thick gray smoke, swirling and churning, curled up behind them and drifted into the sky.

She turned back to the chopper. She was nearly certain they were in the Vallerio. If so, the helicopter most likely belonged to James Corbotch. In fact, it had probably been used to bring her and the others to the forest in the first place.

Fast as fire, she shot through the bushes and entered the field. Her bare feet stung like crazy as she stepped on sharp rocks, lumpy fruit, and God knows what else. But she didn't stop.

The curly-haired head appeared for a second time. Slowly, it lifted out of the grass like a space rocket, bringing the upper body of a man with it.

Mills ran up to the man. She stared straight into his eyes for a moment, seeing vague signs of recognition. "Where is he?" she said. "Where's James?"

"You shouldn't be here." The man glanced over both shoulders. "It's not safe."

"Safe? You want to talk about safe?" Mills was tempted to bash him over the head with the logbook. "Two people died right in front of me, killed by an animal that shouldn't even exist. That same animal chased my friends and me all over this nightmare of a forest. And it's still after us. We're hungry, thirsty, exhausted, and pissed-off. And oh yeah, there's a forest fire heading this way."

"Easy, lady." The man's voice wavered with fear and regret. His gaze, tight and focused, swept the clearing. "You need to listen to me—"

"Where is he?" Mills shouted, not caring who heard her. "Where's James?"

"Right here."

Fury engulfed Mills as she twisted toward the voice. She saw an old man, decked out in a gray sport coat and tailored white shirt. He looked cool and collected, the exact opposite of how she felt at that moment.

"It's good to see you again, Bailey." James Corbotch smiled. "Welcome to the Vallerio."

CHAPTER 53

Mills' brain worked in overdrive, reminding her of all she and the others had endured. She wanted to scream at Corbotch, to make threats she'd never be able to carry out. But try as she might, just one word managed to squeak past her grimy lips. "Why?"

Corbotch cast his gaze upon Mills before shifting it to the approaching Toland and Elliott. "Because you were threats."

"To what?" Toland sneered. "Your precious ego?"

If Corbotch was angry, he didn't show it. "To my work. To *Apex Predator*."

Elliott gasped. Mills clutched the logbook a little closer to her side. She suddenly recalled where she'd heard the term *Apex Predator* before. Elliott had mentioned it back in the cave, calling it some kind of weird project taking place in the Vallerio.

The chopper door slid open and Mills saw the interior for the first time. It was jam packed with people, at least a dozen of them. They were all different. Men and women. Old and young. Tall and short. Different shades of skin color. It was truly a diverse group. But their attire, well, that was something else entirely.

The men wore silk suits, all of which were soiled, and expensive shoes. The women, who were mostly barefoot, wore formal cocktail dresses. The dresses were soaked through with mud and ripped in all sorts of places.

A stern woman with uncanny bird-like features climbed out of the helicopter. She cast a single glance at the growing wildfire. Then she limped quickly toward Corbotch, wincing with each step. "We need to go, James," she said, with nary a glimpse at Mills or the others. "Now."

Corbotch twisted his neck toward the curly-haired man. "Derek?"

"I need five minutes, sir," Derek replied.

"Make it two."

Why are you standing around like an idiot? Mills thought. *This is your chance. Attack!*

"Don't even think about it," a man said.

Mills whirled around and fixed her gaze upon a veritable giant of a man. He stood several inches above six feet and sported the impressive physique of a bodybuilder. As if that weren't intimidating enough, he also carried a gigantic pistol.

"Ms. Mills, I'd like you to meet Julius Pearson," Corbotch said. "My right-hand man."

Pearson didn't smile. Didn't speak. Didn't move an inch. He just stood like one of the Vallerio's indomitable trees, aiming his gun directly at Mills' chest.

Mills turned back to Corbotch, just in time to see the bird-like woman clamber back into the cabin. The woman struggled to find space in the crowded, standing-room only area before finally reclosing the door.

"Looks like a tight squeeze," Toland remarked. "I don't suppose you've got room for one more."

One more? Mills thought. *What an asshole!*

Corbotch arched an eyebrow. "Ahh, Brian Toland."

Toland puffed out his chest in pride. "So, you've heard of me."

"Not you. Your research. My people tell me you've written a lengthy tome about my family."

Toland's chest sagged a bit before puffing out again. "What of it?"

"In the process, you dredged up some long-forgotten stories. Stories like the Dasnoe expedition, for instance. Stories that might draw renewed attention to the Vallerio." Corbotch twisted toward Elliott. "And you're Tricia Elliott, the president of Scrutiny. I take it Randi is no longer with us?"

Elliott's eyes were dull, nearly vacant.

"The two of you spent the last few months building a lawsuit against the Vallerio Foundation," Corbotch said. "You demanded access to all sorts of records. Records that could shed light on *Apex Predator*."

Elliott didn't respond. Instead, she just stood there, silent and unmoving.

Corbotch twisted back to Mills. "Travis?" he asked simply.

Mills' fingers curled into fists.

Corbotch read her body language. "Travis was writing an exposé on the Vallerio Foundation. Specifically, about the impressive scientific minds we've managed to gather under one roof. His work would've thrust us into the spotlight. Experts might've even figured out what we were doing here."

Mills glared at him.

"As for you, Ms. Mills, you wished to take what was rightfully mine." Corbotch shrugged. "Alexander loved this land. He would've never sold an inch of it, especially to a mere logger like Daniel Mills. Even so, your documents posed significant risk to me. What if the courts decided to honor your claim? What if they took the Vallerio from me? I couldn't let that happen. Not now. Not when I'm so close."

Mills wanted to scream, but managed to keep her tone in a tight range. "So close to what?"

"Salvation."

A roar reverberated through the clearing. The Vallerio's density, along with the crackling flames, made it impossible to tell how far it had traveled. But the sound had force behind it. Force which staggered Mills to her core.

"That's the saber," Elliott whispered.

Corbotch gave her a sad smile and began to back toward the helicopter. "That, my dear, is my cue to exit. I wish you all the best. I—" Corbotch paused. His eyes flicked to Mills. "What's that?"

"What's what?" she asked.

He pointed at the logbook. "That."

"Oh, this old thing?" Mills' brain raced as she tried to figure a way out of the predicament. Her odds, she knew, were long. Corbotch had numbers and firepower. Her little group had torn-up feet, cuts and scrapes, and exhaustion in droves. But she couldn't give up. If she wasn't on that helicopter when it took off, she was as good as dead. "Just something I found in an old building."

"What building? Did it look like a barn?" His eyes widened in realization. "That has to be it. The fire's coming from that way."

Mills merely smiled.

Corbotch's coolness melted away. His facial features began to twitch. "What happened?"

"Hmm." Mills rubbed her chin as if in deep thought. "You know, I don't remember."

Corbotch relaxed. His coolness came roaring back at full force. "Give me the book."

The barn-like building and all its mysteries came flooding back to Mills. She wondered about the machines and the workers. She wondered about the strange wheels and the dead body. But most of all, she wondered why Corbotch cared about some old logbook.

"What's it worth to you?" she asked.

Corbotch sighed, shifted his gaze. "Julius."

Pearson jabbed his gun into Mills' back, just below her shoulder blades. Immense pain shot through her body.

"Give me the book," Corbotch repeated.

Fighting to keep the pain off her face, Mills stared straight into his cold, cold eyes. "Make me."

CHAPTER 54

Date: June 19, 2016, 7:54 p.m.; Location: Sector 48A, Vallerio Forest, NH

The blast, abrupt and clear, reverberated through the forest. Caplan's skin crawled. Then more blasts rang out in quick succession.

He stopped and Morgan stopped alongside him. The gunshot had come from the Rexto 419R3's general direction, making Corbotch or maybe Perkins the likely shooter. But why? Were they trying to fend off 1-Gens? Didn't they realize they might be attracting more of them? *There's your dinner bell, 1-Gens,* he thought. *It's feeding time!*

"Damn it," Morgan whispered in frustration. "Every 1-Gen for miles is going to be making a beeline in this direction."

"The more the merrier."

"You can't be serious."

As the reverberations died away, crackles—ferocious and lasting—stretched across the land. They built to a deep crescendo, faded back into the Vallerio, and then began building again.

Caplan's eyes returned to the fire that had captivated him the last few minutes. Flames blazed in the distance, throbbing and trembling with incredible energy. Gray smoke trailed upward, whirling and churning. The whole thing gave off strange energy, as if the fire itself was alive.

As the sounds of splintering wood filled his eardrums, Caplan thought about the earlier fire, the one triggered by the crash. But the *Blaze*'s wreckage was in the opposite direction. So, what had started this new fire?

Switching gears, he thought through their options and discarded them each in turn. They could try to outrun the flames. But where would they go? They were many miles from the outer fence line. And returning to Hatcher was like voluntarily returning to death row. No, there was just one option available to them and they needed to grab it before they ran out of time. "How are your legs feeling?" he asked.

"Like rubber."

"That'll have to do." His instincts reared up as he stared into the forest. He wasn't close enough to actually see the clearing. But he could feel it. Like the good old days. Before all the madness. When he could close his eyes and still sense the trees, the leaves, the rocks, the hills, everything. "Come on."

Slinging his rifle over his shoulder, Caplan broke out into a mad dash. His shoes flew over the pine needles, expertly avoiding roots, branches, and mud holes. Slowly, shiny black metal, tucked carefully between rings of conifers, came into view.

Turning his head, he looked for Morgan. She trailed him by a considerable margin. She ran with a limp and without style, awkwardly tripping over obstacles and kicking up mud with every step.

He zeroed in on her for a moment of time. Her skin was purplish-red. Her cheeks puffed in and out like a blowfish. Her blonde hair was a disaster area of floppy curls and frizz. And her clothes were a mud-soaked mess. But none of that altered the way he felt.

To him, she'd never looked more beautiful.

His head swiveled back to the front and he saw four shadows rushing northwest. Three of the shadows were new to him. But the fourth one sent his brain zooming back to where it had all started, that dark alleyway in Manhattan.

He knew he needed to keep going, to get to that helicopter. But instead, he veered off-course. Calculating the angles in his head, he ran full tilt through the forest. Derek Perkins, seemingly oblivious to his presence, did the same.

Caplan felt an inkling of doubt as they converged upon one another. But he quickly stuffed it away and leapt at Perkins, smashing the man with a vicious shoulder block. Caught off guard, Perkins went down like a glass-jawed boxer. They rolled, exchanging sharp elbows and punches, before Caplan gained the top position. Pinning Perkins, he raised his left fist and prepared to rain hellfire down on the man.

A body, small and petite, crashed into his back. The blow jostled Caplan and he tipped off balance. Swiftly, Perkins slid out from under him.

Fueled by rising insanity, Caplan whirled around to face this newest aggressor. He blinked, did a double-take.

A woman in her early-thirties stood before him. She was three or four inches shy of six feet and couldn't have weighed much more than 120 pounds. Despite the mud caking her tanned body, he could see she was a cookie-cutter knockout. One of those blonde, blue-eyed supermodel types that the media and masses loved to despise, yet still fawned over at every opportunity.

Farther back, he saw two other people. A bearded, bookish guy and a hapless mud-covered woman. They sure as hell didn't look like any of Corbotch's big shots. But what else could they be?

His gaze shifted to the knockout. To the logbook under her left arm and to the large branch clutched in her right hand. She wielded it like a little kid wielding a too-heavy tennis racket. Harmless for the most part, but you still wouldn't want the kid taking a swing at you. Rising to his feet, he yanked the branch out of her hand. Then he spun around to face Perkins.

"Wait." Perkins, on all fours, gasped for air. Blood streamed from his right side, just below his armpit. Slowly, painfully, he lifted his eyes to meet Caplan's. "I'm ... I'm trying to help."

Caplan lunged forward, grabbed the man's shirt. "You work for Corbotch," he growled.

"See that?" The knockout strode forward on bare feet, leaving tiny blood streaks on the pine needles. With her free hand, she pointed at Perkins' right side. "That's a bullet hole."

Caplan cocked his fist. "And?"

"And he got it saving us from Corbotch's man." She gave Caplan a defiant look. "Maybe he used to work for James. But I think it's safe to say he's officially tendered his resignation."

Chapter 55

Date: June 19, 2016, 8:01 p.m.; Location: Sector 48A, Vallerio Forest, NH

He gave you the tablets ... he saved Amanda's life, Caplan thought. *Then again, he didn't say a word when Pearson infected you.*

His fist hung steady in the air, poised to slam into the bridge of Perkins' nose. He became increasingly aware of the others. The bookish guy and the mud-covered woman. Morgan too, freshly arrived from lurching through the forest.

"Punch me if you want. Hell, pummel the shit out of me. Lord knows I deserve it." Perkins' eyes, small and bloodshot, flicked from Caplan to the trio of maybe-big shots. "Just give them tablets and get them the hell out of here."

Caplan's fist wavered. In the distance, he heard the crackling flames. The ground trembled slightly and pine needles fluttered to the ground.

The knockout looked over her shoulder. "Whatever you do, make it fast."

"Why?" Morgan said between gasps. "You planning on outrunning that fire?"

"Something like that."

Reluctantly, Caplan lowered his fist. Then he gave Perkins a shove, sending the man to the ground. "You brought me here," he said. "You let Julius inject me with that ... that ..."

"With HA-78." Perkins swallowed. "Yeah, I know."

"People died. Lots of people."

His face twitched, but he stayed silent.

"Why shouldn't I kill you right now?" Caplan asked, his voice full of venom.

The bookish guy cleared his throat. "I hate to interrupt this fun little reunion of yours—"

"Then don't," Morgan said.

He stared down the barrel of her pistol without blinking. "Yes, you've got a gun. We're all very impressed."

Morgan frowned.

The bookish guy didn't miss a beat. "But we're not just running from the fire. There's a giant on our trail."

Caplan's eyes narrowed to slits. "Giant?"

"He means Julius." Perkins rose to a knee and clutched his side. "Julius is the one who shot me."

Caplan glanced at Morgan. Morgan gave him a little nod. Then she knelt behind a tall cedar tree and looked southeast, studying the forest with great care.

"You didn't answer my question." Caplan looked back at Perkins. "Why shouldn't I just kill you and be done with it?"

"Look, I deserve to die," Perkins replied. "No denying that. Truth is, I let James into my brain. I let him twist my mind and convince me we were doing good things. His enemy list was a mile long. I flew dozens of them here—including these three—on his orders. I abandoned them to certain death and didn't think twice about it."

The mud-covered woman didn't move a muscle. But the bookish guy clenched his jaw. And the knockout's blue irises seemed to double in size.

"But then James said he wanted to kill everyone at Hatcher," Perkins continued. "I started questioning him, doubting him. Doubting everything I'd ever done for him. So, I stole those tablets, smuggled them aboard the helicopter, gave them to you."

"Yeah, you're a real Samaritan."

"I know I should've told you the truth about HA-78. I almost did. But ..." He trailed off.

Caplan stared into the man's eyes. In that instant, he felt Perkins' pain and tortured anguish. Perkins had committed great sins. He'd knowingly caused unimaginable horror and death and he would have to live with that knowledge for the rest of his life.

Caplan's feelings didn't suddenly jump into the realm of positivity. But he reached out and offered a hand to Perkins.

Perkins grasped the hand and rose to his feet. He took a few deep breaths. But the haunted, hollow look remained in his eyes.

Caplan's mind buzzed with questions about HA-78. But other questions also fought for his attention. Questions about 48A. Questions about the wildfire. And questions about the knockout's logbook.

He shook his head, clearing his mind. There would be time for answers. Right now, he had to focus, to prioritize.

He fished the amber pill container out of his pocket. Popping off the cap, he offered a tablet to Perkins.

Perkins shook his head. "I was immunized before the flight."

Caplan turned to the trio, handed out tablets. "In case you didn't follow all that, you're infected," he said. "You need to swallow these down."

The bookish guy made a face. "Without water?"

Caplan nodded at a small mud puddle. "Help yourself."

"What do we look like? Savages?"

"What's your name?" Caplan asked.

"Brian Toland."

"Let me make this simple for you, Brian. Take the tablet, you live. Don't take it, you die."

Toland frowned. But he stuck the tablet into his mouth and swallowed it all the same.

Caplan glanced at the others. "Names?"

"Bailey Mills," the knockout said.

The mud-woman didn't respond.

"Her name is Tricia," Mills offered. "Tricia Elliott."

"And was he telling the truth?" Caplan asked, with a nod at Perkins. "About the three of you being abandoned here?"

"It wasn't just three of us." Mills' eyes clenched tight. "It was five in the beginning."

Morgan's head tilted a few inches to one side. "Did you wake up in a field? Surrounded by strange animals?"

"Just one animal. A saber-toothed tiger." Mills arched an eyebrow. "How'd you know?"

"Lucky guess."

"Well, any enemy of James' is a friend of mine. I'm Zach Caplan and that's Amanda Morgan." Caplan studied the trio, feeling an instant kinship with Mills. Elliott seemed distant, as if lost in another dimension. And Toland, well, the less said about him the better. "It looks like you've been through a lot."

Mills clutched her logbook a little closer to her side. "We lost two people to the saber. And still, it kept chasing us. We thought that barn-like building—"

"Wait." Morgan, still keeping a lookout, paused for a long moment. "What building?"

"The building." Elliott's voice took a wild turn. "The hatch and the basement. Wheels and tubes and—"

"Tell us later." Caplan turned to Perkins. "How's the landing skid?"

"Fixed," he replied.

"Think you can fly us out of here?"

A smile crossed Perkins' face. "Just try and stop me."

CHAPTER 56

Date: June 19, 2016, 8:14 p.m.; Location: Sector 48A, Vallerio Forest, NH

The inferno curled deep within the forest, gaining substance and momentum by the second. Caplan tried to estimate its height, its width. But it was impossible to tell at that distance.

He heard snarls and growls, distant yet close. According to Mills, they came from a saber-toothed tiger, presumably the same one that had slaughtered two of her friends.

Briefly, he thought about his conversation with Morgan, about the possibility that 1-Gens were growing to terrifying proportions. How big could a Pleistocene beast actually get? Eventually, gravity would take over and pull it into the earth. That is, if its bones and cartilage didn't give out first. But such a monster could do a lot of damage before that happened.

The clearing came up fast and Caplan refocused his attention on it. He saw the Rexto 419R3, sitting quietly in the clearing. Corbotch stood alongside it, his gaze aimed at the wildfire.

"No sign of Pearson ... he must be searching the forest." Caplan studied Corbotch from head to foot, searching for signs of weapons. "That means James is alone."

"Not exactly," Morgan whispered. "Bailey told me she saw over a dozen people packed into the cabin."

"The dignitaries?"

"That's my guess. They're probably armed."

"Yeah, but they're not Pearson." Caplan shook his head. "Why would Pearson leave Corbotch by himself? It doesn't make sense."

"I think I can answer that one." Perkins, wincing and clutching his right side in a firm grip, sidled up to Caplan. "He's looking for me."

The truth dawned on Caplan. "You're the only one who knows how to fly the Rexto?"

"Yup. Without me in the cockpit, they're stuck here."

"Then stay out of sight. We can't let them know you're with us." Caplan glanced at Morgan. "James or the cabin?"

Morgan cocked her head to one side. "That depends. Are you going to let me shoot him?"

"On second thought, I'll take James. Here, take this." Caplan shrugged off his rifle and handed it to Morgan. "You'll need it more than me."

She slung the rifle over her shoulder and handed her pistol to Caplan. "Ready when you are."

Caplan spun around, looked at the others. "Don't come out until we say so."

Elliott didn't respond. But Mills, Toland, and Perkins nodded in unison.

Crouching down, Caplan stole into the clearing. He kept one eye on the blaze as he cut through the deep grass. It continued to grow bigger and bigger. He figured they had twenty minutes before the fire turned them into ash.

He paused upon reaching Corbotch and checked his surroundings. Still no sign of Pearson. Warily, he rose to his feet and took careful aim at the old man. "Fancy meeting you here."

Corbotch froze for a second. Then he slowly turned around. His weathered, wrinkled face showed no signs of anger or fear. "I have to admit I had my doubts. But you really are a survival expert."

"And you're a murderer."

"But you're still going to let me go."

Caplan's teeth gnashed in disgust. "And why would I do that?"

"Because this planet is dying." Corbotch exhaled a long breath. "And I'm the only one who can help it."

CHAPTER 57

"Help the planet?" Caplan shook his head. "You wouldn't help a little old lady cross the street unless she paid you for it."

"I'm many things, Zach. Some good, some bad. But greedy certainly isn't one of them."

Out of the corner of his eye, Caplan saw the cabin door slide open. A pistol, clenched in a small hand, appeared.

Morgan popped out of the grass and slammed the door on the hand. A screeching yelp rang out. Wasting no time, she opened the door again and yanked the hand. An aloof middle-aged man tumbled out of the helicopter. Morgan aimed the rifle at him. "Remember me?" she asked with a twisted smile. "Yeah, I thought so. Do yourself a favor and stay quiet."

For the next two minutes, Caplan kept up a steady aim on the cabin. Meanwhile, Morgan emptied it one-by-one, frisking the big shots before sending them to join the others.

"It's okay. I can handle this." Corbotch flashed the panicked big shots a calming smile before turning back to Caplan. "Do you know what's going on here? I mean, what's really going on?"

At any second, Pearson could return. And then there was the fire, still throbbing, still drawing dangerously close. There was no time to waste. He needed to call to Perkins and the others, board the chopper, and get the hell out of the cursed forest. "The better question is, do I care? And the answer is, no, I don't."

"I lied to you earlier. Oblivion isn't inching our way. It's already here."

Caplan wanted to dismiss him. But the sincerity of Corbotch's tone gave him pause. "What are you talking about?"

"The Holocene extinction is about to kick into high gear, Zach. It's nobody's fault. It's merely an inevitable consequence of the strange and massive loss of megafauna during the Pleistocene epoch." Corbotch stared unblinking into Caplan's eyes. "Regardless, the world is in serious trouble. Vallerio Foundation experts expect systemic ecosystem failure to occur across the globe within six months."

Morgan gave him a hard look. "You told us—"

"I told you what you needed to hear, nothing more. The truth is very few people know how bad this is about to get. The only ones that know, besides me and some select researchers, are them." He jabbed his thumb at the big shots, packed close together in the clearing.

"If ecosystems are about to collapse," Caplan's eyes flitted to the forest, "then why do they look so healthy?"

"The Vallerio, along with many other places, look fine on the outside. But on the inside, they're rotting away at a jaw-dropping rate. In the next few years, my experts expect sixty-five percent of all families, eighty-five to ninety percent of all genera, and ninety-five to ninety-nine percent of all species to perish before nature's wrath."

Caplan wanted to leave. But he couldn't, not yet anyway. It wasn't that he trusted Corbotch. He didn't. Not really. He just ... well, he just wanted to be sure. "If that's a fact, then how come this is the first I'm hearing about it? How come the whole world isn't in crisis mode?"

"The smart people—survivalists like you—are prepping. They might not know the exact mechanism, but they can sense the coming disaster. The scientific community, by and large, is aware of the Holocene extinction. But they don't have my equipment, my resources. So, they have no idea how close it is or how bad things are about to get." He shrugged. "As for the general public, they're skeptical of the vague warnings delivered by the scientific community. And who can blame them? Rising politicization has undermined scientific credibility. Plus, the survival of captive populations obscures how many species are truly extinct in the wild. And many recent extinctions have been among life forms that get little attention, like arthropods."

Caplan readied a mocking quip. But then he noticed Morgan, noticed how she was looking at Corbotch. Something had clicked in her facial features, causing her skepticism to fade away. Horrible realization had taken its place. "Don't tell me you're buying this crap," he said.

She blinked, looked at Caplan. And in that moment, he knew that she wasn't just buying it. She understood it. Understood it like someone who had stared at puzzle pieces for years, but had only just now put them together.

"I thought rewilding could stop it," Corbotch continued. "I stocked the Vallerio's ecosystems with proxies. Bison, jaguars, zebras ... they all found a home here. But it didn't work. Remember the horse apple trees I told you about on the way here? Well, elephants didn't spread their seeds like we'd hoped. Not even close. And that's just the beginning. All in all, our rewilding project was a complete failure."

"That's when you hired us," Morgan said.

"Yes," Corbotch replied. "I brought in the finest minds the world had to offer and tasked you with the ultimate challenge ... recreating the entire spectrum of lost Pleistocene megafauna."

Morgan shook her head. "We only worked on megafauna indigenous to North America."

"True. But what makes you think Hatcher is my only research facility?"

Caplan gawked at him. "There are others?"

Corbotch merely smiled.

"I don't understand something," Morgan said after a moment. "Why'd you lie to us? Why didn't you just tell us the real timeline?"

"Make no mistake about it, Amanda. The world as you know it is about to undergo the largest extinction event of all time. Nothing can stop it. And that means people will die. Lots of people. Our entire species if my plans don't work. And even if they do, I'll only be able to save a tiny slice of the population. Those people—the best, brightest, and youngest—have already been selected. If I had told you that in advance, do you think you could've handled it?"

Morgan didn't hesitate. "Of course."

"You've got a sister, right? Lelanie, I believe."

Morgan froze.

So did Caplan. He knew about Tony, but a sister? Morgan had never mentioned her before.

"As I recall, she teaches fourth grade. In Florida, I think. She's clearly a bright woman and probably good at her job. But her skills, pardon me for saying this, will be useless in the coming world." He paused. "Do you think you could've handled that truth? Or would you have wasted time and resources fighting to keep her alive?"

Morgan didn't reply.

"So, she just dies?" Caplan shook his head. "You get a kick out of playing god, don't you?"

"Actually, I despise it," Corbotch replied. "Do you really think I like picking who lives or dies? I'm doing what I must to preserve our species."

You didn't seem to have a problem picking who died in your 1-Gen killing fields," Morgan whispered.

"That's different."

"You're a murderer."

"Those people threatened everything."

"They were innocent."

"They were greedy. Greedy for money, power, influence."

"It's still murder," Morgan said.

"I prefer to call it justice."

Morgan glared at him.

"I wish I could stop this," Corbotch continued. "But I can't. The best I can hope to do is prepare for the future. The Vallerio, Hatcher Station, even the 1- and 2-Gen animals are just a small part of what's to come. I've set wheels in motion across the globe. Wheels no one will see coming, wheels that will bring this planet and our species back from the brink of disaster. That is, assuming you don't kill me right here."

Just kill him, Caplan thought. *What's the worst that can happen? Hell, everyone's about to die anyway!*

But deep down, Caplan knew the issue was bigger than that. Corbotch had linked his very existence to the survival of their species. In other words, kill Corbotch and humanity was on its way out of evolution's backdoor. On the other hand, Corbotch was a master manipulator and a lunatic. A man who'd disposed of his enemies on a Pleistocene-inspired killing ground. Was he really the best person to lead the post-extinction world?

Caplan glanced at Morgan. Her gaze, unreadable, was locked on Corbotch. As he turned back to Corbotch, he saw the inferno. It was close enough that he could see the individual flames, the many strands of smoke.

Another roar rang out. Caplan blinked, stunned by its volume and power. It was louder than anything he'd heard in a long time.

Corbotch glanced over his shoulder. A smile creased his lips. "Do you know what that is?" he asked.

"A saber," Morgan replied tightly. "In case you've forgotten, I was there when they came out of their incubators."

"It's far too loud to be a mere saber, don't you think?"

Caplan cleared his throat. "Some of the 1-Gens might be going through growth spurts."

Corbotch's smile broadened.

"But you already knew that, didn't you?" Morgan's eyes narrowed. "Your guards controlled the unopened incubators. And they controlled the sabers and woolly mammoths via microchips. What's going on here, James?"

"You'll find out soon enough." Corbotch looked at Caplan and Morgan in turn. "Julius went looking for Derek. They'll be back any minute now. And when they do, I want the two of you to come with us. What do you say?"

Decision time had arrived. And Caplan didn't have the slightest clue what to do. If the Holocene extinction was imminent—and based on Morgan's reaction, that seemed to be the case—then Corbotch was probably the only person in the world who could save them. But could they even trust Corbotch? Once they put their safety into his hands, what would stop the old man from executing them?

"Zach!"

Caplan, acting on instinct, had started to turn before he even heard the shout. At the edge of the clearing, he saw Pearson. He saw the hand cannon.

Saw it leveled at him.

CHAPTER 58

Caplan lifted his gun, but a loud blast, followed by a rush of air against his left cheek, froze him in place.

"Drop your weapons," Pearson shouted. "Now."

Caplan's nostrils flared in anger. Had he really come all this way just to die? Why had he allowed Corbotch to captivate him? Why hadn't he just grabbed the helicopter as planned?

His brain skipped through various courses of action. Unfortunately, Corbotch was too far away to be used as a human shield. And he didn't like his odds in a straight-up gunfight. Lowering his weapon, playing the cooperation game ... that was the most prudent option.

But something nagged at him. *Why bother disarming us?* Caplan wondered. *Why doesn't he just kill us?*

Caplan glanced at Morgan. She was in the process of putting her weapon on the ground. He gave her a little head-shake. She got the message and stood up again, rifle still cradled in her arms.

"One last chance," Pearson shouted. "Drop them or die."

Keeping the pistol at his side, Caplan shot a quick glance at the big shots. They made no sudden move for the pile of guns Morgan had taken from them. Instead, they smiled pathetically at Pearson, like he was some kind of avenging angel of death.

Caplan had mixed feelings about Corbotch. But his feelings toward Pearson lacked even a trace of ambiguity. Here was the man who'd injected him with HA-78, who'd heartlessly let him kill dozens of innocent people. "What's the point?" Caplan called out, half-hoping all the commotion would bring a flood of 1-Gens into the clearing. "You're going to kill us anyway."

Pearson marched across the field. His gun didn't waver as he aimed it at Caplan's forehead. "Where's Derek?"

Ahh! So, that explained it. They needed Perkins to fly the helicopter. And Pearson was gambling that Caplan and Morgan knew where to find him. Which, of course, they did.

Not that Caplan was about to admit that.

"Who?" Caplan asked innocently.

"Don't bullshit me," Pearson said. "Where is he?"

The crackling flames turned ear-shattering. Caplan glanced at the fire and saw giant trunks snap like twigs and topple over, adding more fuel to the inferno. The fire was less than 100 yards away. But Pearson didn't seem to care and at that moment, neither did Caplan.

For at the edge of the clearing, he saw bristling grass. Tall blades folded over, only to spring up again as yet more blades were pushed to the ground. Someone—or something—was sneaking through the field, heading straight for Pearson.

Got to distract him, Caplan thought. *But how?*

Nothing clever came to mind. And so Caplan just forced laughter. And not softly. These were giant belly laughs, worthy of the finest mall Santa Claus. And after a few seconds, they became real. Caplan laughed so hard tears started to stream down his cheeks. He laughed away his grief, his pain, his sorrow. He laughed because he was still alive and laughed because he might not live much longer.

Pearson cocked a confused eyebrow at Corbotch.

Corbotch shrugged.

"Hey Julius." Caplan's insides hurt from all the laughter. "You know what's essential for a practical joke to work?"

Pearson frowned. "What the hell are you talking about?"

"A rube that doesn't see it coming."

Pearson's eyes narrowed, then bulged. Abruptly, the grass folded behind him. Something struck his legs. He grunted and flopped onto his face.

Caplan darted forward.

The big shots started to move forward as well, but a single burst from Morgan's rifle kept them in check.

Perkins' head appeared above the grass. His hand, now clutching Pearson's hand cannon, lifted high into the air. Seconds later, he swung it at the ground. Metal struck flesh.

Caplan halted next to Perkins and peered down in amazement. The mighty Pearson lay unmoving on a pile of bent grass and mud. Blood trickled out of the back of his skull and took the gravity ride to the ground, leaving long red streaks on the man's neck.

Perkins raised the gun again. But Caplan grabbed his arm, arresting his movement. "Cockpit," he said. "Now."

Perkins nodded and jumped to his feet. His body trembled from nervous energy as he stuck the hand cannon into his waistband. Then he ran to the helicopter and entered the cockpit. Within moments, the rotors started to whirl at a low speed.

"Bailey, Tricia, Brian!" Caplan shouted as a wave of boiling heat passed over him. "It's time to go!"

Toland burst out of the tree line and ran for the chopper. Mills, who was helping Elliott, followed at a distance.

As Toland huffed and puffed past him, Caplan gave the man an annoyed look. "Whatever happened to chivalry?"

"Feminism killed it," Toland retorted with a wheeze. "Thank the goddess for that."

Ignoring the burgeoning heat, Caplan ran to Elliott's other side and slipped under her shoulder. As he and Mills dragged her toward the helicopter, he felt a small change inside his brain. So many people—too many—had already died. Did he want to add more to the body count?

Corbotch and Pearson had obvious blood on their hands. He assumed the same about the big shots. And they would pay for their crimes. But that didn't mean they deserved to die. It didn't mean they were beyond redemption.

Just then, a woman—Deborah Keifer—shouted something unintelligible. Abruptly, the big shots whirled around.

Morgan shifted her rifle. But the big shots didn't race for the pile of guns. Curiously enough, they didn't rush the helicopter either. Instead, they hurried across the field, waddling like penguins in their Sunday best, and shooting terrified looks at the oncoming inferno.

"What are you—?" Caplan cupped his hands around his mouth. "Get back here!"

A few of the big shots twisted their heads around. But they stared at the fire, not at him.

Then Keifer looked over her shoulder. Her gaze met Caplan's and he saw a look of profound terror in her otherwise-vapid eyes. The sort of terror that couldn't be explained by the laws of this world.

Keifer faced front again. Arms flapping at her sides, she propelled herself to the tree line and past it. Moments later, the other big shots followed her into the forest.

Without breaking stride, Mills, Elliott, and Caplan continued across the field. They passed by the spot where Perkins had attacked Pearson. Caplan saw smooshed grass and little puddles of blood.

But no Pearson.

Immediately, he turned his attention to the pile of guns.

Again, no Pearson.

Caplan scanned the rest of the clearing. But the big shots had trampled a lot of grass, obscuring any clues the man might have left behind.

A loud burst filled the air. Caplan glanced at the fire. It was approximately fifty yards out, as tall as a skyscraper, and seemed to stretch for a whole city block. The flames ran the spectrum of the fire rainbow, from red to orange to white. They moved forward with firm, deliberate speed, still throbbing and trembling. Between and above the flames, he saw billowing gray smoke, along with significant patches of blackness. Loud crackles, along with monstrous roaring, like an airplane about to take off, nearly deafened him.

Caplan and Mills hauled Elliott to the helicopter. Morgan jumped into the cabin and grabbed her by the armpits. Toland frowned in annoyance but he deigned to help out as well. Together, they hauled Elliott aboard.

Mills paused, her eyes traveling to the point where the big shots had entered the forest. "How long do you think they'll last out there?"

"Longer than us if we don't get airborne." Caplan jabbed his thumb at the cabin. "Your turn."

Without hesitation, she clambered into the cabin. Then she turned around, offered her hand to Caplan.

But Caplan hesitated. There was still the matter of Corbotch, the man who had started this whole thing. Corbotch's resources could definitely improve their odds of survival. On the other hand, he was responsible for dozens of deaths.

Hot air engulfed Caplan and his forehead turned slick with sweat. He tasted ash and smoke in the air. The odor of burnt wood filled his nostrils.

If anyone deserved to die, it was Corbotch. But Caplan's instincts told him that was the wrong move. And not just because they might need Corbotch to survive the coming extinction. But because … well, just because.

"Your turn." Caplan rotated toward Corbotch. "Get in …"

But no one was there.

Corbotch was gone.

CHAPTER 59

Date: June 19, 2016, 8:37 p.m.; Location: Sector 48A, Vallerio Forest, NH

The rotors gained speed, spinning faster and faster. Caplan steadied himself against a metal bar next to the open cabin door as a rush of hot air washed over him. The blowing air was loud, but the fire—now just twenty-five yards away—easily drowned it out.

Swiveling away from the fire, Caplan studied the clearing, searching for Corbotch, Pearson, or any big shots that had rethought their plans to flee the oncoming flames. But all he saw was grass.

He glanced over his shoulder. Toland and Morgan sat in the two plush seats directly behind the cockpit. Toland lounged in his chair, eyes closed, as if all was right with the world. Occasionally, a snore would escape his lips. In contrast, Morgan hunched forward, her elbows resting on her knees. Her hands were cupped around her cheeks and she stared straight ahead, a pensive look upon her face.

Mills sat across from Morgan. Her legs, along with her muddied and bloodied feet, were curled upon her chair. Her forehead was plastered against her window. Elliott sat next to her, securely buckled into her seat. Physically, she looked fine. But deep stress lines, probably permanent now, crisscrossed her visage. Her eyes were hazy and unfocused and Caplan guessed that no amount of therapy would change that. Not that it mattered since she, along with the rest of them, would apparently be dead in a few months anyway.

There was an empty seat in the cockpit. But Caplan didn't bother to take it. As soon as they'd flown clear of the fire, he had every intention of taking a page out of Toland's playbook. He'd lie down on the plush wool carpet, prop his grime-soaked head up on his backpack, and grab a few Z's of his own. Just the thought of it caused a small smile to flit across his face.

Gusts of gray smoke shot into the clearing and swept into the cabin. Toland's eyes opened wide. He sucked in a mouthful of smoke and then started coughing. "Close ..." He hacked a few times. "Close the damn door!"

"The others ..." Caplan coughed as well. "... they're still out there."

"They can go to hell."

The rotors picked up even more speed. Tons of gray smoke blew into the chopper. It got in Caplan's lungs and in his eyes. He couldn't breathe, couldn't see. Rubbing his face on his shirt and fighting off more coughs, he cast a look at the fire.

"Whoa," he whispered in awe.

The fire was no longer twenty-five yards away or even ten yards away.

It was here.

Gigantic flames, tall as skyscrapers and bright as spotlights, licked the edge of the clearing with ravenous desire. The colors, brilliant reds and oranges along with an almost bluish white all against a throbbing, trembling black backdrop, captivated his attention.

The chopper lurched a few inches off the ground. It swayed in the air like a pendulum before shooting toward the center of the clearing.

Caplan stumbled. His sweaty hand slipped on the metal bar, but he managed to keep his grip on it. With his other hand, he reached for the cabin door.

A weighty object plowed into his legs. His feet slipped out from under him and his rear thudded against the carpet. His lower half felt like it had suddenly doubled in size and his grip on the bar began to slip all over again.

Morgan unbuckled her belt, grabbed for his hand.

But she was too late.

Caplan's fingers slipped off the bar. The chopper lurched as he tumbled feet-first to the ground. He landed awkwardly, twisting his knee, and rolled to a heap. The fire raged all around him, encircling the clearing and burning away at the deep grass.

Caplan tried to think, but the wildfire completely overloaded his senses. Blinding colors were everywhere he looked. He smelled burning wood and grass. Heard nothing but crackling flames, splintering tree trunks, and those awful roaring noises. Smoke filled his mouth and lungs and the pulsating heat roasted him like he was in an oven.

Confused and disoriented, he tried to get up. But again, he felt the weighty object. It pinned him down, held him flat to the rapidly scorching earth. Looking up, he saw a hazy form mounted on his chest. He blinked a few times. His eyes cleared.

And he saw Pearson.

A heavy fist cracked into his cheek. Caplan's jaw snapped open and he choked out a hoarse cry. Instantly, smoke and ash streamed down his lungs, leaving him coughing and choking for air.

He wriggled, trying to throw off the giant man. But a fist to the collarbone stopped him cold. A third punch slammed into his jaw. His whole body shuddered as if his soul had been knocked clear out of him.

A thick fog settled over Caplan's brain. His pain and fear melted away. It was kind of nice, actually. Languid and peaceful, like the first few moments after waking up from a deep sleep. Where was he again? Why was he here? Did any of it really matter?

Julius is killing you, Zach, his brain screamed. *Julius! Do you really want to let him get the best of you?*

He shook his head. The fog began to lift and his body groaned in protest.

Then the pain appeared.

It roared through him with a vengeance, racking his body and causing him to squirm and writhe on the ground.

Pearson lost his balance and fell to one side.

With pain came clarity and in a split-second, Caplan realized the precariousness of his position. Walls of fire surrounded the clearing, blocking off possible exits and sucking oxygen out of his lungs. The helicopter couldn't be far away. But before he could climb aboard, he needed to deal with Pearson. And not only was Pearson bigger and stronger than him, the man seemed to have lost all concern for self-preservation.

Caplan rose to his feet. Stumbled to one side. Then to the other. Smoke was everywhere, all around him. It felt like he was standing in a caldera, waiting for a volcano to erupt. Lifting his eyes, he saw the helicopter, cloaked in smoke, hovering a couple of feet off the ground.

But before he could run toward it, Pearson rolled to his feet directly between Caplan and the chopper. The giant took several deep breaths, inhaling the smoke as if it were oxygen. It seemed to pump him up and he rose to his full height, swaggering like a professional wrestler.

Looking over Pearson's shoulder, Caplan caught glimpses of Morgan amidst the smoke. She clutched the metal bar in one hand and held the pistol in her other one. But the chopper swung wildly, back and forth, and she couldn't get good stability. Even if she could, he wasn't sure she'd take the shot with all the smoke.

Caplan looked into Pearson's eyes. He didn't bother with bargaining or reasoning. There was no point. Pearson clearly had no interest in boarding the helicopter and escaping the flames. The giant was perfectly willing to die.

As long as he took Caplan with him.

Caplan's thoughts returned to their last altercation. Pearson had sucker-punched him in the clearing and then wailed away at him. Despite the recent beating, Caplan still remembered those earlier punches, still felt them deep in his bones. Pearson was simply too powerful to take on *mano a mano*.

Caplan reached for his jaw, gently massaging it. It hurt like hell. "Is that the best you've got?" he mumbled, barely swallowing his pain.

"Not even close." Pearson slammed his right fist into his left palm. "I'm going to break your face. And I'm going to enjoy it."

"You couldn't break bread without an instruction manual and someone to read it to you."

Pearson's face reddened. "Think you're smarter than me? Then how come I tricked you into taking that HA-78 shot?"

"You didn't trick me. James did. You were just his tool."

Pearson's face grew as red as the flames.

"And you're still his tool. Want to know how I can tell?" Caplan grinned, pouring fuel on the verbal fire. "Because he's long gone and you're still here."

"Not for long. I'm going to kill you and get the hell out of this place."

"Correction. I'm leaving in the helicopter. You're leaving in an urn."

Bellowing at the top of his lungs, Pearson rushed forward.

Caplan raised his fists, adopting a boxer's stance.

Still running, Pearson cocked his fist and took a wild swing.

Time slowed down for Caplan. He saw Pearson's scarred knuckles and taut muscles. He studied the man's footing and range of motion.

Then he ducked.

Pearson's swing missed by a country mile. Digging his heels into the soft mud, he fought to shift course.

Caplan whirled around and gave him a powerful shove.

The extra momentum, coupled with Pearson's awkward movements, sent the man reeling to the side. He fell down, taking a whole section of grass blades with him.

The sound of splintering wood grew deafening. Pines, spruces, and cedars began to sway. Air whooshed and something hot and soft struck Caplan's head. Peering upward, he saw hundreds of fiery pine cones raining from the sky.

Caplan didn't bother to throw more punches. Instead, he raced across the clearing, plowing through burning grass and across patches of baked soil. And all the while, he watched the hovering helicopter, watched Morgan's outstretched hand.

The splintering turned into full-blown cracking. Spinning his head from side to side, Caplan saw trees immersed in hot flames. They disintegrated before his eyes and began spitting out pieces of red-hot bark and chunks of blazing wood.

And then the trees started to fall.

A thick pine tree, some 200 feet tall, was the first to go. It slammed to the earth, just a few feet behind Caplan. The earth trembled and he lost his balance, falling to the ground.

Another pine tree, positioned to the southeast, broke free. It crashed into the first tree, sending waves of sparks into the air.

Caplan leapt to his feet. His eyes shot skyward and ice crept through his boiling blood.

Everywhere he looked, he saw shattering, falling trees. They collapsed in all directions, but the vast majority looked like they were headed for the clearing.

Caplan ran forward and vaulted over a thick cedar tree. His trail-runners hit dirt on the other side and he kept going, picking up speed and trying not to get hit by the plummeting, burning tree trunks.

The smoke thickened. He could barely breathe, let alone see. Based purely on instinct, he leapt into the air. A blast of hot air struck his side as a tree narrowly missed crunching into his skull. Thick smoke wafted around him, enclosing him in its nonexistent grip. He shifted his hand, grasping for something, anything.

His palm struck something ... was that? ... yes! The landing skid! His fingers closed around it, grasping it in a vice grip. His body jolted and he dangled in mid-air for a moment. Then he reached up and grabbed the skid with his other hand.

Morgan's face appeared in the smoke. She grabbed his wrists and braced herself. "I've got him," she yelled to Perkins.

The helicopter rose a few inches. Caplan kicked his dangling feet, trying to wrap them around the skid. Failing, he rested for a moment, gathering his strength. Then he started to kick them up again.

Muscular arms slammed into his legs, wrapping around them. Caplan jolted again and he nearly lost his grip on the skid. Looking down, he saw Pearson clutching his thighs, hovering a foot or two above a fallen and fiery pine tree.

Pearson stared at Caplan. His cheeks were bright red and his lip curled from the effort of maintaining his grip. His eyes flashed with lively insanity.

Morgan's fingertips dug into Caplan's wrists. He tried to shake off the bigger man. When that failed, he attempted to pull himself upward. But Pearson's size acted as a veritable anchor, slowly dragging Caplan into a sea of fire and falling trees.

An enormous roar, accompanied by a fierce gust of wind, slammed into the helicopter and Caplan. The chopper shot to the side. Morgan lost her grip on Caplan's wrist and tumbled into the cabin.

What the hell was that? Caplan thought.

For a single moment, he forgot about the fire, about Pearson, about his weakening grip on the landing skid. His head turned to the south and he saw the massive wildfire. But he saw something else, too. A giant shadow of shifting, thumping blackness.

Trees cracked and splintered, falling to the northwest and northeast. The shadow surged forward and Caplan glimpsed something he'd never expected to see in his entire life. Something that didn't belong in this world, during this epoch or any other. Something that shocked him to his very core.

It was a saber-toothed tiger. But not the sort of saber that had roamed the world thousands of years earlier. This saber was different. It was monstrous. No. It was far beyond monstrous.

It was a behemoth.

CHAPTER 60

Date: June 19, 2016, 8:46 p.m.; Location: Sector 48A, Vallerio Forest, NH

Since he'd first arrived in the Vallerio, Caplan had seen a dire wolf, a short-faced bear, a giant ground sloth, an American mastodon, an American lion, a North American jaguar, and an American cheetah. He'd felt their wrath and watched as they'd dished it out on people as well as on each other. But nothing could've prepared him for the shock of seeing that saber.

He estimated its height at roughly thirty feet. The darkness and blazing inferno kept him from seeing its full length. However, he could see four tree-like legs and a distant swishing tail. Its eyes were lava-orange and blazed hotter than the surrounding fire. And those curving teeth on either side of its jaw were longer than he was tall.

Glad I don't have to feed you, Caplan thought. *And don't even think about feeding on me.*

The saber strode through the wildfire like it was nothing, its enormous paws stomping on shattered and broiling tree trunks. It stopped just outside the tree-strewn clearing and bared its massive teeth for all to see. Then it lifted its head and roared at the sky.

Vicious shockwaves shot across the clearing, striking the chopper and sending it into a tight circle. Caplan's right hand slipped off the landing skid. He jolted and his left hand began to slide as well.

Perkins worked the controls, arresting the chopper's momentum. Caplan managed to grab the skid again with both hands. But the effort depleted his reserves. He was simply spent and no amount of fear or anger was going to change that.

Pearson released his grip on Caplan's thighs. Caplan experienced a momentary wellspring of hope. But it didn't last long. Less than a second later, he felt Pearson's right hand grab hold of his belt. The man's left hand latched onto his shirt.

And then Pearson began to climb.

What does he think I am? Caplan thought. *A ladder?*

Inch by inch, Pearson climbed up Caplan's body. And Caplan was helpless to stop him. He had just two moves left. Let Pearson finish the climb and possibly kill his friends. Or release the landing skid and fall to his doom.

More sweat beaded up on Caplan's hands, further greasing his grip. Unable to move, he resolved to hang as long as possible or until Pearson was in reach of the skid. Then he'd let go. Because, quite frankly, there was no way in hell he was going to let Pearson hurt anyone else ever again.

The helicopter rose a few more feet, shifting wildly from side to side as Perkins fought to dodge dozens of falling tree trunks. The saber lowered its head and stared at the chopper with abject curiosity. As Caplan stared into its giant pupils, he couldn't help but wonder if the saber had any type of self-awareness. Did it know how it had come into this world? Did it care that it had grown to a size nearly double that of a giraffe, the heretofore tallest animal of modern times?

And he wondered how it saw things. What did it make of the chopper? Did it consider the mechanical marvel and its strange occupants to be some kind of rival? A complex predator, possibly?

Or did it see them as mere prey?

Jaws gnashing, the saber bounded into the clearing.

"Look out," Mills shouted.

Perkins didn't flinch. With precision-like movements, he sent the chopper sailing across the smoke-filled clearing, weaving back and forth to avoid the sudden appearance of crumbling, burning pines and cedars.

The saber clambered after them, its paws crunching the cylindrical tree trunks, it jaws drawing ever closer to the metallic rotorcraft.

Morgan regained her footing. Staggering from side to side, she approached the cabin door. But at that exact moment, Perkins swung the chopper into a steep banking maneuver and began to gain height. Morgan toppled back into the cabin and bashed her head against the minibar.

The behemoth followed after it, its eyes blazing with deadly malice. Its long curving canines cut through the smoke time and time again, missing the flying contraption by mere inches.

And all the while, Pearson continued to climb. His head pulled level with Caplan's waist, then stomach. Then chest.

Think, Caplan's brain screamed. *Use your head!*

Perkins threw the chopper into another steep bank before coaxing the craft a couple more feet into the air. A dazed Morgan started to roll toward the open cabin door. But Mills loosened her buckle and wrapped her arms around Morgan's waist.

Caplan glanced to his right. He saw they were above the creature's eyes but within easy reach of its long paws.

The saber must've realized this as well. Abandoning its previous approach, it reared up on its hind legs and swatted at the helicopter with its front paws. Perkins anticipated the move and pushed the craft northwest. Undeterred, the saber jumped forward a few feet and tried again. Again, Perkins was forced to direct the helicopter to the clearing's northwest corner.

"It's boxing us in," Perkins yelled.

"Can you take us through the forest?" Mills called out.

"Not in one piece."

Looking northwest, Caplan saw what Perkins meant. The inferno had ravaged much of the Vallerio's coniferous trees. But many others stood tall, their limbs ablaze, serving as both impervious obstacles and potentially deadly traps.

Caplan's throat hurt from all the smoke he'd inhaled. His fingers, still curled around the skid, stung like hell. The stinging traveled up his arms and directly into his brain. He wanted to let go, needed to let go.

Think, Zach, think, he screamed silently. *Use your head!*

Perkins halted the helicopter a few feet from the edge of the clearing. Quickly, he set to work gaining altitude. But Caplan knew it would be too little and far too late.

The saber jumped close, so close it didn't bother rising up on its hind legs. Instead, it opened its jaws and lunged upward at the helicopter.

"Remember me?" Pearson, sporting a wicked grin, grabbed Caplan's shoulders and pulled himself up to an even level. "Cuz it's the last thing you're going to remember."

Don't listen to him, Caplan thought. *Just use your head. Use … your … head.*

With the last of his strength, he lunged at Pearson. His forehead smashed into the man's skull.

A fleshy, cracking noise rang out. Pearson blinked, clearly startled. His fingers tensed up and he lost his grip.

Then he fell.

Pearson shouted, not out of terror but out of sheer anger.

Caplan watched the man fall, watched as an abyss of blackness, buttressed by giant yellow teeth and an enormous pink tongue, rose up to meet him.

The saber's jaws snapped shut with perfect timing, slicing the still-shouting Pearson neatly in half. Part of the man's body vanished down the creature's gullet. The other part spun through the smoke-choked air, sputtering blood and guts into the waiting inferno.

Despite his aching skull, Caplan's lips curled upward.

And he smiled.

CHAPTER 61

Flames swiftly consumed Pearson's remains and Caplan shifted his smoke-infested eyes to the fiery clearing. Tree trunks were stacked high and burned brightly. They looked like logs in a super-sized campfire.

A snarl, ferocious and loud, assaulted his ears. Wincing, he stared at the saber. It was still close by, still staring at him with those lava-orange eyes.

Caplan's fingers still ached and his muscles were close to exhaustion. But at least he was no longer supporting Pearson's weight. At the same time, the loss of ballast allowed the chopper to climb just a bit faster and on a more even keel.

Morgan wrenched herself to the cabin door and fell flat on the carpet. With Mills holding her legs, she reached out and grabbed Caplan's wrists. With the extra support, Caplan was able to shift strength to his lower half.

The saber rose up on its hind legs. Snarling and spitting, it lunged at the chopper.

Swinging his body, Caplan kicked his legs into the air. The saber's paw passed beneath him, so close he could feel the creature's bristling fur.

Quickly, he hooked his legs around the landing skid. Waves of pleasure and pain flooded his arms as he relaxed his fingers.

The chopper soared higher and higher, rising well above the saber. Then Perkins leveled out the craft and they hovered above the inferno, shrouded in thick columns of gray smoke.

Morgan released his wrists and grabbed his shoulders. With her help, he grabbed onto the cabin door and then dragged himself into the craft. As he flopped on the ground, sputtering out smoke and ash, Morgan slammed the door shut.

"You okay?" Perkins called out.

"Just ..." Caplan hacked a few more times. "... peachy."

Perkins nodded. "Well, where to?"

Where to, indeed? The question sent Caplan's mind spinning off in all sorts of directions. Back to New York? Somewhere else?

And what would they do when they landed? Return to their lives as if nothing had happened? Go underground in case someone came looking for them?

And so on and so forth. Truthfully, Caplan didn't know what to do, now or at any point in the future. It was all just a complete blank. At the same time, he noticed the others looking at him expectantly, waiting for his answer. They would, he realized, follow him anywhere. That fact scared him more than anything. Well, almost anything.

"Just head south," he said. "To the nearest airfield."

"Will do."

More questions filled Caplan's head. What, if anything, should he do about the coming extinction? Should he tell the world, even though he knew no one would listen? Should he put his survival skills to the test and find a place to bunker down, to ride out the storm? Should he invite the others to join him?

His coughs faded away. His breathing normalized. He slid to the minibar and pressed his back against it, feeling its coolness through his shredded and mud-laden shirt.

He felt something in his pocket. Reaching inside, he pulled out the amber-colored pill container. It was chock full of tablets. Glancing at the cockpit, he cleared his throat. "What do you know about HA-78?"

"Not a lot," Perkins admitted. "It was one of James' side projects. I was vaccinated months ago along with a whole bunch of his inner circle."

"He created it?"

"Not him. One of his research teams."

"The tablets ... if I take one, will that cure me?"

"I'm afraid not. The tablets don't cure anything. They just suppress symptoms. So, you—all of you—are asymptomatic carriers."

"So, we're contagious." Caplan frowned. "Forget the airfield. Take us to ... I don't know ... someplace without people."

As Perkins returned to the controls, Caplan stuffed the container back into his pocket. Great, just great. They were infected with a disease none of them understood. All he knew was that anyone who came within shouting distance of them required a tablet to stave off death.

Guess I can forget about New York, he thought.

Morgan looked at Elliott, then at Mills. "Is she okay?" she asked with a nod at Elliott.

Mills shrugged.

"Back in the forest, you said something about a barn-like building," Morgan said. "And she mentioned wheels and tubes."

Mills' gaze shot to the minibar where it lingered for a few seconds. Then she exhaled. "We saw smoke and followed it to a building. An electric fence surrounded it. The power was out, the fence had been knocked down, and the building had been set ablaze. We'd seen these elephant-like animals earlier in the day. One of them probably did it."

"These animals ... were they woolly mammoths?"

Mills nodded.

Caplan exchanged knowing glances with Morgan. The Blare had most likely caused the power outage. Some 1-Gen woolly mammoths had overrun the fences, killed everyone, and set the building ablaze in the process. And that burning building, he thought, might just explain another mystery. "So, that wildfire ... that came from the building?" he asked.

She nodded. "We thought we'd put it out. Unfortunately, it blazed up again."

"And the wheels?" Morgan asked.

"They were in the basement. Tricia and I went down there while Brian kept watch. She opened one and we saw this dead guy." Mills winced. "At first, we thought the wheel was an isolation chamber. But the guy was plugged into it with wires and tubes. Tricia guessed it was some kind of life-support system and that the power failure had killed him. But who builds over a dozen life support systems in the middle of nowhere?"

A barn-like building? Life support systems? A corpse? Apparently, Corbotch's Vallerio-based projects weren't restricted to Hatcher Station. And that thought made Caplan's skin crawl.

He studied Mills for a moment. She was frazzled and in desperate need of a shower. The large logbook he'd seen earlier sat neatly in her lap. She held it with both hands as if her life depended on it. "What's that?" he asked.

"This?" She glanced at the book. "Truthfully, I don't know. I don't even know why I still have it. All I know is that I found it near the wheels."

Caplan's eyes traced the leather cover and he saw the title, etched in fine bronze lettering. *Apex Predator?* he thought. *What the hell is that?*

"Sweet Jesus." Perkins whistled in awe.

Elliott stared straight ahead, apparently still stuck in some kind of mental hell. But Toland, Morgan, and Mills all swiveled toward the nearest windows. They tensed up. Their jaws fell agape.

Caplan, well past the point of physical exhaustion, waited for someone to say something. But other than the whirling of rotors and the quiet buzz of electricity, the cabin remained silent.

With a sharp groan, he struggled to one knee. Twisting around, he looked out the side window.

They'd flown clear of the fire and so he saw pristine evergreen and deciduous forest in the darkness. It was thick and green and full of ancient mysticism. This was the Vallerio he wished to remember. The Vallerio of hidden secrets and youthful dreams. But there was no going back to that Vallerio. For him, the forest had undergone an irrevocable change and …

He frowned. Leaned closer to the window.

Wide paths zigzagged through the forest, veering in all directions. It looked like someone had taken an army of bulldozers to the place, chopping away at the trees with reckless and directionless abandon.

He focused on one of the paths. Pressed his forehead against the window and watched as a patch of textured blackness cut a gigantic path below him. Abruptly, the textured blackness shifted like ripples in an ocean. And then it started to rise.

Caplan recoiled in shock. The textured blackness … it was fur. Distinct wiry fur. He couldn't believe it. It was the same short-faced bear that had chased Morgan and him in the lab facility with one key difference.

It was larger.

Much larger.

The creature's shoulders rose some forty feet off the forest floor. It rumbled through the forest with ease, causing the ground to quake and once-mighty tree trunks to fall before its wrath.

Abruptly, it paused. Then it glanced over its shoulder. As if sensing Caplan's gaze, its orangish eyes shot toward the helicopter. Its body froze. Then it spun around in a slow circle and rose up and up and up. All the way up to its full height of some eighty feet.

Caplan's jaw hung from its hinges. Other than maybe a blue whale, it was easily the largest mammal on Earth.

"I feel like ... like ..." Toland stared out his window. "... like Professor Challenger. Exploring that plateau deep in the Amazonian basin, watching iguanodons and stegosauruses and ... and ..." He trailed off.

Wait, Caplan thought. *He's not looking out of this window.*

Turning around, he looked out the opposite window. He saw a second path. Then a third one. His heart pitter-pattered against his chest. Everywhere he looked, he saw giant animals.

Behemoths.

"There must be dozens of them," Mills whispered. "Maybe more."

"Where are they going?" Morgan asked.

"Every animal that came out of Hatcher seemed determined to go on a killing spree," Caplan said slowly. "And since those ones aren't attacking each other, that must be looking for new targets."

"Oh, my God." Morgan's eyes opened wide. "They're heading for the exterior fence."

"And if they get through ..." Caplan trailed off.

A moment of silence filled the cabin as everyone pondered the implications of the behemoths breaking out of the Vallerio and going on a multi-pronged rampage.

Undoubtedly, the U.S. military would be called in to fight them. But could mere bombs stop animals of that size? Maybe, maybe not. Regardless, Caplan knew one thing for sure. For thousands of years, mankind had reigned as Earth's apex predator. But between the behemoths and the coming extinction, that rule seemed destined to end.

Caplan glanced at Morgan, then at the others. They stared back at him, eyes boring holes into his skull, waiting upon his words.

"Okay," he said at last. "Here's what we're going to do …"

Apex Predator Logbook

Apex Predator Memorandum
Date: October 5, 2011, 11:55 p.m.
To: Vallerio Foundation, Stage II Team
From: Deborah Keifer
RE: HA-78 compound results, recent security breach

With the first round of tests behind us, I thought it prudent to discuss the efficacy results of the initial HA-78 compound. But first, I would like to take the opportunity to offer all of you, most especially Dr. Bishop, a hearty 'thank you' for your hard work on developing the compound. Because of your efforts, I am now confident we can complete Stage II of the Apex Predator project on deadline.

The HA-78 compound showed enormous promise in this, its initial iteration. As you know, fourteen primary subjects were exposed to the compound for various time periods, ranging from three seconds to three days. Each of these subjects was then exposed to three separate secondary subjects of varying age and health.

All primary subjects showed strong symptoms—moist and glassy eyes, purplish lips, foaming mouths, difficulty breathing, etc.—within four minutes of exposure. Similar results were shown in the secondary subjects. And all subjects, primary and secondary, died of asphyxiation and/or massive organ failure within thirty minutes of exposure.

At this point, it appears that the HA-78 compound carries an incubation period and latency period of roughly four minutes apiece. Unfortunately, these results are unsatisfactory for our needs. The compound is simply *too effective*. A short latency period, of course, is highly desirable. But we require a much longer incubation period if we are to spread the HA-78 compound far and wide without raising the eyebrows of doctors and public health officials.

Your task, Stage II team, is to continue to help Dr. Bishop develop the HA-78 compound to its fullest potential. As part of that, I am moving your operations to a new facility in New Hampshire's Vallerio Forest. It is my sincerest belief that this will allow you to achieve greater focus as well as substantially reduce the risk of another security breach.

In regards to the unfortunate and recent breach, please know I'm fully aware of and appreciate the terrible moral implications of your work. All Vallerio Foundation personnel, none more so than myself, know the awesome responsibilities we have undertaken. Please remember the Holocene extinction is imminent and will be upon us in approximately five years. Nothing can stop it and the *Homo sapiens* species will certainly not survive what is to come. This is what makes your work with the HA-78 compound so critical. The only way to save mankind is, unfortunately, to hasten its demise.

Thank you again for your continued support and devotion to this, the most urgent of causes.

END OF BOOK ONE

AUTHOR'S NOTE

Thank you for reading *BEHEMOTH*, my first foray into the *Apex Predator* universe. I've waited many years to write this book and it all came out in a four-month whirlwind of powerful emotions, late nights, and personal milestones, topped off by that incredible moment my wife and I welcomed our first child into this world.

The seeds for *BEHEMOTH* were planted during my childhood in northern Virginia. An ancient forest, dreamy yet dark and mysterious, rested within walking distance of my home. Many weekends, I'd strap on my explorer's belt, take my water-filled canteen from my mother, and hike into the wild with my father. Along the way, he'd regale me with tall tales about 'giant bears' and my imagination would run wild. We never did find those bears (although I often heard odd roars whenever my dad wandered off!), but those outings provided me with a lifetime of inspiration.

As I sit here on this warm September afternoon, my newborn son nestled safely in my lap, I find myself thinking about the cyclical nature of life and relationships. In a way, *BEHEMOTH* is about those cycles—mass extinction and speciation, the extinction and possible de-extinction of individual species, breaking up and coming together again—and how we might handle them.

So, what's next for Zach, Amanda, Bailey, and everyone else? That depends on you. I have many stories to tell and many ways I want to tell them. Graphic novels, lost journals, films, video games, and so on. But none of that will happen without your support.

Please post reviews for *BEHEMOTH* on Amazon, other book sites, and on social media. Tell your friends and family members about it. Create *Apex Predator* art and send it to me (maybe it'll end up in a future book!). Anything you can do to help spread the word is much appreciated.

Finally, make sure to sign up for my newsletter at **eepurl.com/CVjj5** to ensure you're the first to know about upcoming stories.

Thanks for your support!
David Meyer

READY FOR MORE?

Then turn the page for a preview of *CHAOS*, the first book in David Meyer's bestselling *Cy Reed Adventures*.

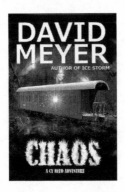

The *Cy Reed Adventures* consists of four books, *CHAOS*, *ICE STORM*, *TORRENT*, and *VAPOR*. Follow along as treasure hunter / salvage expert Cy Reed crisscrosses the globe, searching for ancient relics, battling mythical monsters, and unraveling mysteries of history!

 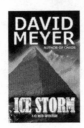 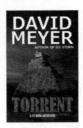 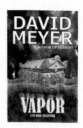

PROLOGUE

The Omega (March 6, 1976)

The long, twisting tunnel should've been empty.

Fred Jenson's heart skipped a beat as he examined the gigantic black shadow that rose menacingly out of the darkness. Why was a subway car still in the tunnel? Had it been damaged by the fire?

Sweat poured from his forehead, soaking his grimy face. His hands shook as he lifted the plastic bottle of bourbon and tipped a few ounces down his throat. It didn't burn. It never burned.

Not anymore.

He stared at the car through bleary eyes. Must be fire damaged. That was the only explanation that made sense. But if that was the case, why did it look so normal?

Jenson inched forward. He didn't want trouble. He merely wanted to see the destruction. The old-timer who slept in the maintenance shack said it was the worst disaster he'd ever seen. Maybe even the worst disaster in the history of New York's subway system.

Earlier that evening, a mysterious fire had ravaged the Times Square station, destroying a five-car length strip of the terminal. The 42nd Street Shuttle had quickly ceased operations. The Metropolitan Transportation Authority, or

MTA, had shut down the route. Maintenance workers had converged on the station, eager to complete repairs before the morning rush.

Three R36 ML subway cars had supposedly been crippled by the blaze. Scores of people had suffered burns, with at least four confirmed fatalities. While the cause remained unknown, the old-timer swore he overheard police officers chatting about it.

And they thought it was arson.

Jenson clenched his teeth as a thousand invisible knives pierced his skull. He dropped to a knee. His vision crumpled from the corners and blackness enveloped him. A roar of pain screeched out of his belly. Slamming his mouth shut, he cut it off, just like he'd done thousands of times before.

Breathe. Just breathe.

Jenson began to count, slowly and methodically.

One. Two. Three …

Ignoring his throbbing head, he continued his count.

Twenty-four. Twenty-five. Twenty-six …

His pulse slowed. His nerves relaxed. Finally, the knives vanished and he exhaled with relief.

His vision firmed up. Lines and shapes began to poke out of the darkness. Just ahead, he saw the concrete trough. The dull running rails. The rotten wood ties.

He still clutched the plastic bottle in one hand. Rising unsteadily to his feet, he lifted it to his lips and poured more bourbon into his stomach. Cheapest medical treatment he'd ever known. And far safer than those horrid Veterans Affairs hospitals. He had that thing that was all the rage these days … what did the papers call it? Post-traumatic stress disorder?

He took a few more swigs from the bottle. Sixty seconds. That's all it had taken. Sixty seconds to normalcy. Sixty seconds for his body to forget those other sixty seconds, the ones that had shattered his soul into billions of pieces.

The moment the boat had hit Iwo Jima, Jenson and his four closest friends had stormed the beach. Unfortunately, it was no ordinary beach. As they ran forward, they quickly found themselves sinking into volcanic ash. Before long, they were waist-deep in the stuff.

And then the shooting began.

Jenson didn't know how he'd survived the battle. The last thing he remembered was seeing his friends bent over at the waist, their arms splayed to the side, their bodies riddled with holes.

After the war ended, he'd returned to his family. He'd gone back to work at Brooklyn Gas & Electric. And for weeks on end, he'd sat in a chair, hunched over a desk, checking transactions for eight hours a day. He'd tried to live a normal life. And it had worked.

At least for a little while.

Admittedly, he hadn't tried that hard. What was the point? He wasn't the same person, not anymore. So, how could he be expected to return to the same life? Sure, living with the other tunnel bums wasn't exactly paradise. But at least they didn't expect anything from him. At least they didn't turn their noses up at him.

What was that?

Jenson cocked his head and listened for a second. He heard noises coming from the general direction of the subway car. An uneasy feeling arose inside him and he felt a small pinprick at the base of his skull.

Taking a deep breath, he clamped down on his emotions. Most likely, the subway car was one of the R36 MLs that had been caught in the inferno. That meant the noises probably came from subway workers. They were preparing to tow the car back to one of the yards for repairs. Yes, that explained everything.

Squinting, he saw two shadowy figures. They climbed through a gaping hole in the south wall and made their way to the subway car. They carried a massive bell-shaped object between them. It looked like it weighed a thousand pounds. And yet, they held it aloft with ease.

The two men reached the subway car. They disappeared into it and then reappeared a few seconds later, sans object.

As they walked back to the hole, Jenson felt a twinge of curiosity. Crouching down, he moved toward the center of the tracks.

But before he could get another look at the strange object, the men returned. This time, they carried a large burlap bag between them. Jenson stared at it for a moment.

Then the bag moved.

Panic filled Jenson's chest. He didn't understand the situation. But he'd seen enough. Too much, in fact. If the men spotted him, his life wouldn't be worth a rusty rail spike.

Spinning around, he darted through the tunnel. Twin lights surged behind him, casting a bright glow on the walls. Cursing, he slipped to the side of the track, opposite the third rail, and put on a burst of speed.

The non-pedestrian track under his feet connected the 42nd Street Shuttle Line to the Lexington Avenue Line. Ordinarily, it allowed shuttles to be taken in and out of service. But now, it served another purpose.

It was his way out.

The ground trembled. Digging deep, he picked up the pace.

The lights grew brighter and brighter. Lurching forward, he ducked into the cross-tunnel. He plastered his back against a wall. His heart slammed against his chest.

The subway car slowed as it passed by him. Jenson couldn't help but stare at it. Like its cargo, it was highly unusual. A rich coat of silver paint covered it, making a sharp contrast to the faded gray paintjobs that adorned most subway cars. And instead of graffiti scrawls, black lettering adorned the low alloy high tensile steel siding. Jenson mouthed the word in his head.

Omega.

The *Omega* slowed a bit more. Jenson pressed his back as hard as he could against the concrete. Someone had seen him. He was sure of it.

But with a mechanical groan, the car turned away from him. It passed into the opposite cross tunnel and pressed forward, heading south.

Relief swept over Jenson. He slid downward, his back scraping against the wall. His haunches came to a rest just above his worn shoes.

A high-pitched shriek reverberated through the tunnel, ping-ponging from wall to wall. Jenson glanced to the south and watched as the *Omega* slid to a stop. For a moment, it stood quietly in the semi-darkness. Then metal scraped against metal. Three shadows hopped out of the subway car's side and ventured to the front.

"Running rails," one of the figures announced. "How the hell ...?"

Jenson squinted. Long metal slabs lay perpendicular across the tracks. He didn't remember seeing them earlier.

Gunfire erupted. One of the shadows jerked backward. The other two retreated to the *Omega*.

Invisible knives sliced back into Jenson's skull, sending waves of debilitating pain down his spine. He sank to the ground.

More shadows appeared out of the darkness. Swiftly, they swarmed the subway car, peppering it with gunfire.

The barrage ended almost as quickly as it started. And as the tunnel fell quiet, Jenson felt more screams barreling their way toward his throat. He shut his mouth and fought them back with all his strength.

Blackness reappeared at the corners of his vision, eating its way toward the center. Straining his eyes, he looked toward the *Omega*. Its rear door had come open during the gunfight and he could see the bell-shaped object looming before him. At last, he understood its secret.

And it scared the hell out of him.

Darkness swept across his eyes, consuming his sight. He felt himself falling into a deep abyss. And then he felt nothing.

Nothing but blackness.

ABOUT THE AUTHOR

David Meyer is an adventurer and the international bestselling author of the *Cy Reed Adventure* series and the *Apex Predator* series. He's been creating for as long as he can remember. As a kid, he made his own toys, invented games, and built elaborate cities with blocks and legos. Before long, he was planning out murder mysteries and trap-filled treasure quests for his family and friends.

These days, his lifelong interests—lost treasure, mysteries of history, monsters, conspiracies, forgotten lands, exploration, and archaeology—fuel his personal adventures. Whether hunting for pirate treasure or exploring ancient ruins, he loves seeking out answers to the unknown. Over the years, Meyer has consulted on a variety of television shows. Most recently, he made an appearance on H2's #1 hit original series, *America Unearthed*.

Meyer lives in New Hampshire with his wife and son. For more information about him, his adventures, and his stories, please see the links below.

Connect with David!
Website: www.DavidMeyerCreations.com
Mailing List: eepurl.com/CVjj5
Facebook: www.facebook.com/GuerrillaExplorer
Twitter: www.twitter.com/DavidMeyer_

BOOKS BY DAVID MEYER

Cy Reed Adventure Series
CHAOS
ICE STORM
TORRENT
VAPOR

Apex Predator Series
BEHEMOTH

45918716R00202

Made in the USA
Lexington, KY
15 October 2015